ALSO BY S.I. HAYES

(The Roads Trilogy)
In Dreams... The Solitary Road
In Dreams... The Unavoidable Road
In Dreams... The Savage Road

Centuries of Blood: Becoming

Heart of Stone

Battleborn
Sweet Girls
Administrative Duties

(Manhattanites Series)
Xander & Asher

(The Natural Alpha Series)
California Moon

(Guardians of Grigori Series)
Fated Binds
Midnight Run
Branded Wings
Faery Road

Written with Will Van Stone, Jr.
Awakenings: The Wrath Saga

Written with J. Haney
(A County Fair Romance)
Stolen Moments
Winter Kisses

Spring Fling
Freedom Rings

(A Sex, Drugs and Rock Romance)
Vegas Lights
Hell In Heels

ALSO BY J HANEY

(Hudson Bros. PI Series)
An Unexpected Love

(A Heart Strings Love Affair)
Kentucky Blues
Playing House

Written with S.I. Hayes
(A County Fair Romance)
Stolen Moments
Winter Kisses
Spring Fling
Freedom Rings

(A Sex, Drugs and Rock Romance)
Vegas Lights
Hell In Heels

ACKNOWLEDGEMENTS

First, we'd like to thank Rebecca Baldridge aka Jess's Mom for being our awesome editor. This one was a little outside our expertise, but we thought why not? Let's write some rockers and so we did.

We want to thank the Beta Readers; Samantha Soccorso, Rebecca Waggner, and Victoria Berfet, as well as the Bloggers and Reviewers for being a part of this journey with us!

To our amazing fans: Thank you so much for reading Steve and Crystal's aka Beast and Bella's story. This story was something that we started on a whim and had no idea where it was going, but it's finished. We hope each of you have enjoyed reading it as much as we enjoyed writing it.

J. Haney & S.I. Hayes

DEDICATION

I had trouble coming up with this dedication, but only because it's supposed to go with the book. This book was so much. One of the key things was to have faith and remember even if you think you're in the dark there is an angel there watching over you whether you know it or not.

1

STEVE

"I MISS YOU, DADDY," Peggy Sue, my oldest says into the phone and my heart breaks. She's been in Colorado for the last seven months to keep her away from the prying eyes of the press. See, she's having herself a baby, which should make for a joyous event, but she's just this side of sixteen. How pissed was I when I found out? Ever seen a bear get shot and not die? Yeah, I was about right there. The father? A good for nothing rocker from one the bands that opened for us while we were touring in Australia. We found out just after we got home, adding to an already smoldering fire.

See, it hasn't been all wine and roses for Kellie, Crystal, and me. Not for a while. Three's company, but four, five, and six? Well, that's not sitting with me like it used to. Here lies our dilemma. Kellie likes our arrangement. I, however, want something different, something more like monogamy, but how do I get that and not break up our family?

"Daddy?" Peggy Sue asks, pulling me back from my thoughts.

"Yeah, honey?" I answer with a catch in my throat.

"I said I miss you." She sounds so tiny on the other end.

"I know, honey. Maybe Crys and I will come up this weekend. Bring the girls."

"Not Mom?" she asks curiously.

"She sees Damien," I deadpan and she goes quiet. Peggy Sue is at the age where we've pretty much made her aware of our lifestyle. Not the nitty gritty, but the overall gist of it.

"Oh," she replies, her answer telling me she's got the same opinion I'm beginning to have, that it's time Damian take a long walk off a short pier.

"But it'll be good, yeah?"

"Yeah," she sighs. "You should see me, I'm as big as a house."

"Any word from Harrison Lagrange?" That's the sperm donor. He hadn't said one word to her when we tracked him down and slapped him with the papers for responsibility. He's just eighteen, so no legal charges could be filed, but his response has been to send money every month and that is it.

"Nope, just the checks, but they have gotten bigger."

"What's bigger?"

"This last one was for ten thousand."

I suck air in through my teeth. "Have you deposited it?"

"No, Daddy, I've not deposited any of them. I've been putting them aside for the lawyer like you said, for after the baby comes, just like you said."

"Good girl," I say, swishing my Scotch, staring at the fire I've made. "Good girl. I'll talk to your mom, maybe she'll forgo her weekend to see you. If not, at least it'll be us. Okay?"

"Alright, Daddy. Oomph…"

"What?" I ask with concern.

"He's a kicker is all. Must be feeding time." Peggy Sue laughs. "I'm gonna go. I love you, Daddy."

"Love you too, my Peggy Sue."

She giggles, hanging up, and I throw my tumbler at the fireplace, smashing it with a growl.

"What *are* you doing?" Kellie asks and I turn to face her. She's standing in the doorway, looking freshly fucked. She's been with *him* tonight, and God knows who else, leaving Crystal and me with the girls.

"You're home early," I bark, not quite drunk enough to want to deal with her.

"And you're drinking? With the girls home?" she asks with venom in her voice. "I thought we talked out this?"

"Damn it, woman, what I do in my own home is my fucking business. I'm not drunk. I had two drinks, which I needed after the day I had. Is that okay with you?"

She walks over to me and her stilted steps tell me she's probably got some good bruises on her ass from tonight. I shake my head as she looks me in the eyes. She submits for her Dom, but here at home, she's always aggressive. "What happened?"

"Just a rough one. Between Brent and Marissa getting ready to have the babies, and Angelica and Maverick just coming back from Aspen after getting hitched last month, it's just getting to be too much. Everyone has so much going on it's like they've all forgotten we have an album to promote, and no one is even talking new material. Even Ringo is in his own little world, which is not like him.

"Bear, it's life. We all have one, maybe it's time you got back to yours." She puts her arms around me and fishes for a kiss. I groan against her lips, tasting the blackberry lip balm. She smells sweet and clean. Damian's rule, she always comes home to me properly bathed, no matter how badly he's used her.

I grab her by the ass and she winces then purrs. She likes the pain as I push my cock against her stomach. I'm not hard, but it's still a beast and she knows just what I need as she unzips my jeans and pulls me toward the couch.

She sits and slides my cock into her pert little mouth, wrapping her lips tightly around it, her hands stroking the length that doesn't fit down her throat. I grab her hair and pound into her mouth. Fuck, it feels good. I wrap my hand into her dirty blonde hair and pop her off my dick. She looks at me, confused until I rip open her blouse, sending the buttons flying.

"Hmm, someone's in a mood," she whispers.

"Shut up," I grit out, hiking up her skirt and pushing her panties aside as I pull up her leg to open her pussy to me. I drive my thick, pulsing cock into her and she whimpers from the force as I lift her off the floor, wrapping her legs around my hips. We haven't fucked like this in a while. I've been too busy with the band and we've been fighting a lot, but tonight, I'm just too fucking horny to care about any of that. It doesn't last long, but when I feel her clench up around me, I know I've done my part and can come too. I drop her down on the couch and zip up my pants, leaving her panting and astonished as I go clean up.

2

KELLIE

DAMN HIM. I'd be pissed about how he left me if it didn't get me wet. Steve and I have something of a love/hate relationship. I hate to love him and he deals with his need to hate me for making him the man he is, but whatever. We make it work for the kids. We have Crystal, he has his floozies, and I have Master Damien. Mmm, the things that man can do to me makes the little bits of hair I have left on my body stand at attention. Steve doesn't really like Damien, probably because he's only twenty-four and built like a brick shit house, but that's how I like my men. Big, I like being man handled. Steve just isn't the type to really grab and go for it, though, tonight he was in rare form. Tonight, he'd been *drinking*. I know it's sad to say, but I sometimes miss him on something. God, we'd fuck like rabid wolves back in his cocaine days. It was the heroine that I couldn't deal with, the dangers of the needles, the way it strung him out, his need for more and more. We got lucky, *he* got lucky that he never got a dirty needle.

I don't know what the girls would do without him,

they love their daddy very much. *Me?* I have loved that big teddy bear for eighteen years. The two years we dated and the sixteen we've been married, but I need my spice like I need oxygen. I give him his and I take mine, that's just how it works. Always has, always will.

I slip off the couch and head for one of the four bathrooms that we have on the main floor and strip down, climbing into the shower to hose down before sinking into the deep tub to soak. I keep clothes in a closet down the hall for nights like these. They're rare as I said, but frequent enough that I like to be prepared. I don't like going to bed unwashed. Once I finish here, I'll go upstairs and climb into my big bed with my husband and Crystal and find my oblivion.

I have to be at the hospital at noon, I'm working a swing shift. I know, I'm the wife of a Rockstar, I know, but there is only so much shopping, lounging, and schmoozing one can do before you get bored. I need to work, I've got degrees I worked my ass off to get, and I'm gonna use them. I'm a registered nurse and physician's assistant, which is why I am so useful to the guys when they have any issues or go on benders. I get access to everything and they all have me down as their primary PA, so I bill for most of it. I go on tour with them most of the time when they are here in the states, where my licenses are legal. It works.

I'll go up in a while. Right now, the hot water feels too good on my bruising flesh.

3

CRYSTAL

I WAKE PINNED UNDER THE BEAST'S ARM with the sounds of snoring in my ear. I try to push him off, which fails miserably. Instead, Steve stretches, pulls me into him, and kisses my head, which just has him spitting my hair out of his mouth. I try to wiggle free and the Beast groans in my ear.

"Mmm, Bella," he moans, grabbing my tit.

"I need to get up," I say, turning my head to face him.

Steve's lips meet my neck, then he grabs me by the hips and turns me to face him. "It's a holiday."

"I have to feed the girls and we have to get ready soon."

Steve groans against me then finally lets go. "Rain check?"

"Always." I give him a quick kiss. "Now go shower. We're going to Angelica and Maverick's."

I roll out of bed and head to the kitchen where I see Kellie making her coffee. She's already in her scrubs, but she doesn't even look among the living yet.

"Morning," I say as I'm grabbing the pancake mix.

Kellie looks at me. "Good morning, Crys. Bear awake?"

"Supposedly, but you know that just means I'll have to go in there and beat him with a pillow."

Kel smiles and nods her head as she grabs the coffee creamer out of the fridge. "Yeah, he was in rare form last night, bent me right over the couch."

"I noticed, so I kept the girls entertained till bed."

"You guys, um, what you are doing for the day?"

"After breakfast, we're supposed to go over to Angelica and Maverick's."

"Ah, is the whole crew going to be there, or just you guys?"

"Everyone, including Kyle."

Kellie's eyes pop. "Hmm, if you feel the need, my bag is down the hall… Just in case."

"It may be necessary once Angelica lets the cat out of the bag to Kyle."

"She still hasn't told him? I'm glad I'm not going to be there for that. Could you make sure the kids aren't around for that? You know how Kyle can be."

"I usually do."

"Great, I'm off to work."

"See ya later."

Kellie leaves and I get to making breakfast. I'm so used to it just being the four of us anymore. Kel and I haven't gotten along for a while, but we're both good at pretending for Steve and the kids. She knows I don't agree with the shit she does. We've had conversations which usually turn into arguments.

I've got breakfast on the table when Mary Ann and Sue Ellen come bouncing into the room. "Morning, girls, hungry?"

"Morning," Sue Ellen says and I just get a grunt from Mary Ann. She's much like her father, not a morning person.

The girls are eating, so I grab Beast a cup of coffee and head for the bedroom. I shake my head as I shut the door to our room. He's still asleep. Setting the coffee on the night stand, I climb on the bed and grab a pillow. With my feet on either side of Steve, I give a good bounce and then hit with the pillow. Once, twice more, and he growls and grabs me, dragging me down on top of him.

"Pillows to the face? These are not the pillows I wanted," he teases, burying his face in my breasts.

"Beast, you gotta get up; the girls are eating breakfast and Kel's gone."

"Good, we got time," he mumbles as his hands are sneaking up my shirt.

"What are you doing?" I ask, feeling the vibration of him chuckling against my chest.

"Getting you out of these clothes so you can join me in the shower. I figure we can do our part to save the planet. You know they got a drought in California."

"Good thing we aren't there, huh?" I push so I'm in a seated position on top of him.

"So, no?"

"And if your girls were to walk in?"

"We'll be in there."

"Have I told you lately how absolutely horrible you are?" Steve gives me that cocky grin he gets from time to time. "You know we need to be on alert today, right?" I ask as I lean down to cuddle him. I love our moments like this, when it's just us and I can almost forget about Kellie.

"Yeah, Kyle's going to be there today, right?"

"Yup, and he doesn't know she's pregnant yet."

"Right, yeah. We'll be fine. Maybe she can put off telling him for another month or so. Maybe she doesn't have to tell him at all."

"She's just starting her third month if I'm correct and you know as well as I do that Maverick is feeding her all the fucking time."

"Yeah, well, Kyle's not the brightest crayon in the box. Didn't he promise he'd behave if he got an invite?"

"Yeah, but he's promised that before. I don't know, I guess I'm just worried about the girls. If it were just us, I wouldn't think too much about it because it'd be stopped. We usually just keep this shit away from the girls."

"Speaking of the girls..." Steve says and clears his throat. "I talked to Peggy Sue last night and I told her we'd come out and see her next weekend. Is that doable?"

"We can do that. Kellie won't be here though. Do you want to stay the whole weekend?"

"I was hoping Friday to Monday. We'll fly out commercial. I don't want the guys to know where we're going."

"I can get the tickets and everything as soon as we're home. Thinking about that, are we staying there tonight or coming back home?"

"I don't know, just pack some bags and put them in the car."

"Will do. You ready to get up yet?"

"I'm up... To something."

"Aren't you usually?" I ask as his hands slide down the back of my pants.

"You gonna take that shower with me?" Just as I go to kiss him, Sue Ellen walks in the door. Steve slides his hands out of my pants and up my back as he looks over at Sue Ellen and asks, "What's the matter, baby?"

"Just wondering when we're leaving."

"Shortly, but we need to pack a bag just in case we stay all night. So, get your sister, grab a few things, and include bathing suits please."

"Okay," Sue Ellen answers and shuts the door.

I look back to the beast under me. "Now you're going to have to get up."

"Can't, you're sitting on me."

"Any other time, you'd have moved me by now."

"The only place I'm moving you to is the shower."

❖ ❖ ❖

I finally got Beast satisfied and packed. Now we're all in the car and heading for Angelica's house. I've started feeling weird being around everyone. I've been able to keep it to myself, but I guess the everyone having babies' thing gets to a girl who can't have any.

The girls are in the back seat in their own little worlds. Mary Ann has her nose in the Kindle while Sue Ellen has hers in a book. I wonder what Peggy Sue is doing about now. It's sure gonna be nice to see her. I'm betting she's grown so much. I tried so hard to talk them out of sending her away. I told Steve and Kellie both that I'd stay home with her when they went out, but it was a no go.

I look up at Steve when I feel his hand on mine. "Bella, where are you?"

"Right here." I smile.

"You sure?"

"Positive."

"Nothing on your mind that you want to share."

"Nope, just what we talked about earlier."

He gives me that look that tells me he knows I'm not telling him everything, then he nods and squeezes my hand once more.

4

STEVE

CRYSTAL IS EDGY TODAY. She says it has to do with our going to Angelica's and Kyle being around the girls, but I'm not sure I buy it. Kyle knows better than to do anything stupid around my kids. He knows I won't hesitate to bash his fucking head in. No, she's got something else weighing her down. I know her well enough to know it, to see it in those emerald eyes of hers. After almost nine years, you start to know these things about a person and I know my Bella.

We get to Angelica's and Brent's Navigator is right in front of us. I see Blake's long dark arm as it hits the pass codes for the gate and we follow them up the driveway. I hop out and the girls follow my lead, running up to Brent with laughter. He stops them for a moment so he can help Marissa out of the truck. Holy cow, she's popped. She looks great though, pregnancy, even this far along, seems to agree with her. She's got on a little white summer dress and flip flops with her brown and pink hair tied up in a bun. Her eyes are covered with matching pink sunglasses. She looks radiant.

Angelica steps out the front door and I can't believe my eyes. It's only been a month, but it seems like longer. She's put on some weight and it's a healthy look for her. Her waist is thicker and her tits are sitting higher in the bikini top she's got on. Damn, she's looking good.

Crystal must see me staring because she ribs me, bringing me back to the real world. "Sorry," I mumble under my breath.

"We don't need you fighting with Maverick now too." Her country twang comes rustling out like it does when she gets to scolding. The rest of the time, she's prim and proper, but when she gets mad, hoo-wee!

Just as we are approaching the Navigator, Kyle gets out too. He sees me and nods. "Hey," he says, smiling."

"Sup, man?" I ask, giving him a hug. "You doing okay?"

"Hanging in there today," he answers glumly.

"Hey, it's a holiday, let's make it a good one. There's good food, friends, and family." I put an arm around him and walk him to the door.

"I just don't want a repeat of last time."

"Look at it this way, this time you were invited." I laugh, patting his back.

"This is true," he agrees with a smirk. "This is true."

"Hey, guys," Angelica shouts, "don't bother goin' in, we're all round the back! C'mon!" She waves us to the pool, so we follow, my girls running off ahead with Crystal right behind them. It's gonna be a long night.

❊ ❊ ❊

I leave Kyle as soon as we get around the back and

find Maverick has made himself the grill man. I haven't seen the man in over a month, so I mosey on over.

"Maverick!" I say, clamping my hand on his shoulder to get his attention.

"Why are you hollering?" he asks, looking at me.

I laugh. "Excited to see the would-be daddy is all, how's married life treating you?"

He sighs. "About the same as before, pretty sure I'm going to Hell."

I can't help but chuckle, the man has no idea what being married is. They're still in the honeymoon phase. "Oh, just wait. How are you adjusting with Angela?"

He scratches his head as he answers, "She's about as moody as Angelica, I'm pretty sure that one of them is trying to kill me."

"Oh, I'm sure." I pat him on the back. "Just think, in seven months there will be one more, but it'll be yours."

"That's if I make it that far." He wipes his forehead.

"You will. You're resilient. I believe in you!" I condescend.

"At least somebody does."

"Alright, gimme the tongs and go be with your woman."

He hands them over. "Where's Kellie?" he asks, looking around.

"Working at the hospital," I say flatly.

"Everything okay?"

"Just the same old routines. Different days. We're okay," I answer, watching Crystal as she strips down to her bikini and gets into the pool. God, she's got a great little body on her.

"You know if you need to talk, I'm always here, right?"

I look back at him. What would I say to him? That

my wife's a deviant who prefers her twenty-four-year-old Dom to her husband and children? Yeah, I don't even want to think it, let alone say it out loud. "I'm good, man, but thanks. Now, go to your wife."

I watch as Maverick goes over to Angelica and stands her up in the middle of a conversation with Marissa. He sits down and proceeds to pull his wife onto his lap. Seems he's staking his claim. I smile and get to the cooking.

5

CRYSTAL

WHAT HAPPENS WHEN YOU HAVE THREE rambunctious girls that won't go to sleep? A splitting headache and much needing of a drink. After finally getting them down, I head back out, looking for Steve. He's sitting in front of the fire pit alone. Brent took Marissa to bed earlier, Angelica and Maverick are in their room, and Kyle and Ringo left after the food was done.

I stand behind Steve, wrap my arms around his neck, and kiss him on the cheek. "What are you doing out here all alone?"

He stretches his legs out in front of him and arches his back. "Wishing I had a cold beer in my hand and a hot woman in my lap."

I smile against his cheek. "Shucks, I'm all out of both."

"Can't win em all."

"I've heard that," I say, coming around and settling on his lap.

Steve wraps his arms around me. "So, you gonna

17

tell me what today was about?"

"What are you talking about?"

"I'm talking about the mopey face you had every time nobody was looking, or at least you thought nobody was looking," he says with curiosity and seriousness in his eyes.

"I've had a bit of a headache today. I'm okay."

"You sure it's just a headache because earlier you said it was nothing."

Damn him for always listening. "It's nothing I can't handle. Don't worry so much."

"If I don't worry about you, who will?" he asks as he runs his hand down my cheek.

"It's life, Beast, and things I'd rather not talk about."

Steve drops his head. "You know if you need to talk, you talk."

"I've talked enough, so it's not necessary."

"Alright, if you say so."

"You ready for bed or are you staying out here for a while?"

"No, I think I'll stay out here for a little while longer. You go to bed. I've got to put the fire out anyhow."

I nod and give him a quick kiss before I'm off. I make it to our room and into the bathroom, stripping my clothes quickly. I need a shower and I can cry in here without anybody ever knowing. I step into the shower and let the hot water run over my body as the tears fall.

I know this shouldn't bother me anymore, but every now and then, the fact that I won't and can't ever have kids gets to me. The doctors told me years ago that my body just wasn't made for babies. If by some miracle I actually conceived a child, I couldn't carry it. I think my shot was one in a billion. So, I gave up and never saw another doctor for it. I didn't need anyone else telling me that I failed at being a woman.

Kellie makes her digs when Steve isn't around about me being the little girlfriend that he can fuck and dump in because I can't get pregnant. I honestly don't know why she hates me so. I know she's asked Steve to get rid of me. I heard it one night coming back from putting the girls to bed. I've just never let on to knowing anything.

I finish showering and clean myself up so I can get into bed without Steve knowing anything's wrong. He's apparently been watching me all day. I get dried off and dressed before walking out of the bathroom to find Steve sitting on the edge of the bed waiting for me.

Once he sees me, he stands, grabbing and pulling me to him before kissing the top of my head. "What are you keeping from me, Bella?"

"Nothing, you know everything."

"Absolutely not if you're crying your eyes out in the guest bathroom."

I pull back and look up at him. "Beast, it's life. Sometimes a woman just needs to cry to feel like a woman."

He looks down at me and shakes his head. "No, I'm not buying it, I've known you too many years. Did Kellie say something to you? Or one of the guys here?"

I place my hand on his cheek. "Nobody said anything. It's just part of being me. You know, the reason you all wanted me to begin with." Steve shakes his head at me. "The fact I can't have babies. It was your way of getting to have fun without the consequences."

Steve's grip on me loosens. "What do you mean you can't have babies? Aren't you just on birth control?"

"You didn't know?"

"Do I look like I knew?"

"But Kellie said…"

He huffs. "Kellie. Of course."

"It doesn't matter, let's just forget about it."

"No, I mean…" Steve trails off, looking at me with compassion in his eyes. "Have you seen doctors? When did you find out?"

"I've known since I was a kid. I just thought you knew."

"No, I just assumed you didn't want any, so you were being careful. I remember we started off with condoms and it just sorta fell off, so to speak."

"Nope, can't have them. The shot of me actually getting pregnant is something like one in a billion, according to the doctors. Kellie and I talked about it not long after we started this thing. She wanted to make sure I was on birth control so there weren't any accidents."

"Not like that's her call to make. Not alone, at least. She never told me."

"She was just doing what was best for you. I was just some kid that was supposed to be there to teach your girls, then we ended up together." I swipe at the tears falling down my face.

"What about IVF or any other countless fertility things out there now."

"I'm almost thirty, Beast. I'm well past the age that could handle a baby. Plus, the doctors told me that even if by some miracle I got pregnant, I couldn't carry the baby."

"Doctors are wrong all the time. Shit, look at Marissa. Look at Angelica, how tiny she is, and this will be number two for her."

"Why are we discussing this? It's not like you want more and Kellie wouldn't agree."

"If it's what you want…"

"It doesn't matter. It can't happen, and if it could, I'd have to find someone else because Kellie's made it pretty fucking clear that you don't want any more kids."

Steve straightens his back. "With her, she doesn't want any more children. She got fixed right after Sue Ellen."

"I know."

"I love my children, and if you had gotten pregnant, or if you were to get pregnant, it wouldn't bother me at all. Kellie would have to suck it up."

"She's your wife, you have obligations there. I won't step in the way of the two of you."

Steve chuckles. "I'd never put you in the line of fire, but if it's something you want, you let me know and I'll make the arrangements, call the doctors. Let me worry about Kellie."

"I don't want you all fighting worse than you already are because of me."

"What she and I are fighting about doesn't really have anything to do with you. Not yet anyhow."

"It has more to do with me than you think." The big beast just *hmm*'s me. "Are we going to bed or do you need a shower? It's sorta been a long day."

"I think we're just going to bed. I don't like Angelica's showers. They're not big enough. I feel like a squirrel shoved in a toilet paper roll."

I push him back toward the bed. "Ya know, not everyone has a beast in their house."

"Yeah, well, maybe they should."

Steve and I get into bed, cuddle together, and we're out before we can even say goodnight.

6

KELLIE

NINE IN THE MORNING AND I'M JUST coming through the door. One of the other APRN's didn't show, so it was mandated OT for me. Sleeping on a cot for a few hours wreaked havoc on my back and I just want a shower and my bed. No such luck, Steve is sitting in the parlor and he looks pissed. Now what?

"You got a minute?" he asks as I try to walk past.

"Not now, I'm tired. I just want to sleep." I look around and the house is too quiet. "Where are Crys and the girls?"

"I left them at Angelica's for the morning, so we could have a talk."

"Uh-huh, about?" I drop my bag and sit in the chair opposite him with a thud. Now, what's his problem, did one of his band mates fall off the wagon... *Again*?

"Crystal and I were talking last night and she told me about her not being able to have babies."

I raise an eye at him. "That's old news, thought she told you years ago."

"Did you? Really? Somehow, I doubt that," he says

in a tone that clearly says his bullshit detector is going off.

"Well, yeah, I mean you haven't used a condom in what? Seven years? I just figured she'd told you and it was moot to discuss further."

"Right, because you decided that helping her or talking to her about it was useless, right?"

"Is she telling you she wants babies all of a sudden? Is that what's going on here? She wants us to shell out for fertility treatments or some shit?" I roll my eyes. "I don't want any more little kids running around here. Ours are about the age that they can do shit on their own, finally."

"No, Kell, they're really not. Look what happened with Peggy Sue, a little freedom and Bam! Pregnant. They need us, now more than ever."

"Maybe what they need is a better education. I've been looking at some private schools. Something more formal. I-"

"Not happening, you don't get to say Crys has to go, not while you continue to see Damien. Especially after I've asked you to cut that back."

"Cut it back? I see him once a week."

"Him and how many others?"

"That's my business," I growl, standing up. "Maybe if you were more of a man and could give me what I want, I wouldn't have to get it somewhere else," I spit. "Now, if you'll excuse me…" I start to walk away, but he grabs me by the wrist.

He turns me to him, grabbing my hair and wrapping it tightly around his hand. "I should snap your neck." He pulls my head back roughly and I half laugh, half moan as he teases my lips.

"You don't have it in you," I sneer as he silences me

with a kiss. His mouth is hungry and the kiss is rough as his tongue runs along mine. I bite him and he draws back.

"Bitch," he snarls.

"Yes, but I'm your bitch."

He watches as I drop to my knees. Unbuttoning his shorts and dropping them, I take his cock into my mouth, sucking him until he gets hard. He grabs my head, making me go harder, faster, as he pumps into my mouth. My eyes tear; I'm gagging, but he doesn't seem to care as he slams his cock into my open mouth.

"Take off your pants," he orders me and I kick off my shoes and pull off my scrubs and panties.

He wrangles me up off the floor and pushes my legs apart, bending me over the high-backed chair and pushing into me hard. It hurts, I wasn't wet enough, but soon, he's got me soaked and he's hammering me hard. His cock fills me up and makes me moan and pant.

"That's it, take it like the whore you are," he berates me, yanking my head back by my hair with one hand as he assaults my nipple with the other. Squeezing and teasing, I feel him begin to tense up and I'm almost there too. Just as I'm about to come, he pulls out of me and I lose it as he comes all over my back.

"You want to be treated like some common trash whore, I can do that," he barks as he pulls up his pants and smacks me on the ass. "Go clean up, your kids will be home in an hour and will expect their lunch to be in progress."

Watching him walk off, my body reacts and I come right there where I stand.

STEVE

I LOVE MY WIFE. I just don't like her right now. Keeping secrets and acting like a skank doesn't go over well with me. Would it go over well with any husband? Fucking her and leaving her like I did was my way of showing her I could be the bastard lover she wants, but it does nothing for me. Putting on that face is exhausting. I'm a bear of a man, but it's a Teddy Bear. I know it and I'm man enough to admit it.

I hear a car pull up and see that it's Brent's Navigator, and out pop my girls. They look adorable, all in white summer dresses with little hats and sandals to match. Crystal, my Bella, looks like an angel with her blonde hair reflecting the sunlight in gold and platinum hues.

I walk out to the parlor to meet them at the door. Mary Ann and Sue Ellen rush me, hugging me.

"Daddy! We went to the Aquarium! Saw the sharks!" Sue Ellen chirps excitedly.

"Did you have fun?"

"Oh, yeah!" Mary Ann exclaims. "So much!"

"That's wonderful. Now, you know you'll have a lesson later, on the place, so go write in your journals for a half hour, then read till lunch is done. Understand me?"

"Yes, Dad," they acquiesce, not nearly as excited as they were a second ago, but that's life, disappointments around every corner.

I look at Crystal. She looks worried and hasn't actually come inside yet. "Bella? What's troubling you?" I ask, putting out my hand for her to take.

"How'd your conversation go?" she asks, still not coming inside or taking my hand. I furrow my brow and step outside to join her, closing the door behind us.

"It went. She claims she thought you told me, don't know that I believe her."

"You know the only way to get rid of Damien is to get rid of me, correct?"

I look at her, confused. I hadn't said anything to her about wanting Damien gone. "I never-"

"I can read it all over you."

I shake my head. "I've gotten rid of other boyfriends over the years and not lost you. He's no different, just a little younger than the rest of them is all."

She sighs. "She didn't like them as much as she likes him."

"Doesn't matter, we have our rules for a reason. This open relationship was changed years ago to include you. The only way you go is if you leave. That was the agreement." I wrap an arm around her, pulling her into me. "You're part of this family, what would we do without you? What would *I* do without you?"

"You'd live a normal life," she mumbles against me.

"I'm a Rockstar, what's normal?"

"When you're not on the road and you're not traveling, then it's normal. You see your kids, you take care of your kids, you're here like a normal father."

"With the exception that I have two beautiful women who I dote upon profusely."

"Yes, most only have one."

"I'm not most men, you should know this by now," I say, thinking about when Kellie broached the topic of us taking on Crystal almost ten years ago. We had been having problems then and I was ready to leave. I had been running around on her because I couldn't stand to look at her knowing that I was locked down. I was only twenty-three and already had two kids with the third on the way. Peggy Sue was already starting school and I was losing my mind. My addictions were starting to take hold of me even then.

Crystal grabs me by the arm, pulling me from my internal ramblings. "Are you okay?" she asks me, concerned.

"Yeah... Yeah, I'm good. Just thinking about the past a bit. You know, I think you probably saved my marriage."

"How would I have done that?"

"I was ready to leave it all before you came along. Kellie, the girls. You made it all seem like it was doable. Life, the kids, life with kids, you took it all on and were so good at it. Hell, you stuck around during my dark period. You saw us through some pretty gnarly shit. You were there for Kellie while I went off for weeks at a time with a needle in my arm. I don't think she'd have stayed if it hadn't been for you. I know I'd have never come back if it hadn't been for you."

"Back then, all I was seeing was someone had what

I couldn't and they were gonna lose it all. I had to do what I could to stop it."

"You risked a lot, though, coming into those places to find me. You could have been hurt or worse. Seeing you, knowing that you'd seen me at that low a point, it made me wanna get clean again. You pulled me out. That's why you aren't going anywhere. I don't care what anyone thinks."

"Like I said, you have kids you need to be home for. If that meant I had to travel hours to find you, then I traveled hours to find you," she states matter of factly, looking up at me.

"I've never really thanked you for it." I wrap my arms around her.

"And you don't need to now. You got clean, that was all the thanks I needed."

"My Bella," I say, kissing her gently. "You have nothing to be afraid of, I'll always be here and I'll always want you."

She doesn't reply, just hugs me tightly as I turn us and lead her back to the house. I can smell the pizza Kellie's made. Her sauce permeates the house, it's one of the few things the woman cooks really well.

8

CRYSTAL

I'M WORKING ON DINNER WHEN I HEAR Steve and Kellie talking. From the sounds of it, they are heading this way. I was hoping to not have to deal with her tonight, seems I'm out of luck. I've got chicken frying, potatoes cooking, and the gravy and corn to go on last. I head over to fix the salad just as Steve comes in the room.

"Something smells awfully good."

"I was in the mood for something fried. Hope that works for everyone," I say with a glance at him and Kellie before going back to cutting vegetables.

"Ugh, I was really trying to avoid the fried foods. After the last awards ceremony, it seems I put on a few pounds," Kellie grumbles.

"There's a salad too."

"Where'd you gain? In your ass? Because you know you could use it there," Steve says to Kellie and grabs her by the ass playfully.

"It's not funny," Kellie snaps and smacks his hand away.

"Ya know, Kell, having three kids and your age will do that to your body. Can't always look like a kid."

Kellie looks at me. "You know what? I look damn good for three kids. Not all of us can look twelve forever. I earned these tits."

"Whoa- whoa- whoa! Separate corners. What is this shit?" Steve's in between us with his hands up. I'm not batting a lash and just keep working on dinner.

"You heard her dig at me," Kellie spits, "she's being very hostile toward me."

"The only one here that's hostile is you. If anyone started this, it's you, starting in about dinner. If you were gonna go on some stupid diet, you could have said something *before* Crystal started to cook. I don't know if you're on the rag all of a sudden or what, but you're going to fucking apologize and you're going to do it now."

"No, it's cool, I usually ask what you all want. I didn't today, so it's my bad," I say, hoping to smooth things over.

"No, Crystal," Steve says before looking at Kellie. "Well?"

Kellie's standing there with her arms crossed, tapping her foot and glaring at the both of us. "You know what? I'm sorry, but I'm not sorry," she says through gritted teeth and walks away.

I take a deep breath and go back to the stove to flip the chicken. Just as I get the chicken flipped, I hear a car peel out. I run a hand through my hair. "Just fucking great."

"Ya think?" Steve asks and I jump and turn toward him.

"I thought I was alone. Sorry."

"It's the right reaction. I don't know what's gotten

30

into her."

"It's my fault. I should have asked what you all wanted."

"I don't really think this had anything to do with dinner." Steve runs his hands over the top of his head.

I walk over and wrap my arms around his waist. "Beast, you shouldn't have said anything about me, you've got her on edge."

"I couldn't let it go." He wraps his arms around me.

"I know this. Remember, I slept with you last night. You were all over the bed."

"I'm sorry, I hope I didn't crush you."

"Nope, just pushed me out once."

"I'm sorry, can I make it up to you?"

"You have nothing to be sorry for. You had a lot of news dropped on you last night. If I'd have known she hadn't told you, I would have."

"Ah, it's alright, I know now and that's all that matters."

"The girls asked if we could watch a movie after dinner and I thought maybe you'd want to watch it with them. I was hoping Kellie would too. They need some time with the two of you."

"Well, I'll watch it with them, but God only knows where their mother went. What about you? Family movie night means *family* movie night."

"I've been working on lesson plans. They haven't started their new school year yet because I'm still waiting on materials and now that I'm adding Angela, I've got to rearrange the room."

"Do you need help? If it can wait till tomorrow morning or later, after the movie, I'll help once we put the girls down."

"I'm sure it can, I just thought maybe you'd want

some time with just them. You still have to tell them about Peggy Sue before we get there."

Steve rolls his shoulders. "I haven't figured out how to do that."

"Yeah, I've been trying to figure out the same thing. Is it wrong of me to wish she was coming home with us?"

"I just don't want the press to get wind of it and cause her any extra stress. Teen pregnancies are high risk and so far, she's had it really easy."

"I know, I just hate her being so far away and alone."

"I know, Bella, but she's doing well and sounds happy."

"She does. I get a call at least every other day from her."

"Do you now? She only calls her old man once every couple of weeks."

"She's usually wanting me to make something and mail it to her. She's been craving lots of brownies."

Steve laughs. "That doesn't surprise me. When her mother was pregnant with her, she wanted blondies all the time."

"Haven't you noticed me baking more than normal?"

"I smelled it and was wondering where it was going. I figured you were taking it over to Brent and Marissa or something because you know that psycho never leaves the house."

"Who are you kidding? I was shocked he let her come yesterday."

"I think he just couldn't get away with hiding her anymore. She probably threatened to kill him in his sleep if he didn't let her out of the house."

* * *

I wake with a start, my eyes fluttering as I try to figure out what's going on. I finally get myself awake enough to realize that Kellie's kissing on me.

"Kellie, what are you doing?" I whisper, trying not to wake Steve.

"Rendering my apologies. I was a cunt," Kellie says. I can taste and smell the booze on her.

"You're forgiven. Now, let's get you in the shower so nobody sees you like this."

"So, you're coming with me?"

"I'm going to help you into the shower, but then I'm gonna go get your clothes."

"Mmm, poo. Fine, whatever."

"Kel, you're a mess. You don't need the girls seeing you this way."

Kellie crawls off the bed and stands up, but she's wobbly. I walk her into the bathroom and start the shower. Once I get her in, I head out into the bedroom and start pulling some pjs out for her.

I grab what I need, then head back to the bathroom, stopping dead in my tracks when I see Steve holding Kellie up in the shower.

"You come home like this? You drove home like this? Are you trying to get yourself killed?" he grits out.

"Get the fuck off me. I didn't drive home, you asshole," Kellie shouts.

"Kellie, calm down, the girls are going to wake up," I say, placing the clothes on the sink.

Kellie starts crying. "I said I was sorry, what more do you want from me?"

Steve looks at me as he lets her go. "And you're

forgiven, but you're getting too loud."

Kellie collapses onto the shower floor and she's bawling. Steve throws his hands into the air. "I don't know what to fucking do with her right now. Can you deal with this? I've got a meeting with Christy in the morning."

"I've got it. I was trying to keep from waking you."

Steve looks at Kellie before walking over to me and kissing me on the head, then he's out the door. I strip my clothes before getting in the shower and fixing the temperature.

"We need to get you off this floor and cleaned up. Okay?" Kellie nods and stands. I get her showered and then dry us both off before getting her and myself dressed. "He's asleep, so I'm gonna hold you till you go to sleep, okay?"

She nods. "Yeah, I really am sorry about earlier. I didn't mean to be such a- whatever."

"It's okay, you just need to sleep it off."

"Yeah, maybe."

I get Kellie into bed and it takes twenty or so minutes to get her to sleep. Once I'm awake, there's no going back to sleep, so I leave the bedroom and head straight for the kitchen. I need coffee today. With coffee brewing, I fix my cup with creamer and a ton of sugar, then I pour coffee in the cup and walk to my classroom.

I take one look around the room, then go about rearranging tables. I've got three different ones because I will have three different grades when Peggy Sue comes home. It'll take me most of the day to get this room the way it needs to be, but the distraction will be good for me.

9

KELLIE

I WAKE UP WITH MY HEAD POUNDING. I went to the Martini Bar last night and had a lot of appletinis with nothing else on my stomach. I wake up at about nine-thirty and I'm starving. The bed is empty, so I pull myself out and get dressed. It's gonna be a hot one today, the weatherman says ninety-eight with a severe thunderstorm warning for later this afternoon. That's just perfect, explains the thumping in my head, because I never get hangovers from fruity drinks.

I head into the kitchen and find a fruit plate set up in the fridge with my name on it. Crystal can be thoughtful when she's not running her mouth and whining to Steve about shit that's ancient history.

I grab the fruit and fix it with some fresh spinach and peanut butter in a couple wraps, fix my coffee, and head out to the patio. The clouds are already getting dark. The sounds of my kids laughing and carrying on grab my attention and I turn to find them playing badminton in the yard with the net set Steve put up for them. Compared to the rest of the band members, our house is modest. It's only got eight bedrooms total, including our master. It's got two levels and two wings, three rooms to each side upstairs. The downstairs has two, one that I typically utilize on nights like last night, but I was feeling rather guilty for my actions. I'm not always a total bitch and can admit when I've stepped over a line and yesterday, I was just in a mood. I've gotta go find Crys and make sure we're good. Steve won't have us fighting, he's a stickler for us getting along.

I finish my food and head down to the den. Crys had it modified into the classroom for the girls since it was huge and gets lots of natural light from the bay windows. Steve thought it was a good idea since we had the big open parlor with the fireplace to entertain anyhow. Not that we ever really do, Steve never quit drinking and since Brent is totally sober but can't handle the temptation, Ringo and Kyle are the only ones who ever come over and that's pretty rare. I don't keep many friends, what few I have are from the scene and Steve doesn't like them, so I hang out with them when I see Damien on Saturdays.

Crystal is rearranging furniture and keeping an eye on the girls through the open bay windows when I enter the room and clear my throat.

"Morning," I say softly.

"Good morning," she responds.

"You look like you could use a hand there," I say, coming in and grabbing the other side of the big desk she's trying to move. We lift and carry it across the room, setting it down in the far corner.

She motions to the whiteboards, asking, "You wanna move one over to the two desks by themselves and I'll get this one over there?"

"Sure." I grab the large white board and move it along. "You know, about yesterday... And not telling Steve... It wasn't outta spite. I just figured you cried it out to me, you must have done so with him."

"I wouldn't have told him at all if I'd have known you didn't, but the way you'd made it sound was like he already knew."

"Like I said, I thought he did. My bad," I say, grabbing the third white board and looking around. "Where do you want it?"

"I need it in the middle with that desk." She's getting a little snappy at this point, must have been something I said. Oh well, this is my house, I'll do and say what I please.

I move it over and look around. The place is neat and clean as always, one thing she's a crack at is keeping these kids organized. She tends to them, I tend to the better parts of the house, and we split most of the chores. Steve never has to worry about coming home to a messy house, even with two kids running around it all day.

"I'm going to have to head out. I Uber'd home last night and have to go pick up the Lincoln before it gets towed. So, I guess you'll have to get lunch today, but I'll handle dinner. How do steaks with a fresh mozzarella and tomato salad sound?"

"That's fine."

"Do I need to grab anything else at the store? Is he low on beer or anything like that, do you know?"

"Nothing was mentioned."

"Alright, well, could you double check? He was hitting the bourbon hard the other night. Just text me if I need to hit the liquor store." I turn on my heel to leave as she answers in the affirmative. I could look myself, but just don't feel like it right now.

10

STEVE

I'M SITTING IN THE CAR AND CAN'T WAIT to get home. My meeting with Christy wasn't as I had hoped. We were supposed to be going over the tour schedule for the fall, but Brent made it clear that he won't tour until he's got Marissa and the babies settled, and Angelica won't tour while pregnant. Like at all. He's pissed to say the least. So, he had me, Ringo, and Kyle in to see what kind of press we can muster up because our sales are apparently not as high as he and the studio projected. It's only gone gold and they expected double platinum by now just like Nephilim had.

Without us doing appearances, it's just not getting the traction it needs. Brent's song *Nightmares* has just dropped as a single and is climbing the charts though. That's promising at least. I'm tired. I need food and a beer and maybe the lovin' of one, if not both, of my girls to make me feel better about all of this.

As I'm hopping off the highway, the sky opens up and thunder shakes so hard, my truck actually vibrates. Damn, I hate these storms. I have to slow down because

I can hardly see past the nose of the truck. Fuck, man, I just wanna get home.

The twenty-five-minute drive becomes an hour long one with these storms and I'm pulling up to the house at about two. I get soaked running from the carport to the front door. I mean completely drenched. "Damn it!" I huff. "Crys! Kell! Somebody get me a fucking towel!" I shout, standing in the doorway.

Crystal comes to the door with a towel, looks me up and down, and asks, "Did you go swimming?" A smirk plays on her lips.

"Ha! It's pouring out there like nothing else." I take the towel and dry my face, then strip off my shirt, handing it to her. It's so drenched, she could wring it out if she were so inclined.

She shakes her head at me. "I've got the girls gathering up candles and flashlights right now."

"Good idea, they say when this shit is gonna end?"

"Couple of days."

"Ugh, figures. Well, let's batten down the hatches, then, shall we?"

"Everything is taken care of and the girls have eaten already. They had sandwiches, do you want anything?"

I look down, my cock's half way to full attention. "Apparently, I'm liking you in that tank top and those shorts." I smile.

"Well, you're outta luck, your girls are awake and Kel still isn't back."

"Isn't back? Where'd she take off to now?" I snap.

"She had to go get her car. She said she'd be back in a bit, but she hasn't returned yet."

"Uh-huh." I tap my foot. "Okay, I'm gonna toss this stuff in the wash and rub one out in the shower since you won't oblige me. If she's not home by then, we'll just have to find her ass, won't we?"

"Yup," Crystal answers, patting my chest. I just take the towel and shirt back from her and head down to the washroom to strip and grab a shower.

❈ ❈ ❈

Cleaned up and not even remotely satisfied, I come out of the bedroom and go make myself a sandwich. It's just about four o'clock and I'm starting to get pissed about Kellie not being home. I've called four times and each time, it goes straight to voice mail. Ugh, I swear if she went to see him, we are gonna have a war on our hands.

I go to call again just as the door swings open and her heels click-clack on the tiles.

"Bear? Come help me with the groceries I bought. There's rum raisin in it for ya."

I get up from the dining room table and find her juggling a bunch of bags from the grocery store. Seems she's actually been doing something useful today. Although, it also looks like she's had a manicure and a fresh waxing, she's still a tad red around the brows.

"Chloe get you a little close, did she?" I smile, taking the bags from her as she huffs a thank you.

"She lost out on her tip for it too. Burned me twice and we won't talk about where the second burn is... *Okay*?"

I chuckle. "Ouch. You should just get the laser, I said I'd pay for it."

"I'm considering it, believe me."

"Crystal says it was worth it."

She looks at me and rolls her eyes. "Whatever, let's

get me inside and dry."

"Sure thing, Sweet Cheeks."

She heads off to our room as I get the food taken care of. Seems we're having steaks tonight, good thing our patio is covered. I'd hate to broil them and ruin a good cut of meat.

I get everything put up and season the steaks when Kel comes back down. She's dry and looking cute as ever in her jean shorts and racerback lace top. God, these women and the way they tease me. I growl in my throat and she laughs.

"Not anymore today. I'm not feeling it if you get me."

"Ah, yeah, not looking to make a mess."

"Certainly not. Go sniff around Crys if you're horny." She pats my shoulder and kisses my cheek. "She's probably in need of the stress relief, what with taking on the new kid and all."

"Speaking of kids, I'm going to see our Peggy Sue this weekend and you are coming with us."

"Um, I have plans."

"Yeah, and they are going to Colorado because your daughter comes first, Kellie, don't make me cut up your credit cards and take away the car."

"You wouldn't."

"For our kid, I would. You haven't seen her in months, it's the least you can do after last night."

She bites her lip and drops her head, then nods. "I'll cancel my plans."

"That's a good wife. You tell Damien he can see you when we come home."

"Okay." She goes over to the stove and puts on the kettle for her afternoon tea as I go see what my Bella is up to.

Walking into the classroom, I find her sitting at her desk going through papers and books. She looks like she hasn't stopped all day and from the looks of the place, I'd say she hasn't. She doesn't hear me as I come into the room or see me as I step up beside her.

"You need a break," I tell her.

"No. I need to finish."

"No, you need a break," I repeat, pulling out her chair and turning her to me. "Kellie's home, why don't we take a little walk?" I raise my brows suggestively.

"A walk where?"

"I was thinking that the billiard room needed some dusting and I'd like to watch you bent over in these little shorts... That, or maybe just down the hall to the bedroom where I can strip you down and give you a full body massage with my tongue."

"Somebody is in rare form." She arches her brow at me.

"Hmm, it's been a while since we've done either, and I'm feeling like I need to pamper you a little right now."

"If you must, lead the way." She puts out her hand and I grab her up, throwing her over my shoulder and smacking her ass. I carry her to the empty bedroom down here, the one Kel doesn't use, but I know is cleaned twice a week just the same. Crystal is laughing as I put her down on the bed and lock the door behind us.

"Can't have the kiddos finding us, now can we?"

"They'd get a lesson if they did."

"Ain't that the truth." I snigger, taking off my shirt and walking over to her. I pull off her top and stand her up, unbuttoning her barely there shorts and letting them drop to the floor. She's got on a silky red thong and

43

matching bra, which I also quickly relieve her of. I lay her down on the bed, face first, and straddle her. I start at the top, kissing her neck, her shoulders, licking with my thick, firm tongue, rubbing with my huge strong hands.

Crys lets out a deep moan as I rub down her back, getting it to pop from neck to ass then up again. She lifts up as I rub down and over her ass, giving her little licks and bites. I swipe her clit and she bucks slightly, her head turning toward me.

I chuckle as I move down her legs, rubbing her thighs, her calves, then taking off her socks, I rub her feet. Here's where the moaning really starts. The poor girl spends so much time on her feet, I'm sure they hurt, like all the time. She lifts her leg to me so I can better reach and really get in deep, then I tap her ass and she looks at me in question.

"Roll over, Bella."

She rolls over and I work my way back up her body, my tongue leading the way. This time, I give her kitty a lick and find her getting wet. I'm going to enjoy that shortly, that's for sure. I take to her arms and her hands, I did promise her whole body, after all. Her moans get deeper and I kiss her to silence her as I hear the kids come running down the hallway.

She laughs softly as I pull away, my hands trailing down her sides, my mouth finding her pert little nipples. I love how perfectly pale and pink they are against her flushed skin. I roll them in my teeth, making them long and hard before making my way down to the little patch of hair she keeps just for me. I take in her scent and feel the heat she is throwing. God, she smells good. I open her up, ping her clit with my tongue, and she lifts off the bed, her back arching exquisitely as she clutches the sheets in her hands.

I press my thick tongue against her as I slide my long fingers into her, curling them toward me as she presses down, riding my hand. I love the way she moves her body. She's so tiny, I can just bend and twist her so easily.

Putting her legs over me, I lick and suck on her until I feel her quake beneath me. My cock is so hard it hurts, but I want to make sure she comes again, so I hold out, my mouth singing for her. She comes again, her nails digging into my shoulders, knees locking against my head. It's a good one this time. I pull off my shorts and boxers, letting the monster free.

She licks her lips and nods her head in approval as I climb up on the bed and pull her up to me. "Ride my cock?" I ask her and she pushes me down, putting herself over me. She drops down slowly, letting me feel every inch of my manhood as it's swallowed by her tight little pussy. I love to watch as my cock disappears into her. She lays back, rising and falling against me, her hips doing these little figure eights that drive me wild as she pushes off my chest with one hand and clutches my balls from beneath with the other. The woman knows what I need. She lifts and drops faster, harder, and soon I can feel the boys tighten up, I'm gonna come. I grab her by the hip, gaining her attention. She looks at me and I pull her down for a kiss as she plays with my nipples, sending me right over the edge. I pump into her, coming. She stays folded around me as we both calm our racing hearts. No need to hurry to move, we're good, Kel wouldn't dare go anywhere, not right now. Not today…

11

CRYSTAL

TODAY HAS BEEN EVENTFUL. Starting with me helping Kellie pack last minute, then dealing with the fact that we had to cover up so nobody noticed us in the airport or on the plane. We're now unloading in Colorado, then we have to wait for our bags and hope Sonny is here to pick us up. Nobody really understands how hard it is to hide a Rockstar till said Rockstar is a *Beast*.

Just as we grab the last of the bags, someone yells, "Steven, is that you?" I turn to see an older and much more preppy version of our man. Thank God Steve does not look like this.

"Sonny?" he yells, then looks at me. "That can't be *my* brother." Kellie runs over and gives Sonny a hug and I stand back, helping the girls with their bags. Kel and Sonny walk toward us. "What the hell happened to you?"

"Got me a good woman, but we'll talk about that in the car. Let's get you guys loaded up."

"I want you to meet Crystal. Come here, Bella."

Steve puts his hand out and I walk over to stand beside him.

"Oh, yeah, the *teacher*. We gotta talk about that," Sonny states and Steve gives him a funny look. "Let's go," he says as he grabs our bags.

Judging by the way Sonny called me the *teacher* and the looks he's giving me, this weekend isn't going to go over well. We get outside and our stuff is being loaded into a minivan. Thank God I got the other brother.

Steve's laughing his ass off. "What happened? A minivan? Ten years ago, this guy would have given Kyle a run for his money."

"A lot has changed, Steven. I'm sober and I found God," Sonny says and all I'm thinking is this weekend just went from hell to I'm killing myself to end it.

We all get loaded with Steve up front with Sonny. "It's about a thirty-five-minute drive down to the house, so do you guys need to use the restrooms or anything like that before we go?"

When all decline, Steve asks, "Sonny, what's going on? Quit stalling."

Sonny starts the car and explains as we pull away from the curb, "Uh, Beth Ann, my wife, she doesn't exactly know about your unorthodox relationship. If she did, it wouldn't go over so well in our house. She's got a couple of kids and it's just not appropriate for them to see. So, for the weekend, can you just do separate bedrooms?"

"So, what you're telling me is I have to hide her like some dirty little secret just to appease your woman?" Steve asks with a growl. "And as far as kids are concerned, I've got kids and it ain't hurt them none."

"Steven, your girls have come up with this all around them. They've been raised to embrace your

47

lifestyle. Beth Ann is not going to understand it, and she's not going to want her sons anywhere near it. Yes, you've got kids, and I'm sorry for it."

"What's that supposed to mean?"

"Nothing, man, nothing. I just… It's been rough having Peggy Sue here. Look, I took her because you're my brother and she's my niece. That's what family does. So, please do me this solid for everybody's sake."

Steve turns, looking from me to Kellie. "What do you want to do, ladies? We can stay in a hotel."

"It's just the weekend. So, it's really up to you," Kellie says. I bet she's fucking loving this.

"You came to spend time with your daughter. You need to be there for Peggy Sue."

"Are you sure, Bella? Tell me, are you alright with this?"

"It's their house. I know people don't agree with the way we live. I was also raised to respect others in their homes."

Steven cracks his neck and gives a little growl. "I guess we're going to your house."

Kellie is downright loving this; you can read it all over her face. *Bitch*. Steve isn't happy, but he needs to be there for his girl and like I'm always told, I'm just the girlfriend. Let the weekend of hell and hatred begin.

12

KELLIE

A WEEKEND WHERE CRYSTAL ISN'T PAWING all over my husband. Hmm, I might get used to this. It's about time she remembers what it's like to be the help. Steve wants me to cut it back with Damien, well, maybe I want Crystal to fade to black too. She's been with us too long and gotten too damn comfortable. She's not a wife, she doesn't have the level of say that I do, but she's getting dangerously close to it.

Can't have that, I know I've slacked here and there, but these are my kids, this is my daughter out here, and I'm not going to forget that it was Steve who sent her here. I didn't agree with it. Hell, it was one thing Crystal and I agreed on. He just had to have it his way, said it was better for her. I'm not so sure now. These people, while it's funny that they are so uptight as to make Steve give up his toy, they are judging us. Judging me and that, I don't like. That doesn't sit well with me. It makes me wonder how they've been treating my Peggy Sue.

Our first born turned sixteen in February and was already nearly three months pregnant. Steve was furious, *I* wasn't surprised. She may have been fifteen, but she looked every bit of twenty. Peggy Sue takes after me with long honey blonde hair, full hips, and an ample chest, much to Steve's chagrin. I knew she was flirting, I just didn't think she was being left alone with the boy. What was his name? Doesn't matter, he's of no consequence. She doesn't need him. Maybe if I'd left Steve when we got pregnant, I'd be in a different place. I could have taken his daddy's money and run, but instead, I married him and we struggled for years. His addictions were bad, then his first band tanked and he got worse. Then we met Crystal. I guess she saved us. Saved him. She has her good points. I just feel I've had enough of her.

We get to the house and the girls are excited to see Peggy Sue. We told them about the baby on the plane, figuring the last minute was best, fewer questions that way. They are just happy to be seeing their big sister. Boy, is she ever big!

My eyes water at the sight of her, her belly full and round, as she stands on the porch to greet us in a flowy dress cut down to her ankles. Sheesh, she must be hot. I remember that phase, being that far along, I was always getting flashes. Her long hair is gone, cut up to her chin, her curls thick and wild like her father's when he lets it go. She smiles, holding her belly as the girls run up to her.

"Hey, Mary Ann, Sue Ellen." She is beaming now as she hugs them, one to either side of her belly.

"She looks like you," Steve whispers as he takes my hand and gives it a squeeze.

"I know. It's uncanny."

We walk up to our girl and hug her. She embraces her father with loving arms, but is tentative with me.

"What's that about, young lady?"

"I- I just didn't think you'd come. I'm surprised to see you," Peggy Sue answers, smiling past me at Crystal as she comes up the porch steps with some of the bags.

"Crys," Peggy Sue asks with a laugh, "why are you carrying shit?" She covers her mouth, looking inside. "Sorry, stuff. You got Daddy for that."

"Don't worry your pretty little head, just talk with your momma and your dad," Crystal answers, heading inside. Yeah, keep walking, get used to it. You'll be doing a lot more of it and soon if I have my say.

Steve watches as the girls look around.

"Hey, who wants a drink?" Sonny comes outside, holding a platter with tall glasses of sweet tea on them.

The girls look to us and I nod, so they each take a drink and say thank you. Sonny hands a specific one to Peggy Sue. "You're caffeine free, no sugar, my dear."

She makes a face, but takes it anyhow. "Thank you, Uncle."

There is something off about this whole situation. I'm not feeling the vibe here at all. I squeeze Steve's forearm and it tells him we need to talk and soon.

"Is this your family?" a woman asks from inside. "You should probably have stayed with them." I look up to see a woman with black hair escorting Crystal back outside. "Hello," she says, extending her hand, "I'm Beth Ann, Sonny's wife. You must be Kellie and Steven. I've already met the nanny, Christine, was it?"

I hold my snicker.

"It's Crystal, and she was just trying to help us get everything inside since Sonny here disappeared," Steve replies through a forced toothy grin.

"Well, she should have asked for the protocol first. We don't allow shoes in this house, especially those that will scuff up the hardwood, like those heels," she says as she points to my feet.

"Good to know." I force a smile. Bitch better have clean as fuck floors.

"We also don't just open random doors."

"Uh, that was me, dear. I told Crystal which rooms were which in the car."

"Shush, buttercup." Beth Ann puts a finger to her lips and Sonny puts his head down. Christ, she must have some damn good pussy if he's this obedient.

"Uncle, Aunt, it's warm out. Do you think we could go inside now?"

"Did you finish your hanging?"

"Yes, it's all out back, neatly folded, I just can't lift it anymore."

"That's fine, Jimmie and Ralph can get it when they get home."

"I'm sorry… Hanging? You have her doing chores at eight months pregnant?" I ask and as my voice raises, Peggy Sue grabs my arm.

"Momma, it's fine, really. I don't mind earning my keep."

Steve steps forward. "You don't have to earn anything, I've paid well and good for you to stay here. What the fuck, Sonny?"

"Oh, well, I-" Beth Ann puts a hand on her chest. "You're a bear."

"Damn straight, and you're a bitch who's got my little girl slaving while you do what? Crochet doilies of the stations of the cross?" Steve looks at me, then to Crystal as he adds, "This shit ain't happening. I'm not hiding you, and I'm not hiding my little girl here anymore." He growls, stomping into the house.

"Sonny, stop him!" Beth Ann screams.

"From doing what? Taking his child? Not I." He moves out of the way. "Best to let the man have it his way unless you want broken furniture."

13

STEVE

LIVID. Absolutely enraged. These words do not come close to describing how I am feeling right now. I pack all of Peggy Sue's belongings and make sure she has all the checks from Harrison Lagrange before glaring at my brother one last time. I had Kellie call the car service and we load up, heading for the nearest hotel with master suite openings. It's an hour drive but worth it to get my girls, all of my girls, away from that crazy house.

"I'm so sorry I sent you out here."

"It's okay, Daddy. You didn't know."

"Why didn't you tell me? Or Crystal? She said you talk almost every day."

"Because I was never alone. If not Uncle Sonny or her, it was one of them boys around, spying."

"Ugh! I could kill him."

"It wasn't Uncle Sonny, really. He was always kind and generous with his time and helping me and stuff. It got him in the dog house more than once with Aunt Beth Ann."

"That woman ain't no Aunt to you, you hear? She's a crazy woman that got her hooks in your Uncle, that's it."

"Yes, Daddy." She lowers her head, holding her belly.

"You okay?" I ask, concerned.

"Yeah, just gassy."

Kellie looks her over as I make the flight arrangement. I call the studio and explain that I'm in Colorado Springs and need to be out of here as soon as possible.

"They say that the plane is in for maintenance, but will be available in the morning. I guess we're staying the night."

"Well, that's good, because we're headed to the hospital. You're gonna be a grandfather."

* * *

Fourteen minutes past six pm on September eighth and I'm holding the most perfect little boy. He weighs nine pounds and three ounces and is twenty-three inches long. Peggy Sue did great and is resting soundly with Crystal and Kellie at her side. The girls are sitting with me as I coo and haw over him. His name is Brayden Michael Falcone, and he's my grandson.

I take a picture of us and send it to the band, so excited that I forget they don't already know about Peggy Sue's pregnancy.

Within minutes, the texts start pouring in.

MAVERICK: Congrats, but, dude, seriously? Ya could have told me!

RINGO: Congrats, man, why didn't you say

anything?

KYLE: Dude! WTF? You getting old on us, forgetting to tell us that kinda shit? Congrats, man! Where the hell are ya?

BRENT: What the fuck, a grand baby? You didn't say anything? Some friend you are.

Wow! Seriously, these guys are a hoot and as I'm setting up a group message, I get another from Brent.

BRENT: I'm supposed to apologize, but I'm not sorry.

STEVE: Stranded in Colorado, the plane can't come get me till morning. Won't fly commercial with the baby, now I'm not sure if I wanna fly at all. Is it safe with a newborn?

MAVERICK: Yeah, yeah, it's safe, just make sure the doc approves. You need me to get anything before you come home?"

STEVE: EVERYTHING! We aren't prepared yet! HELP!

Everyone responds to my plea with *on it*.

"You about done communing with the cellular gods over there?" Kellie asks me as she comes over and rubs down my chest.

"Sorry, told the band. They are on baby prep duty, we'll be hooked up by the time we get home."

"Least they can do."

"Hey, let off."

"No, we do plenty for them. I work my ass off nursing them for a pittance. The least they can do is help your daughter out."

"Momma? Please don't fight with Daddy, not now," Peggy Sue pleads groggily. The drugs they gave her are kicking her ass right now.

I get up and go to her, giving her son to her. She

cradles him and smiles. God help me, I hope she has more patience than I did at her age.

14

CRYSTAL

I WAS RIGHT WHEN I SAID THE DAY WAS
going to be crazy, only instead of crazy, it was
downright insane. Steve's gone to take Kellie and the
girls to the hotel because they don't need to be sleeping
here. I've barely held Brayden while Kellie was here.
Right now, Peggy Sue is sleeping and the little man was
hungry, so I'm in the rocker feeding him when Peggy
Sue says my name. I look up to find her watching me.

I stand, walking over and sitting on the edge of the
bed. "Where's everybody?"

"Your daddy took them to the hotel to sleep. He'll
be back in a bit. How you feeling?"

Peggy Sue nods her head. "I'm okay, tired and
achy. I gotta pee."

I smile just as Brayden falls back to sleep. "Let me
lay him down and I'll help ya."

"Okay."

I get little man down and go back to help Peggy Sue
to the bathroom. "Do you want me to stay in here or
step out?"

"It doesn't matter. Can I talk to you?" My Peggy Sue sounds like that little six-year-old again.

"Always, you know that."

"I need you to talk to Daddy."

"About?"

"Harrison."

"What about Harrison?" This isn't going to be good with the way she's watching me.

Peggy Sue finishes up, then washes her hands, but she keeps staring at her fingers. The baby wants to get married. She turns quickly and looks at me. "He sent me a ten-thousand-dollar check and engagement ring. He wants to marry me. Daddy's going to kill me, but I said yes."

"Peggy Sue, why would you do such a thing?"

"He's my baby daddy."

"Oh, my God! Whatever you do, never ever say that again."

"It's true." Peggy Sue starts crying. "He loves me. He's just afraid of Daddy."

"With damn good reason. I'd be scared of your daddy if I didn't know what a big teddy bear he is."

"His band got a deal here in the states in California."

"I can't promise anything. You're sixteen."

"Daddy was sixteen when he married Mom."

"I know that, but things are different. He's different."

"Please, Crys, I love him. I don't want my baby to be a bastard. All I have to do is call him and he'll come."

I shake my head and keep my tears from showing. "I'll see what I can do, but let's get you back in bed."

"Okay." Peggy Sue wraps her arms around me. "I wish you were my mom." I don't say anything to her because she's upset. If her momma was here, it'd be different.

Once Peggy Sue is asleep, I walk out into the hall and let my tears fall. They fall because she has what I've been craving. They fall because she wants to leave us and they fall because I know the love of my life is going to hate me when I tell him. I pull myself back together and go back into the room to two sleeping babies. Peggy Sue may be sixteen, but to me, she's a baby. She was only six when I came to live with them and we've been close ever since.

I'm nodding when Steve comes into the room and I look up to see him standing over little man, then he moves to the bed and kisses Peggy Sue on the forehead. He walks over to me, kissing me with his hand in my shirt. "How're my girls?"

I push his hand away. "Be good, and she's doing really well."

"And the boy?"

"He's an eater."

"Yeah, so was I and so was she."

"Wanna go grab a coffee while she's sleeping?"

"Think it's any good here?"

"Do you really want to go any further?" I ask and he shakes his head no before helping me up. "Yeah, I didn't think so." As we're walking down the hall, Steve puts an arm around me. "Girls go to sleep okay?"

"It took like three stories and two glasses of milk, but yeah."

I smile. "I guess I should have warned you."

"Well, it's been a while since I put the girls to bed."

"I enjoy it."

"I should help more often when I'm home."

"Or we could do it together."

"That'd be nice too."

Just as we get to the cafeteria, I see Steve is trying to adjust himself and it makes me giggle, but I cover it with a cough. "Do you want food or just coffee?"

"We can get food later, let's just do coffee. I've afraid to eat from here. Nothing smells right," he says, but still grabs a tray and if it's in a package, he grabs at least one.

"No food huh?"

"Shush, you, at least I know what it'll do to me."

"Now, Beast, you've known me what? Ten years? Have I ever actually shushed?" He looks at me with a cocked brow. "Get those thoughts out of your head right now."

"I've got no idea what you're speaking of."

We head to the register and Steve is noticed right off the bat.

"OMG, you're Steve Vicious from the band Fallen Angels. What are you doing here?"

"Yes, I am," Steve says. He sidesteps and the girl notices me.

"OMG, Crystal's with you. Is Kellie here too?" I'm going to kill him.

"Kellie is not here at the present, no. Can I sign something for you, or can we just pay?"

The girl pulls out a napkin and hands it to him. "Please."

"Pen, marker, blood of your first born…" he says, then I smack him.

"He's only joking, he's a bit of a beast when he needs coffee and sweets."

Steve growls, only it's the one that gets my girly bits in an uproar. "Got a name, honey?"

"Misty."

Steve clears his throat and I know we both just thought of Marissa. "Now, don't go selling this unless it will keep you off the pole. If you need the money, I'll give you another signature."

I slap him again and pay for our stuff so I can push him on. "Bye, Misty, it's nice to meet you. Remember to stay in school."

We get to the table and I'm positive I'm going to kill him. "Would you quit?"

We take our seats. "With the day we had, we needed a laugh."

I take a sip of my coffee as he bites into his muffin. "I talked to Peggy Sue while you were gone." Better to jump straight in than to beat around the bush.

He chews his muffin slow and takes a sip of his coffee, then makes a disgusted face. "How is she? You said she was fine. The look on your face doesn't say she's fine."

"She is fine, but she's also sixteen and thinks she knows what she wants." He gives me a raised brow and starts tapping his fingers at me. "You got to promise not to get mad at me."

His fingers stop tapping and he looks at me, confused. "Why would I get mad at you and what is this about?"

"You know, kill the messenger, and it's about your girl."

"This isn't Sparta."

"So, Harrison sent her a check and, um, a ring." Steve's teeth grind together. "Apparently, he got a record deal and is in California. She wants to go."

Steve's really quiet and looking around like he's searching for something in his head. "So, she's been talking to him all this time and lying to me."

"I didn't know this either. She told me she loves him."

"She has no idea what she's talking about. She's known this boy for half a minute."

"I know and I tried to talk her out of it." I shake my head. "Do you want to know what her response was?" He waves his hand for me to go on. "You were sixteen when you married Kellie."

"And it was one of the worst and best things I ever did."

"Don't say that, Beast. You love your wife."

"Yeah, but we had it rough. Before you met us, things were bad. There wasn't always money. What little we had sometimes ended up in my arm or up my nose. Hell, Kellie wasn't much better. I'm surprised Peggy Sue survived those first couple years, but she doesn't know that. She doesn't need to know that. It wasn't till Kellie's dad died, till we got the money, that we had a little bit of breathing room. I just, I don't want to see her struggle. No safety net and if this boy loves her so much, where's he been all this time?"

"I know you have addictions, I've seen them, but I've also watched you overcome them. As for Harrison, I have no idea. I don't like it any more than you do. I've been with her for ten years and helping her have Brayden... It killed me watching her in pain. If I could have done it for her, I would have. She's still a baby, but it's not my place to give her an answer."

"I suppose she's already made up her mind. She is her father's daughter after all."

"She wouldn't have asked me to talk to you if she hadn't."

"What do you think I should do?"

"I can't answer that."

"Come on, Bella, she's as much yours as she's mine."

"Kellie will kill you if she knows you listened to me."

"I'll handle her. I'm asking you because you know Peggy Sue best."

"I'd say take her home kicking and screaming, but once she turns eighteen, she'll take Brayden and we won't see them again. At least this way we get to see them when we want."

"Well, I guess we're gonna meet the boy, huh? Because she's not eloping to California."

"Thank fuck."

Steve laughs. "If she's gonna get married, then we're gonna do it right. We can take that ten thousand as a down payment for her dress."

"If Mary Ann and Sue Ellen make me go through what Peggy Sue has, I'm making them tell you."

"Don't worry, I'm ordering them chastity belts. We're gonna lock that shit up."

"Come on, Beast, let's go back up to our girl."

15

STEVE

"YOU AGREED TO WHAT?" Kellie is screaming at me through the phone. I have just told her I've agreed to meet Harrison Lagrange. She's swearing and carrying on, but I'm too busy watching Crystal with Brayden and Peggy Sue. My mind wanders and I am imagining what she would look like with a swollen belly, carrying my child, her breasts heavy with milk, her nipples darkened, pulling me in for a taste. It's been a niggling at the back of my mind since she told me that she couldn't conceive, but now, I know that I'm going to do everything I can to knock her up, that is if she's willing to let me, of course.

"Kell, I don't rightly care if you like it or not. We're meeting him as soon as we get back to Vegas, so suck it up." I hang up the phone and look over at my girls. "So, it's on like Donkey Kong." I smile.

Crystal doesn't say anything, only sits down beside Peggy Sue as I walk over to them. I bend down and kiss her, a little bit savagely, but what do you want? All my head is thinking is *I wanna put a baby inside you.*

She pushes me back and I growl deep in my throat.

"Not in front of the kids."

"Please, I'm pretty sure she's figured out what goes beyond this, seeing as we have him here." I chuckle, pointing to Brayden.

"Um, do I need to go for a walk or something? Give you guys some privacy, Daddy?" Peggy Sue asks with an awkward laugh.

"Beast, you're scaring your daughter. Stop," Crystal orders me sternly.

I drop my head, my arms on either side of her on the chair so I have her enveloped and blocked from Peggy Sue's line of sight. "What if I told you I wanna make a baby with you?" I whisper. She freezes and doesn't say a word. I reach down, sticking my hands between her thighs. "I wanna plow this field and sow my seeds till you're ripe and swelling from it. I want to make love to you, Bella, and watch you grow with life inside you."

"We talked about this…" she says through her teeth.

"I want to look into it further if you're willing," I answer, kissing her behind the ear.

"Kellie's not going to agree," she finally whispers after a painful silence.

"I don't plan on telling her unless we succeed. What's the sense in upturning the house if it doesn't work, but if it does," I pause, coming around the chair, "it'll all be worth it." I kiss her again and Peggy Sue laughs.

"Okay, you two, seriously, go get a room. I'm fine here. Really, they are taking good care of me. I'll see ya in the morning."

I can't help but laugh as Crystal snorts. "Okay, my

Peggy Sue, we'll go, but we'll also be back bright and early."

"Fine, just go sow your wild oats away from me!" She waves her hands. If she only knew just how spot on she is.

We get to the car and I look at Crystal. "I don't wanna go back to Kel and the girls tonight."

"Where do you wanna go?"

I pull out my phone and look up the nearest hotels with five-star amenities. "How about this hotel?" I hold up my phone, showing her a room with full room service and a hot tub on the balcony. "It's got one opening left if we hurry."

"It-it's fine," she stammers as I wrap my hands around her, pinning her to the car.

I kiss her again. "Okay, so we're doing this then?"

"What are we doing exactly?" she asks with innocence.

"I'm taking you to this luxury hotel where I'm going to ravage you over and over again, preferably, until I have to carry you out of there."

"What's gotten into you?"

I snake my hands up her sides and under her top, running my thumbs across her nipples through her bra. "I told you, I wanna have babies with you, and I only know one way to do that… Fuck like bunnies."

"You're serious?" She pulls my hands from her top, lowering them to our sides.

"I wouldn't joke about something like kids, Bella. I know what that means to you. Seeing Peggy Sue tonight, seeing Brayden, it reminds me of when the girls were little, what you and Kel were like. Seeing you holding that little boy, it seemed like the most natural thing in the world. You deserve to do that with our children…

Yours and mine."

"I don't know if it can happen, I don't want you getting your hopes up."

"We make an appointment to see a fertility specialist, not just some OBGYN who thinks they know it all. We'll see what they recommend and move forward from there. In the meantime, practice makes perfect."

She looks at the ground and then up at me. "Okay."

I kiss her again, lifting her up and putting her in the car.

16

CRYSTAL

STEVE AND I HAVE NEVER DONE ANYTHING like this. Not gonna say I didn't enjoy it because God knows I did. It's just a lot to go through. Steve's in bed next to me, snoring like the beast he is. I've got no clue where our clothes, phones, or hell, my purse is. He told me he wants to make a baby with me even after I explained to him that it would be impossible. He wants to see a fertility doctor and find out our options.

I just can't help but wonder what will happen when Kellie finally tells him it's her or me. What if I'm already pregnant? Do I just get sent off like Peggy Sue? Will he try to take my baby after I've had it? I can't help the thoughts rolling around in my head as I sneak out of bed and head for the shower.

Stepping into the shower with the hot water rolling over me, I'm sore in all the right places. I've just finished washing my hair when a strong arm snakes around my waist and I'm pulled into my Beast.

"You snuck away," Steve says kind of sleepily.

"I needed a shower and it's almost seven."

"Almost?"

"About a quarter till, last time I checked."

"I told Kel that we'd pick her up at nine. You know how she likes to sleep," he says with his hands on my tits.

"I know, but we have to get Peggy Sue and Brayden." I try to say it normally, but it comes out breathlessly.

Steve nuzzles into my neck. "Just till seven."

His knee is trying to part my legs. I turn, facing him. "We both know better than that." Steve's lips are on mine as he's lifting and pinning me to the wall.

He fucks me into oblivion once more, then holds me up to shower us down. He wraps a towel around his waist, then one around me before carrying me back to bed. My body is pretty much mush. Steve goes to find our stuff, then helps me dress before dressing himself. He's very tentative when he wants to be.

After checking out, we head to the hospital. It's time to pick up Peggy Sue and Brayden. We make small talk about nothing in particular on the drive there, like it's just another day.

Steve walks into Peggy Sue's room before me and stops dead in his tracks, which has me running into his back.

"Beast?" I question.

Steve growls. "What is he doing here?"

Oh boy, sounds like somebody showed up early. I try to push him out of the way so I can see what's going on, but it's no use. "Steve, let me in, people are staring."

Steve sidesteps and I walk in too.

"Mister Falcone, it's so nice to finally meet you. Peggy Sue has said nothing but good things." Harrison walks up to Steve with his hand extended.

I glance at Peggy Sue, then watch as Steve looks the boy up and down, then he proceeds to look through him.

"Peggy Sue?" Steve says.

I place my hand on the beast to try and calm him. We need no blood shed here. I look back over at Peggy Sue and notice she's got on this cute little pj set. "D-d-Daddy, Harrison got here just after you guys left. He's been with me all night. He wanted to make sure we were okay," Peggy Sue stutters out in a rush.

Someone needs to shake the boy's hand because he's still standing there with it out to Steve. I reach over and shake it. "Harrison, it's a pleasure to meet you, but we weren't expecting you till we made it home."

Harrison looks at me. "I couldn't stand the thought of her here in the hospital without me. She went without me long enough."

"I understand that, but it wasn't your place to decide."

Steve walks past Harrison and goes straight to Peggy Sue. "You should've called."

"I didn't see a reason. He's got a right to be here. It's his son. What would you do if someone kicked you out of my room when I was born?"

"I'm sorry, I felt I needed to be here."

"Daddy, don't send him away."

Steve pats Peggy Sue on the leg before turning to look at Harrison and me. "You've, ah, got bags I assume?"

"Just carry on, Sir."

Steve lets out a deep growl. "You come with us on one condition. You keep your trap shut that we weren't here last night."

"As far as I'm concerned, I just got here, Sir."

Steve looks at me. "You gonna be alright while I go get Kel and the girls? I'm sure Peggy Sue has paperwork and whatnot she's gotta do."

"I'll be fine and get her all taken care of," I answer quietly.

Steve kisses Peggy Sue on the forehead before walking over to me and kissing me goodbye. He looks at Harrison one more time before shaking his head and walking out the door.

"You know who I am. Are you the wife or the mistress?" Harrison asks.

I stumble over my words as Peggy Sue starts laughing. "They usually call me the girlfriend. Name's Crystal."

"Well, it's nice to see one other smiling face."

"It's how I was raised. Do I like the situation? No, I don't. I think both of you are too young. It's just not really my place to say anything. But, since Steve didn't say it, I will. You hurt our girl and you won't have to worry about any more children because I'll cut your dick off and feed it to ya. Got it?"

He raises a brow. "Well, damn."

"Crystal, really?"

"At least I won't starve to death," Harrison says before walking back over to Peggy Sue.

"Don't 'really' me. I'm the one who's had all the talks with your father for you. So, I have every right to tell him what I'd do."

Harrison looks at me then and quietly says, "Thank you for that."

"No thanks needed. I'd do it for any of the girls, they all know it."

"Just the same. I'm starving. Peggy Sue, do you want anything from the cafeteria?"

"Um, ginger snaps if they've got them. Otherwise, I'm all right."

Harrison looks at me. "Do you wanna come with or do you want me to bring you something back?"

"I'm fine, thanks."

"I'll be right back." He kisses Peggy Sue, then he's out the door.

I take a deep breath, then look over at Peggy Sue. "So, paperwork?"

"My discharge stuff and they're giving me a pump to unload these things. They've got to show me how to use it."

"So, you've decided on breastfeeding?"

"He won't latch on, but they recommend my milk, so we're gonna do a bottle. I'm just gonna have to pump."

"I think that's a good idea."

"Um, where did you and Daddy go last night."

I click my tongue and try to answer, "Just out."

Peggy Sue raises an eyebrow. "Out? What'd you do, sleep in the car? You look well rested."

"No, we didn't sleep in the car."

"So, you got a room without Momma?" Peggy Sue smirks.

"Damn man doesn't know when to keep his mouth shut. Can we, uh, keep it between us?"

Peggy Sue shrugs her shoulders. "What'd you think of Harrison? He's pretty, isn't he?"

I walk over and sit beside her on the bed. "I think we're both in for a world of hurt."

"Why do you say that?"

"Because we're both young, stupid, and in love."

"I don't think I've ever heard you say you love Daddy before. I've always assumed, considering you've been with us forever. You've just never actually said it before."

"That's something else that stays between the two of us."

"Okay, I'd tell him if I were you though. He kind of needs to hear it. Momma doesn't show him love anymore."

"Peggy Sue, she loves him, they just have a funny way of showing it. Plus, I'm not supposed to fall for the Beast."

"We're not supposed to do a lot of the things we do, are we?"

"I can't believe you're leaving me again."

"Um, I don't know if were going very far."

"What are you talking about?"

"Well, I'd kind of like to finish high school and it's only a couple hours commute for him. When he has to go out there at all."

"Are you asking your daddy if you all can stay at the house?"

"Oh God, no! Do I look like I have a death wish or look like I want to be a widow before I'm a bride?"

"Well, you aren't making much sense at the moment."

"I'm just thinking that with all the money he's sent and what he's got now... Just give me my phone please."

I hand Peggy Sue her phone just as Brayden starts crying. I get up and grab him. I'm humming as she's searching for something.

Peggy Sue flips her phone so I can see it. "It's a cottage just fifteen minutes up the street from Daddy and you guys. I could ride my bike."

"Not with a newborn, you couldn't. I'm not telling him this time."

"Well, do you think he'd be happy about it? At least I'm not going to California."

"I'm sure he'll come around. You know how he can be. He's been a bit more of a beast than normal lately."

"Well, not much he can do. It's either this or I move away."

"You don't want to give him ultimatums because you won't like his decisions. Remember, you are still sixteen, meaning you still need to watch how you go about things." Peggy Sue sticks her hand out and I hand the phone back. "Don't get mad at me. I've always been straight forward with you and you know it. Ten years with your daddy and I've learned a thing or two."

Peggy Sue isn't saying anything, so I place Brayden back in his little bed. I'm turning back to her when she huffs, "You know, if Daddy thinks I'm going to stay under his roof and let him teach me how to screw up my kid, he's got another think coming."

I just nod at her and walk out into the hall where I lean against the wall. I'm trying to keep in mind that she just had a baby and is still hormonal. I'm also dealing with my own shit and don't need the dramatics of a sixteen-year-old.

17

KELLIE

"SIX CALLS! Between the two of you, Steve. What the fuck were you doing all fucking night?" I can't let it go, we're in the master bedroom on the private jet and I'm furious.

"Kellie, I told you I left the chargers with you last night, our phones just died. I had no idea you called till I plugged into the car this morning," Steve growls. He's defensive and aggressive. I know something isn't right, I just can't pinpoint exactly what it is.

"Uh-huh. Right, and what about the boy? He just showed up outta thin air?"

"No, Peggy Sue called him while Crystal and I grabbed food in the cafeteria, then he showed up this morning."

"You should have called me."

"Dead phone!" He waves his hands in the air. "Damn it, woman, listen to me for once in your life, would ya?"

"So, you're going to let her marry this boy? Is that what it boils down to? No consulting me first?"

"I don't know that we have a choice, Kell, she'll get herself emancipated if we don't allow it, or she'll simply run off with him like you did with me. Do you want that for her? For Brayden? Do you want them to go through what we did? Because I sure as fuck all don't."

I sit on the bed, tears behind my kohl lined eyes. "No, I don't want that for her, but I don't want her rushing headlong into a marriage that may only look good on the surface, but could turn out to be a huge mistake for them in the long run."

"Huge mistake? Is that what you think of us? That we've been a huge mistake?"

I look at him, part of me screaming YES! Yet another part of me still clings to the love I have for him. It's that love that answers him.

"Bear, no. Sure, we had some really rough patches, but you're the best thing that ever happened to a girl like me. Let's face it, I was white trash straight from the trailer park, but you never saw that side of me, you always saw my potential. You pushed me to stay in school, to get my APRN license. You've kept me well all these years. I've just always thought I held you back, kept you from reaching your potential. I've never felt good enough for you. I worry that you regret me."

Steve walks over to me and bends down, kissing me gently. "You are the mother of my children and my first love. Kellie, I don't fight you like I do just to have something to do with my day. I fight you because I want you, need you, love you, and damn it, I miss you too."

"I miss us. Like we were when it was just us."

He pulls away. "What are you driving at?"

"I think it's time we closed our relationship."

"You're going to give up Damien?"

"If you'll give up Crystal."

77

He shakes his head. "No, that doesn't work. Crystal is a part of this family. She's been with us for years, Kellie. How heartless can you be?"

"It's simple, Steve, if you're fucking her, you're no longer fucking me," I say matter-of-factly.

He nods his head. "Yeah, let's see who breaks first." He walks out of the room, slamming the door.

* * *

"I can't take the stress anymore, Damien, Sir, I need to see you," I whisper into the phone. I'm standing on the patio at home, watching as the girls help their father with the bags. They're so cute, each with their own rolling suitcase. Harrison will be staying with us for I don't know how long. I wasn't paying attention to the conversation. Instead, I was thinking of the terrible things that Damien could do to me if I go see him.

"Your needs don't interest me, nor do your wants. Have you been fucking him too? Like the little whore that you are?"

"Yes," I answer obediently. "Twice this week alone."

"Hmm, not near enough to cultivate a healthy bond between you. You need a reprimand. Meet me in two hours. You know the address."

"Yes."

"Yes, what?"

"Yes, *Sir*."

I pack my overnight bag and slip out of the house while everyone else is in the kitchen and living room getting comfortable. Steve wants to play a fucking game, I'll play and I'll come out satisfied. He hates that I see Damien as it is, maybe if I see more of him, Steve will realize just what he's doing in pushing me out the door. If not, well, I still win because I get the pleasure of a twenty-four-year-old stallion between my legs while he deals with a broken doll.

I get to Damien's place and he isn't alone. He's got two of his playmates with him, Ricky and Racine. Ricky is a submissive like me, but Racine is a Switch, meaning she can be both. Typically, when she's here, she bottoms for me at Damien's request.

"Hey, pretty lady." Racine smiles, kissing my lips and caressing my ass. She smells of liquor and cigarettes, and the taste in my mouth isn't at all sexy. I pull away, wiping my mouth and Damien laughs.

"Come here," he orders and I go to him, dropping to my knees and crawling in my dark green pencil skirt with matching black and green leather corset. My thighs rub together and I can already feel the wetness between them.

"Thatta girl. Now, come greet your Master like a good little kitten."

I sit up on my knees and come up between his legs, crawling up into his lap and curling into him, kissing him. He reciprocates, his hand going up my skirt to make sure I am pantyless, which of course, I'm not.

"Tsk, tsk, my little one. You know better, one would think you like being punished. Do you like the sting of my hands on your ass?"

"Yes, Sir," I answer truthfully. "I do, Sir. I've been bad."

"Seems so." He sits back, pulling a joint from his cigarette pack. He lights it up and blows smoke into my face. I cough softly and he laughs. "Come here." He turns the joint in his mouth so the head is inside and makes me take the hit he blows against my lips. After a few more, I'm comfortably numb and lying languidly in his lap, that's when he flips me over and begins to lash me.

I yelp as he hits me and his other hand goes fishing into my corset and grabs my breasts. He keeps hitting me and as he does, the orgasm builds inside me. My yelps of pain become moans of pleasure as I transcend one head space for another. He pulls my panties off and lifts me up, placing me on the fucking machine, the dildo just at my entrance. He manacles my wrists above me, hoisting me in the air, I'm his to do with as he pleases. His pleasure is to see me thrust upon this machine tonight as Ricky takes me from the back.

My body is used and abused, and I couldn't feel any better. Steve will never understand the need deep in my core to be treated like this. He's too good a man to ever do so. This is why I have Damien and his toys.

18

STEVE

IT'S BEEN A ROUGH WEEK. With my baby girl having a baby and then the would-be father showing up, and Kellie being Kellie, I've barely had time to talk to Crystal since our night in the hotel. I'm so exhausted by the time she comes to bed that I just can't wait up for her, so though we wake and sleep together, there's been no more *sleeping* together, and no real conversation.

Peggy Sue showed me the cottage she wants to move into. It's close to us, it's not in California, and while I would rather have her home, I don't think I can deal with the fiancé. Yes, I've said it. Fiancé. With or without Kellie's permission, I've decided to allow this insanity to go on, but only because with Maverick's help, I'm pretty sure I can gain some control over it. That man can plan anything to a T. If he weren't married to Angelica and about to have a baby of his own, I'd swear he played for the other team.

Right now, I'm on my way to the hospital. Brent called and Marissa is in labor. The twins are arriving today. Crystal and the girls stayed home since Peggy

Sue is still at the house and we don't know how long it's going to be. I didn't want her here with Brayden. I walk into the labor and delivery ward and see Angelica, Maverick, and a pacing Kyle? "Where's Brent?"

"In with her. He's so anxious. They're doing a C-section, as we speak," Kyle says, his hands shaking.

"What's going on? Ky? You alright?"

He pulls from my hand on his shoulder. "Y-yeah, I'm good, just worried about them." He's stressing hard and looks to be coming down off something harder.

Angelica is watching him and her hands are over her belly as Maverick sits beside her, practically blocking her from view.

"Hey," I say, sitting next to him and Angelica.

"How's the grandbaby?" Maverick asks casually, though, like me, he's watching Kyle twitch.

"Gorgeous, I need your help when you have some time."

"Okay. Something goin' on?"

"You could say that. I need to plan a wedding and a move for my Peggy Sue."

"Okay. Which one do you have me doing?'

"I was hoping you could help on both fronts. Peggy Sue's just this side of sixteen and she's really disorganized. Me, I'm all thumbs with this stuff, and the girls are making a production of it. I need someone who's level headed involved."

"Well, first things first, she needs a prenup."

"We don't have one, why would you even go there?' Angelica smacks him on the arm.

"Yeah, I thought about that. The thing is he's got the money, and I do, but she really doesn't have anything."

Maverick looks at his wife. "If I'd wanted your

82

money, I'd have taken it while you were still in rehab." He waves her off and she smirks, grabbing his face and kissing him.

"Yeah, but then you'd be going to hell alone."

"Just shush and let the big men talk."

"Whatever, Steve, you give that little girl whatever she wants. The Vera Wang dress, the fountains at the Bellagio, the works. She'll love it and you'll get to walk her down the aisle."

"Cupcake, shut up," Maverick orders and she purses her lips, crossing her ankles and her arms. "She may not have the money, but because you do and the boy does, I would do a prenup for everybody's sake."

"I'll have to call the lawyers in the morning for that. What else do you suggest?"

"Well, she's sixteen, you'll have to get the papers drawn up so she can even get married. I'd also take her to the doc as soon as possible and get her put on birth control."

"That we already picked up before leaving the hospital, I wasn't playing that game again."

"Good, yeah, I wouldn't."

Just as I'm about to ask another question, the delivery room doors open and out comes Brent with the world's biggest smile.

"It's a split, I got one of each!" he exclaims, hugging Kyle. We go over to him and embrace him. He's in such a state of euphoria that he doesn't seem to care that he's crying like a baby.

❖ ❖ ❖

Seeing the twins reinforces my determination. I do a search for fertility clinics in the area and find one that is well rated and discreet. I call to make an appointment and they can see us tomorrow. Wow, I didn't think it would be that fast. I head home and Kellie is at work according to what her schedule says, and Crystal is in the kitchen making dinner.

I come up behind her and wrap my arms around her, nuzzling into her neck. "My Bella."

"They have the babies?"

"A boy and a girl. Two perfect little peaches."

"Oh, those poor babies." She sighs.

"Nah, they have Marissa, remember? She's a whirlwind, they'll be okay."

She crosses her arms. "We'll see, you know once he gets them all home, he's gonna lock them down."

"We just have to make sure it doesn't stay that way. Go over there more, bring the girls, invite Angelica and Maverick. Force him to interact. It's high time he broke out of that shell of his."

"The girls will like it, they always love going over there... How was Kyle?"

"A mess, but I don't know if he was on something or just feeling what Brent was."

"Honestly? I think he's been on something for a while. H's always on edge, he reminds me of you before we got you clean." She wraps her arms around my waist.

"Yeah? Well, I don't know what to do about that, but I do know that we need to have us a talk."

"Everything okay?"

"Yeah, it's about what we talked about earlier in the week."

"Okay?"

"Don't be mad, but I called a specialist and they can see us tomorrow at ten. I already asked Angelica if she could take the girls for a couple hours and she said yes."

She pulls away from me and goes back to stirring the sauce on the stove. She pauses, thinking, then finally says, "I guess I didn't expect it to happen so quick?"

"Oh, me either, but I suppose it's a good sign, Somebody up there is looking to help us get this done."

She's quiet and I can see her stressing. "If you don't want to do this, I can cancel. It's not just me that we are doing this for."

"It's not that, I've gone for years thinking it wasn't possible," she says with a shake of her head.

"And that very well may still be the case, but we won't know until we see the specialist." I wrap my arms around her again, turning her to me once more.

"I don't know if I'm more scared that there is a slim possibility I can, or that there is that high risk that I can't."

"Bella, it's just a preliminary, nothing invasive they say, a pelvic, blood work, and a conversation. Where is the harm in that?"

"Okay," she finally answers and goes back to stirring her sauce.

19

CRYSTAL

WE DROP THE KIDS OFF AT ANGELICA AND Maverick's, meaning Sue Ellen, Mary Ann, Peggy Sue, Brayden, and Harrison. Man, there's a lot of kids under our roof all of a sudden. Steve's driving us to the clinic and I can't help but be worried. I'm afraid he's getting both our hopes up. I'm watching out the window, stewing in my worry when he puts a hand on my thigh.

"We can still turn around if you're having second thoughts. I don't want to push you into this."

I turn to look at my Beast. "I'm not having second thoughts. I'm just worried, I suppose."

"I know, this is a trip."

"Are you having second thoughts?"

"Not in the least." He doesn't hesitate, which makes me feel a little better. "All I hope for is a boy."

"God knows we have enough girls in the house."

"You're telling me. I practically sit to pee."

"Well, you have Brayden and Harrison." Steve shakes his head with a grunt and I figure now is as good a time as any to ask, "Beast, how are you and Kel?"

"Um, she's trying to hold out on me and I'm winning."

"Are you?"

"Oh yeah, she's starting to look at me like a piece of meat. Why do you think she's taking on all these extra shifts?"

I watch him, confused for a moment. "She's going to kill herself if she keeps going the way she is."

Steve shrugs his shoulders. "She'll level off. She always does. If you remember, she did this a couple years ago too."

"I remember. It was right after I overheard you all talking. She wanted me gone. Was it the same reason this time?" Steve takes a right before looking at me and nodding his head yes. I take a deep breath. "I don't like coming between the two of you."

"Bella, you're not coming between the two of us. She's coming between the two of us." I just nod, then go back to looking out the window because I'm not sure what to say to him. Steve reaches across the car and pushes my hair out of my face. "You know I love Kellie, have since I was sixteen years old. But I love you too, and I'm not giving either of you up without a fight. You know me, Bella, I don't like to lose."

I bite my lip, looking at him. He just said he loves me like he's been saying it forever. Just as casual as can be. We pull up to the clinic and he parks, but I've yet to say anything because honestly, I'm a little shocked. I knew he cared for me, I just didn't know he loved me.

"You're going to chew that lip off in a second." Steve chuckles and my eyes shoot to his.

"You, you said you love me," I stutter out.

He nods at me. "Does that surprise you?"

"Honestly, yes."

"I don't see why. Ten years is a long time to be with someone and not love them."

"When this started, it was just fun. Yes, I was a kid and fell head over heels quickly. I just figured you cared but not that you could ever love me."

Steve turns in the seat, grabbing me by the face. "I've loved you for a long time. I just didn't have the balls to tell you."

"Well, don't we make a pair?"

"So, are you saying you love me too?"

"Beast, I've loved you for almost ten years."

His lips connect with mine and I grab him by the shirt, wishing I could pull him closer. He crawls across the seat and is over me in seconds. Deepening the kiss, he drops the seat back and I let out a low moan. Steve's got his hand in my pants and his fingers are teasing my entrance. I grind against his hand and he pushes two fingers into me. His thumb is circling my clit as his fingers pump in and out me. I've got one hand in his hair, holding him to me and the other digging in his shoulder. I can feel my walls tightening around him as I reach my orgasm. He lets me ride it out on his hand before coming up for air.

"We ready to go in here and see about making some babies?"

"Babies? I thought it was one baby?"

His lips curl as he crawls back across the seat and I right myself. Steve gets out of the car, then comes around to help me out.

"Remember, we may not get the news we want."

Steve nods and we walk inside. He takes me by the hand and we walk up to the front desk where I let him do the talking.

"Welcome, can I help you?" the older woman

behind the desk asks with a smile.

"Yes, hi, Steve Falcone, we have an appointment for ten."

"Yes of course. Let me get you the paperwork," she says as she's riffling around her desk. "Here you go. Just fill out this packet, Mrs. Falcone. Mr. Falcone, I need you to go in the room just to your right and fill this at least a quarter high." She hands me the paperwork and Steve a cup.

"Um, why? We're here for her."

"It's standard to check both people in the relationship."

Steve takes the cup. "Do I get any help?" he asks, looking at me.

"There are magazines and videos in the room, Sir."

"I don't want to use that sticky shit," he says, then walks off, still muttering under his breath.

I find a seat and sit down. I am looking over the paperwork and trying to figure out how to answer some of these questions. My last period. Hell, I don't know when my last period was. Steve sits down beside me.

"How's your paperwork coming?"

"Horrible. What name do I put on here?"

"Crystal, it's fine. Put Falcone if you want, or put Howard. I'm paying cash, it doesn't matter."

"It does matter. We're going to get these questions."

Steve squats in front of me. "Bella, calm down. They are general questions. What don't you know?"

"Apparently, my name and my last period."

"Well, your name is Crystal Howard, though we should have made a Falcone out of you a long time ago. Your last period was around the tenth of June." I look at him, confused. "You woke up and said, 'son of a bitch,' and kicked me in the balls. I wasn't going to forget. When you do get it, you sync up with Kell."

"How long have you known this?"

"Known what? That your periods are jacked? Years. I thought you took that seasonal shit, or one of those other weird birth control pills."

"You notice way too much for a guy."

"I'm married, it comes with the territory."

"Not to me."

"Well, practically common law. I should become a Mormon."

"You aren't bringing anymore crazy into this life we have."

"Well, maybe a little more." He leans up, kissing me on the nose.

***

We've gone through all the necessary tests, blood work, ultrasound, and pelvic exam. Now, we're sitting in a stark white office and I'm a bit on edge. I've been looked at from the inside out and I'm starting to feel twitchy. My leg is bouncing a mile a minute.

Steve reaches over, putting his hand on my thigh and giving it a little squeeze. "Bella, it's okay, calm down."

"I don't have a good feeling," I say just as the door opens.

"Mr. Falcone, Miss Howard, how are you feeling?"

Steve takes a breath. "I think we're a little anxious to know what you found."

The doctor smiles, shaking hands with us.

"Firstly, let me introduce myself, I'm Dr. Ang. I'm a specialist in dealing with PCOS, also known as

Polycystic Ovary Syndrome, which, Miss Howard, your ultrasound findings indicate you have been a long time sufferer of. We will have to wait for your blood results for conclusive findings, but the preliminary outlook put you in my caseload."

"Okay," I answer, but in my head, all I can think is okay, what's that? How do I get rid of it?

"Polycystic- Blah, blah, what does it mean? Can we get pregnant or not, Doc?" Steve blurts out.

"It's not that black and white. We need to treat the symptoms of the syndrome. First, I'll need to run down a list of some other symptoms if you have a few moments." He looks at me with soft and caring eyes.

I rub my face and squeeze my forehead as I nod.

"Your periods are irregular. When you get them, are they unusually heavy or very light?"

"Heavy, but they only last a couple days and then they're gone."

"Okay, excessive hair growth, usually on the face and abdomen."

I nod. "I've had electrolysis for it though."

"I see." He makes a notation and I wonder if I did something wrong? Should I have not had the procedures? Will it be hurtful to us?

"Any pelvic pain, aside from when you have had a period?"

I shake my head no.

"How about mood swings, depression, or anxiety?"

"Um, I don't think so."

"Uh- actually she does get these moments where she's all doom and gloom. It's rare, but it takes days for her to snap out of it and she doesn't wanna get out of bed typically," Steve interjects and I just look at him. The Beast really does notice everything.

"Okay, good, and how long have you been trying to get pregnant?"

"Um, we just started, but we've been having sex without condoms for years and never had so much as a scare. I was told I couldn't have babies."

Dr. Ang sighs. "I'm assuming this was many years ago, before the discovery of PCOS. We've come a long way since then. I'm going to prescribe Metformin, it will help to level your insulin and if we're lucky, regulate your periods. Once we get that under control, given how long you've been dealing with fertility issues, I would suggest forgoing oral stimulation and going with injectables. Now, the chance for multiple births is about twenty percent, but in cases like yours, worth the risk in my professional opinion."

Multiple births? Like how many are we talking, not the Kate plus eight crazy, I hope. "Um, multiple?" I manage.

"About twenty percent for twins, seven for triplets and three for quadruplets or more. But the odds are low," the doctor insists.

"Then, pregnancy is possible?" Steve is lit up like a Christmas tree at midnight. Great.

"Oh, about ninety percent that we can get your girl here to ovulate, then it's up to you to get the job done, so to speak. Unless you want to do IVF? That will increase your chances tenfold, but it is costly."

"With the injectables, we can conceive the old-fashioned way though?" Steve is suddenly all chatty Cathy.

Dr. Ang nods. "Well, yes, but injectables and IVF is more conclusive."

"Always trying to sell a Lamborghini when a Corvette will do. Let's see what the blood work says, let me and the little lady have a talk, and we will get back to you." Steve stands and puts his hand out to me. I'm in a daze, all this new information, tests, injections? Talks? What am I supposed to be thinking here besides run for the hills?

20

STEVE

"I KNEW IT WAS GONNA BE POSSIBLE," I say with a laugh as we get to the car and I pick Crystal up, swinging her around.

"He said there's a chance," she says with some bite in her voice.

"Bella, that's more than we had an hour ago. If they get you to ovulate, I'm betting my boys can make the swim to knock you up. Hell, all I had to do was spit and I got Kel pregnant."

"They have to get my period regulated first."

"And we'll get the medicine, and hopefully, it will help. I've got faith that this is gonna happen for us. In the meantime, we keep trying like we have been."

She sighs as we get in the car, not saying anything more. As we drive, she finally speaks, "I think it's just gonna take time to sink in, we're banking on a lot."

I reach over and take her by the hand. "I say we don't stress over it, we have fun with it and we enjoy it. I know I am gonna have fun figuring out ways to keep it interesting," I say as I pull the car into some tall standing trees off the highway. They envelop the Escalade and cast a twilight glow on us. I unbuckle my seat belt and turn toward her.

"What are you doing, Mr. Falcone?" she asks with a suspicious tone.

"Keeping it interesting." I point to the back seat with a grin.

"If we get caught, it's your face on the tabloids, not mine," she warns as she takes off her seatbelt.

"Move that pretty little ass, Miss Howard, before I come over there and strip you myself."

She crosses her arms and her legs, facing me. "Is that supposed to be a punishment?"

I reach across the seat and pull her to me, backing us into the bench seat of the Escalade. I hit the button and it falls down, giving us a good, flat surface to play. My mouth crashes against hers and my hands make quick work of her yoga pants and panties. God, she's wet already. I love it! She pulls off her top and the sports bra goes too. Now, she's exquisitely naked before me. I pull off my shirt as she unzips my fly. Our bodies clash and I'm being ridden backward, her ass bouncing up and down as she clings to my ankles. I grab her by the hips and grind up into her, and she moans out my name as she comes.

She falls down over me, then slips off only to pull me to her so I am on top of her. I bury my cock deep inside her as she digs her nails into my back and shoulders, spurring me on. I take my time, kissing her, licking her nipples, sucking on her neck. I mark her, but I don't care, she's mine, all mine. The idea that she's gonna be able to have my baby sends me over the edge and I come. I lay to the side of her, pulling her to me as I continue to kiss her and fondle her tits.

"I don't wanna move, I just wanna lay here in the shade and wait to get hard again," I whisper.

"That would be nice, but we have to go grab the kids, and Kel will be home soon."

"Right, I'll just have to embed you into the mattress later." I chuckle.

"I think you've turned into more of a beast than you already were." She plays with my ponytail and sits up, looking for her clothes. Her ass in the air has me hard again and soon, I'm right behind her, my cock tapping at her from behind.

"Yup, you're a beast," she coos, going down to her elbows as I push inside her once more.

"All right, enough, I'll pick up pizza! Sheesh," I holler when the kids all bitch and moan that they're hungry and want Italian. "Crystal, call Luigi's and order the usual plus a couple salads."

Crystal smiles at me, pulling out her phone and making the call. We've got a car load with Peggy Sue, Harrison, the baby, and Sue Ellen and Mary Ann managed to wrangle Angela for the night from Maverick and Angelica. Now, to get food and supplies. I swing by Walmart and send Harrison in for s'mores supplies since no one knows his face yet. This way, we can have a nice night by the fire and not have to worry about paparazzi.

"It'll be twenty minutes, Steve," Crystal says, then lets me know how much the pizza and everything else came to. I nearly choke.

"A hundred and fifteen dollars? Seriously?"

"You are feeding a small army, Daddy." Peggy Sue chuckles.

"No kidding, you all had better eat it all too, or never again! Ya hear?"

"Yes, Daddy."

"Yes, Mr. Falcone," Angela answers too.

"Oh, for heaven's sake, no pouty faces. We are gonna have fun tonight, pool time, play time, and pizza, the three P's," I insist and Crystal looks at me like I've lost my ever lovin' mind. "What? I'm feeling playful today."

"Yeah, caught that." She shakes her head. Oh, I'm sure she did, seeing as I've been extra frisky.

* * *

Food's devoured and we've all waited the forty-five minutes suggested by some random pool guy forever ago. Kel has even gone to put on her suit to come and join us in the volleyball match in the pool. Just as Crystal returns from the bedroom in her black halter bikini, Peggy Sue snickers and Mary Ann looks at her strangely.

"Crys? What happened to your neck?" the little one asks curiously.

Crystal stops in her tracks as Kellie appears. "Is there something wrong with my neck?"

"Yeah, you look like a leopard," Kellie spits before stomping off. Fuck, now her feathers are ruffled and there are way too many people here for me to let it go.

I look from Crystal to the back of Kellie's head as she stomps away and back again. Crystal is pinching the bridge of her nose. Fuck it, I'm not ruining the play time because Kellie is overreacting.

"Who's ready to play some ball?" I shout and the girls all yell happily. "Alright, grab the ball and I'll be right out." I walk over to Crystal and pull her hand from her face. "Hey…"

"I'm going to kill you."

"I couldn't help it, you were digging those nails into me and I had to do it, had to leave my mark on you. I'm sorry, Bella."

"We're gonna have to be more careful," she whispers softly.

"Nonsense, you and I are just expanding our horizons. I put up with Kellie and those bruises all the time, she can suck it up. She wants me to be a prick, consider this my prickish move."

She shakes her head. "Beast, we have other stuff we are trying to do and we are gonna get caught. I already feel like we're sneaking around."

I wipe my face. "It shouldn't be like that, I'm sorry, Bella. How do I make it up to you?"

"It's something new that we're gonna have to work it out… Figure it out… I don't know." She's getting frustrated again.

"Okay, let's just go have some fun, huh? Play a little with our girls and see if that boy has any athletic ability."

"And if he doesn't?"

"Then I know I can catch his ass if he ever hurts our Peggy Sue."

"Um, I may have taken care of that."

"Really, did you threaten him well and good?"

"Well, you didn't and somebody needed to, so I told him if he hurt her, I'd cut his dick off and feed it to him."

"Ouch, appropriate, but still, ouch." I lace my fingers into hers and lead her toward the patio doors.

21

KELLY

THE NERVE OF HIM, marking her up like that. People are gonna see it. I don't care if he wants to brand his cow, but I do care that our kids are looking at it. I mean, sure, Peggy Sue knows and the little ones look at her as a second mommy, but there's no reason to parade it around. I have my marks and you can't see a single one, even in my bikini. My ass and my tits are covered, thus, so are my marks. Besides, most of my pain and pleasure is psychological. Degradation, humiliation, being put on display. These things get me off. Having my power stripped away, being fucked, and fucking are different things.

Steve and Crystal spend so much time together, more than I do with Damien and the others, but my time is always fun. They deal with the mundane while I transcend it.

After walking away from them, I head to my room that I keep on the first floor, get dressed, and go to bed. I have to work in the morning. I've been taking on extra shifts and seeing Damien on the sly all week and I'm sore all over, but at least I've not given over and let Steve win. I've kept from him and his big swinging cock. Like I said, as long as he's fucking Crystal, he's not fucking me.

22

CRYSTAL

IT'S BEEN ABOUT A WEEK SINCE STEVE AND I saw the specialist and we've both been kind of anxious waiting for our results. It's Wednesday, and I've got the kids here doing their studies. I've had an extra two kids in my room because Harrison is pretty much stuck up Peggy Sue's ass and with him comes little Brayden.

My phone rings on my desk and I walk over to grab it and look at the number. I answer it and walk out of the room. My results are back and I need to tell Steve what's been found out. I step back into the room.

"Harrison, I need to run down the hall for a minute, can you help the girls if they need it?"

"Oh, um, yeah, sure. Yeah, I can do that." Seems I caught him off guard.

"Great, answer key is on my desk, just don't give them the answers."

"Will do."

I shut the door and make my way into the living room. Steve and Angelica are playing *Rock Band* while Maverick is watching them. Poor guy. "Um, I hate to interrupt, but can I borrow you for a second?"

"Angelica, Angelica, pause it- pause it."

"You snooze, you lose," Angelica says.

"*Steve*?"

"Yeah, yeah, I'm coming, I'm coming." He puts down the drumsticks and gets up, following me out back. I head over to the pool. It's away from the house and I can see if someone is coming.

I turn to face him. "I got the call."

Steve stares at me blankly for a second before realization dawns. "Oh! And?"

"Well, things around here are about to get a lot crazier."

"*Okay*?"

"There's a prescription for me at the pharmacy and I have to go on a Maverick diet."

"What? Why?"

"Because if we do this right and you knock me up, I'm likely to have gestational diabetes and this way, I'm already on the diet."

"Okay, and the prescription, I'm assuming, is the injectable."

"Yeah, once I start my period, we start the injections and I take those for two weeks."

"Okay, I'll go pick the prescription up now. Are you ready for this?" Steve snakes an arm around my waist and pulls me to him.

"Beast, it's a lot more real and I'm scared."

Steve pushes my hair behind my ear. "There's nothing to be afraid of, I'm here and will be with you every step of the way. I love you, Bella." He kisses me.

"I love you too, Beast. We're gonna have to go to the store for Maverick approved food," I pout.

"Hey, why don't we just go now? Angelica and

Maverick are here and they can watch the kids for a few minutes. We can just get it over with. If they ask, we can tell them your blood sugar's high and we've got to change your diet because that's what I'm telling Kellie. That is, you know, if she speaks to me this week."

"She's really upset with us."

"She'll get over it, she always does. She's the one being irrational."

"I suppose I can show Harrison what to give the girls next."

"There you go, and I'll talk to Maverick about getting them hitched. I did ask him to help and the fucker hasn't done anything yet."

"Okay, let me go show him what to do. If he's going to be stuck up Peggy Sue's ass, he can work for me."

"Work, work, work, put him to good use. I'll go talk to Maverick," Steve says as he turns to walk away.

"Hey, Beast?" I call after him.

He turns around and looks at me. "Bella?"

"You might want to get that look off your face. You look like the cat that ate the canary."

Steve's grin gets bigger than it was and I didn't know that was possible. I take a deep breath, then head back inside and to my classroom. After giving Harrison instructions, I meet Steve by the car and we head out. We head into the local Walmart so we can do the one stop shop and grab my prescription, then go home.

I grab a buggy. "Do you have a list of what I'm allowed to have and not allowed to have?"

"I can pull one up. Google," Steve says into his phone.

"This was your idea. You have to help me keep track of this shit."

✻ ✻ ✻

We get our shopping done and head home with everything. One thing has been bothering me and now is the best time to ask, so I turn to Steve.

"Beast, what time is Kel supposed to be home?"

"Unless she's gotten mandatory overtime, she should be home around six. Why?"

"I wanted to hide the prescription before she came in."

"I'm way ahead of you. I bought a new lock box today."

"At least we're on the same page."

✻ ✻ ✻

"Shit! Fuck! God damn it!" I shout, pushing Steve away from me and getting out of bed.

"Bella, what the hell?" Steve rolls over, groaning.

"Get up, I need to strip the bed."

"What? Why?"

"Because there's blood everywhere!"

"What? Wait, are you okay?"

"Do I look okay?"

"Do you want me to answer that?"

"This is all your fault, you know," I snap.

"Me? You bleed all over the bed and it's my fault?" he asks, helping me strip the bed.

I put my hands on my hips. "Yes, your fault. You and your stupid ideas."

"Oh, Christ."

"Go grab the bleach while I clean myself up," I order, shooing him away.

He nods his head. "Okay."

I grab clean clothes and head for the shower. I get showered, then dry myself off and dress before bagging up my clothes that are now garbage. Walking back out into the bedroom, I look at Steve.

"You suck, you know that?"

"Bella, baby, sweetheart, I can't do what I'd normally do to get out of this because you aren't in the shower anymore. So, tell me what *can* I do?"

"Kill me."

"I can't do that."

"The doctor could have warned us that I was going to get twenty some odd years of periods at once. It fucking hurts."

"You want the heating pad? Snacks? A giant teddy bear to snuggle."

"No, I've got to make breakfast, then get ready for a day of school."

"How about I make breakfast and you just get ready for a day of school."

"Beast, I'm not liking this so much right now."

"It'll get better, I promise."

I just laugh and drop the bag of garbage by his feet before walking out of the room. I head for my classroom and start setting out what each kid will be working on today, then make notes for Harrison because I've decided I'm going back to bed and everyone can suck it if they don't like it.

23

STEVE

I LOOK LIKE I MURDERED HER. Is that much blood normal? We definitely need to talk to the doc. I shower, then get the sheets and bloody clothes all bagged and out to the trash. Just as I'm starting breakfast, Kel comes padding into the kitchen, still in her pj's.

"Morning, bear," she mumbles, heading for the coffee pot. She pops in a pod and stands there shaking her ass.

"You aren't working today?" I ask, watching her. She's still looking good and I can tell from the tightness of her pants that she's not wearing any panties. I internally groan.

"Switched with Kerri. I don't go in till three, then it's a double."

"Okay," I answer and start to pull out pans for breakfast. As I'm bending down, Kellie's small hand caresses my ass. I stand up and look at her, wondering what she's up to.

"I hate that we're fighting," she pouts and her lips

get that fullness I love.

"Well, you're the one who pushed yourself out of our bed and moved into the spare room and all. I'm just riding the tides here."

"I know, I've been terribly unfair to you. Here I am, getting every hole filled with cock, and you're just pumping into the same old model. How bored you must be." She smirks, the woman knows just what gets a rise out of me. I know that she fucks other men, I just don't want to hear about it.

"You've been seeing more of Damien, I take it?"

"Well, of course. I have my needs too. I'm sure you've been fucking Crys at every possible turn, being you can't go more than a day or two without slipping your cock into a pussy or mouth. But, tell me, don't you miss a big pair of titties wrapped around you while you get sucked off?"

She is fucking good at that, her tits being the larger of my girls. I watch as she unbuttons her night shirt, leaving her breasts exposed. "C'mon, you know you wanna." Her finger trails down my chest, stopping at my waistband with a flick.

"Fuck," I half moan as she kisses me before falling to her knees. Pulling her top over her shoulders, she takes my cock into her tits, sliding me up and down. My head swims as she sucks and slides. I grab the kitchen island, letting her do her magic.

"Daddy?" I look up to find Peggy Sue in the doorway. Fuck, I'm glad that the island is solid, so she can't see her mother as I instantly blow my load all over her face and tits.

"Fucker," she spits, but can't move with our daughter standing there.

I hold my laugh and covertly drop a kitchen towel

to her. "Yeah, baby?" I answer my little girl.

"What's for breakfast and where's Crys?" She looks around, confused by my presence in the kitchen.

I right my pants and walk over to avoid her coming to us. "Um, she's not feeling well today. It's that time, you know. So, I'm sure she just went back to bed. I'm making bacon, fried potatoes, eggs, and hash this morning, you wanna tell the girls?" I put up my hand to turn her and head her back out of the kitchen.

"Okay, Daddy." She kisses my cheek and heads off.

I laugh and Kel pops up, her shirt back to rights and a glare on her face.

"You did that shit on purpose."

"Probably, but I got the sense you liked it."

Kellie walks up to me and grabs my cock. "Maybe if you were more of a bastard in bed, we'd have more fun times. You know where to find me." She slaps the kitchen towel against my chest before walking away.

✼ ✼ ✼

I feed the girls and Harrison, then make sure they have everything they need and head upstairs to check on Crys. She's changed the sheets and is curled up on the bed in a ball.

"Bella?" I ask, climbing in the bed with her and wrapping my arms around her. "Can I get you *anything*? I'm so sorry."

She grunts at me and shrugs me off her.

"Please, I feel like I should be doing something." Anything so that I don't go find Kellie. I'm horny as fuck and her tight little ass is just what I'm craving about now.

"You need to read the instructions on those boxes.

You wanted to do this, you do the hard work. I'm just gonna lay here and bleed to death, let me die in my misery."

"Bella, I had no idea it would be this bad." I roll her to me, pressing on her tummy. I know Kellie always likes that, the pressure helps. I kiss her softly. "I'll go check the stuff, but it'll have to be a bit later. Kel is home until three and Maverick and Angelica will be here in about ten minutes."

"I left everything out that they need to do, Harrison can help them today."

"You seem to be trusting the boy with an awful lot," I observe.

"He's in there every day, he sees what I teach him. I trusted him yesterday and he did good, didn't give them answers since they still got stuff wrong. It's not that much, he can handle it. If he's gonna be in there, he might as well be useful."

"I guess. They are moving into the cottage this weekend, so at least it will be quieter here after classes."

"I was supposed to help decorate."

I told her that you're having your period, I'm sure she'll understand."

She shakes her head. "You gotta be careful, Kellie knows I don't have them like this."

"I know, but we can say the insulin meds are doing it. The Metformin is used for blood sugar, she knows that."

"Looks like you've thought of everything," she condescends. I know it's the cramps talking, but her being testy isn't gonna help our cause, especially if we're trying to do this quietly.

"Like you said, I need to be on the ball," I respond, looking around. "You sure I can't get you something?"

"A stiff drink."

"Bella, even I can't have one of those anymore."

She looks at me, confused.

"The doctors told me everything looked fine, but said that a diet high in iron and protein would be better and that if I drink, I need to cut out alcohol because it decreases mobility of the sperm. We want optimal movement, so I'm not drinking anymore, not till we get you babyfied at least."

"This house is going to go crazy... Fucking insane," she cusses, which isn't a good sign since she rarely swears, if ever.

"All aboard the crazy train."

"You know I'm blaming you for this, right?"

I nod and smile. "As well you should." I lean in to kiss her again when the doorbell sounds. "Maverick and company." I get up. "I'll be back in here later to check on you."

"I'll still be here *dying*," she shouts as I go out the door. Poor girl, I feel so bad for her. I wish there was more I could do for her. I head downstairs and Mary Ann is letting Maverick and Angela into the house, no Angelica.

"Hey, man, where's the wifey?"

"Spa day." He rolls his eyes and I chuckle.

"I need a spa day. I wanna switch with her, marry me, Mav?"

He shakes his head. "Um, no, not into the dude thing, but from what I understand, Brent and Kyle are, so you might wanna hit one of them up."

"Wow, you went there?"

"You started it."

"Been a long bit," I say, letting Angela run along to the classroom.

"Where're the ladies?" Maverick asks, looking around the house.

"Oh, um, well… I…" I don't know what I should tell him. I now he won't tell anyone, but still.

"Let's go out back so you can spill your guts because you look like you need to talk to somebody." Maverick puts out his hand, walking me through my own house and out to the back patio. I reach into the cooler and pull out a beer, popping the top and slugging it down.

"Shit," I spit it out, tossing the beer over the fence and down the mountain side. I look at Maverick, who's got a hand over his face as he sits down.

"You ready to tell me what's going on?"

"So much stuff…" I huff. "First, I find out Crys might not be able to have babies, then Peggy Sue has her's and my daddy instinct kicks in. So, I tell Crys I wanna see a doc to see if she can have babies, then Brent has his kids, and Kellie and I are fighting because she wants Crys gone but won't stop seeing her Dom, Damien. Kellie starts holding out on me, then Crys and I see the specialist and they say we can get knocked up with some help, so we're taking fertility drugs and now, she's bleeding like a stuck pig and miserable. Meanwhile, Kellie is trying to seduce me in the kitchen with her titty fucking and telling me I know where to find her. Shit, man, all I know is I wanna drink, or fuck, or something because I feel like I'm gonna explode, but I can't do either right now. If I drink, I'm hurting our chances for a baby, and if I fuck, then I'm giving up my control to Kellie. Fuck, man, just… Fuck!" I'm pacing and running my hands over my head.

"Am I to assume that nobody knows about you and Crystal?"

That's all he got outta that? Really? What the fuck? I nod with a huff. "Because it's so risky, we don't want anyone to know until it happens."

Maverick is sitting there as cool as a cucumber while I quickly fall to pieces.

"Alright, so, let me get everything straight. You find out after however long you've been together that Crystal can't have babies, then your daughter has a baby and nobody knows. We on the same page so far?"

"I didn't want the press getting wind of a teen pregnancy."

"I get it, just hold on, I wanna make sure we are together so far."

"Yeah, man, you got it."

"You and Kellie are fighting because she want's Crystal gone and you don't, but you want her Dom gone and she doesn't?"

"Crys has been with us since Peggy Sue was six, Mary Ann was an infant, and Kellie was pregnant with Sue Ellen. She's pretty much my fuckin' wife too. This idiot, twenty-four-year-old has only been in the picture for the last two years on an off. He's a blip on the screen. Crys is family and I love her."

"You, my friend, have yourself a dilemma. You need to tell your wife that you're in love with the girlfriend. You also need to deal with the fact that you started an open relationship and if you don't want that open relationship to continue, then you need to come to terms with your wife. Honestly, it would do you all some good to talk to somebody because you may not see it, but I do... There's tension all through your wife and your girlfriend."

"Maverick, Kellie knows I'm in love with Crystal, has known for years, it's why she's tried to get me to end the relationship in the past. It was just that I never told Crystal, not until recently. The thing is, she loves me too."

"Well, hell, I could have told ya that."

"Hey, I was busy trying to keep up with them both and didn't notice. Kel and I came to an understanding about Crys, at least I thought we had, but she's started again, then today, she's all up on my shit like nothing's changed. I don't know what to do with her."

Maverick sighs. "Oh, yeah, you all need some major counseling, you're all fucked up."

I laugh. "Thanks, man, thanks a lot."

24

CRYSTAL

IT'S ABOUT A QUARTER AFTER ONE AND I'M still lying in bed dying. If I knew this is what it'd be like, I would have said forget it. My head's pounding, ovaries and back are screaming, I'm bloated, and to beat it all, I've already ruined three pairs of panties and pants. So far, this is not much fun.

I hear the door open and close and, of course, I expect it to be Steve coming in to check on me. This time, I'm wrong, it's Kellie and the shrill of her voice today is making everything so much worse.

"What are you doing out of commission? You're never out of commission," Kellie quips as she disappears into the closet.

"Apparently, I'm not perfect."

"Ohh, were snappy," Kellie yells. "Are we not getting enough? Steve not taking proper care?"

"What do you want, Kellie? I leave you alone when you're like this, can't you, at least, do that for me?" I sit up so I can see her.

"I'm sorry, since when are you ever on the rag?"

Kellie asks with a bag full of clothes in her hands.

"Since I had to start a new medicine. What's it to ya? Are you writing a fucking book? If so, kiss my ass and make it a love story," I snap.

Quick as a whip, Kellie is on the bed and has me by the face. "You watch your fucking mouth with me. I've only got to say one word and you're gone. Believe me, divorce scares the shit out of Steve," Kellie hisses, shoving me back and walking out of the room.

I'm done, I'm not doing this anymore. I get off the bed and start packing what little I showed up with. I've got tears falling down my face when Steve enters the room.

"Ding-dong, the bitch is gone," Steve says. I ignore him and finish doing what needs to be done. I stop and take a deep breath when he places his hand on my shoulder. "You going somewhere, Bella?" I turn to face him, tears still streaming. He tilts my chin, looking at my face where I'm sure Kellie's left a mark. "What happened?"

"I can't do this anymore."

"What are you talking about? There's a lot of *this* going on."

"Me and Kellie, we've been going at it for years, but never once has she laid a hand on me till today. I can't do it anymore."

Steve's head ticks to the side. "Kellie did this? What happened?"

"She came in and you weren't here, so she was being her natural, bitchy, I can't stand Crystal self when you're not around. She was going on and on about me never being like this and wanted to know why." Then, I give him what happened, verbatim, and the action that went along with it.

Steve pulls me against him and his heart is pounding out of his chest. "She put her hands on you and threatened me. I've had it, this ends today."

"What do you mean?"

"It means Kellie and I are about to have ourselves a little talk." Steve steps away and grabs his clothes.

"Beast, she came first." He ignores me and keeps getting dressed.

"You're not going anywhere, put your shit away. Kellie and I had an agreement and she's broken it. Apparently, she's been breaking it for quite some time."

"I love you, but she's your wife and she doesn't want me here," I say as my tears flow faster. I'm not used to all these hormones and I'm not sure how to control them.

Steve visibly swallows before walking back over to me. "I'll deal with it. Don't you worry." Steve kisses me, then grabs his sunglasses off the rack and walks away.

25

KELLIE

WHY IS IT THAT THE LINE FOR COFFEE IS always longest just when you need to be someplace else? Here I am, feeling pretty sure I've managed to scare Crystal right in to finally packing her shit. The little coward, she won't fight me, she knows she'll lose. Always has, always will. Steve may think he loves her too, but he's loved me for seventeen years, we have three children, no prenuptial agreement, and Vegas is a no-fault state, meaning in a divorce, I get half of *everything*.

I get my Trenta Iced with vanilla and cream, and head to the hospital. Is that the Escalade? What the fuck is Steve doing here? I pull into a parking space and watch through my rearview mirror as, sure enough, Steve gets out of the car. What the actual fuck? I get out of my Lincoln and before I can say word one, I'm pinned to my door.

"You liked putting your hands on her? How's it feel?" Steve grits out. Oh, he is spitting nails. Guess the little minx finally went and told on me.

"Bitch had it coming, running that mouth of hers. She's lucky all I did was grab her." I laugh as he squeezes my arms.

"No, Kellie, you are. See, I've been thinking about our relationship a lot lately. Especially since you cock blocked me. I think you're wrong."

"Oh? What about, bear? That you're pussy whipped, or that you're just a pussy?"

He slams me against the car and I chuckle. "Is that your worst? Damien hits harder with a feather crop."

"I'd rip you in half if it wouldn't give you fuel in the divorce."

I stop laughing. Did he say it? "You wouldn't dare."

"You brought it up, and I think for the first time in months, we finally agree on something. You want your freedom? Wanna get gangbanged on the regular? Fine, have it your way, and I hope your pussy shrivels up and falls the fuck off." He slams me against the car and stomps away, leaving me breathless and stunned.

26

STEVE

WELL, I'VE GONE AND DONE IT. I've said *the word* to her. *Divorce*. After seventeen years, I've finally come to terms with the fact that Kellie and I are through. Fact is, I think I should have left years ago. The minute I admitted I was in love with Crystal, I should have taken the girls and run. It would've saved us years of fighting to save a marriage that we didn't really want to be a part of. She stepped out on us long ago, stopped paying mind to our children, and has pretty much sucked the soul right out of me. I'm exhausted from trying, trying to hold it together, trying to be the good, understanding man. She opened our marriage, saying it was for us, for *me*, but I think that it really has always been just to feed her deviant needs.

I pull up to the house and the driveway is packed. There's Maverick and Angelica's BMW, Brent and Marissa's Navigator, Ringo's Hummer, and even Kyle's Monte Carlo is just chilling like it's the Fourth of July and we're having a party.

I walk into the house to find Angelica and Marissa

cooking dinner, the girls sitting at the counter reading books and Kindles, and the guys are all in the living room just talking like it's nothing strange. I see everyone. Everyone but Crystal.

"Where's Crys, Peggy Sue? And what are you all doing here?" I ask as Angelica comes over to me, wrapping her arms around me in a hug.

"Your daughter called in the Calvary. Can't have you going through the crazy alone. It's not how we work, not anymore," she answers, kissing my cheek. "You okay?"

"Where's Crys?"

"She's upstairs, still in bed." Peggy Sue stands up. "Did you find Momma?"

I nod. "Does everybody know what's going on?" I whisper, looking at the faces all turned on me.

Maverick gets up, walking toward me. I tense up, my fists balled. "Calm down." He puts up his hands, open palmed as if in surrender. "I didn't say anything. This was all Peggy Sue." He looks to my little girl and so do I.

"Peggy Sue?" I ask sternly.

"I went to see Crys and she was so upset, crying, and I just listened. Daddy, Momma is outta control. Between you and her fighting and Damien and her shackin' up, it's too much." She takes my hand. "We need family right now, so I called them."

I sigh, looking at Maverick.

"After you left and Peggy Sue came down, she knew everything, I asked her if Crystal had eaten and she said she hasn't, so I went up to check. She's... You gotta get her to eat."

"I'll go up to her now, what are ya cooking?" I ask as I hear babies cooing and crying. Christ, my house is full of insanity, but the sound of the kids is easing my nerves. I go over to the stove and see chicken and veggies sautéing with a big salad being chopped up and set to the side. Good, healthy eating. What I wouldn't give for a bloody steak right now and a bottle of Scotch, but I promised myself no more drinking, not while Crys and I are going through this. "Alright, well, I'm gonna go up to her. Hopefully, I can get her to come down, now that the cat is outta the bag, complete with kittens."

"Dude, we're here for ya, Kellie can go screw. I always liked Crys better anyhow," Kyle says, coming over to us. My little ones look up at me and I can see the confusion on their faces.

"Kyle, not now, alright? Peggy Sue, can you take the girls outside for a bit, let them stretch their legs?"

"Sure, Daddy. Hey, guys, let's go play outside."

I nod, heading up to see Crys and try to get her to show herself to the masses.

I find her pulled into herself with the covers over her head. I reach out and pull them back, revealing her in an entirely different outfit. "Crys, Bella, I'm back." I sit on the bed next to her.

"Everybody leave?"

"Not at all, they're worried about us. From the looks of things, they are looking for places to sleep at this point if we don't get our shit together and fast."

"There's nothing to get together."

"Actually, I need to pack up some things."

She grabs her head. "What did you do?" she whines.

"I told Kellie we are done. I want a divorce."

She sits up and stares at me, her mouth open a tad. "Why would you do that?"

"Why?" I groan. "Look around, her shit is here, but

121

she's gone. She's been slowly walking out for more than a year. You think I don't notice that some of her stuff has gone poof, never to return to this house? I'm not blind, I just refused to face what's been crumbling around me because I didn't want to break us all up... Because of the girls. It's not worth us all being locked in hatred and discord just so Beth Ann and Sue Ellen feel like everything is okay. They are bigger now, they can learn to understand. They're old enough to get that it has nothing to do with them and everything to do with their momma and me."

Crystal is shaking her head, looking at everything but me. "I should have just kept my mouth shut."

"Frankly, I wish you would have told me sooner. We could have been past this all and happy by now, but I understand, Kellie can be overwhelming."

"I don't have the right mindset to deal with what I have to deal with. I can't do it."

"What are you saying to me?" She wraps her arms around me, cuddling against me. I stroke her hair and kiss the top of her head. "Bella, we need to go downstairs."

She shakes her head no against me.

"We need to, you haven't eaten anything all day, it isn't good for you. Also, I know we have a lot on our plate, but we need to add the injection to it tonight. Even with everything going on, I don't want to stop that process."

"I'm not hungry," she quietly whispers.

"Hungry or not, you need to eat. With all the blood you're siphoning off, you need something in you besides Motrin." I pull her into me, lifting her off the bed. "Let's go."

"Not giving me a choice, huh?"

"Seems I need to become a dominant prick like Maverick to get anything done around here." I kiss her, carrying her out the bedroom door.

"I'm not Kellie, I don't do the submissive woman thing. If you smack me, I'll kill you."

"That's my girl."

We appear and the kids are all absent as I put her down. Angelica is also missing, while Marissa is tending to breastfeeding the twins on my couch. At least she's got a blanket over her, my girls don't need to see that, not yet at least.

Ringo and Maverick are talking in hushed tones by the patio doors. "Great, the councilors have found each other. What do they have in store for us?" I ask as I take Crystal by the hand. Brent and Kyle just smile at us as I look around and the councilors follow us into the kitchen.

"So, are we gonna eat or what?" I ask, trying to deflect whatever these two have in their heads.

"We've been thinking... You wanna get pregnant, correct?" Ringo asks, looking over at Crystal, who's squeezing my hand for dear life as I nod, clearing my throat.

"Well, you're gonna need help," he adds.

"Um, we have doctors for that, but thanks," I say.

"No, you need somebody to take the girls. It's gonna take a lot of alone time." Maverick clamps his hand on my shoulder and I just stare at it.

"*Right...*" I draw out the word, still not clear on their thoughts.

Ringo looks at us and huffs. "Maverick, we're gonna have to throw it out for him, cause he's apparently not smart enough to understand it."

Maverick leans into me with his hands out in front

of his body. "All right, let me break this down into smaller pieces for you. I know I've dealt with cases like yours, and in said cases, you have to have certain windows of opportunity. In those windows, you have to go at it like rabbits, so to speak. You can't do that with kids here. We're suggesting that we take them off your hands when that time comes. Plus, you're gonna have doctor's appointments and other stuff you have to do."

I look at Crystal. "He's making some good points."

"We're already turning their world upside down. We don't need to do it more."

"Crys, we're not giving up this shot for us. If we do, we're letting her win. I'm not backing down on any of it. What I did, what I said, I mean it, it's done."

The guys are looking at me and even Brent and Kyle have confused looks as they try to process what I've said.

"I don't wanna stop trying either," Crys says, "but we also have the girls to think about."

"Could you guys come here? Like, instead of us uprooting them, maybe have one of you help with the schooling and everything else?"

"We thought about coming here, but then we thought about the sounds that you two would be making and didn't think it would be suitable for little ears."

"Nothing different than a Tuesday night. Their rooms are on the opposite side of the house and if you kept them down here, or maybe Crys and I could go someplace else? What do you think, Bella?"

"I think this is getting so confusing," she says, sitting finally, her hands in her hair.

"There has to be an easy way. There's just gotta be." I rub her shoulders.

124

"We're not even to that point yet. Do we need to talk about it right now?"

"I think we need a plan, fourteen days comes up fast when you got shit to handle." I look to the patio doors to check on the girls in the pool. At least they are well occupied. "Why don't we do this? Let's try you guys coming to us, if it doesn't work, then we'll do it your way."

Before Maverick or Ringo can answer, Crys takes my hand. "I don't wanna leave here, I don't wanna go someplace where I'm not comfortable. Of course, here isn't comfortable at the moment, either."

"Once I pack her shit, it will be."

"You put her out?" Kyle stands up. "Good for you! About fucking time, man."

"Wait, what?" Marissa turns, putting the babies down. "I thought this was just a fight? Are you talking divorce?"

Brent moves to stand by Kyle. "What the fuck, dude? Have you lost your fucking mind? You've been together for years."

Crystal pulls from me and starts to walk away. I race after her. Turning her to me, then us to them, I say, "No more running." I wrap my arms around her and pull her to my side. "Yeah, Brent, we've been together for years, but aren't you forgetting that so have Crystal and I? Kellie and I have been having issues for over two years. Now, I know you guys like her and there are redeeming qualities about her, but the way she's treated me, treated Crystal, it just isn't worth it anymore. We deserve to be happy too, don't we?"

"I just figured it was a fight, you'd work it out," Brent huffs.

"Don't get all huffy with me. I know you got

yourself a hang-up. She's saved your ass a few dozen times over the last three years, but you don't know what she's like when the cameras are off, or we're behind closed doors. That's a different woman. A woman I can't keep happy anymore. We aren't the same people we were before the band, or even before the girls came along. I'm a grandfather now and I want to do it right. I wanna be a good person, do the right thing, and sometimes what seems like the scoundrel thing is really the right thing. In the long run, she will be happy free of me." Crystal hugs me as they stare. "Look, either you are here for us, or you're not, it doesn't matter. Side with Kellie, she needs friends in this too, it ain't gonna hurt me. Just don't let it break up the band and we'll all be good." I look to Crystal. "Now, I'm gonna get some food into this one, are you all gonna join me or are we eating all that food alone?"

"Well, I'm starving." Marissa stands up, looking to Brent.

"Let's eat," he answers defeatedly.

27

CRYSTAL

THE PERIOD FROM HELL IS FINALLY OVER and Steve and I are heading for our first injection and shot at getting knocked up. To say this has been a long week would be an understatement. I have to take a test every morning to check for ovulation, then Steve has to stick me in the ass every night.

Angelica and Maverick are at the house with the kids. I showed Harrison what the girls would need to do today and he took over without a problem. I think he rather enjoys helping around the house. It's been weird not having Peggy Sue, Harrison, and Brayden at the house at night since they moved down the road on Saturday. Angelica and Marissa helped me decorate with Peggy Sue as the guys moved all the heavy stuff. Friday, we painted the entire house, then it took Saturday and Sunday to get them completely moved in.

Steve and I have been bickering more than normal and more than once, we've slept on opposite sides of the bed. It's getting to be more often than not that we're fighting. This time at the specialist is much different than last time because Steve hasn't touched or talked to me. I'm sure it's got a lot to do with the fact that Kellie hasn't been home in a week. I honestly don't know if she's coming back or not.

I went through all the bloodwork and ultrasound. Now, we're sitting in that stark white office once again, waiting for the doctor. A few minutes go by and Doctor Ang comes in.

"Well, we have good news, it looks like you have a couple of mature follicles, which is just what we're looking for. So, we're prepared to give her the HRC today, but before we do that, I'd like to have a conversation with the two of you. How are you?" he asks, giving us a pointed look and folding his hands on the table.

"We're peachy, just regular, everyday, life stuff."

"It's not uncommon in the first stages of treatment for couples to be a little frustrated."

Steve clears his throat. "You're tellin' me." This only gets an eye roll from me. "All we're doing is bickering about everything from the way I gel my hair to the corner on the bed sheet."

Doctor Ang nods his head. "The hormone treatments can make communication difficult and abstaining from sexual activity can be cumbersome for a couple used to being intimate more often. It's essential to remember why we're here; that you two love each other and that you're trying to bring a new life into this world. While it's not going to be easy, I promise you that it's worth it."

Out of the corner my eye, I see Steve turn toward me, then he turns my chair so I'm facing him. "Bella, I'm sorry I've been a jerk."

"I'm sorry for not having more patience."

"I'm sorry I let not being *with* you keep me from you."

"You're a man that knows what he likes."

"I'll try to be more understanding and when I'm not, you need to smack me upside the head. Only, use your hand and don't throw anything at me."

"I can't reach your head when you're standing."

Steve reaches out and kisses me. I melt into him as soon as our lips touch. It's hard not to. I've missed him.

"Okay, now that we're all back on the same page, let's see if we can't get you ovulating. Miss Howard, please come with me." I step behind the curtain and to my displeasure, it's another shot in the ass.

"Ouch."

We walk back around to where Steve is sitting with that stupid grin on his face.

Steve stands. "So, now what, Doc?"

"Within the next twenty-four to thirty-six hours, she should begin to ovulate. Then, from that time, you have about 40 hours to attempt insemination. After that, the window for pregnancy closes dramatically. Thirty days from now, you'll come back in to see us. That's just about the time you'd be starting your next period."

"Okay, thank you. Come on, Crys," Steve says.

We make it out to the car and I sit down gently. Steve looks at me. "When we get home, I'll kiss it and make it better."

"Oh, no, you won't. We only get one shot at this. I've not gone through hell for you to fuck it up."

Steve laughs, starting the car and driving off. "So, are we calling everyone to pick up the kids for the week?"

"What do you think we should do? Sue Ellen and Mary Ann are starting to ask questions."

"We've looked into everything except how we're going to do this."

"We've not really been getting along."

"We have to work on that."

"No shit."

"How's about when we get home, we take a nice long bath?" I give him a raised brow. "When I say we, I mean you."

"I've got to pack the girls up."

"I'll call Maverick and Angelica."

"Beast?"

"Yeah?"

"I'm scared."

"It's just us, I'm not suddenly going to start spinning you like a plate."

"I don't think it's a good idea to spin me like a plate."

Steve laughs and we head for home.

28

KELLIE

A WEEK, AND NOT A PEEP FROM STEVE. Not a phone call or a visit to the hospital. Damien isn't particularly pleased with the situation. I was warned about cultivating my marriage. When I arrived at his place, crying and suffering from Steve's assault on me, he scolded me, bent me over his knee, and took the riding crop to me. I've been opened up and put on display as his little harlot, and men have jacked off to me and on me for days. The humiliation was exquisite and just what I needed to get my ass back in gear. Time to go and see my husband.

Mary Ann and Sue Ellen are playing in the front yard when I pull up with Damien. I step out of the car and my babies run up to me.

"Mommy!" Sue Ellen cries as they both hug me. I've missed them terribly. I kiss their little faces and look around. Nothing is different, but I don't see or hear Peggy Sue.

"Where's your sister?"

"Her and Harrison moved into their cottage up the

road," Mary Ann answers. "It's pretty and has a nice garden. Lots of flowers."

"I see." Steve has let our daughter shack up with the man who got her knocked up. Some father he's turned out to be. I let them go and Damien comes up to me.

"You think this is still a good idea?" he asks. "If he's still pissed..."

"You're here, he won't act like a fool with a witness." I look at the girls. "Babes, why don't you go and find Crystal? Mommy has to go and find your father."

The girls run off as I walk into the house. I see Steve playing with his phone, a huge grin on his face. He hasn't seen me yet, so I approach, letting my heels do the announcing for me. He picks up his head, stopping in his tracks as he turns to me.

"What are you doing here?" he asks sternly, then looks beyond me, no doubt seeing Damien. "And what's with the toddler in tow?"

"That's Damien, you know that; you have met once or twice," I snap. "As for what I'm doing here? I live here."

"No, see, not anymore. We're getting a divorce and you're leaving," Steve states matter of factly.

"Is that so? Just how do you presume to put me out?"

"It's already been done. I have a PTO to keep you fifty feet from our girls and the property once you've collected your things."

"I see." The bastard has gone and gotten the courts involved. What a fucker. "So, let me collect my things."

"Done. Everything that is yours is in the bedroom down the hall, neatly packed, and itemized with receipts. You'd do well to put it in a safe place since all of your jewelry is there."

"Humph. You just think of everything, don't you?" I ask, stomping past him and heading for our bedroom.

"Where are you going?"

I have something to retrieve, you fuck. Stay away from me."

He follows on my heels as I barge into our bedroom. I look around and see a hypodermic needle on the dresser.

"What the fuck is this?" I ask, pointing to it. I pull out my phone and take a pic. "Oh, this will go over well when I sue for custody."

"Yeah? You think I'm gonna let a degenerate pig like you have my kids? I'll snap your neck first."

"G'head, try. Lay hands on me and I'll really have your ass," I say, getting closer to the needle. That's when I see the bottle next to it. I know this cocktail. It's a fertility drug.

I pick it up and hurl it at his head. It just misses and smashes against the wall. "You're trying to knock her up? You son of a bitch!" I scream. As I do, Damien and Crystal both appear in the doorway. Damien is at my side instantly and Crystal is being pulled into Steve's arms.

"That's our business. Now, if you would kindly retrieve your things from the bedroom…"

I put up my hand and go into the closet. Tapping the underside of a drawer, I pull a roll of cash out that I had been saving for over a year. There is almost ten thousand and it's all mine.

"I'll be on my way now," I say with a smirk as I walk past them. "I hope your ovaries shrivel up and die," I sneer and Steve lunges for me, but Crystal holds him back.

"Beast, no," she says softly.

Yeah, let the little cunt subdue him. I'll get my things and be on my way, but he hasn't heard the last of me.

"Those kids are mine and I won't give them up without a fight," I singsong.

29

STEVE

"Are you okay?" I ask as I hold Crystal while Kellie screams like a banshee through the house.

"I'm fine."

"Today of all days, she shows up," I say, turning her in my arms. "I'm sorry."

"It's not your fault."

"I shouldn't have let her in the house, I should have blocked her from coming upstairs, and what was that bundle of cash?"

Crystal looks down, her face laced with guilt.

"Crys?" I ask again, lifting her chin.

"She's been hiding money for a while. She thought nobody knew. She's wrong. It started about the same time she told you to get rid of me the first time."

I roll my shoulders uncomfortably. "You think she's been fixing to run?"

"Things have disappeared here and there, things I know she left in but haven't seen since."

I sigh heavily and realize that the house has gone quiet. I sit down as I hear the car peel out. "She's gone, for now."

Movement catches my eye and I look up and see my daughters standing in the doorway.

"Mommy left again," Sue Ellen whispers with a sniffle.

"Where's she going with all that stuff? On a trip?" Mary Ann asks.

I put out my hands and the girls come to me. I take them each on a knee and pat the bed so Crystal can sit beside us.

She sits, but I can see the stress on her face, in her manners. I rub her thigh and look at the girls. "Your momma loves you very much, know that. It's just that she doesn't love Crystal and me the same way anymore. When people stop feeling that way, sometimes they need to be apart. So, your momma, she had to leave, but just because she left us, doesn't mean she loves you any less."

Crystal has her hand over her face. I probably could have said things better, but I'm not sure how. The girls look at the floor, then Mary Ann hugs me.

"We love you, Daddy, and we're not leaving you."

"Nope." Sue Ellen hugs me too, then they hop off me and grab Crystal.

Crystal hugs them back and they look back at me. "Um, are we still going to see the horses at Aunt Angelica's?" Mary Ann asks.

Thank God for the attention span of a child. "Yes, are you all packed?" They nod. "Then, go wait downstairs."

I turn to Crystal who falls back on the bed with a stressed sigh. I place a hand on her belly. "We are so going to get through this."

"It's not feeling like it at the moment."

"Maverick and Angelica will be here any min-" Car doors interrupt me and I get up to look out the window. Maverick is just approaching the house. "They're here. Are you coming down with me, or are you gonna take that bath?"

"I'm going to the bath."

"Alrighty, I'll be up in a few to keep you company."

I head downstairs and let Maverick in. He must see the tension in my face, or feel the heat of it radiating off me because he's looking me over.

"What happened?"

"Kellie showed up with her Dom and raised a bit of hell. Got the kids asking questions and I had to tell them she left."

"Crystal?"

"Taking a bath."

"How's she dealing?"

"Stressed, and I don't blame her. Kellie also found out about the fertility treatments."

"Oh?" He sounds surprised. "How'd she handle the news?"

"Called me an SOB and threw a seventeen-hundred-dollar prescription at the wall, smashing it."

"This is gonna be a fight."

"I think so. She also said she was suing for custody."

"She can try."

"I know she won't get it, but she can make me miserable while trying, can't she?"

"Yeah, she can."

"Ugh, I don't need this. We don't need this. I should have someone just strangle her and be done with it."

"Then, you go to jail and your kids go to her,"

Maverick says as Angelica comes in. I notice in the light that she's starting to show with the slightest bit of curve to her belly.

"I just want this," I say, pointing to Angelica. "Is that so wrong?"

"Oh, Steve, you guys will get it, I can feel it." She smiles as the girls come rushing to us, dragging their suitcases behind them.

"Time to go?" I ask as they smile. They nod and Angelica walks them out after kisses.

I look at Maverick. "I guess you should wish me luck?"

"Good luck," he says. "Are we praying for one or multiple?"

"One at a time, don't wanna damage the merchandise." I grin as he shakes his head.

❆ ❆ ❆

Crystal is laying in the tub when I come upstairs again. I swish my hand in the bubbly water and she looks up at me.

"What are you doing?"

"Just coming in to see if you need me to wash your back or your front," I smirk.

"Um, no?"

"I was reading and according to the clinic website, sperm can live up to three days in the body. They recommend sex every other day leading up to, and including, the ovulation day."

"How can you think about that right now?"

"How can I not? It's been nearly two weeks since I've touched you. I don't wanna think about all the shit that went on today because it will still be there after our

138

window closes. Right now, I want to climb into the tub and make you blush, then I want to take you to bed and relieve some much-needed stress."

She nods her head and I start to take off my clothes. Boy, am I glad I sprung for the Jacuzzi tub. I slip into the water and pull her to me with ease, my hands gliding over her tits and down between her thighs as I kiss her deeply. She grabs my head and turns over in the tub, straddling me as my fingers work into her. She kisses me and digs her nails into my shoulders as I thrust my fingers up inside her, flicking her clit with my thumbs.

It doesn't take long before she's coming against my movements and I'm lifting us from the tub and carrying her to the bed.

"You're gonna get it soaked."

"It's just water." I laugh as I pull back the covers and putting a pillow under her ass, I climb on top of her. She wraps her legs over my shoulders and I'm diving in, a man on a mission. That mission is babies.

❊ ❊ ❊

It's after midnight when we come up for air. "I'm starving, do you want me to make us a couple sandwiches? I can grab them and some water from the fridge?" I ask, still panting from our sixth time tonight. She's laying there with her legs propped against the wall, letting my boys do their job.

She looks at me and her situation, then laughs.

"Okay, I'll wait the twenty minutes with you, then you can come down and raid the fridge with me."

"I'm tired."

"Food, then sleep."

"Not good food."

"I've got a couple Ho Ho's stashed, but you gotta come get them." She smiles as I kiss her. "So, kitchen?"

She nods. "I'll be down in a few."

"Okay." I get up, not bothering to put on clothes since we have the house to ourselves.

The next four days are a blur of sex, food, and sex with food. The whipped cream she sucked off my dick was inspired and got me hard in seconds. The chocolate sauce I cleaned off of her was perfectly drizzled and extra dark. By day five, we are spent and do nothing but hold each other and make love sleepily. We have to get up though, the kids will be back today. I already called Peggy Sue and she and Harrison are coming for dinner, mostly so we can pass back out as soon as possible.

30

CRYSTAL

FIVE DAYS. It's been five days of sex, sex, and a little more sex. My girlie parts are screaming that they can't take anymore and for once, I think the Beast is truly satisfied. Steve and I have been cuddling together, dozing, since the girls are supposed to be home today. I need to actually make myself get up and go downstairs to make dinner. I'm just not sure if I can walk. Every time I've tried, Steve has carried me around upside down.

I roll over to force myself to move. It's then that I hear people in the house and I know by the sounds, it's not just the girls. I push Steve to try and wake him. "Beast, get up. Someone's here."

He lets out a low growling moan, then I smack him.

"Steve, someone… Well, more than someone is in the house. Get up!"

"Christ." He gets up, taking the sheet with him.

"Hey! I need that."

"There's still a sheet on the bed," he says, walking out the door. A few minutes go by and I hear my Beast yell. "Bella."

I sit up on the bed, putting a pillow in front of me just in case one of the girls comes in. Steve walks into the room and gives me that crooked head look he gets from time to time.

"Who are you trying to hide from? I've already had my mouth all over every inch."

"I didn't know if you were coming in alone."

"We have to get dressed."

"But I kind of like the naked in bed thing."

"So do I, but if we don't get dressed, they are going to come up here. All of them."

"All of whom?"

"Fallen Angels has moved in."

"What?"

"They're here, all of them. Babies in tow. You should see the banner."

"Banner?"

"Baby Batter Rise."

"Kyle?"

"And Angelica."

"How'd Maverick handle that, I wonder?"

Steve scoops me up into his arms, carrying me into the bathroom. "Beast?"

"Yeah?"

"Can we go back to bed?"

"No, not yet. We have to make a clean appearance. I have to shave."

I bring my hands up and scratch his face. "I don't know, I kind of like it and I know where I *really* liked it."

"Well, I can keep a goatee and try it out."

"It's something different." Steve sits me on the sink while he shaves. I'm kicking my feet back and forth, watching him. "So, the clothes in bed thing... Is it still a rule?"

"Do we still have two small children that can randomly jump into bed with us at any given time?"

"Yes, but I was thinking about that." He stops shaving and looks at me. "They make these detectors and they can alert us to when anyone is around."

"Or we can start locking the door."

"That would change your open-door policy."

"Yes, but not everyone has one. We can make it more of a metaphor."

"I like the no clothes thing and I know you do. You've made it very much known over the last five days."

"Well, it makes things so much easier when I wake up in the morning. Like, hello and good morning."

"Or anytime during the night when you roll on top of me?" I ask with a raised brow.

"That too. As long as you're prepared for that, we can start locking the door. Don't say you haven't been warned."

Steve finishes his shaving, then leans over and kisses me. I don't know how, but I can feel myself getting worked up from just a kiss. If this man only knew what he does to me.

A hand travels to my boob and Steve breaks the kiss. "You naked is so much temptation." He pulls me to the edge of the counter.

"Maybe so, but I guess one of us will need to be stronger than the other," I smirk, then I feel the tapping of his cock against me.

I shock him and me both when I put my hands on his shoulders and lift myself off the counter and onto his cock. He pushes forward slowly and I gasp as his shaft swells and then begins to fill me. He continues to push forward until his body is pressed against mine. He remains motionless for a few seconds, letting me adjust to the feeling of having him inside me, yet again, so soon. Slowly, he starts to move back and forth. My knees become weak and I lean back against the counter. His hands rest on my thighs as he pulls me toward him. One of his hands slide up my body to my tits and I feel my hard nipples slip between his fingers. He pinches and pulls before giving it a flick, then doing the same to the other.

He keeps at a slow and steady pace, rocking in and out of me. I feel that familiar feeling starting to build. My breathing increases and I know my orgasm is fast approaching. I feel him take my nipples between his fingertips and roughly pinch them. The semi-intense pain immediately sends me over the edge as the waves of my orgasm wash over me. Involuntarily, my hands leave the counter and his hands are on my hips, pumping me against his cock. All the while, he continues to slowly fuck me through my orgasm.

He is aggressively pounding me now, which feels incredible. I find it difficult to remain where I am, I need to kiss him. I push myself up to press my lips to his. The slapping sounds of our bodies coming together grow louder and I can hear his breathing start to change and become shallow. I know he has to be close and I can feel myself begin to climb again as those familiar shock waves start to travel through me. His hands are on my hips and he uses my body to give him increased leverage to thrust into me harder and deeper. I start to shake in orgasm as his hard thrusting abates and he grunts loudly, coming inside me. After his orgasm subsides, he falls forward onto my chest, which in turn, presses me back down on the counter. For several minutes, we remain motionless as our breathing returns to normal.

I feel his cock lose its rigidity and slip out of me and he kisses my neck, then whispers into my ear, "I love you, Crystal Marie Howard."

I pause, looking at him. "That's the first time you've actually said you love me and my name."

"Well, I mean it."

"I love you too, Steven Robert Falcone." I run my hand through his hair.

"Stop that unless you want me to ravage you again."

"We need to shower and get downstairs. We smell like sex and our room reeks of it."

We take our shower, then get dressed before casually making our way downstairs. Steve's hand in mine, we find everyone outside on the patio. The girls are in the pool with Brent, Angelica, Kyle, Peggy Sue, Harrison, and Brayden. Maverick is beside the pool with just his feet in the water.

Steve looks at me with a finger to his mouth to be quiet. He sneaks up behind Maverick and picking him up, throws him in the pool.

Maverick comes up sputtering. "What the fuck, dude?"

"You never get wet," Steve shouts.

"I get plenty wet, you just can't see it," Maverick says and then disappears as Angelica dunks him.

Steve takes off his shirt and dives into the pool. I'm standing back and leaning against the steps, watching everything. It's weird without Kellie here, but sometimes, that's how life goes. I can't help but wonder what's going to happen over the next few weeks with the divorce and the girls. Kellie can be vindictive, I just hope for the sake of the girls, she loves them enough to not put them through hell.

A hand on my shoulder startles me and I jump, turning to see Marissa. "You scared the shit out of me."

"I'm sorry, you looked like you were really deep in thought."

"It's been a long week."

"Tired?"

"Tired, stressed, and worried."

"Have you guys heard from Kel yet?"

"She showed up five days ago."

Marissa laughs. "She called me."

"She did?"

"Yup, wanted to, uh, get to together for coffee."

"Uh *huh*."

"I said I couldn't, I had the twins. I'm not leaving them alone with their father. He'd have them color coded and alphabetized the second I walked out the door."

I glance back to the pool and smile as I look at Marissa again. "You know, the bad thing is I could so see him doing that."

"I know, right? Like little Post-it notes. I'd come home and they'd be covered."

I just nod because, honestly, I'm not sure what to say. I didn't usually get to talk much. Kellie made sure I was doing something while she hung out.

Next thing I know, I have arms around me and I'm soaked. "So, we have a bun in the oven yet?" Kyle asks.

I elbow him in the stomach. "Seriously? Dick!"

Kyle groans, then Steve yells, "Keep your hands off my woman."

I smile at Kyle. "It takes longer than a couple days to get knocked up."

Kyle shrugs his shoulders. "So, what's for dinner, sis?"

I look from Kyle to Marissa, confused. Marissa just rolls her eyes, then turns around and walks away. "Awkward."

"We're still working out the kinks."

"I thought you did that already."

"Shut up. I'd tap it again, but Brent would kick my ass."

"Brent or Marissa?"

"Touché."

"What are you doing out of the pool?"

"Came to see what's going on with the food and you look lonely."

"A lot's been going on and you're sober."

"I have my days. I'm not always high."

"I like you better like this."

Kyle looks at the ground, then looks at everybody else. "Some days, you just gotta party and other days are for family."

"My partying days are over or haven't you heard?"

"You'll pop out a baby, then go back to all the fun you can handle. You managed it raising his other girls."

"Because I would drink one or two, then be done. Someone needed to be level-headed for you bunch." I glance around again, just noticing I haven't seen Ringo. "Where's the other brother?"

Kyle looks around. "Good question. RINGOOOOO!" he sings.

"Would you shut the fuck up? You're going to wake my kids," Marissa hisses from inside and Kyle just laughs.

"So, Kel showed up," I tell Kyle.

"Steve may have mentioned that."

"Why do you and I always get stuck in the messes?"

"Why do you and I always get stuck in the messes? Cause we're outsiders. Well, you were," he says.

"I don't feel like an insider yet. Technically, I'm still on the outside."

Kyle puts his arm around my shoulder, turning me toward the pool. "See that big hunk of man over there? He says you're in, then you're in."

"That beast of a man is the biggest teddy bear I've ever met."

"Don't let him hear you say it."

I look at him like he's daring me. "Hey, Beast?"

"Yeah, Bella?" He raises his head as he swims to the edge of the pool.

"Tell ding-dong here that you're a big teddy bear."

Steve pulls himself out of the pool and strolls over to us, shaking the water out of his hair on the way. When he reaches us, he grabs me and pulls me to him.

"I'm only a teddy bear till you stick your fingers in my honey pot." I burst with laughter and end up having to hold my stomach. "Kyle, go stir something in the kitchen with Marissa."

"Beast, be nice, we're just talking."

"This is me being nice," Steve says and I can't hold in the eye roll.

"I'm out of here," Kyle says and is up the steps.

"Now you've gone and scared him off."

"Why don't you go get your bathing suit? Come play with us."

"I'm pretty sure we've played enough for a while."

Steve chuckles. "No?"

"I'm not sure what the chlorine would do to... You know."

"You've got a point. Yeah, stay out of the pool for the next three days."

"You know it's a vacuum seal down there, right?" Ringo quips and we both laugh.

"Where the hell'd you come from?" Steve asks.

"I was inside with the twins."

"Yeah, man, well, strip and get in the pool. You missed Maverick's entrance."

"No, I didn't."

"Ah, Ringo, don't ya wanna play with the boys?"

"Not particularly. Two are brothers and the others are bigger than me."

I scratch my head at that and look at Steve as Ringo disappears back inside. "What the fuck?"

"Nothing? He's a weirdo, you know them gingers."

"All of you confuse me. Go have fun. I think I'm gonna go lay down."

"You sure?"

"Been a lot going on. I think I just need some rest. Just get the girls to bed at a decent hour, so I don't have to fight them through schooling."

"What about dinner? Aren't you gonna eat?"

"I'm not really that hungry."

"Alright, I'll make sure the girls get to bed."

I pull him down so I can kiss him, then head inside to our bed. I need like a week of sleep to catch up.

31

KELLIE

"WHERE DO YOU EXPECT ME TO GO?" I ask Damien as he starts to pack up my shit.

"You can go to Hell for all I care. I told you this wasn't a permanent thing between us. I like using you, and you submit to most of my whims, but I've grown bored of your mouth and your other more useful holes. Besides, your fucked up situation just brought a sheriff to my doorstep. If he'd have come inside and looked around, it would have been my ass going to jail. I can't risk my business for a ho like you."

I stare at him, mouth agape. I want to tear his fucking head off. I lunge for him and he tosses me across the room like a rag doll.

"You've got no respect, none for your husband, none for me, and certainly none for yourself. This was supposed to liberate you and you've managed to let it tie you down like everything else in your life. Take your money and your shit and go. I already called you a cab."

I cradle my arm and hold back the tears, I'm pretty sure it's broken, but I won't give him the satisfaction of seeing me cry again. Steve did this, this is all his fault. He chose that little cunt over me. Me, the woman who's given him three girls and seen him through his addictions. Not once, but twice. I let Damien put my stuff on the street and have the cab take me to the nearest hotel. I check in and they bring it all up to the room. It's not the Ritz, but at least it doesn't smell like cat piss and pot.

I get situated and then I look over the paperwork that I was served with. It's divorce papers from Steve's lawyers. It's got the Imogen heading, so he's using the record label muscle to try and push me out. He's going for sole custody of our kids and wants to offer me a settlement rather than split it all like I'm entitled to. Well, fuck that. I want to see my children. I want what I've earned over the years. I was there when we had nothing and starved while he shot Heroin in some flop house for days at a time. I stuck through the booze, pills, and everything else he put in his body. I deserve my half. It's time I get what I deserve and Steve gets his.

32

STEVE

"WHAT THE FUCK?" I'm standing at the ATM and my card is being denied. I've got money in this account; I know I do. Hell, I've got more money in here than I know what to do with. Crystal is sitting in the car with the girls; we are supposed to go to the Zoo and I wanted some cash on hand. I look over at her and hold up a finger as I go inside the bank.

"Yes? Can I help you?" the teller asks without looking up.

"Hi, there seems to be something wrong with my ATM card."

The girl looks up and I see she knows my face. "You- you're-"

"I'm a customer, a very wealthy one, who'd like to take out some cash and take his kids out for the day." I hand her my card.

"Yes, Sir, right away." She taps on the keyboard. "Umm, one sec." She walks over to a man in a tie who looks me and my card over and then comes to me.

"Mister Falcone?"

"Yup."

"Can you come with me?"

"What seems to be the problem?"

"This is highly unusual and I apologize," he says, walking me into an office. "Mister Falcone, your account has been frozen. We received a writ from the Kline law office and it stipulates that any accounts belonging to both you and Mrs. Falcone need to be stopped and seized. I'm assuming you're going through a divorce?"

I nod. "How do I unfreeze them?" I ask, my fingers digging into the chair.

"You'll need to talk to her lawyers, and your own, and come to a financial agreement of some kind. I know if you have children and are in possession of them, it moves faster because you need access to support them."

"Okay, but what do I do in the mean time? I need money."

"You can always do those fast cash places, or borrow from someone, or we could run you a new line of credit."

"Yeah, do that. I'll take that."

"It'll take just a few minutes."

"Thanks."

Fifteen minutes later and I'm getting back into the car with a fifteen-thousand-dollar credit limit. We should be okay for a while. I look at Crystal and sigh. "Who's ready for the zoo?" I ask as she puts a hand on my shaking leg. The girls all yell happily and we take off down the road.

We have Peggy Sue and Brayden but no Harrison, he's had to go out to L.A. for a few meetings with his band mates and won't be back for a couple days. She's pushing Brayden in the stroller ahead of us and keeping an eye out for the girls.

"Kellie froze my accounts," I whisper to Crystal as we are walking.

"What?"

"She's managed to freeze my bank accounts. I can't touch them. Neither can she, but something tells me she made a sizable withdrawal before she did this."

Crystal rubs her face. "So, what do we do?"

"I took out a new line of credit, so we won't starve, and I've gotta call the lawyers and see what all they can do."

"Maybe I should look for a job."

I look at her like she's got a second head. "No, we're too close to our goals and you teach the girls and take care of me, that's a full-time position."

"It didn't work," she whispers. I look at her and swallow hard.

"How do you know?"

"A feeling."

"Then we try again, they said it could take a couple rounds."

"We don't have the money."

"I'll get it. Fuck, I'll take out another loan someplace else if I have to." I stop walking and take her hands. "I'm not giving up, she did this for this exact reason, to prevent us from getting pregnant. I know it, it's all out of spite."

She's shaking her head at me. "We've got kids to feed, we've got two girls to raise, we can't just make it about us."

"And if we stop now, you become resistant to the drugs and it may not work later. Fuck that, no, I will figure it out. I'll give her what she wants. Whatever that is."

"If I had to guess, it's the girls. You can't do that to

them."

"I know I can't give up my children, but I also know Kellie. She wants freedom more than she wants our kids. I'll give her half, but I need to sell the house and fast."

"Then we have to find somewhere else."

"Nope, I'm figuring Kyle could use a little property to invest in."

"So, Kyle would be living with us?"

"No, Bella, he'd be our landlord. He buys the house from me for what's left on the mortgage, I split the price with Kellie, and we don't go anywhere. Hell, with him being a first-time buyer, I bet the monthly payments will be low as fuck. We take over that and are golden."

"We need to get it done if that's what you think will work. Either that or find someplace else because these girls need somewhere to live."

"I'll call the lawyers when we get home."

✻ ✻ ✻

When we get to the house, Angelica is sitting on the steps with Maverick and Angela. "What are you guys doing here?"

"Can we go inside?" Maverick asks. We get in and the girls go upstairs.

"What's going on?" I ask, concerned by their silence.

"We got served with notices to appear in court to testify for Kellie," Angelica hisses.

"Testify? For what?"

Maverick looks at us as I hold Crystal's hand. "It could go one of a few ways. Either she wants the girls, she wants half of everything, she wants everything, or she just wants you miserable." At this point, he's looking at Crys and not me.

"Yeah, miserable and broke, she froze my accounts."

"Wait, what? What are you doing for money?" Angelica asks as Maverick puts up his hand to silence her.

"You told me she found the bottle when she showed up, correct? Smashed it against the wall?"

I nod.

"She's an APRN, she knows how much something like that costs and it's not cheap, and if I had to guess, she figures Crystal talked you into it. Not the other way around."

I'd never told him who initiated the baby talk, but he's a quick study. "I came to a similar conclusion, and she's gonna succeed in stopping it unless I can get the accounts unfrozen in the next two weeks. We will have to start all over again and our opportunity decreases the longer she's off the medications."

"Well, hell, Steve, if you need me to float you a few hundred grand, just say it. I'm not gonna let you guys miss out on this," Angelica says, holding her little pooch tummy.

"I've gotta-" Crystal points to the bathroom and briskly walks away before I can say or do anything.

"I-I don't know what to say to that. It's very generous."

"I've invested well lately, had some good returns, I can afford it," she says as if a couple hundred grand is just sitting around the house. "I'll write you a check. Better yet, I'll make it out to Crystal."

"That would solve a lot of problems."

"That's me, the problem solver. Since I got sober,

I'm a lot clearer."

Maverick walks away as Angelica and I figure out what we are going to do and how.

33

CRYSTAL

I'M IN THE BED, CRYING. Between what I've found out today and the fact that I couldn't get pregnant, I don't feel like much of a woman right now. Sure as hell not one Steve needs hanging around if he wants more kids.

There's a knock at the bedroom door and then, Maverick pokes his head through. "Crystal?"

"I'm okay."

"No, you're really not," he says, coming into the room and sitting on the bed beside me. "You need to talk to someone. I can read it on you and it radiates off you in waves."

"It didn't work. It's my fault, my body isn't made for this. I hate that I can't give him what he wants. I mean what kind of woman can't give children to the man she loves? Not much of one, I'll tell you that."

"Crystal, this is part of your issue, you need to be calm. With everything going on with Kellie, you're not very calm. Your lives have been turned upside down. Just talking about it will help you. It doesn't have to be with me, but if you want to, whatever you say to me will stay between the two of us."

"Maverick, I really doubt I could actually be helped. Does Steve know you're up here?"

"No, but I'm sure he'll figure it out once neither of us comes back."

"Then go, because there's nothing you can do to help me. I suck as a woman and Steve deserves better."

"Crystal, please listen to me. I know what I'm talking about. If you want to conceive, a lot has to go into it besides five days of fucking."

I stand and start pacing. "Maverick, what the fuck don't you get? It didn't work and I doubt it's going to. I know I'm supposed to be calm, but please tell me how to do that when everything is being turned upside fucking down!"

"I get that, but do you want this with Steve?"

"*Of course*, I want this with Steve. I've not spent the last ten years of my life here for shits and giggles."

"Okay, then why do you think it won't work?"

"I swear to God, Maverick, if you ask me stupid questions one more time, you won't have to worry about any more kids because I'm going to cut off your dick and feed it to you."

"I get it, you're upset, but my dick? Really? That would fucking hurt."

"Do I look like I'd care?"

"Not really, but I think once you've calmed down and thought about everything, you'll be upset with yourself. Just know I forgive you."

"UGH!" I scream, turning away from him. "Why must you men think you're so fucking smart. Always thinking you know everything and us, supposed to be women, even if we can get pregnant, know fucking nothing."

"Crystal, tell me what you want."

"I want it to be over. I want to be able to get pregnant without having to bleed through every fucking thing I own or get shots in the ass for two weeks. Better yet, being able to sleep with the man I love and not have to wonder if this is the time he knocks me up. I want to not have to worry about where we are going to be living with the girls from one day to the next. More importantly, I want to know that Kellie won't take the girls from Steve. He's always here for those girls and doesn't deserve the shit she's put him through all these years. I watched it for the last decade and kept my fucking mouth shut because I've loved him and didn't want to see him hurting any more than he already was." I drop to the floor as the tears fall. "I hate that she's tearing us apart and trying to take all of our friends from us. All we did was fall in love, is that so bad?"

"No, that's not bad at all. I've been told some people only find love once in their life. Steve's been able to find it twice. I've got a saying hanging in my office. 'Some people come into your life to stay while others are just a lesson.' The question is, is Steve staying or is he a lesson?"

"If I'm going through hell, he's stuck with me because if he tries to put me out like he did Kellie, I won't go. I may be small, but by God, I'm mean when I need to be."

"Then you need to clean yourself up and you need to talk to someone about all these bottled up issues because they are going to keep coming back. Steve loves you, or he wouldn't be here now."

"Maverick, can you go away now?"

"No, you're still crying and haven't told me you'll

talk to someone yet."

"Fine, Maverick, I'll talk to someone. Can you go away now so I can have my bed back and wallow alone?" I ask, then mutter to myself, "Stupid fucking men."

"I can go, but you aren't alone."

"Great, just fucking peachy."

Maverick stands and passes Steve as I'm crawling onto the bed. "She needs to talk to someone and it needs to be more than once. She's got a lot bottled up and it's going to cause problems for you both. Oh, and if I had to gauge her mood, she's getting ready to start again. Need to get prepared. Angelica and I will make dinner and keep the girls entertained."

"Go the fuck away, Maverick!" I shout.

"Thank you," Steve says, pushing Maverick out the door and shutting it.

He walks around the bed and pulls me to him. "Bella, everything's going to be just fine. I've got it all figured out. Well, most of it."

"Easier said than done."

"We don't have to worry about money."

"Does it grow on fucking trees?" I ask and he shifts to hold a piece of paper in front of my face. I can see what it is, but I still can't comprehend it. It's a check for half a million dollars made out to me. What the fuck? My gut rolls and I take off for the bathroom. My head is over the toilet just in time for what we ate at the zoo today to come up.

Steve's behind me, pulling my hair back and getting me a wet cloth. When I think it's over, I flush, then lay my face against the cold tile floor.

Steve lays down on the floor next to me and just looks at me. "Feeling better?"

"No."

"Do I wanna know what happened?"

"Why did she write me a check?"

"Because if it's in your name, nobody can touch it but you. She wants us to be okay."

"How much of what I said did you hear?"

"Enough."

"Do you agree with him?"

"For the most part. I think you do need to talk to somebody. I think we both do. It might as well be him."

"He just has this way of going about it."

"He's a bit of a prick, but he's effective."

"Dick is more like it," I say and Steve laughs. "I'm sorry it didn't work."

Steve reaches out, touching my cheek. "One thing's for certain, the metformin is working. You're regulating."

"What are you talking about?"

"I'd say you're getting ready to start your period again."

"How do you know that?"

"Well, you're a little cranky and the rest of your emotions are all over the map. You also tried to eat my lunch on top of your own."

"I think you're crazy, but whatever."

"Just trust me on this one."

"So, tell me this grand scheme of yours."

"Well, there's enough money there for your medication, to pay the doctors, and to put a down payment on this house in your name. The rest can go into your account and we'll use it when we need it till my accounts unfreeze."

"She's trying to hurt me. She thinks I'll leave just because there's a money issue. She's always thought of me that way."

"Well, she's wrong. We're going to show her."

"I'm so stressed that I don't know if I'm coming or going."

He cocks a smile. "Well, I can help you figure that one out."

"No, you can't. Not if you really think I'm going to start."

"Windows of opportunity." He grabs me and pulls me across the floor to him. He looks me square in the eye. "Take off your pants."

"I'd rather not."

Steve runs a hand up my leg and grabs me. "Take. Off. Your. Pants."

"Did Maverick rub off on you? You're getting awfully commanding."

He just looks at me. "I'm not going to tell you again," he states as he pulls off his shirt. Finally giving in, I strip my pants, but leave my panties. Steve lets out a low growl as he sets my ass on the tile floor and grabbing one side of my panties, he rips them open. He throws my legs over his shoulder and dives in. Fuck me if this man can't make me come in seconds this way.

34

STEVE

HENRY LOGGINS IS MY CONTACT WITH THE Imogen lawyers, he's a partner at the prestigious Loggins, Glade, and Fern and was procured by Christy for me. They will pay the retainer and I just have to take care of the rest after the case is handled. After the issue with my accounts, I called him and now Crystal and I are sitting in his office waiting to hear the news.

Henry comes in and he reminds me of Blake, Brent's bodyguard, instantly, only in a better suit. He could be a twin with the same bald head, dark sun-kissed skin, and broad shoulders. Even his deep voice is similar.

"Mr. Falcone, Miss Howard, it's good to meet you. Now, I've filed the papers to unfreeze your personal accounts as they do not have her name attached and were created before you were married. Seems you liked your bank." He smiles.

"Okay, how long will that take?"

"If she doesn't fight it, a few weeks."

"Ugh, moments to freeze, but weeks to fix, this is fucked up."

"I know it's frustrating, but she's put in a complaint that you were appropriating funds to impregnate Miss Howard without Mrs. Falcone's knowledge or consent. Based on the cost of these treatments, the judge was sympathetic. We will, however, need to paint a better picture than she has. She wants your kids, so you must show that she can't handle them, or that she is unfit in some manner while establishing that you and Miss Howard can provide a loving and safe environment. As for the assets, she wants the no fault amount of two-hundred million and she will walk away. It's her lawyer's estimate of what you're currently worth."

I look at Crystal. That amount would cut me deep, but I can make it back. "What do you think, Bella?"

"It's a lot of money. What he just said is she'll take the money and walk, isn't that proof enough that she's unfit.

"With a division of assets also comes split custody," Henry explains, it's something of an unspoken arrangement."

"She hasn't spent more than a night with them in years," Crystal says with worry.

"Miss Howard, if you have something to say, now is the time. As I understand it, you've been the children's caregiver for close to ten years now. Your say holds great sway."

She rubs her temples. "She lives a particular lifestyle, one that the girls have no part of."

"You are referring to the relationship with Damien St. Andrew. She claims that it is over."

"There've been others," I respond.

"She's had countless lovers outside your marriage, but so have you, so we can't go with prior bad acts. The State of Nevada doesn't leave much room for it anyhow, which is good seeing as you are a recovering addict, Mr. Falcone." Henry shifts in his seat. "Would your oldest be willing to testify? Her understanding of your very public relationship could be useful, as would her stating where she plans to live."

"She doesn't live with us," Crystal says quietly.

"My daughter had a baby recently, Mr. Loggins, no one knows about it but family. She's engaged to be married and lives with her fiancé. I would rather her be kept away from this. I want my grandson to have a normal childhood."

"Well, I can work within your parameters. It will be hard, but not impossible, you tell me what you want to do."

"Offer her the two hundred and visitation, every other weekend and two weeks in the summers, given she is in a stable living space and is not engaging in any activity that will put my girls in harm's way."

"Sounds like you've talked it out somewhere already."

"It's good to be informed, going into these things," I say, standing. "Thank you, and do let us know what you need."

"Will do." He shakes our hands and we are off to see the doctor to see how the hormones are doing. Hopefully, the growth rate is on schedule.

We are in the car and I look over to her, watching her. She looks at me and sighs. "This isn't getting any easier."

"It is though, at least we know what she wants. What's gonna make her go away?"

"It's not feeling any easier." Her voice breaks and I pull the car over, unbuckle myself, then her, and pull her to me.

"I know this is overwhelming, but we need to focus, concentrate on the girls, on each other. Let the lawyers do their jobs."

"I know that, but it's not easy." She sniffs into my chest.

"What do you say we skip out this month, go over to one of the big hotels and let them pamper us, get massages, hang out by the pool, get room service, instead of staying here? It could be fun."

"What about the girls?"

"I'm thinking we do it during our little window, they'll be with Brent and Marissa this month."

"Can they handle that?"

"Maverick says he'll come over and do the schooling, check them out."

"I'll have to get everything taken care of beforehand."

"What can I do to help?"

She slowly shakes her head against me. "Take away the cramps."

I press on her belly firmly as I kiss her. "Here, does that help?"

"Not really."

"Well, I tried. I'd do more, but we need to reserve the swimmers."

"Let's just get this day over with." She pushes me back into my seat.

35

CRYSTAL

I'M IN THE CLASSROOM, TRYING TO GET everything ready for the week approaching. I still need to pack the girls for the week because god knows, if I asked them or Steve, they wouldn't have everything they need and it'd just be thrown in a bag.

Lesson plans are done, but now I need to gather everything and sort it by days. I've got bins set out for each day and grade. Sue Ellen and Angela are in third grade, so I have double of everything. Mary Ann started fourth this year and Peggy Sue is a Sophomore. It's a lot to handle, but it's what's needed to make sure the girls get everything they need and can live normal lives when they're older.

I look up as Maverick walks in and takes a seat at my desk. Mister Counselor is expecting me to talk and I don't much feel like it today. I keep working as he watches me.

"You going to talk today or be a stubborn mule?" Maverick finally asks after watching me for a good fifteen minutes.

"What do you want me to talk about, Maverick?"

"Everything."

"And if I say I don't want to?"

"Then I'm going to assume you're not ready to get pregnant because it's not going to happen with you wound so tight."

"You think you're just so perfect, don't you?"

"No, even I have my faults, but I've dealt with my shit. You haven't and it's holding you back. You need to deal with it and move past it. There's a good possibility that it could take years and if that's the case, I'll be here to help you." He pauses, watching me for a second. "How about today we start with your family and where you come from."

"I've done well to keep my past hidden and I'd rather nobody ever found out."

"I've noticed that when you get pissed, you have this bit of twang and if I had to guess, I'd say you come from Kentucky."

He's watching to gauge my expression and I fail to keep it controlled. "Nobody else has figured it out. How did you?"

"It's how you pronounce things. Remember, I actually pay attention. It's kind of my job."

"I really hate how you can see through people so well. You suck."

"Actually, I lick, but that's a different topic for another day."

I finally give up and just spill. He isn't going to go away. However, I keep working, which also means he winds up following me around the house while I talk. He somehow gets to me to talk about Kentucky and my life there. He also now knows my real name isn't Crystal Howard, but Hayley Berlet Ayres. My past is a lot like the rest of our little group, only mine has a mix.

I'm more like Steve than he'd think. I was emancipated at the age of sixteen. This was after my father and mother had spent those first sixteen years abusing me in one way or another and just after my father went to prison for murder. I can't help but wonder sometimes if my fertility issues come from the fact that my parents started sexually abusing me when I was a six-year-old and went on till I got away.

Most people going through the shit I went through would have given into drugs and drinking, but I never did. Somehow, I managed to get away, finish high school with honors, and then put myself through college while working minimum wage jobs.

I was fresh out of school when I met Steve, Kellie, and the most precious little girls I've ever known. It didn't take me long to fall in love with Steve. He was attentive and always asking me how I was handling everything, even when he started going down the drain again with the needle. He doesn't know it, but I fell for him before we ever slept together the first time. How could I not? He's this big teddy bear that just needed someone to show him the love that Kellie withheld.

All these years, I've known he wasn't actually mine, but I never treated him any different. When Kellie would be gone, I made sure everything was taken care of. Food was always cooked and the house was clean. I think that's why Kellie hated me so much, because I always had everything taken care of and never really asked for help.

When I finish, I'm in the kitchen, working on dinner with tears falling down my face. I'm not exactly sure how long I've been talking, I just know it feels like a weight has been lifted off my shoulders. Maverick is sitting at the island and when I look out the sliding glass door, I can see Steve where he sits on the patio. He just happens to turn this way and our eyes meet. He smiles at me and I wave, then go back to my task at hand as Maverick takes everything in.

"You know you need to tell him everything," Maverick finally says and yet again, I can feel him watching me.

"I don't see why he should have to hear the shit I was put through. It's just going to make him look at me with pity and I've done well to keep anyone from looking at me like that."

"Trust me, for you to ultimately move past this, you all need to have a talk. Don't get me wrong, I'm still here for you, but the smile that's on your face tells me that my job is done." He gets up and walks out the patio doors.

The doors open and close again, but I just keep working on dinner. I know it's got to be healthy, so I'm trying not to make anything I really want but can't have.

"Do you need help?" Steve asks from behind me.

"Not really, it's almost done. Are the girls still in the pool?"

"No, they're on the patio with the Kindles. I told them to get some reading done."

"Way to go, Dad, now they will be upset with you and not me."

Steve wraps his arms around me and I place the knife I'm using on the counter. He puts his head on my shoulder. "There's something you need to talk to me about?"

Maverick. "What did he tell you?"

"Just that you wanted to talk to me. Is everything alright?"

I take a deep breath, then finally turn to face him. "I think you better sit down for this."

"Should I be worried?" he asks, pulling back from me a bit.

"I don't think so, but Maverick is so adamant that I tell you everything."

Steve sits down, pulling me onto his lap. His hand travels down my back and I finally give in and tell him everything... My past, the last ten years, and everything that's been going on lately. Of course, he has to let me go so I don't burn our food, but I can feel the different emotions coming from him as I talk. They range from pity, to rage, to love, to sadness, and so on, but I keep going until dinner is done and I'm standing in front of him, waiting for a response.

"How do you do it?"

"Do what?"

"Keep all of that bottled up into such a tiny little package."

"It's something you learn after years of abuse. I busted my ass to get to where I am and I didn't want anyone to think any different than what each of you have, until now."

Steve swallows and sighs, just watching me. "You're still my girl, have been and will always be. I don't love you any differently just because I know more about you. In fact, I think I may love you more."

"It would have made a difference if you knew back then."

"If I'd known back then, all I wouldn't know is that I was hiring a very strong woman and hoping that my children could have an ounce of that strength."

"Kellie wouldn't have let you hire me."

"Kellie didn't have a say when I hired you in the

first place. She thought you were too young and too pretty. She's always thought that of you."

"I'm not really that much younger, I just look it."

Steve chuckles, grabbing me. "You're my beautiful angel. My Bella." He kisses me and I wrap my arms around his neck.

"Are you mad at me for never telling you?"

"No, I understand that some secrets need to be kept."

"Well, they're all out in the open now."

36

KELLIE

MY NEW CONDO LOOKS OVER THE STRIP. It's got three bedrooms and plenty of space for my meager needs. The cash I stowed away was perfect for the down payment and some essentials, and I'm only a stone's throw from work. Steve has made his counter offer, and I'm like, um, no. Why should he get the happy ending?

I'm at work in the quad, having my supper when I see Peggy Sue. She's got Brayden with her and is sitting on a bench, feeding him a bottle. Fuck it, I'm going to go and see my little girl.

"Peggy Sue?" I ask and she looks up at me like she was expecting me.

"Momma."

"What are you doing here?"

"Brayden needed a checkup and I wanted to see you."

"You know we're not supposed to talk, your dad put out a restraining order."

"Yeah, well, I'm not telling him I saw you, so how

can we get in trouble?"

I nod and have a seat next to her. Brayden has gotten big in the past few weeks. "How fast they grow," I say, watching her with him. She reminds me of me in so many ways. Though she's the age Steve was when we had her, she's got my touch. Brayden fusses a bit and she adjusts him.

"We need to talk, Momma."

"About?"

"You, Daddy, and Crys."

"You need to mind your business about all of that. It doesn't involve you."

"Like hell it doesn't. Those are my sisters you all are using as pawns to hurt each other."

"That's not-"

"Really, Momma? You've ignored us for the better part of two years and now, you want us? I don't buy it. You work all the time. To keep up your lifestyle, you're gonna have to keep working, pay a sitter, or get another live-in nanny. You really have the time for that and to keep your precious boy toys?"

I look at her, fury rising in me. Who was she to tell me how to be her mother?

"Don't, Momma." She stands up. "I love you, but I don't like you very much, not like this. Not anymore. You leave Daddy alone, or I will testify about how you've left us, how you took me to meet Damien, the things I've seen over the years. All of it, even the stuff Daddy doesn't know."

I suck in air. "You would betray my trust like that?"

"What trust? You lost my respect the moment Daddy asked you to leave Damien and you refused. He was supposed to be a dalliance, but you made him more."

"What about Crystal? She wasn't supposed to be what she became either."

"Ten years, Momma, and you expected what? For her to just disappear? You think we'd allow that? She is a mother to us too."

I scoff.

"She kissed the scrapes, taught us to ride bikes, held me when I had my heart broken, and loved me even after I got knocked up. She never judged and never will. She's always had my back and I will never forget that. You do right by Daddy, or I will make sure you never see me or this baby again." She walks away, then turns back. "I still love you."

I sit on the bench. It seems I have a decision to make.

37

CRYSTAL

IT'S THAT TIME AGAIN. As Steve says, 'It's operation baby maker week.' We just finished with the doctor, where I got yet another shot in the ass. Steve made a pit stop at Walmart Plaza, where he told me to wait in the car. Did I mention he also packed our bags for this little trip? I don't know where we're going or what we're doing besides sex for another five solid days.

I'm sitting in the car, waiting for Steve, when I get a call from Peggy Sue.

"Hey, everything okay?" I ask.

"Um, yeah, everything's fine, but Daddy got a package from the lawyers."

"Small or big?"

"Medium envelope. One of those manila folders, but it's only moderately thick."

"Okay, I'll let him know and we can run home."

"Okay."

"See you soon." I hang up as Steve puts something in the back of the car, then slips into the driver's seat. "Beast, we have to go home."

"What is cutting into my time with my girl?"

"Package from the lawyers."

"Okay."

It takes about fifteen minutes to get back to the house and he jumps out, telling me not to move. He runs in the house and right back out, jumping into the car with the package in tow.

"What do you think it is now?" I ask quietly.

"Feels like a contract, like the one I sent her."

"What else could she be wanting?"

"Hell, if I know," Steve says and I drop my head in my hands and just sigh. Steve slips the package onto my lap. "We can open it now because it's a bit a ride or we can wait till after operation baby maker."

I look up at him. "It might be something important."

He nods his head. "Well, open it."

I open the package and start reading to myself. I get through all the legal crap and get down to the fact that she's accepted the offer. She's not fighting. I look up at Steve with tears in my eyes.

"Is it that bad?" I shake my head no. "Then what is it?"

"She's accepted everything and it's signed." Steve looks at me in shock and the car swerves. "Um, could you not kill us?"

"Trying not to, trying not to." His breathing is increased and he's smiling. "So, that's it, I just have to sign the papers."

"Pretty much, and give her the money, then we start visitation."

He nods his head and is white knuckling the steering wheel. Steve reaches out and rubs my thigh. "That's it, it's over."

"You know we don't I have to do this right now. A divorce is a big thing."

"No, I have plans and we're okay." He pulls over onto the side of the road. Cars are honking as they go past us, but he doesn't seem to care. "I know you got a pen in your bag." I shuffle in my purse and find the pen, then hand it and the paperwork to him. He signs the papers.

* * *

We get to the hotel just outside of town and Steve and I walk inside after he grabs a bag from the back of the car, letting the Valet know everything else needs to be brought to our room. I stand beside him and he checks us in. The lady at the counter lets us know that they are waiting for us in the spa.

I give Steve a raised brow. "Spa?"

He pulls me to him. "I want to pamper you this time."

"And here I thought you were just going to fuck me senseless."

"Well, you got to prime the pussy." I smile and then frown when he tells me to give him my phone.

"No."

"No interruptions and no Candy Crush."

"The girls may need us."

"And they know how to get ahold of us here."

"Just so we're clear, I don't like this idea." I take my phone out of my purse and pop it into his hand.

"For the next five days, we are on radio silence."

"Beast, in ten years, we've never had radio silence. You're going to lose your mind."

Steve kisses me. "I have ways of keeping us

occupied. Let's go."

We get into the spa and he tells them I'm here for the Pure Decadence package which includes the You Rock massage, Desert Rain, hydrating facial and WELL spa manicure and pedicure. I'm also getting the Glam Me package which includes shampoo and blowout, Just Eyes makeup and Strip lashes, and express file and polish for hands and feet. I look at him, confused, and the only thing it earns me is a happy as a peacock smile. Men!

He then lets them know that he's here for the Bromance & Swagger package which includes an on the deeper side massage, men's executive refining facial, and a MAN-icure.

After four hours of pampering, I'm feeling luxurious all over. Steve and I walk back to the locker rooms to change into our clothes where he kisses me, then disappears. I walk straight to my locker and open it, but in place of my clothes is an emerald dress. I pull it on and it's a halter that falls to just above my knees with a flowing skirt. Then, I see the silver, strappy heels and clutch to match.

Once I'm finished getting ready, I grab the clutch and walk out of the locker room to see my man leaning against the wall. He's in black slacks and a black button down with the sleeves rolled up to his elbows. You can see the dragon tats on his forearms and the Fallen Angel on his chest. His hair is down from its usual high and tight pony and falls with the slightest of curls. I lick my lips and finish looking him over. He's got a silver belt buckle that matches the gauges in his ears.

He's still not noticed that I'm standing here. I smile and yell for him. "Hey, Beast, who are you waiting for?"

He looks at me, smiling, then curls his finger for me

to come to him. I walk over to him and I still have to look up at him even with my heels.

He bends, kissing me on the cheek. "Bella, you look lovely. Do you like your presents?"

"Thank you, though it seems someone is holding out on me."

Steve smirks at me. "One more gift, well, one more for now." He holds up a pair of panties. I grab them from his hands and they are a tad heavy, which earns Steve a look. "Go, put them on."

"Tell me what we're doing first."

"We're going to have dinner and maybe a little dancing."

"Why do feel like something's going on that you aren't telling me?"

Steve laughs. "Go put your panties on."

Fucker wants to play games, I'll play games. I hand him my clutch before slipping the panties on. No sooner than I straighten out my dress and I feel a vibration, which has me falling against him.

"Fucker."

"Soon enough." He sticks his arm around me and leads the way to the restaurant.

38

STEVE

"COME FOR ME," I whisper into Crystal's ear as I turn up the vibration in her panties. When I stopped at Walmart Plaza, I sidestepped the big box shop and went into the adult store there in the strip mall instead, picking up a few provisions to make things more interesting this time.

We are sitting in the back of the Killawatt restaurant in a dark corner booth, having just finished our cucumber salads. I told the waiter to take his time with the entrees. She's breathing heavy, her hands fisting in her lap, trying hard not to succumb to the feeling rushing through her body.

"I-I can't, Beast," she whimpers, so I turn up the power another notch and she falls back against the seat, her leg lifting as she begins to pant. "Oh God!" she whispers, her chest heaving as she comes. I slowly dial back the vibration, letting her ride it out. She's moaning gently, her eyes squeezed tightly shut as she licks her crimson lips. "You're wrong. We're in a public place."

"Do you want to do it again, or shall I wait until

you're eating your New York strip like I planned?"

"I think you should stop till we're upstairs."

"Mouthy? Hmm." I hit the low button and she writhes. As torturous as this is for her, it's killing me. I'm hard as a fucking rock. The food comes and so does she, which is hilarious since the waiter is taking the dessert order from me and she digs her nails into my thigh. I'm pretty sure she's just drawn blood.

I order the cheesecake. To go.

Teasing her is fun, but touching her is so much better. Our room is a penthouse level, so I take her hand and we get on the elevator. We're not alone, but I can't keep my hands to myself. I slip my hand under her dress, caressing her ass through the lace panty.

She lifts onto her toes as I reach under her, parting her thighs and pulling her to me as the last passenger exits. I kiss her and she wraps her arms around my neck as I slide her panty aside and get my fingers drenched.

"I can't wait to bury my cock in you."

"What's stopping you?" she moans and I hit the penthouse button on the elevator wall. Lifting her up, I unzip my fly and push her panties aside. I thrust up into her and pin her to the wall, my body connecting with hers as we travel up the floors. When the elevator dings, I pull out of her only long enough to get us through the doors, then I'm back inside her faster than the doors can slam shut.

"Your pussy feels so good," I pant, working her little body on my cock. She grabs the door frame, using it for leverage as she slams against my cock, taking every inch I have to give. It doesn't take long and as she comes, I erupt inside her. It feels good, feels like home.

I put her down on the bed and strip her as she puts her legs up over a pillow for the next twenty minutes. I kiss and caress her, licking and sucking her nipples. She holds my head, but stays quiet.

"A penny for your thoughts, Bella," I say as I hold her.

"Thoughts? What are thoughts?"

"Oh, no, I've broken you," I say, my cock twitching against her thigh.

"You act so worried."

"I figure if I can fuck you into a coma, I can fuck you back out."

"Is that what you're trying to do?"

I get up from the bed and go to my bag of tricks. I pull out a set of fingertip vibrators. "Among other things." I open the package and disappear into the bathroom to clean them, then return to her.

I have them on my fingers and turn them on low. Slowly, I rub her tits, the vibration making her nipples stand instantly. She arches her back, lifting off the bed and pushing up on her elbows as I run my tips down her body, to reach the very center of her. Rubbing her clit makes her call my name as she grabs my hair and tugs. The pain shoots through me and I bite her nipple, sucking hard enough to turn it purple.

"Easy, Beast."

"Shh, or you'll be lopsided." I grab the other breast and make a similar marking as I continue to circle her clit, bringing myself down on her for a second go.

❧ ❧ ❧

I'm up before her each morning, ordering food and collecting towels from the maid service. We've forgone them coming in until late evening, when we're out. Every night, I've made sure that we've gone out for either dinner, a show, or just to gamble a bit. We won't get to do these things as much once we're pregnant, so I figure we'll get it in now.

I have a good feeling about this time. Most of our stress is gone and now, it's all a matter of waiting. It's our last night and I still have a few things to present to her. She's fresh from the shower and wrapped in a towel when I turn to her.

"I have a couple more presents for you."

"I don't want them," she says, completely straight-faced, and I fall out laughing. "Between the panties, the magic fingers, the chocolate body painting and the anal vibe, what the hell else could you possibly have?"

"Oh, you'd be surprised," I say, pulling out a baby blue bag with a white bow.

Her eyes pop out of her head as I swing it and my cock, walking over to her. "What is it?" she asks cautiously.

"Open the bag."

"Don't want to," she pouts.

"Ugh! Christ, woman." I gently dump the four boxes on the bed and I hear her audibly exhale. I can't help but laugh. The ink isn't even dry on my divorce yet, not ready for a ring. "Will you open them now?"

She rolls her eyes and opens the boxes to find a diamond set. Four carat studs, tennis bracelet, anklet, and matching diamond solitaire necklace. "Did I miss something?"

"The accounts unfroze the other day. I checked the ATM card on a whim and everything is back in proper order. I decided to celebrate by covering you in ice."

"And not telling me?"

"It's why they call it a surprise, Bella. Will you put it on?"

"This whole week has been a surprise." She puts her hands on my bare chest. "I don't need jewelry and I don't need all the extravagances you used to do. I just need you."

"I get that, I do, you never ask for things the way Kellie always did. I get that you don't need this stuff, but I want to give it to you, I want to finally show my affection."

"They're beautiful, just one question. Where the hell do you expect me to wear them?"

"Right now, I want you to wear them while I make you come like Niagara Falls. After that, you can wear the earrings all the time, they're studs, and the bracelet and anklet when you are out about town in your cute little Capri and tank ensembles.

"So, you plan on letting me out of the house at some point without you?"

"Yeah? Why not? I just come because I don't like being alone and you always take the girls. You've never asked me to watch them or anything."

She looks up at me, confused. "I asked Kellie once and she told me no, so I always took them with me and had them help."

"Crys, if you need some you time, you just gotta tell me. We all need to be alone once in a while."

"I'm so used to having the girls around that it's weird when they're not."

"We've managed, so far," I say, putting the bracelet on her.

"That doesn't mean I don't wish we were home."

"We leave in the morning, right after breakfast, then it's time to Trick or Treat." I get the rest of the jewelry on her and look at her. She looks sexy as hell. "Just one last toy for us," I smirk.

"Oh, sweet Jesus," she half cries as I wrap a towel around my waist and grab the ice bucket, heading out of the room. "Where are you going?"

"We need ice," I answer with a smile.

When I return, she's lying on the bed on display. I put the ice next to the bed and get the last thing we have to play with. A cock ring that has a vibrating clit stimulator attached. I'm half-mast, so I can get the sucker on, but as she touches herself playfully, the rig tightens around the base of my shaft and my erection is firm and ready for her.

I watch her and she looks at me as she bites her lip. Fuck, I need to be doing that. I crawl across the bed to her and kiss her deeply. Pulling her to me, I grab a few ice chips and taking them into my mouth, I circle her nipples. Then, with a bit more ice, I slip my frozen tongue into her hot and aching core. It's our last night here, so I'm going to make it memorable.

39

CRYSTAL

ANOTHER FIVE DAYS COME AND GONE.
Only this time, I was pampered *and* fucked. Steve made
sure to take care of everything. I think he's pretty
confident that this is it and we will have a baby. Me? I'm
holding out hope, but I'm not certain. We pull up to the
house and once again, it's packed.

"Is this going to happen every time?" I ask as Steve
shuts off the car.

"God, I hope not. I'm not the one who invites
them."

"You do know who it is, right?"

"Peggy Sue. I'd ground her, but she doesn't live
here anymore."

"I'm gonna string her up by her toes."

"Careful, she's her mother's daughter, I'm afraid
she might like that."

"Thank God I got to her when she was young. I'm
pretty sure I've taught her the right ways. I don't think
she's as sadistic as Kellie."

"Let's hope not. Otherwise, I'd have to feel sorry for

that boy."

"Beast, he's already pussy whipped."

"He's not the only one."

"You can do whatever you want and you know it. That boy doesn't leave her side."

Steve smiles. "Well, I suppose it's because he'd like to keep his dick."

"Don't go there. You didn't take care of it, so I did," I say and then jump as hands hit my window.

I grab my chest and Kyle says, "Come on, get out of the car."

"You going to kill him, or am I?"

"I got him."

"Let's grab the bags and go see the girls."

We step out of the car and Kyle is bouncing around. "You guys are in trouble!" he singsongs.

I just look at him like he's crazy and go around the back of the car to help with the stuff. I take a deep breath and try to get past him but can't because he's all over the place.

"Kyle, if you don't chill, I'm going to hurt you. You're going to hit me with all the bouncing you're doing."

"Kyle! Slow your fucking roll or go the fuck home," Steve yells and I stand still, waiting for him. I'm thinking it's a good idea to put Steve between Kyle and me.

Kyle puts his hands in the air and backs off, then Steve puts an arm around my shoulder. "Why don't you go in the house and I'll get these bags. Go relax."

"We're gonna have to start hiding shit if he keeps showing up like this."

"It's not going to come to that. Please, just go in the house. I'll talk to him."

I nod. "Okay," I say, then carry the couple bags I

grabbed into the house.

"Honey, I'm home!" I yell out as I shut the door since, apparently, everyone is here.

"Aww, baby, we missed you," Angelica says, wrapping her arms around my shoulder and kissing me right on the mouth.

"Angelica, we have a house full of people and some of them shouldn't see this."

"But you didn't say you didn't like it," she says and pokes my nose.

Kyle's high and Angelica's lost her mind. Just fucking perfect. Too much is going on, so I just pass everybody up and go straight up the stairs. I drop the bags in the closet, then sit down on the bed. I fall backward with a groan as the door opens.

I turn my head to see Marissa. "Hey, you got a minute?"

"Is this about your brother-in-law being high again?"

Marissa shakes her head. "That's an issue all its own."

I sit up and look at her. "Did you have problems with the girls?"

"No, they were angels. They even tried helping with the twins."

"Come on and sit down. What's wrong? You're starting to worry me."

"This is about you, Steve, and a certain penthouse elevator ride."

"What the fuck? How could you possibly know that?"

"Because I don't know if you're aware, but all those hotel elevators have cameras... Video cameras."

"Fuck me."

Marissa shakes her head. "It went viral in two hours. They called the video Fallen Angels flies high."

"Is it bad that I'm just glad that the divorce papers are signed and Kellie can't use it against him?"

"You're taking this a helluva lot better than I did. You realize this is a sex tape, right?"

"It happens every day. Not a lot we can stress about now. You know we each have our fuck up, this is mine and Steve's."

"That, along with the pictures of you guys all over the hotel. What exactly were you doing in the booth? Everybody is speculating."

I cover my face with a laugh. "Did they get a picture of me putting on panties?"

Marissa covers her face and nods her head. "You were in the middle of the lobby."

"He wanted to play games, so I played, only his came with a remote."

Marissa laughs so hard she snorts. "So, you both won. You came while America watched."

"That's why *that* happened in the elevator. I was losing my mind just as much as he was."

"He's going to catch some hell for it, but you guys will be okay."

"You don't actually think he cares, do you?"

"No, I suppose not."

"I guess we should go downstairs so he knows I'm not up here freaking out. I just needed a break because Kyle came close to knocking me on my ass."

Marissa sighs and drops her head. "I'm sorry, he's getting out of control, but I seem to be the only one that notices. Brent looks the other way, it's his brother."

"I notice, he's acting the same way Brent does. If I couldn't tell them apart, I'd have sworn it was Brent."

Marissa just shakes her head. "Come on, let's get you downstairs."

We get downstairs and I see Steve out on the patio on the phone. I ignore everyone and go straight to him. "Fine, I'll pay the God damned fine. Just send me the bill." Steve says, hanging up the phone.

"We fucked up," I say, looking at him.

"Are you okay?"

"It's a sex tape and some pictures, nothing we can do about it now."

"At least we look good doing it." He turns his phone to me.

"We do look pretty good. Though, everyone is trying to figure out what was going on in the booth."

"Wouldn't they like to know."

"Marissa does."

Steve wraps his arm around me, kissing me. "You wanna use the ring again tonight?"

"Of course, but we have to take the girls out first."

* * *

We're all getting ready to go out to take the kids trick or treating. I'm Little Red Riding Hood and Steve's the big bad wolf, only he's got a collar and leash, so I can lead him around. Sue Ellen, Mary Ann, and Angela are the three little pigs. Angelica and Maverick are Harley Quinn with the black and red jumpsuit and the Jack Nicolson Joker. Brent and Marissa are Hugh Heffner and a Playboy bunny, and the babies are little bunnies. Kyle is dressed as Two-Face, which I'm sure got a rise out of Maverick. Ringo is full on Oliver Queen aka The Green Arrow. Peggy Sue is Supergirl, Harrison is Jimmy Olsen, and Brayden is Superman.

We don't actually make it back to the house till almost ten at night and I'm worn out. I leave Steve to tell everyone goodbye and take the girls upstairs to start getting them ready for bed. I lay down in the bed with them and start reading a story when they are finished with their showers.

I wake to Steve saying my name. "Huh?"

"Bella, I need your help so we can go to bed."

"Help with what?"

"Getting this shit off my face." He takes my hand and I feel a nose, which only makes me laugh.

I pout, "I don't want to walk."

He picks me up and carries me to the bathroom, sitting me on the counter. I smile at him. "You know, you kind of look like a beast now.""

"Just help me out of this, please."

I get him all cleaned up and admire my work. "There, all better."

He rubs his face and then looks at me with a cocked brow. "Hey there, Red."

"What do you want, Mister?" He takes off his gloves, tossing them on the counter before howling. "Quiet down, you're going to wake the girls."

"I already locked the door."

"Did you now?"

He raises his brows and I don't take another second before I pull him to me. Our lips crash together, then he's picking me up and taking me to the bed. I unlatch the collar around his neck and he removes my wig. All my blonde hair comes falling out.

He runs his hands up my stockings. "I kept hoping you were going to drop something tonight. I love you in this short skirt."

"Show me how much," I say with a smirk.

He growls, tearing my panties off me and it's on.

40

STEVE

ANOTHER THREE WEEKS, ANOTHER MISS.
Crystal is on a razor's edge with her moods, which only means one thing, she's getting ready to start her period again. That means I failed again and she's going to have to go through another round of the injections. She hates that part and I hate giving them to her. Maye it's time we look into other options. IVF, perhaps. I didn't want to go that route, having my baby created in a lab. I wanted us to make him or her together, the way it should be. I wanted to have a conception story worth telling.

It's the day before Thanksgiving and Crystal has given me a list of last minute things she needs. I head out to the grocery store, leaving her home with the girls and Adam, our body guard. Since the sex tape and the other photos came out, there has been a lot of activity around the house. Before this, we didn't have issues, but since this and word of my divorce leaked, it's becoming a problem. I used to feel like I was enough to protect my girls.

Adam is armed security and seems to be a good, trustworthy guy. Blake introduced him to us, so I'm inclined to trust the guy, though I have had Maverick install a security and video surveillance system as well.

I get to the shopping and am just turning into frozen veggies when someone whispers my name. I look up from my list and am face to face with Kellie.

"Um, hi." I don't know what else to say. She's in her work scrubs and has a basket with just a few items in it.

"Feeding a small army?" she asks, pointing to my basketful.

"Um, yeah, the band is coming to the house for the holiday." Why is she being civil? I am trying to wrap my head around it when she speaks again.

"You know, I never stopped loving you, Bear. I just could never handle you loving her too." She walks up to me, kisses my cheek, and walks away.

Our divorce finalized last week. I got the papers from Loggins along with the bill from Imogen. Why would she bother to tell me she loves me, especially after everything she did to the contrary? My head is swimming as I finish the shopping. I collect the items and head home.

✻ ✻ ✻

Crystal is prepping for tomorrow. Her mood? Lousy. I go into the parlor and feeling rather sorry for myself, I grab the scotch and my notebook. Maybe if I get the shit in my head out on paper, I'll be able to get through this craziness.

I start with a drum beat and the next thing I know, I'm writing lyrics.

Release me
Steve Falcone

A man on the edge, just tryin' to survive
Tappin' that vein, once, twice, just to feel like I'm alive.
Once, I ran the streets, but now I've got it all.
But now all I think about is when will I fall?

Fall, like the angels. Rise, to the heavens,
I'm just a man, I have no plan.
Release me. God. Release me.

I write a stanza, I take a drink, I write some more.

Met a girl who took me for a whirl,
Turned me right round, slammed me to the ground
Made it alright, new ways to take flight
How the years take their toll, so afraid we're gonna fall!

Fall, like the angels. Rise, to the heavens,
I'm just a man, I have no plan.
Release me. God. Release me.

What's there left to lose
When the fires rise and the waves crash
When there's nothing left of what you thought would
last
This world has me caught and I can finally see
The person who's always been standing in front of me,
and so I fall

Fall, like the angels. Rise, to the heavens,
I'm just a man, I have no plan.
Release me. God. Release me. Release me.

I'm sitting on the floor, a mess of myself. The song is my past, my present, and my future. I just wish I could sort it all out in my head. I try and get off the floor and slip, the glass shattering under my hand.

"Fuck, that hurts!" I growl.

"Beast? Is everything okay?" Crystal asks and I am frantic, she can't see me like this.

Her feet shuffle on the floor and I collapse to my knees. "Whoa!" she exclaims. She must smell the liquor I've spilled, it's all over the floor and me and I've got blood all over me now as I'm trying to pull the glass shards out of my hand.

I look up to see her standing over me. She looks around. "What's wrong?"

I rip the last piece of glass out of my hand with my teeth and spit it out before tearing my shirt and tying it around my hand. I heard her, I just don't know what to say.

"You're drinking?"

I try to get up. I can hear the accusation in her voice. "I know, I've fucked it up. It's all my fault. I couldn't keep it together," I say, slurring.

"Slow down, wha-what happened?"

"She still loves me, she says. Yeah, love doesn't hurt like that," I say with a wry chuckle.

"What are you talking about?"

I reach for my notebook, "It's there... All there," I whisper-shout.

She picks up my notebook, looking it over. I don't want her doing that, it's personal, it's raw, it's my broken heart.

I reach for it, trying to say something, but the words fail me. I watch as she swallows.

"It- it's too much, right? Too honest?" Her response is to get down on the floor and crawl to me, hugging me to her. I wrap my arms around her and erupt into a sobbing mess.

"Tell me what happened," she whispers.

"I-I'm failing. I'm falling. Everything is wrong. The only thing that makes sense to me is *you*."

"What are you failing at?"

I laugh. "*Life*. I'm a terrible brother, lousy husband, well ex-husband now, as a father, I'm a fucking joke. I can't get you pregnant, and now, I can't even get off the floor because I decided to drink and make an ass out of myself when I promised I would stop. I can't keep promises, I'm just a failure."

She cups my face, making me look at her. I try to pull away, but she holds me firmly. "We're done, we're stopping this now. You can't handle it, you knew there was a possibility that it wouldn't work. I already told myself if it got to be too much for you, I'd stop it. I love you, the girls love you, but you've been here every day. You've not slipped in three months. You've done so good, what happened that you aren't telling me?"

"I saw Kellie today. She said she loves me. What am I supposed to do with that? How am I supposed to react to that? She completely mind-fucked me with one little sentence."

"And you still love her, you always will. You have three amazing girls together. Maybe you made the wrong choice."

I push back from her. "No! No! Don't say that! Don't you dare say I've made a mistake here. You're the only thing I'm sure about."

A tear rolls down her cheek and I pull her to me. "I wouldn't be upset, I would understand."

"Then understand *this*... I'm so sure of us that there is a ring that matches the rest of your diamonds. I was going to wait until Christmas to propose, but you seem to need the reassurance now. Crystal Marie Howard, I love you more than words can say. Marry me."

She pushes off me and stands up, backing up to the fireplace. "It's too soon. You're barely divorced and you're drunk. I'll call Maverick to come clean you up." She's crying. What did I do? I love her, I know that much. I've told her, I've asked, and she's what? Gonna run out on me?

"We've been together ten years, we're trying to get pregnant, marriage is the rational step in this irrational situation." I stand up finally, a little off on my feet, but I go to her. "You're the one that I want. Don't make me beg." I drop to my knees again, holding onto her, my face against her abdomen.

"You're drunk. We can have this conversation again when you're sober, but not until. I've got everything done in the kitchen and I need a shower, the girls will be up in a few hours. I'm gonna call Maverick before I get in the shower to sew you up because I can't do it. I'll be in bed once you're taken care of and cleaned up."

❆ ❆ ❆

"So, I asked her to marry me, and she freaked out." I've filled Maverick in on everything that happened and he's been listening without response for the last twenty minutes.

"Well, you are a bit drunk."

"Which makes me incapable of telling a lie at this point."

"Honestly, I think she's just worried."

"That makes two of us."

"Steve, I'm pretty sure it's that time again with as moody as she's been."

"You think I don't fucking know that?"

"Hey, I'm on your side here. I'm just trying to figure out why she is the way she is and to help you understand. Maybe all this," he says with a wave of his hands, "is she might just be having a moment."

"Well, I had one, so she's entitled… Look, man, I'm tired, I'm drunk, I don't know half of what I'm saying. Thank you for the help and the ear, but I think I'm going to go upstairs, strip down, and climb into bed with the woman I love. She did say I was welcome after you fixed me, so there's hope for me yet."

"Go to bed, I've gotta go back home and be ready to be back here in like three hours."

I stand up and walk Maverick out before climbing the steps and going into my room. Crystal is sound asleep as I go and take my shower. When I get back to the bed, I snuggle up to her and wrap my arms around her. She wiggles against me and I groan, but ignore it, I need sleep and so does she.

41

CRYSTAL

I FEEL MY STOMACH ROLL AND I PUSH Steve off me, making a mad dash for the bathroom. I barely get my head over the toilet when I start puking. I automatically start trying to figure out if I ate something wrong, but I didn't eat anything different than everyone else and they're not sick.

"Bella, are you okay?" Steve asks.

I try to answer, but just start puking some more. When I finally think I'm done, I flush the toilet and lay my face, yet again, against the cold, tile floor.

I force myself to swallow before talking. "What's today?"

"Thanksgiving?"

"No, the actual day."

"It's the twenty-third." I start counting days in my head. "Are you okay? Did you eat something messed up? Did you pick at the raw turkey?"

I groan, pretty sure my calculations are correct. "You suck."

"Why do I suck?"

"Because this is your fault."

"What did I do?"

Before I can answer, my head is over the toilet once again. I flush again and reach for a cloth since, apparently, Steve has lost the ability to help me.

"I need my phone." Steve walks out, then comes back a few seconds later, carrying my phone. I take it and hit Maverick's name. I'm not sure what time it is.

"Hello, Crystal."

"I need to speak to your wife."

There's a shuffling of the phone, then Angelica asks, "Did he roll over and squish you? Do we have to bring a forklift this time?"

"I wish."

"Are you still not over last night?"

"Forget last night! I woke up puking my guts out."

"What's today's date?" Maverick asks, his voice muffled through the phone.

"It's the twenty-third," I snap. Angelica is laughing. "I need you to bring me something."

"I'm way ahead of ya. We'll be there in about an hour."

"Thank fuck because right now, I've got an overgrown beast staring at me like I've lost my fucking mind."

"We'll be there in an hour. Goodbye." She hangs up and I toss the phone on the floor.

Steve crouches down in front of me, staring me in the face. "Did we do it?"

"I'm pretty sure I'm not puking my guts up for any other reason," I snap.

Steve's got that stupid grin on his face. He picks me up and hands me the mouthwash. Just as I go to use it, my stomach rolls again and my head is over the toilet.

"Bella, we did it," he says and my hands fly in the air.

"What can I do?" he asks just as I flush again and lay back on the floor.

"The girls need breakfast. They will be up anytime. Ham needs to be basted, but the rest has to wait for me." I sigh.

"Alright, I'll go feed the girls and then, I'll be back to check on you. Do you want me to bring you anything?"

I just wave him off.

❈ ❈ ❈

I've spent almost two hours, on and off, with my head over the fucking toilet. I'm lying on the floor when the bedroom door opens and closes.

"Crys, you in here, honey?" Angelica calls.

"Dying," I groan.

"Look at you on the floor like a kitty cat," Angelica says as her feet come into view.

"It's cold."

"I don't miss that. Wait, because it lasts all day."

"I hate you," I whine.

"That's nothing new." She comes over and sits on the floor beside me with a bag in her lap. "Marissa's downstairs, making your tea. Come on, sit up." She pats the floor in front of my face. "Come on, get up. We didn't get to whine about it and neither do you."

I groan, sitting up. "Marissa doesn't count. Bitch didn't get any symptoms."

"Don't you hate her for that? She carried two babies and not a peep between them of a symptom," Angelica says.

I crack a smile. "They are Brent's kids. You know they are gonna be anal as fuck."

Angelica starts digging in her bag. She pulls out a big green tin and I look at her, confused. "Soda crackers, they murder nausea. They taste good with jam, honey, peanut butter, and pickle juice."

I cringe, "Can we not talk about food please?"

"You're going to become very good friends with these, I promise you."

"And the test?"

She hands it to me. "Here you go. It's really simple, it will say pregnant on it when it's done."

I look at the test and back to Angelica. "Are you going to watch me piss?"

"No, I'm going." Angelica gets up and out the door, she goes.

I force myself to stand long enough to pull my pants down and take the test. Then, I set it on the counter and clean myself up. I flush the toilet and wash my hands. I'm finally brushing my teeth when the bedroom door closes again.

There's a knock, then the bathroom door opens and Steve quietly calls, "Crystal?" I turn toward him, still scrubbing my mouth. "I brought your tea."

I just groan and nod my head toward the counter. I finish up, then use the mouthwash. Spitting it out, I wipe my face and finally look at Steve. "Sorry I snapped."

"It's okay, Bella."

"You just kept talking and I sure as hell couldn't answer."

"It's okay. Is that the test?"

I nod. "I'm afraid to look. What if I'm wrong?"

"What if you're *right*?"

205

"If I'm right, then this morning is completely your fault."

"You may have helped a little."

"Other than throwing out a couple of eggs, I didn't do a lot."

Steve passes me, putting the tray on the counter. He picks up the test and I hold my breath. He looks at it, then looks at me and just nods his head yes.

Tears fall down my face. "We're having a baby?"

"We're having a baby!"

I bite my lip "That means no more shots in the ass."

He shakes his head no. "No, no more shots in the ass." He drops the test to the counter, picking me up and sitting me next to it. He kisses me and when he pulls away, we're both crying. He pulls me to him. "Operation baby maker is a go. We've got a bun in the oven."

"Thankfully, we've got an appointment tomorrow."

"Yup, double confirmed, triple confirmed. Whatever needs to be confirmed."

"Is everyone here?"

"Yes, except for Kyle, but you know him, he'd rather sleep in anyhow."

"So, I'm also to assume everyone knows?"

"Um, I think Angelica told them."

"That doesn't shock me. Bitch laughed at me on the phone," I whine.

"Well, have your tea and hopefully, you won't puke your guts up anymore."

❊ ❊ ❊

Thanksgiving has come and now, it's gone. Thank God! It's been a stressful day between them talking

206

about Angelica's bump to them asking Brent and Marissa as well as Harrison and Peggy Sue when they'd plan on trying again. Most of the conversation stayed on the fact that Steve and I did it. We're pregnant and all I can think is how, with all the stress going on.

It's almost like they don't understand that for Steve and me, this first trimester is going to be hard and long. We have to be careful with everything we do. They told us when this process started that if I was to actually get knocked up, that it'd be very high risk and it wouldn't be easy. Like anything about this process has been easy.

I got the girls to bed just like I always do, now I'm working on putting the kitchen back to order. Steve said he'd be back to help me, but I've got no clue where he went. Of course, Adam is off to the cameras to watch the house. It's kind of creepy having someone watch us every day. I would like to say no, but I already know Steve doesn't hear a word of that.

I'm working on loading this dishwasher when I turn to grab a plate. I grab the plate, then notice the ring on the counter. I look at it for a second, then go back to loading the dishes.

Steve snakes an arm around me while he's picking up the ring, then holds it in front of my face. "I love you. I'm sober. Marry me."

"The ink isn't dry on your divorce."

"It's dry enough."

I turn to face him because he needs to see my face to understand. "You need to let things settle for the girls."

"I'm not saying to marry me tomorrow. I'm asking you to marry me sometime in the future."

"We've done everything so backward and then, today, Kyle and Angelica wouldn't shut up. The girls questioned me when I put them to bed."

"What did they say?"

"Sue Ellen asked if I was her mommy now. Mary Ann asked if I was going to marry you. Then they both wanted to know if we are having a baby."

"What did you tell them?" he asks.

"I told Sue Ellen that Kellie will always be her mommy and I just plan to be exactly what I've always been. Mary Ann didn't like my answer much when I told her maybe one day, which started a discussion on why we weren't already married because I've always been here. I've taught the girls too damned well because they are too smart. As for the baby comment, I just told them maybe one day."

"I know that this is risky, but that's no reason for us not to move forward. I just want you to wear my ring."

"I'm apparently already carrying your baby and now you want me to wear your ring too."

"I don't want my baby born a bastard. I want to give you the name you've more than earned, you deserve it. As for whether or not you're the girls' mommy now, you always have been. You've taken better care of them than their mom ever did. In my eyes, actions speak louder than words. You're bound to those girls by something more than blood."

"Steve, I won't take on the mommy role. That isn't fair to Kellie. I hate that everything has happened the way it has. I hate that she hasn't seen them. She can hate me all she wants, but I will never take her place. It's not fair to her as their mommy. One day, and I'm not saying anytime soon, I'll be their stepmom, which keeps me as just what I've always been in their eyes and I'm okay with that."

Steve sets the ring on the counter next to me. "You

could at least look at it," he says, sounding so defeated.

I look at him, confused for a moment, then it dawns on me that the idiot didn't understand me. I put my palms against his cheeks. "Beast, you didn't understand me. When I said that one day, I'll be their stepmom, I was saying yes to you."

Steve looks surprised, then smiles and opens the box. "Give me your damned hand." I give him my left hand and he slips the ring onto my finger. It's a solitaire and it's big, but it's nothing too crazy like everyone else has.

"I love you, Bella."

I pull his face to mine and kiss him. "I love you too, Beast."

42

STEVE

BLACK FRIDAY AND BABY CONFIRMATIONS. Crystal had me up by three a.m. She wanted to hit the shops for the deals and so did Marissa and Angelica, apparently, since they were waiting for us at the car.

"So, who's minding the little troopers if we are all leaving?" I ask, still trying to wake the hell up.

"Peggy Sue and the guys. I'm not shopping with Maverick around; it will ruin the surprise."

'Yeah, and I hardly get to shop, so I'm tagging along," Marissa adds with a smile as she gets in the back. "C'mon, I'm freshly milked and ready to go."

"Not without me, Ma'am," Blake says as he comes around the back of the car.

"Damn it!" Marissa pouts. "Don't you sleep, like ever?"

"Yes, but Brent heard you planning this last night, so I was tasked with joining you."

"Just get in," I bark, putting on my trucker hat and hoping that it's enough to get us left alone.

"Sir?"

Ugh, it's Adam. That's it for me.

"Seriously! Is everyone just coming along?"

"Sir, you have three women to keep track of and two are with child. I'd say you are gonna need the extra hands."

"Yup, I guess so, just c'mon before the kids wake up and I have to bring them too."

"Let Adam hang on to the cart and just sit down." I take Crystal by the hand and force her down into a chair in the baby section of Walmart. It's a glider rocker combo and looks rather comfy.

"I would have left you at home with the other guys if I'd have known you were gonna drive me crazy," she says seriously.

"I'm just… Sorry, I want to make sure you're doing alright. How's your nausea?"

"I'm fine."

What do you think about this chair? It looks cozy."

"It's okay."

"Do you want it? For the nursery?"

She looks at me, flabbergasted. "It's too soon."

"I can't help it. My head is all over the place." I squat in front of her to look in her eyes. "I'm so excited."

"I'm afraid to buy anything. What if we jinx ourselves?"

"We worked too hard for a jinx now. I just know we're gonna be okay."

"It's just so early." She sounds worried and I pull her into me, kissing her head. She's afraid and I need to be her rock.

"Bella, we see the doc in a few hours. I'm sure he's gonna say everything is okay. We've been doing everything they say."

"I know that, but there's still that tiny part of me that's worried I might screw up."

"There's nothing to worry about, you're not gonna screw this up and neither am I. We are going to have a baby and we are going to get married. It's finally coming together like it should."

She covers her face, the light of the place bouncing off her ring.

"Are you two…" Angelica asks suddenly. "That's a mighty fine rock ya got there."

Now, still hiding behind her hands, Crystal shakes her head vigorously.

"Angelica, not now."

"Well, you may wanna move because people are starting to stare."

I pull Crystal into my arms and stand us up as I kiss her. "We're gonna be alright."

"We're losing our minds."

"Can't lose what you didn't have in the first place," Marissa says, patting my shoulder. "Let's get more stuff. I still need to go over to the jeweler to pick up the new wedding set."

I look at Marissa, confused.

"Oh, I'm getting Brent and me a new set for our anniversary on the ninth. I've got a whole night planned – dinner, dancing, debauchery. Ringo is taking baby Brent and Brenna for the night."

"Sounds like fun."

"Some much-needed fun," she responds.

"Just don't get knocked up again," Angelica smirks.

"Shush, you, don't go getting that in my head. The

twins are more than enough and I'm just getting my abs back."

❋ ❋ ❋

We ran into overtime with the shopping, the Escalade is packed, and we have things being delivered by various shops. The girls are all getting new ATVs, it's time they learn. We even picked up one for Harrison. With so much shopping causing a time crunch, we had to bring the motley crew with us to the fertility clinic. They are in the car while Crys and I see Dr. Ang.

"Well, congratulations, series two is a success. You are officially three weeks pregnant." Dr. Ang smiles, sitting down with our charts.

"So, what's this mean for us? What's our next step?" I ask, holding Crystal's hand.

"We have a team of doctors at your disposal. Doctors like me, who are willing to see you through this, help you with diet details, an exercise regimen that is safe for you and the baby, and whatever else you need. While you can go to your private OBGYN, they may not be the best in regards to your PCOS. We here at the clinic, know your case and are prepared to get you through to holding your healthy baby."

Crystal squeezes my hand. "Okay, and what of the risks? We've read that a PCOS pregnancy is high risk for miscarriage in the first trimester. What can we do to avoid that?"

"Keep on your diet, no lifting or carrying of objects over ten pounds, especially if you are laying them against your abdomen. If you are to continue sexual activity, we suggest woman on top or from behind as it puts less strain on the body. Sex is safe in these positions, but finding other ways to be intimate is also suggested, especially early in the trimester. By week thirteen, we will be out of the woods, but we like to tell our clients that what works in the beginning, usually will be what sees you through to the end."

"What's the rate for miscarriage?"

"If we can't keep your insulin levels down and your hormones in check, thirty to fifty percent. However, you have not had any issues so far from taking the Metformin. Your hormone levels are a little low, but that's caused by the PCOS. We are going to keep track of you, so every two weeks you will come in and we will do blood and urine cultures. While you are not going to be on insulin because there doesn't appear to be a need right now, we will be sending you home with a blood glucose meter to keep track of your sugar levels. When you come in, you will bring the meter. It will show us how you are doing and help us to pick the right course of action for you. For today, I would say go home, put up your feet, and have a glass of red wine or Concord grape juice, it's good for you both."

"So, no more Black Friday shopping then?" I ask, looking Crystal over. She looks frightened, her skin is pale, and her heart is racing; I can feel it through her hold on me.

"Not unless it's online and with your credit card, Mr. Falcone."

43

CRYSTAL

IT'S BEEN TWO WEEKS SINCE IT WAS confirmed that we're pregnant and we saw the doc a few days ago. Everything is going smoothly, so far, but I can't help but be on the nervous side. There's a thirty to fifty percent chance I'll lose the baby, so I can't help but stress.

Steve's been making breakfast every day, so I can rest a little. He says his love bun needs to rest more. He usually comes to let me know when it's ready, so I can join them. I'm in the bathroom, stretching my back before I start the day when I notice it. There's a fucking bump. Ain't no fucking way. I head for the closet to grab a bra and one of my shirts to slip on. From the front, with no shirt, you can't really see it, but turn to the side and by God, it's there. However, with the shirt, it doesn't matter which way I stand, you can see it. Jesus Christ, I'm barely five weeks and have already popped.

I let out a growl, stripping my shirt and dropping it to the sink before going to grab one of Steve's. I've finished brushing my teeth and I'm fixing my hair and makeup when Steve comes in.

"Did you forget to get dressed?" Steve asks and I just pull up his shirt so he can see my shorts but continue what I'm doing. "Why are we wearing my Iron Maiden shirt?"

"Because, apparently, I'm carrying a beast."

Steve walks up to me and puts his arms around me, but stops midway and traces the bump. "Should you have this yet?"

"Like I said, I'm carrying a beast." I look in the mirror and see the grin forming on his face.

"You can't wear my Iron Maiden shirt."

"Fine," I say taking it off and throwing up my hands as I move to the closet for a different one.

"Bella?"

"What?"

"What are you doing?"

"You said I couldn't wear that one," I yell.

"What's the matter with your clothes?"

"They all show it."

"And?"

I stomp out of the closet with a *Fallen Angels* shirt on. "And we aren't telling the girls."

"Maybe it's time we do. We didn't hide Mary Ann or Sue Ellen from Peggy Sue."

"Was she high risk?"

Steve just looks at me. "We had blood pressure issues, later on with Mary Ann, but not in the beginning, no."

"Exactly. Our case is different from yours and Kellie's. We've been having this same argument for two weeks." I'm standing in the closet doorway with my hands on my hips, watching him.

"Well, from the looks of it, we aren't going to be

able to hide it much longer. No matter how big my shirts are on you. We're going to have to explain why your shape is changing and Peggy Sue is bound to notice."

"Shouldn't I get to make this decision? It's my body."

Steve runs his hand down his face. "Fine, Crys, wear what you want. I just think it'll be easier if we told them. What if one of them runs into you like they usually do. You're going to yell at her, she's not going to understand why, and then you're going to feel even worse."

"I don't ever yell at the girls. I can't think of once that I've even raised my voice to them," I say as the tears start falling.

"Oh, Bella, Bella, Bella," Steve says, pulling me to him. "I just want you safe and I think the girls will understand. Like you said, they're too smart for their own good."

"They won't understand if I lose the baby."

"I just don't see how you'll hide it with you popping already. So far, the doctors say everything's going good."

"I'm going to have shirts overnighted. We're only starting our fifth week. I just don't want to put the cart before the horse."

He sighs against me. "Alright, we'll do it your way."

❖ ❖ ❖

The girls are all working on spelling, which gives me time to handle a few things around the room. I've just finished filing last semester's graded papers in a file box on my desk, so I pick it up and start to carry it to the corner.

Next thing I know, it's being jerked out of my hands by Maverick. "What the hell are you doing?"

"Putting files away," I say, confused.

"You know you can't be lifting over ten pounds," he shouts at me.

"Could you lower your damn voice? You aren't my daddy and you sure as hell are not my husband."

"Where do you want this?"

"In the corner. What are you doing in here?"

"Steve told me to come let you all know that lunch is ready."

"Go get lunch, we can pick back up after you've eaten. They know, now get out," I snap at Maverick as the girls file out.

Maverick throws his hands in the air and walks away. I just growl and look out the window. I catch a movement out of the corner of my eye and jump, startled. I thought I was alone.

"You're pregnant," Peggy Sue states. I turn to face her and just nod. "Why haven't you told us?"

"Because there's a really big chance that I'm going to lose it."

Peggy Sue furrows her brow. "So, what are you guys doing to lower the risks?"

"The same things we were doing before to get pregnant."

"Diet and exercise. Are you taking your prenatal vitamins yet?"

"Yes, I take it every day."

"Right," she pauses, "so, what can we do to help?"

"There's nothing anyone else can do, it's my body that has to do it."

"Okay, well, I mean, if you need help around here

or with the girls, just ask."

"Peggy Sue, I'm all right."

"You're already wearing Daddy's clothes. That's why I'm concerned."

"Well, mine tend to show things I'm not talking about."

Peggy Sue just nods her head. "I popped by week eight is all I'm saying." She turns and walks out of the room.

I just drop my head and take a seat at my desk. I should probably go eat, but I don't want to with my emotions all over the map. I hit the mouse on my laptop and start a search for maternity clothes. I scroll a little, then click one or two items before scrolling again.

"Shopping, Bella?" Steve asks. I guess I was lost in my thoughts because I didn't even notice him entering the room.

I keep to what I'm doing and answer him, "I need clothes that fit."

He places his hands on my shoulders, massaging them. "You won't have to worry about needing new clothes if you don't eat."

"I'm not hungry."

"You can't be skipping meals like this. It's not good for you."

"I also can't go in there with my emotions all over the place."

"So, I'll bring it in to you. Just tell me what you need."

"I don't know what I need. I don't even know what I want," I say, turning my chair to face him, which causes Steve to step back with his hands in the air.

"What do you mean by that?"

"I don't know... Nothing makes sense. This was

supposed to be easy, but it isn't getting any easier. We've done nothing but argue for two solid weeks. We haven't finished shopping for the girls because we can't agree on anything."

"First of all, who said this was going to be easy? And as for shopping for the girl, is this about the ATVs again?"

I look at him with disgust. "You bought them?"

"I bought them on Black Friday. It was a good deal. It was like buy one, get two free, pricewise."

"We didn't agree on them. Is that how this is going to go? You make the decisions and I just have to deal with them? What happens when you leave? Will I just be stuck here taking care of the girls and going through this alone?"

Steve places his hands on each side of my face and gently wipes tears away that I didn't even know were falling. "Who says I'm going anywhere? If the rest of them can put us on hold for their pregnancies, you think I'm not gonna for ours?"

"I don't know these things. I just figured if the band had something, you'd go. I mean it's not like they can go without you. I don't know how this works. I'm not even sure what we're doing."

He looks at me, confused. "What do you mean, what we're doing?"

"Is it just us or is it open like you and Kellie. I don't want anyone else, but I know you have needs and that's what you're used to. You have to understand, I don't have anything to base this on. I never actually dated or had serious relationships before you and Kell."

Steve sits back on his knees. "We're nothing like Kellie and I were. She was the one who said to open the relationship. It was her idea because I had already been running around. I was twenty-two years old, hitting different clubs every night with the band, and I already had three kids. Women would throw themselves at me. When pussy chases that hard, you can't run that fast… At twenty-two, you don't really want to run that fast. So, she told me I could do what I wanted as long as I stayed and it worked. We stopped fighting, but then I found you. You weren't like other girls. You knew who I was and it didn't affect you. After you helped get me sober, I knew I had to have you, which is why we brought you into the relationship. Kellie didn't want that because I think she saw how I felt before I did. I'm not going to find that with anyone else. I don't wanna try. All I want is you. It's enough. I'm not that twenty-two-year-old kid anymore. This beast has been tamed."

"But we've done nothing but argue."

"That happens. Your hormones are all over the place. It will level off."

"I hate that we aren't getting along, but I have no idea how to change it."

Steve takes me by the hands. "This is how we get past it, by *talking*. The more we talk to each other, the more we tell each other, the better we feel. We don't need Maverick for that."

"Could you not talk about him? I'd still like to rip his head off," I say seriously and Steve laughs. "I'm dead serious. The fucker screamed at me."

"From what I understand, you were lifting more than ten pounds, you've got to be more careful. You've got Harrison in the room, utilize him. Make the oaf do something."

"Pot, meet kettle. The box wasn't that heavy."

"Just know what I was told."

"Maverick better mind his business or Angelica is

going to be husbandless."

"I will relay the message. Why don't you come on out? I'm sure everyone is done eating by now. It's only soup and sandwiches."

"Okay, let's go."

Steve kisses me and leads me to the kitchen for lunch.

44

STEVE

BIG TALKS, MONOGAMY, AND SHOPPING. This has been my life for weeks. Finally letting Crystal know where we stand as a couple was important. She needs to be reassured that I'm not going anywhere. I've called Christy, told him I'm not available for anything that leaves town. I haven't told Crystal this, but I can't have him setting me up for a press thing or show that would have me leaving Crystal. I just promised I wasn't going anywhere. Christy was pissed, said he had things lined up for me and Ringo to attend. I told him tuff titty, not only are we pregnant, but we're also getting hitched.

He scoffed, but was glad for the heads up as opposed to hearing it on the news like the rest of the band and their relationship news. He said to let them know when we plan on doing it and the company would handle the announcement and press releases. I agreed.

It's just after supper and Crystal is in the shower while I finish up the dishes. The girls are in their rooms, reading, and I'm thinking that it's high time Crystal and I reconnect. I've been reading articles on PCOS and high-risk pregnancy and am confident that we can be more intimate. I have been afraid that my size would be an issue, but I've found positions that make for shallow penetration and allowing her to orgasm more effectively.

I look in on my girls and Sue Ellen has fallen asleep with her nose in her book and Mary Ann is playing a game on her Kindle.

"Hey, baby."

"Hi, Daddy."

"Bed in two hours."

"I know."

I go to close her door when I hear a coo come from her that makes me look back up. "What's up, Mary Ann?"

"I was thinking about Momma. When are we gonna see her?"

I come into the room and sit on the bed. "Your momma, she's been busy working and getting her place set up for you and Sue Ellen. According to the call I got though, you will see her this weekend."

"What about Peggy Sue and Brayden?"

"That's up to Peggy Sue."

"She's really mad at Momma, so is Sue Ellen. Me, I just wanna see her." Mary Ann's voice is tiny and full of sadness.

"I know, baby. You'll see her Friday, that's when she'll be coming to get you, and you'll be staying with her till Sunday afternoon."

She nods and hugs me. "I love you, Daddy, and I'm glad you have Crystal to make you happy again."

"I love you too, little bear." I hold her for a few minutes, then excuse myself. As I step out into the hallway, I see Crystal leaning against the wall by the door.

"That went better than expected." She half-heartedly smiles.

"Did it? I just told her the truth. What else could I say?"

"I think it did."

"You gonna be alright with her coming here to pick them up Friday?" I walk her back toward our bedroom.

"Will you be mad if I stay away?"

"I wouldn't blame you, but I also wouldn't mind you there to keep her mouth in check."

"You think she'll hold it in check when she figures out I'm knocked up?"

I shake my head. "Probably not, but as long as she doesn't go spouting off to the tabloids, I don't give a fuck what she thinks."

"Okay," she answers me and I run my hands up her back.

"How are you feeling?" I ask, pulling her to me and tugging on the knot she's tied into another of my band shirts.

She lets out a deep sigh. "I'm okay, it's been a crazy day."

"Yeah, we could use a bit of stress relief, don't you think?" I smirk, inching my hands up her sides and lifting the shirt some so I can touch her velvety skin.

She purses her lips. "And here I thought you weren't touching me."

"I may have had to do a bit of research before I could. Been afraid I might hurt you," I say, kissing her neck and behind her ear.

"And what did your research show?"

"Safe positions we can try, things I shouldn't do, and it says that orgasms are good for you and the baby.

225

If I do it right, it also says that at this point in the pregnancy, you can become multi-orgasmic, and I don't know about you, but I'd love to feel you locked up around my cock for more than a few seconds at a time."

"Then what are you waiting for?" She reaches for the button on my jeans and I lift her, sitting her on the dresser.

She pulls her shirt off as I go for her shorts and she wiggles out of them and her panties. I kneel down, needing to taste her on my tongue and she leans back, giving me full, open access. From between her folds of flesh, I can see her clit already starting to swell from her arousal, the little pink button glistening with her juices. I lick her and she lifts her leg. I push it up and back on the dresser, so I can drive my tongue into her. Her moans start low, then grow as my fingers travel up her body, gently flicking her sensitive nipples. She starts to gyrate on the dresser, changing up the speed of my mouth on her. I suck on her clit as she grabs my head, her legs shaking as she tries to gain footing and barrels over the edge, coming in my mouth so hard that she squirts, getting it all over my goatee. Her whole body is lit up like a firecracker and as I lick and suck her clit more, her nails catch in my head and neck. I pull away and she's breathing heavy, her smile wider than I've seen in a long time as her hands rest against her thighs. I wipe my face covertly with my T-shirt before standing and taking it off.

"How do you feel?" I ask, lacing my fingers in hers. My cock wants to play, but I need to be sure she's okay first. That orgasm was intense, so much so that I damn near came and I've barely touched her.

She looks at me with lidded eyes, her head nodding as she opens her mouth to speak, but cannot seem to form the words.

"That good?" I lick my lips as she reaches for my waistband. I guess she's good to go.

* * *

"The wonder of the multiple orgasm. Dude, I made her squirt and now, she wants me all the time. I came down to make breakfast for the girls and the next thing I know, she's talked me into bending her over the kitchen island and eating her out from the back. I think I've created a monster," I say to Maverick as I'm watering the roses and I'm betting he's sorry he asked how my week has been.

"Welcome to month two."

"Yeah, but I don't remember Kellie being anything like this. Then again, I'm pretty sure she was getting it from someplace else too, so that's probably why."

"Didn't you all have an open marriage?"

"Yeah, but it's who she opened her legs to, and that they didn't wrap it up."

Maverick looks at me, confused. "What are you talking about?"

"Nobody knows this, not Crystal, not the band. This stays between us?"

"Doesn't everything else?"

"Mary Ann and Sue Ellen aren't mine. They're my brother, Sonny's."

"Oh?" Maverick sounds like a man at a loss for words.

"It's why I agreed to give her the money she wanted, and some form of visitation. If I'd tried to keep them from her completely, I could have lost them totally."

"Does she know that you know?"

'I don't know, I've never said anything and never shown any inkling toward the girls. I didn't start to suspect until they were three and four. By then, I was in love with them, they were mine no matter what, ya know?"

"Yeah, I know." He turns his head, looking for Angela, who's playing with Sue Ellen in the tomato patch.

"So, she's coming to get them in like an hour, how do I handle it?"

"You just treat her like a friend, not a lover or an ex-lover. Just treat her how you want her to treat you in this situation."

Seriously? The treat others how you want to be treated adage? Kill me. I shake my head. "Thanks."

* * *

Maverick and Angelica have left, but we'll be seeing them at the Anniversary party for Brent and Marissa in a couple hours. I'm staring out the window, waiting for Kellie to arrive. She's fifteen minutes late and the girls are sitting on the couch with their suitcases. It's pouring rain outside, so I'm assuming that is what's taking her so long. She's always hated driving in the rain. I sigh hard when I feel a hand on my shoulder, I don't need to turn to know it's my Bella.

"You've got to calm down, you're setting the girls off."

"I'm just nervous as all fuck," I say under my breath so that they can't hear me. "The lawyer set this up, so I didn't have to talk to her. So, what if she doesn't show up? It'll break Mary Ann's heart."

"Then she doesn't show up and they come with us."

I wrap my arms around her and gently kiss the tip of her nose, getting a giggle out of my girls, then I hear the car pulling up, followed by the squeal of brakes that need tending to. Looking outside, I see it's the Lincoln. A man steps out of the driver's side and opens an umbrella, letting himself get wet as he holds it up and opens the back door. I watch as Kellie steps out.

She's in a pair of fitted jeans, candy red heels, and a matching red halter top. She looks good, all that money at her disposal seems to agree with her as she looks around and walks up to the door. A moment later, the bell rings and I look at Crystal.

"Show time." She takes my hand in her's and we walk to the door.

I open it and Kellie is standing under the awning with her driver is off to the side. "Kellie," I say with as little contempt as possible.

"Steve, Crys, good to see you. Where are *my* girls?" She looks at me pointedly, almost as if she is trying to make her point. That she could have proven that these were not my children, that I only have them because she is allowing it.

I swallow. "Mary Ann, Sue Ellen, your momma is here." I step back, letting the girls approach, but not enough that Kellie can get inside.

Mary Ann goes to her mother first, hugging her. "Hi, darling." She kisses Mary Ann's head. Sue Ellen has Crystal by the side and front, and if she's not careful, she's gonna reveal the bump. Crystal pulls down her top and Kellie's eyes roam over her. She looks at me and raises a brow.

"Seems congratulations are in order," she sneers.

"Good luck pushing out one of his bastards." She grabs Mary Ann's hand and reaches for Sue Ellen. Sue Ellen pulls away.

"I don't wanna go." She hangs on to Crystal tighter.

Crystal squats down in front of my little angel. "It's your momma, why don't you wanna go?"

She shakes her head and wraps her arms around Crystal. "Just don't wanna."

"Baby, you have to go see your mommy."

"Why? She doesn't have to see me. Hasn't even called. I wanna stay home... *With you*."

Crystal looks up at me as Kellie snaps, "Oh, I don't have time for this. Sue Ellen, c'mon." She reaches out and I step in between her and my girls. "It's my weekend, it's bad enough that you all poisoned Peggy Sue against me, now this one too?"

"Maybe next time," I say as Sue Ellen grabs my pinky finger.

"Fine, whatever. I'll just take Mary Ann."

"I'm not going without Sue Ellen!" Mary Ann exclaims, running back inside and behind me, almost knocking Kellie right off the porch with her suitcase as she flies by.

Kellie stumbles backward, but I reach out, catching her just before her head hits the pavement. I'm getting drenched as she holds onto me in terror.

"Th-thank you," she says, swallowing hard as I stand us up.

"I couldn't let *my* girls lose their mother. Come back next week, they'll be ready to go then. Okay?"

Kellie nods as she's joined by the driver.

"Have your brakes done by then too. I won't have the girls in an unsafe car." I turn back to the house and head inside. Closing the door, I let out a hard-held breath.

Crystal is on the floor with the girls wrapped around her.

"So, that happened," I half-cry, half-laugh, sinking to the floor. "Who wants to go to a party?"

45

CRYSTAL

AFTER KELLIE LEFT, I TOOK THE GIRLS upstairs and got them dressed in their party dresses so we could head out. Now, we're at Brent and Marissa's anniversary party and it's been crazy. That Sir Mix-A-Lot song that everyone knows and can sing is playing and us girls are all dancing and singing together. The guys are mostly just standing around.

Marissa and Peggy Sue start twerking just as Sue Ellen and Mary Ann start bouncing. Of course, I bounce along with them till Steve cuts in. Steve takes my hands and is dancing with me.

"Come on, let's go."

"Where we are going?"

"We're going off the dance floor," he says, taking us off the dance floor, but he's also slowing down.

I pull my brows together. "Why?"

"You're bouncing too hard."

"So?"

Steve places his hand on my bump. "Our love bun."

"Oh," I say with a pout.

"Don't look at me like that, Bella."

"I can't have any fun."

"Moderate fun."

"You can't dance moderately."

I Do by Jessie James Decker begins to play and Steve pulls me to him and starts swaying back and forth. He sings the chorus to me, which brings tears to my eyes. As the song ends, he kisses me and the tears are flowing by the time he pulls away.

"You aren't supposed to make me cry." I push him.

"I wasn't trying to, Bella. I was just trying to tell you that I love you."

"I love you too, Beast."

A few hours pass and I need to sit down. My sides are starting to hurt a little. Everyone else is over where this music is pounding. Steve's dancing with Sue Ellen and Mary Ann. My phone goes off in my purse, so I grab it to see what's going on now.

It's an article and reads...

Kellie Vicious, former wife of Fallen Angels' drummer, Steve Vicious, was in a car wreck this evening at eight fifteen. The coroner says she died on impact.

I can't read any further, my phone falls from hand, hitting the ground, and I look to find Steve. All I can think is the girls would have been with her if Sue Ellen would have gone. The tears are falling so hard that I can barely see through them. I need to get up and go to Steve, but I can't make myself move.

Next thing I know, I have a belly in my face and I look up to see Angelica. "What's the matter?" She turns her head and yells, "Steven Falcone, get your ass over here... Now!"

"P-p-phone," I stutter. Angelica grabs my phone.

"What's going on? What's wrong?" Steve rushes to my side. "Are you okay?"

"Steve," Angelica says softly before handing Steve my phone.

Steve looks at my phone. "We've gotta go. Angelica, can you get the girls?"

"Yeah, go do what you gotta do," Angelica says.

"Crystal, do you want to stay here or go with me?"

"It could have been the girls," I say and just cry harder. "Sue Ellen knew. Steve, she knew," I say, looking up at him.

Steve looks toward the girls, shaking his head.

"What's going on? Is Crystal okay?" Maverick asks, and he's already got his hand on me, checking me.

"It's not me."

"I've gotta go. Crys, are you coming with me or not?" My hands are on my shaking head. Steve picks me up and cradles me to him. "Brent!" Steve yells.

I don't see Brent, but I hear him. "Is she okay?"

"She will be. I need to lay her down somewhere."

"Just take her to your room."

Before I know what's going on, I'm being carried into the house and taken to a bedroom. He lays me on the bed, then sits with me.

"Bella, I need you to stay here and calm down. The girls are fine. I'll be back as soon as I can. I love you." Steve kisses me on the forehead, then leaves the room.

I feel the bed dip beside me and look up to see Maverick. "Sue Ellen wouldn't go. She knew something was wrong. That could have been them."

"Crystal, you have to calm down, you're stressing the baby out," Maverick says as he holds my wrist in his hand.

Arms wrap around me from behind and Kyle says,

"Crys, baby, you gotta drink this." He's not making sense. I shake my head no. I feel spread being tugged and then, I'm under the cover and wrapped in Kyle's arms.

A bottle is pressed to my lips. "You gotta drink this, please." The bottle is tilted and I take a sip, then turn my head away. Kyle turns my face back to the bottle. "We gotta get your temperature down. You're burning up." I take one drink and then another. "That's better." His hands run across the top of my head.

"Her pulse is coming down. Keep going," Maverick says.

"That's it, just breathe. Are you in any pain?" Kyle asks. I nod. "Where are you hurting."

I swallow. "Sides."

"Sharp, dull, throbbing?" I feel a hand on my thigh. "I'm just checking."

"I don't see any blood. What about you?" Maverick asks.

"No, she's all right."

"She was dancing a lot. Could have a bit to do with the hurting."

"The girls. It could have been them."

"The girls are fine. They're just in the other room," Kyle says, trying to reassure me.

"Steve's gonna start drinking and it's going to be my fault. I didn't hold it together."

"He may think about it, but he promised you he wouldn't when you all started trying to have a baby," Maverick says softly.

"That man ain't nothing if he ain't worth his word."

Kyle's smoothing my hair and is humming to me. When he starts to rock, I feel my eyes get heavy.

46

STEVE

I'm sitting in the waiting area at the morgue when I check my phone and see a missed text from seven thirty tonight. My chest constricts and it is taking every fiber of my being not to fall apart. Crystal freaked out. God, I hope she's okay. I hope the girls are okay. I open the message and it's from Kellie...

Bear,

Thank you. If you hadn't caught me tonight, I could be dead. That's just like you. When I'm at my worst, you were always at your best. Rising up and catching me whenever I fell. I never did that for you. That was Crys, I know that now. Just like I know that you took on the girls, knowing the truth about them. It's why you have them. They love you, they know you, they deserve a parent that will always catch them when they fall. You're a good man, and as much as it kills me to admit it, you and Crys deserve to be happy. I'll always love you, in my way, but it's time I let you fly to have the life you deserve. I'll not interfere any longer. Kiss my girls for me, tell them I love them, and I'll see them again soon.

That's it, the flood gates are open and I'm in tears. Kellie, my first love, the mother of my girls, she's...

"Mr. Falcone?" I'm pulled out of my self-induced sorrow by a man's voice. I look up, seeing the coroner. "We're ready for you now," he says, holding open the door.

I nod, standing and following him down the long empty hallway and into the main room where they keep the bodies. I see the slab and the body on it. I know the silhouette, I know my Kellie. I hesitate, a sob billowing up from my chest so hard it hurts as it erupts and I have to bite my hand to relieve the pain.

I get to her and the coroner pulls back the top of the sheet, revealing her head and shoulders. Her long blonde hair is down around her shoulders and there are signs of bruising around her neck. It looks off, like her head isn't sitting quite right. Her face is scraped, but you can tell they tried to clean her up before I got here.

"What- How?" I can't form the words to ask just what happened.

"The car hydroplaned in the storm and the brakes failed, putting them in the path of a semi. She was tossed hard, breaking her neck. Death was instantaneous, she didn't suffer," the coroner answers my broken thoughts. "Is this Kellie Falcone?"

"Y-Yes," I say. I can't stop looking at her.

The man puts his hand on my shoulder. "I'm sorry for your loss. Would you like a few moments with her?"

"If I can." I manage. He walks out of the room, leaving me with her.

"Kellie." I stare up at the ceiling, trying to quell my tears. I wipe at my face and look at her again. She's motionless, and too quiet.

"Fuck, Kellie, wake up, fight with me, you bitch.

You can't leave it like this." I grab her, pulling her up into my arms. "Please, Kel, you can't leave the girls, they're not ready yet."

I smooth back her hair and kiss her face, but she's cold. My Kellie was always hot, always a little too much so. I can't stop the sobbing, even in my anger. My Kellie is gone. This, this is just the shell that held one of the most incredible women I have ever known. I lay her back down, smooth down her hair, and kiss her mouth for the last time. "I'll always love you, Sweet Cheeks," I whisper before turning from the table and walking out.

"I want her transferred to the Jacoby-White Funeral home, and please, be discreet. She has children who still don't know."

"Of course, Mr. Falcone. Again, I am sorry for your loss."

I nod and head for the exit.

❊ ❊ ❊

I don't know how long I've been sitting in my car at the hospital with this bottle of scotch, just staring into it, but the next thing I know, someone is tapping on my window. I wipe my face and see it's Peggy Sue, her mascara is running and there are more tears in her eyes.

"It's true?" she sobs as I get out of the car and hug her. "It's true and I... She thought I hated her," Peggy Sue cries hard into my arms.

"She knew better than that," I say, breathing hard, pulling myself back from the edge of my reasoning. I need to pull my shit together. I need to be here for my girls, for Peggy Sue, Mary Ann, and Sue Ellen. I need to be here for Crystal, I can't just disappear into the bottom of a bottle, no matter how badly I want to. I rock my little girl as she cries.

"I need to see her."

"No, honey, not right now, please wait. Wait until the funeral."

"No, Daddy, now. Please."

I swallow, taking her hand and leading her back the way I had come.

I watch her from outside the room. They had already moved the body to a fridge, so they had to pull her out. Kellie was deathly afraid of tight spaces and the idea of being in a box or in a coffin would have terrified her. Peggy Sue looks and spends some time before finally coming out and hugging me.

"The girls are gonna be lost," she says as we head back toward my car. "If you need anything, you call us." She sniffles and kissing me on the cheek, she leaves me to my bottle.

I look at it and take it by the neck. Sighing, I pour it out and toss the bottle across the grass. That's the last bottle I'll ever touch.

* * *

I get back to Brent and Marissa's house just around midnight. It's still all lit up and all the cars are still here, including Kyle's Monte Carlo. He wasn't here when I left, I wonder what his condition is. If he showed up wasted, I swear I'm gonna kill him. My girls don't need that on top of what I have to tell them tonight. As I walk up to the front doors, I'm met by Brent and Marissa. Marissa wraps her arms around me.

"I'm sorry," she whispers, kissing my cheek. I nod as Brent clamps his hands on my shoulders, the closest he comes to hugs. I nod, looking inside.

"My girls?" I manage to sound okay, I'd been practicing in the car all the way here, making sure I wasn't going to crack again.

"They're asleep in their room." Brent points down the hall. "Crys is right where you put her, plus two. Kyle and Maverick are with her."

"Uh huh." I get past him and head for Crystal. I need to know she's alright, then I can figure out how I tell my little angels about their mother.

Walking into the room, I find her lying on the bed in Kyle's arms. She's covered up, mostly, except one leg is just sort of hanging out on display. "How is she?" I break the silence of the room and Kyle looks up as Maverick turns his head.

"She's going to be okay, but you're gonna have to watch her."

I nod, walking over and motioning for Kyle to move his ass. He gently and quickly changes places with me. "Crys? Bella, I'm back," I whisper against her cheek, pulling her to me. She's quiet, but she's warm, she's still here, but gone. "How long has she been like this?"

Maverick looks at his watch. "Since about twenty minutes after you left."

I look at Kyle. "Thank you for being here when I couldn't."

"Hey, man, that's your woman, can't leave her to the wolves."

I dip my head and look back at Maverick. "Thank you for going into Doc mode."

"It ain't over yet."

"I know, today's stress can be next week's miscarriage. I just need to let her rest, though, right? Keep her off her feet and no strenuous activity. I'll call the OBGYN's scheduling in the morning, explain, and see if we can get her in before our appointment on the twenty-first." I sound like a man desperate for someone to tell him he's doing the right thing.

Maybe I am, I couldn't help Kellie, couldn't save her from the world, I have to be able to get Crystal back together. I can't lose her too, and losing the baby would devastate her. I'll be blamed, me and my drama. I'll be blamed for talking her into all of this in the first place. Pushing for it, urging her to do it. It'll all be my fault, and it is all my fault in a way. My secrets, my past, my way of keeping things.

If I had told Crystal how I felt and been honest with myself years ago, then maybe this wouldn't have happened. Maybe it could have all been avoided. Kellie certainly wouldn't have been on that highway tonight, and I wouldn't have to go and tell my daughters that their mother is dead.

"I don't know if it's that simple. She's having some side pain. She couldn't go into detail, but it's enough to cause a scare. There's no blood, so that's a positive, but what she's going to need, you can't be. You're-"

"What are you talking about?" I cut him off. "What can't I do?"

"You can't be with her every minute, you can't stop the nightmares that are coming, you have girls that need you. When she comes out of this, she's going to feel guilty because she wasn't here for you, she wasn't here for them, and the only thing she's going to know is that you all needed her and she failed you. Steve, you can't start drinking, she's only made two statements, you drinking is one of them."

"I- I had a bottle after I identified Kellie's body. It was a bottle of Scotch I'd had stashed under the seat for those fuck it all days. I didn't drink it, I poured it out."

I turn to Kyle. "I need you to do me a favor. I'm not going home tonight, I'm afraid to move Crys. So, will you go over to the house and clean out the liquor cabinets in the parlor, kitchen, and living room? I don't want the shit in the house."

"Yeah, man. No problem." Kyle hugs me from behind and makes his way to the door.

"Hey," he says, looking at Maverick, "you're not half bad in a crisis." He nods and is gone. I look at Maverick and he's got a look of stunned confusion on his face.

"That's the closest I think you'll ever get to a compliment from Kyle Casey, which is saying something because he never gives them."

"Didn't really expect one."

I sigh, "Peggy Sue showed up at the hospital."

"How'd that go over?"

"About like you would think, tears, blaming herself for how they left things. She went in to see her. That seemed to help her."

"I can talk to her if you want."

I shake my head. "I think she just needs to process, she's more worried about the girls and me. She's really growing up, and Kellie's gonna miss it all." I breathe hard and blink as the tears fall. "I'm sorry." I wipe at my face. "I just can't seem to turn it off."

"It's okay."

I reach into my pocket for my phone, unlock it, and hand it to him. "She sent that minutes before the crash."

"What did they tell you?" he asks softly, still staring at the message.

"That the car hydroplaned into the path of a semi, that the brakes failed, and she was tossed hard enough to break her neck."

"They didn't give you any other information?"

"Like what?" I'm watching him and he's looking back and forth between me and the phone. "Like what?" I growl.

He sighs heavily. "I received a letter like this once. It was the same reason Angelica was able to break me so easily. I was fifteen, my father had already killed himself, my sister and I were separated, and I got news along with a letter just like this, she'd killed herself."

"No, Kellie wouldn't have done that. I mean she's fucked up, selfish, and narcissistic, but she loves her babies. You should have seen her when we were pregnant, she loved it. The first time, holding Peggy Sue, you could tell she just had to be in love." I shake my head.

"They said it was an accident, with the rain, she hated to drive in the rain. When she came, she even had a driver, so she didn't have to. The driver? Did the article say if anyone else was in the car?" I swallow hard. *Please God, I know it's wrong to hope, but don't let her have been alone, don't confirm Maverick's insane theory.*

Maverick scrolls through my phone, he swallows so hard I can hear it over Crystal's breathing. I watch as his eyes scan the phone.

"I'm sorry."

I drop my head. "She was alone? It doesn't have to mean- I mean she had everything she wanted. Why?"

"She didn't have everything she wanted," Maverick barely speaks the words, but I hear him. Like a mosquito buzzing in my ears, I hear him.

"This wasn't my fault. We had problems, they had been compiling, we never should have married, we were too young, too stupid, and too... I don't fucking know. I know that I had to end it, I couldn't go on staying just

243

for the kids. It wasn't fair to either of us." My breathing increases as I grind my teeth, trying to keep from screaming. "Everyone thinks 'Poor Kellie, Steve picked the girlfriend over the wife.' It wasn't that simple, I told you about Mary Ann and Sue Ellen. The only mistake I made was not running with Crys the moment I realized how I felt. Instead, I listened to Kellie, I went for the open relationship, all so she wouldn't have to give up her lifestyle. With Kellie, it was always take, take, take. Gimme, gimme. Even before I got rich, I'd steal for her in my broke days. You know what? She knew it too, but as long as I kept bringing her nice things, she didn't care about how or where."

"That's not what I'm saying. What you did, you made the right decision, and she knew it. That doesn't mean it didn't bother her. It plainly states that she knew Crystal was better for you. That's where the problem's coming from, just because she knew it, doesn't mean she had to like it."

"But why do this? Why not fight me, make me miserable, take it out on me?"

"Could she?"

"She could have, she could have told Sonny about the girls, made me fight harder to keep them. She could have kept coming to get them and being the snide manipulator she's always been. Anything.. But this? She's going to destroy the girls for what?"

"She knows the girls will be taken care of and loved. Kellie isn't the problem here. It's your love for her. You walked away, but you weren't ready."

"Ready? There's no way to prepare yourself for leaving someone you've spent half your life with." I lay Crystal down and get up. Three steps is all it takes to be inside Maverick's personal space. "Have you ever loved someone to the very core of you? So much that you don't know where you start and they begin? No, probably not, not yet. See, you haven't seen that person bring a life you created together into this world, hold it in their arms, and tell you how much they love you. You've never felt completed by someone, only to have them rip your heart out and throw it in the trash and then smile about it. Had that same love manipulated and twisted until it and you are unrecognizable, then find yourself lucky enough to find someone else who sees the broken mess that you are and love you for it anyhow, stand by you, and stand aside, idle and silent in their love, because they, like you, think the first love is the greater love? No, you've never had to go through that. I pray Angelica can keep her shit together for you. That you never have to feel the betrayal of her going back to the coke, or the pills. Those women saw me through my addictions, not once, but twice. Do I still love Kellie? Fuck me, yes, I do. How could I not? But, my love for Crystal, it burns hotter, brighter, and deeper. You say my love for Kellie is the problem? Fuck that, that love got me here, brought me to Crys, and I'll never say a day was wasted because of it."

Maverick smiles at me with a cocksure grin. "Now, you're ready."

"Get out. I don't need your mind fuck right now. What I need is to be alone with my fiancé. Get out before I deck you because I'm close, and if I hit you with the rage I have pent up, I'll fucking knock you into Christmas."

"Okay." Maverick stands up and I take a step back, letting him past me.

"Thank you," I grind out just before he leaves the room.

47

CRYSTAL

I WAKE WITH A START AND SIT STRAIGHT up in bed. "Steve! Someone has to get Steve! He's at the hospital with a bottle in his hand. Please."

Maverick and Kyle are gone, but then I hear my beast. "Bella, I'm here."

He puts his hand on my shoulder as I turn in the bed to face him. I don't think twice before squishing myself to him. "You're okay."

"I am now."

"But I saw you open the bottle."

"Did you see me pour it out too?"

"No."

"Then you should've looked a little harder."

"I couldn't."

"Well, I didn't drink."

"I couldn't see anymore because I saw Kellie." I swallow hard as the tears fall. He looks at me and holds on. "She's safe and she wants you to know she loves you and the girls."

"Shh, it's okay, Bella."

"Damn it, listen to me." I sit up, out of his arms, so I can see him. "I'm not losing my mind."

"Okay." He swallows.

"I know you think I'm crazy and if I were in your shoes, I'd think I'm crazy too. Kellie and I talked. We talked for the first time since you sent Peggy Sue off. We talked about things I had no idea about, but then, she thanked me for always being there to help no matter how bad she treated me. You know, everyone may think I hated Kellie, but I didn't. I loved her just as much as I loved you."

Steve pulls me into him. "I don't think you're crazy." He tilts my chin, kissing me. "I love you."

"I love you, but we need to take the girls home. We need to be at home when we tell them. Before you stop me, I'm okay, and so is the baby. When need to tell them everything." He looks at me, confused. "No sense in hiding it anymore. Once they've had time to heal, we need to tell them about the baby and that we're getting married. We just need to remind them always that Kellie is their momma."

"Right, let's go home."

Steve and the girls are sleeping in our bed together. They asked if they could just have him in there. Of course, who was I to say no? So here I am, at four o'clock in the morning, in my classroom because I can't sleep and I need something to do. My talk with Kellie is on replay in my head. She told me secrets that Steve will probably never tell me. She also told me the sex of the baby. I'm not shocked because I had a feeling it was anyhow.

Right now, everyone is treating me like I'm delicate and need to be locked in a bubble. Sorry about their luck, I'm not John Travolta and they aren't putting me in a plastic bubble anytime soon.

You know it's too quiet in the house when you can hear someone walking around upstairs. I just keep working because I figure if someone needs me, they will let me know. I look up when I hear someone coming down the hall, and I see Sue Ellen as she turns into the room.

I stand, walking over to her. "What are you doing out of bed? It's really late." Sue Ellen shrugs her shoulders at me. "Do you want a drink?" She shakes her head no. "Something to eat?" She's staring at her feet. "You gotta tell me what's wrong, baby, or I can't help you." I squat in front of her.

She wraps her arms around my neck and hugs me. "Can you be my mommy now?" she whispers.

I fall back onto my ass and bring her into my lap. "Kellie's your momma, but I'm not going anywhere."

Sue Ellen puts her hands against my bump. She looks at me with a small smile. "Did she tell you?"

I smile at Sue Ellen because I know exactly what she's talking about. "She did, but we need to keep it from Daddy." She looks confused, so I explain. "We need to make it a surprise."

She nods at me. "We have to tell Mary Ann, she's not going to be happy."

"No, she isn't, and she may not like me for a while."

She twiddles her fingers. "I love you."

"I know, and I love you too."

"Will you come back upstairs with me? Daddy needs you."

"Yeah, let's go," I say, sitting her on the floor and standing up, then giving her my hand to help her up.

Shutting the light out, I walk up to the bedroom with Sue Ellen. I put Sue Ellen on the bed next to Steve, then get in beside her. I lay an arm over her and touch Steve's arm.

He lifts his arm just enough to rub my forearm. He knows I'm here and that's all he needs. I fall asleep with a hand on Steve and Sue Ellen hanging onto me.

It's been a week since Kellie's death. It's been hectic with Steve planning the funeral. He wouldn't let me help and honestly, we've barely spoken. I know he feels guilty for what happened. Just as much as Mary Ann and Peggy Sue do for being upset with her. More times than not, he's fallen asleep in the bed with Mary Ann and I've slept with Sue Ellen.

The funeral was hard on the girls, but everyone rallied together and helped us keep it together. Maverick has texted and asked me every day how I'm feeling. I've not had the girls doing any work because there was just too much going on, so he's not been here. I tell him I'm fine and he's never satisfied with it, but just lets me know he'll message me tomorrow. I'm beginning to wonder if Steve knows because, from the way people talk when they call, he's not spoken to anyone.

I've got a doctor's appointment today and I'm not sure if Steve's going or not, but Sue Ellen has asked me if she can go. I just told her I'd ask her daddy, which is what I'm going to attempt to do. Steve's in the parlor, which is where he stays when he's not with the girls.

I knock on the door before walking in. He's sitting in the chair, staring at the fireplace. He's got a glass in his hand and I drop my head. "Can I come in?"

"Yeah, Bella."

I walk over so I'm standing where he can see me, but I don't approach him. "I have an appointment today. Were you planning on going with me?"

He's sitting with a hand over his face and he's holding the top of the glass. He does this when he's been drinking. He looks up at me. "Yeah, what time's the appointment?"

"In two hours, but you don't have to go. Adam can take me and Sue Ellen wanted to know if she could go." He gives me a raised brow and takes a sip of his drink. I sigh defeatedly. "She came to me that first night, after you were asleep. She already knew."

"Does Mary Ann?"

"Not yet."

"Guess we should tell her then, huh?"

"I don't think she's ready. She isn't speaking to me any more than you are."

He furrows his brow. "Sorry, I know I'm not here like I should be."

I give a small shrug. "You have every right to be the way you are."

He bends down, putting the glass on the floor. "Come here." I watch him closely, trying to figure out if he's closer to drunk or sober. When he drinks, he tends to get a bit rougher and I know he doesn't mean to. He sits up straighter in the chair. "Come here." I finally give in, walking over to I stand in front of him. My bump's bigger than the last time he touched me. He wraps his hands around the back of me and pulls me in with a sigh. "I've been working through some stuff. I know I haven't been nearly attentive enough, but I want to try to be because you deserve it."

"I told you it was okay. I understand."

"No, don't. I'm sick of you feeling like you always

need to stand aside. You're not second fiddle. You aren't the booby prize. I love you and I'm in love with you. I just need you to know that."

"And I love you," I say. I'm just not exactly sure if he's him or the idiot he becomes when he's drinking.

His hand comes from around the back of me to the front and he lifts my shirt. I suck in just a little. "Stop that. You're beautiful." He kisses me above the belly button. "I love this bun of ours too."

I put a hand over my bump. I think for a half a second about telling him what we're having, but I already promised Sue Ellen she could help me surprise him. "It's going to be a big baby."

He nods his head. He sits back and goes to pull me onto his lap, but I pull away from him. He looks at me, confused. "I need to get ready for my appointment."

He stands up, but doesn't stumble. He kisses me and I don't taste any liquor, which shocks me. He pulls back. "I'll get the girls ready."

"You aren't drinking."

He laughs at me. "Is that what you thought?"

"Well, when I walk in here to you sitting in that frumpy way with your hand slung over your face and barely holding your glass? Yes."

"Bella, there hasn't been a drop of alcohol in this house since the night Kellie died. I had Kyle take it all out."

"What'd you do to Maverick?"

He shakes his head. "Not a damn thing."

"You're sure?"

"Yeah."

"Well, he checks on me daily and from the way Angelica talks, he's chomping at the bit to know how I'm doing. Apparently, I worried him a bit."

"You worried everybody, me especially."

"I didn't try to, it just all happened so fast. I remember sitting down because my side was hurting and then my phone went off."

"Yeah, we all got surprises in our phone that night."

"Some got more than others," I say, turning to the door.

"Maverick thinks she killed herself," he says quietly.

I glance at him. "I know, and I knew by my dream."

"Do I ever tell them?"

"Not unless they ask because no kid should ever have to think of their mother in that way."

"Yeah, you're right. I know you're right."

"I try not to always be right."

"You fail miserably at that."

"Comes from living my life."

He sighs. "So, could you forgive your Beast for being an ass?"

"I'm sure I can with time," I say and walk out the door.

48

STEVE

"Where are we going, Daddy?" Mary Ann asks me as I'm getting her and Sue Ellen dressed.

"Crystal has an appointment with a doctor, so we need to go with her."

"Is she sick?"

"No."

"I only see the doctor when I'm sick."

"This is a special doctor.

"How come?"

"Well, this doctor takes care of mommies to be."

"Like babies? Are you and Crystal having a baby?"

I smile and nod my head. "Yes, little bear."

She crosses her arms in a pout. "But I don't want a little brother or sister, can we cancel it?"

"It doesn't work that way, honey. C'mon, both of you, and please behave in the office."

❖ ❖ ❖

Dr. Ang isn't exactly known for his bedside manner, but when he saw my girls, he smiled, and offered them sugar-free lollipops. They took them happily and we all filed into the exam room. They did the usual blood draw, took the card reader from the glucose meter, and then Crys got ready for the transvaginal ultrasound. I kept the girls at the head of the exam table while the doctor did his work.

"What's he doing?" Mary Ann asks as the room fills with a sound like hummingbirds under water.

"What's that?" Sue Ellen asks as I grin like a fool.

"That's the baby's heart." I hold Crystal's hand and she squeezes as the doctor turns on the monitor, letting us all see the baby.

"It looks like a peanut." Mary Ann giggles. "How can that be a baby?"

"It grows, silly," Sue Ellen answers defensively.

"I'm not silly, you're silly and stupid," Mary Ann barks.

"Hey now, cut it out, or I'll tan both your hides when we get out of here," I say, pulling Sue Ellen away from Mary Ann before they kill each other.

"Ah, a little sibling rivalry is never a bad thing. They'll learn to channel it into their teen personalities." Dr. Ang chuckles.

"Yeah, no. Nipping this right in the bud. Nipping all the buds right now." I say to a shrugging doc.

"Okay, well, the baby is progressing nicely. At nine millimeters, it's a little larger than average, but look at the father. Were you a big baby, Mr. Falcone?"

"Eleven pounds and twenty-three inches, and I was three weeks early," I answer.

"Well, I'd say you were a big boy, and nothing much has changed. As for this little one, we'll continue to track things on a by-weekly basis, but so far, everything appears to be going well. Sugar levels are optimal, so keep up the good work with the diet plan. Are you attempting any type of exercise?"

Crystal points to the girls.

He laughs. "How are things between the two of you? I understand there was a passing, I'm sorry for your loss, has it affected your intimacy levels? Have you been finding time for each other?"

Neither of us knows quite how to answer that, especially in front of the girls, so the good doctor plows ahead.

"Right. It's important that you continue to maintain your bonds, especially during the next few months. Momma may be feeling off about her body and need more reassurance than before. Watch for the dry spells and try and keep your moods elevated, if you understand me?"

Crystal nods and I smirk, being told to go out and have more sex is a strange thing. Stranger when your kids are in the room and the doc's gotta speak in code.

❖ ❖ ❖

All the way home, we had questions, questions, questions from both Mary Ann and Sue Ellen. The covered everything, from what sex I wanted if I could choose to what names I like best. A boy, of course, which got boos and snickers alike. Sue Ellen did ask one useful question though. She wanted to know which room the little beastie, as she is now calling it, is gonna live in.

"I suppose the empty room on our side of the house. This way, if the baby cries, it won't wake you guys up." I answer, looking at Crys.

"That works for me," she answers abruptly, then goes back to holding the little love bun and staring out the window.

I smile and reach for her hand, lacing my fingers with hers.

Once home, the girls head inside before us and I grab Crys by the loops of her pants.

"Can I help you?" she asks coyly, watching my hands as they snake up her front.

"Don't think that I haven't noticed these dangerous new curves under development in the past couple weeks. I just wasn't in the headspace to devote myself to you. But sometime soon, I'd like to explore each and every inch of you, preferably with my tongue." I run my hands over her tits, they're at least a cup fuller than they were. "Yeah, sometime very soon." I bend down and grab her by the ass, lifting her up slightly as I make my move to kiss her.

She pulls back, a mischievous look on her face. "Curves? What curves?"

I smile. "Let's see, there are these mountainous peaks," I say as I trail fingers across her nipples through her top, "then, below the inner valley," I add as I trace her sides, "is the ever-changing bump, and around here, is an ass just begging to be bitten while I ping your clit with my nimble fingers until you lose your mind."

"Promises, promises."

"Shall I make good on them now? Or must I wait till sundown?" I press my hardon against her.

"Well, you can't very well do it right now, your girls are awake."

"Mary Ann, Sue Ellen!" I holler and the girls appear in the doorway. "You want to watch Pete's Dragon?"

"Yeah!" they answer and I smirk at Crystal.

"Alright, c'mon, I'll put it in for you. Daddy and Crystal need to do a few things around the house, so after the movie, read your chapters and then we'll all go out for pizza, how's that sound?"

The girls nod and agree while Crystal laughs. I stand up as the girls get cozy on the couch together. Adam comes walking in, looking at the TV.

"Is this the original?" he asks.

"Of course, the other one makes him look like a damn cat," I answer.

He leans against the wall as the music swells for the opening credits. Seems he likes the movie. Good, he's working as an impromptu babysitter. I nod at him.

"Have a seat, the girls are just gonna watch it. If you want, there's popcorn or kettle corn in the cabinet."

"Sure, thanks. Girls?"

"Kettle corn," they answer together.

"Okay." Adam laughs. "On it."

I walk over to Crystal and take her by the hand, leading her away.

49

CRYSTAL

MY PANTIES ARE WET BEFORE WE REACH the top of the stairs. He takes his time with me, undressing me slowly, his hands gliding over my body. I can't believe the changes in just a couple of weeks. First, it was just this little bit of excess flab, and now it's firming up and starting to look like an actual bump.

Steve doesn't seem to mind the added packing. In fact, I think it turns him on more. He's attentive and yet, seems to know that my tits, while needing to be touched, are sensitive. A light touch from the pads of his fingers is all I need to respond to him. He strips me down and then takes off his clothes, climbing onto the bed with me. He sits up with his back against the headboard and crooks a finger at me. I crawl to him and he pulls me onto him. I can feel his huge cock as it teases my opening.

I lift and guide him inside, taking him with a bit of a pinch. Seems things are tightening up down below and I wasn't as wet as I thought. I back off and he slowly lifts to meet my downward thrust. I hold on to the headboard for leverage and ride him fast and hard. We haven't done this in weeks and I just want to come. My pelvis rubs against his and the friction of his hair against my clit sends me right over the edge. As I come, he rubs my clit with his fingers, making me topple over again, my orgasm playing through me like the hard beats of his drums. He doesn't let me come down either as he flips me over, onto my hands and knees and enters me from behind, pounding against my ass. God, how he fills me up. This man moves me in ways he'll never understand.

He comes and pulls me to him, kissing me. His cock still hard, he slowly keeps at me while deeply probing my mouth with his tongue. His fingers working me too, this time when I come, he does too and we fall forward into a pool of orgasmic bliss.

As we come down from our high, Steve grabs his tablet and pulls me to him. "You mentioned something about finishing the shopping. I say we do it from here."

"What are you thinking?"

"Well, I've got Santa covered. I'm going to string up the ATV's like reindeer and fill a sleigh with toys. There will be stuff in there for our girls, Angela, Brayden and the twins."

"Okay, makes sense. Christmas Eve is just us. The question is what are we planning on doing?"

"I don't know, the usual. I mean it will be a little different this year without their mom. I don't want to change things too much on them."

"Too late for that." I place a hand on the bump. "This year is a lot different."

"But good different. Wonderful different."

"What color or colors would you paint the nursery?" I ask.

"I wouldn't go with the traditional pink and blue.

259

It'd be cool to do a night sky theme. That way, it wouldn't matter if it was a boy or a girl. Paint the room in blues and purples and then use the little stickups so we can put stars on the ceiling and walls. That way, it's surrounded by the universe."

"I like that idea. I was thinking maybe dark oak for the crib?"

"Like natural wood finish?"

"Yeah?"

"That would look nice and instead of a mobile, some kind of dream catcher with stars, moon, feathers, and web."

"I think if we do oak for the crib, the rest of the furniture needs to be the same."

"Yeah, get you that chair at Walmart, but better?"

"Yeah, something that's going to hold me and the beast both."

"And maybe me?"

"You are not knocking me up again right off the bat."

Steve laughs. "I like you like this."

"Like what?"

He reaches down, rubbing his hand on my belly. "Swelling with the life we created. There's nothing sexier except maybe when you are on top of me."

I push the tablet out of the way and straddle him. "You mean like this?"

"*Exactly* like this," he says and I lean down, kissing him.

✼ ✼ ✼

Steve and the girls want pizza. I, however, want French toast with bananas. So, we've been arguing for the past twenty minutes on who's going to give.

"How about you all go get pizza and I make myself French toast?"

"How about Adam grabs the pizza and I'll go over to *Waffles Café* and grab your French toast with bananas?"

"It's not the same as if I made it."

"Actually, what about this?" he shows me a French toast from I-Hop.

"No, I know what I want."

"The girls will eat this as long as they get ice cream and you get what you want."

"But they won't make it how I want it," I whine.

"How do you want it?"

"Extra fluffy, deep fried, layered with bananas and syrup." I cringe, I know I'm not supposed to have stuff like this.

"From the looks of the I-Hop, they do all that plus powdered sugar and whipped cream."

"Beast, take the girls for a daddy day and leave me alone."

"If I didn't know any better, I'd say you're trying to get rid of me."

"Would I do such a thing?"

"Yes," he says with no hesitation.

"Daddy, I like the idea of it just being you, me, and Mary Ann," Sue Ellen says. I really love that little girl.

Steve looks at Sue Ellen suspiciously before looking back at me. "I smell a rat, but I promised pizza. Go, get your shoes on. Adam, stay here and make sure she eats."

"Yes, sir," Adam says and I roll my eyes.

Steve walks over to me and I look up at him. He bends, giving me a searing kiss. "See you in a few hours."

"Dick."

Steve and the girls leave and I look at Adam. "I'm not eating French toast, but I plan on eating. If he asks, you heard what I was supposed to be eating, correct?"

"Yes, Ma'am."

"Anything you hear from this moment forward is not to be repeated."

"Okay."

I set to making a salad as I call Kyle.

"Yo?" Kyle answers and it's hard to hear him with all the noise in the background.

"Wanna take it to a dull roar?"

"Uh, hold on." I can hear him moving and he's talking to someone. "Excuse me, sorry, honey, pay you when I come back." Then it sounds like some chick is screaming into the phone. Finally, quiet. "Yeah, what's up?"

"Apparently, you." I laugh.

Kyle just chuckles. "What do you need? How are you feeling?"

"I need you."

"Oh?" he sounds mildly intrigued.

"Well, you have to be sober for a week. Can you do that?"

Crickets on the other end of the phone. I can almost hear the Jeopardy theme as I wait. Eventually, he responds, "Yeah, what do you need?"

"I need you to help with a surprise."

"Kay? Ya wanna be more specific."

"It's the nursery."

"Okay…" The idiot is going to make me spell it out.

"Jesus Christ, I know what I'm having and want to surprise the beast. So, you need to be here about noon tomorrow to start painting."

"Alright. Do I have to pick up the paint too or just shoot me a list."

"I've got someone else handling that. Just be here and sober."

"Okey doke."

"Bye." I hang up and enlist the aid of the twin. "Crystal?"

"Hey, Brent, I need a favor."

"What's up?"

"Steve wrote this song and he needs to be the one to sing it, but I'm going to talk him into coming over there tomorrow. Your job is to figure out a way to keep him there all week. He can come home at night, but during the day, he's all yours."

"Okay, I'll figure out something."

"Perfect! Is that wife of yours around?"

"Yeah, one sec. Princess, phone."

The phone changes hands, then Marissa says, "Hello?"

"Princess, I need your help," I say through a laugh.

Marissa chuckles. "What can I do you for?"

"I'm working on this pretty big surprise, but I'm going to need everyone's help to accomplish it."

"Okay? What do you need?"

"I'm sending Steve to your house tomorrow with a song he wrote. He and Brent can work on it. He's supposed to be there every day, only to come home at night. I just need a call from you when he leaves."

"That shouldn't be a problem."

"I've got Kyle coming tomorrow and I still need to call and get Maverick over here. I want to surprise Steve with the nursery done."

"You pick the theme?"

"We did and a name."

"Kind of putting the cart before the horse, aren't you?"

"Not really, I know what I'm having. Don't ask how because you'd never believe me."

"Okey doke."

"You're spending way too much time with Kyle. Anywho, talk to you soon," I say, hanging up.

I hang up with Marissa and finish the last few bites of my salad before making my next to last call. I hit Maverick's name and it rings.

"You doing okay? Steve still okay?" Maverick asks. No hello, just straight to business.

"We're fine. You in a place you can put the phone on speaker without Angela overhearing us?"

"One sec. Cupcake, outside, let's go. Angela, stay in your room." I hear a door open and shut. "Okay, you're on speaker."

"We're here, all of us."

"Baby kicking?"

"Like a field goaler."

"Got any plans for the week?"

"What do you got in mind?" Angelica sounds much like me, dying to get into something.

"I want to surprise Steve with a finished nursery."

"That's sweet, but I don't know what that has to do with me and the price of tea in China," Angelica says.

"How can you finish the nursery before you know what you're having?" Maverick asks.

"Because I know?"

"It's too soon, there's no way you can already know."

I hear a smack. "Don't tell the girl what she does or doesn't know."

"You quit hitting me, or we won't be able to help

the girl," Maverick says.

"Don't worry, Crys, we got you covered and *you* can smack him with the yard stick later."

"That sounds painful. Just be here at noon tomorrow."

Angelica giggles and Maverick hangs up. I'm pretty sure there will be some noises coming from their house. I stand, cleaning my bowl and fork before putting it away. I head for my classroom as I hit Ringo's number.

"Hello?"

"Ringo, I need a favor."

"Sure thing."

"I'm sending you a list now of items I need you to pick up and then be here by noon tomorrow. It's going to be a weeklong process, but I need help keeping the crazy twin in check."

"You got it. See you then." He hangs up.

✼ ✼ ✼

My feet are propped up and I'm watching the food network when the girls come into the house. Both girls have ice cream sundaes in their hands. Steve comes in with two containers both in his hands.

"Just as I suspected, you didn't deep fry a thing. Now, I don't know if I should give you this." He looks from me to Adam. "What did she eat?"

Adam's head drops and I smile. "Don't ask him. I ate what I ate, now shush."

"I don't know if you *deserve* this," he says, swinging the ice cream in my face.

"Maybe not, but I know what I do deserve." I look at him with a raised brow.

"My hands are full." He turns and walks away. He

walks to the freezer and puts one ice cream in, then leaning against it and begins eating his own.

"Girls, go to your room and read after your ice cream, please. Adam, go away," I say, but never take my eyes from the Beast.

"Well, if you don't need me any more tonight, I'm going to head home."

"Later. "

The girls go upstairs and Adam leaves. I stand and watch Steve as I walk past. I take off my shirt and drop it at his feet, then smile and walk on past. I get to the middle of the stairs and take off my shorts. About half way to the bedroom, my bra hits the floor. The last thing I slip off are my panties and I leave them on the door knob before shutting the bedroom door and climbing onto the bed.

He's not even touched me and I'm already drenched from playing with him. I slip my finger down and flick my clit, inserting one finger and then another into my core. My head falls back as I work myself over.

Steve comes into the room and shuts the door, then I feel something cold hit my chest, followed by a hot mouth. I let out a moan and keep going. My hand isn't as good as Steve's, but it works when you want to play.

I wrap my other hand in his ponytail and hold him tightly to me. He comes up and kisses me, then pours more ice cream down the length of me before licking it up. Then, he drizzles it down my legs and licks almost to my hand. My breathing quickens and my hand is going as fast as it can. I can feel the orgasm coming. I come hard on my hand and it goes all over the bed.

Steve grasps my legs and pulls me to the end of the bed. He takes a bite of ice cream before diving in for something else. My hand is in his hair and I'm moaning his name before I even get to think about what's going on.

50

STEVE

AFTER THE STICKY SITUATION, WE MOVE TO the shower, where I take Crystal from behind. I love how she pushes back, riding my cock. Once we're cleaned up, I turn her, letting her ride my cock from the front, her legs over my forearms as I pound her, biting and sucking her huge nipples. She falls apart again and I drop to my knees to lick and flick, drinking up her orgasm. I love the way she tastes, especially now, somehow pregnancy has made her sweeter. We finish up in the shower and I carry her to the bedroom once again. Her legs are like jelly and her core is still on fire. I sit her naked on top of the dresser as I strip the soiled sheets from the bed.

"I don't know why I'm bothering, I'm just gonna make you come all over the fresh set."

"Then what's taking you so long?"

I smirk, getting the new sheets, when Crystal's sweet voice stops me.

"Hey, Beast, I love you."

I stand up from my position on the floor and look

her over. "What have you done?" I ask. "Will I need to punish you?"

"Possibly..." she answers with her hands on the love bun.

I raise my brow. "Well, spill it and we'll see just what I need to do to you for it."

"I told Brent about Release Me. He wants you to go over tomorrow around noon."

I look at her sternly. "That song was just for you and me," I say, straightening up. "It doesn't even have any music to it yet."

"I think the world needs to hear it." I watch her out the corner of my eye, she is just sitting there with her legs dangling. I walk over to the dresser and open the top drawer. She moves her legs and I go into it, pulling out the bullet vibe I bought for us. I palm it and head into the bathroom to grab a large band aide.

I return to her and calmly say, "I'll go, but you are in for it, for taking the song to him without asking me first."

"If I'd have asked, you wouldn't have done it. I figured it was better to ask forgiveness than to get permission."

"My sentiments exactly," I say, opening her legs and sliding the bullet up to her clit, fixing it in place with the band aid. I turn it on low and watch as her eyes pop. "Forgive me?" I ask, taking her hands in one of mine and putting them above her head as I guide my cock to her entrance with the other.

I slide in and out of her gently, and I can see the fury in her eyes as I take long deliberate strokes. The intensity of the vibe is like a dull hum against my cock inside her. I turn it up and it gets faster, louder, as it pulses against her slippery lips. I watch as her face takes on the exquisite flush from the multiple orgasms that I know she is having.

She growls at me, trying to free her hands, but I hold them up high. I kiss her and she bites me, drawing blood! I can taste it on my own lips as I push beyond her bite and deepen the kiss. Her back arches with my thrusts and soon, I can't hold back anymore. I come deep inside her, my cock throbbing and humming from all the vibrations as I pull out of her. She's panting and fussing with another orgasm, shaking her head and moaning. I kiss her again, finally turning the vibe down and then off. I go to peel the band aid off and it's so slick it just drops and the vibe falls to the floor as I let her arms go at last.

She falls forward against me and I lift her from the pool between her legs. I'm going to have to really wipe down that dresser later. I carry her to the bed, pull back the sheets, and lay her down, then I grab my jeans and slip them on.

"I'm gonna check the girls," I whisper and she just nods, her eyes shutting. I have done my duty as a horny fiancé.

51

CRYSTAL

I WOKE STEVE UP THIS MORNING, SUCKING his cock and fondling his balls. I hear him growling and trying to move his hands, but they are tied to the headboard. I smile and go back to sucking him into my mouth. I keep going until I can feel his body tensing, then I sit up on my knees and look at him.

Steve's panting and pulling at the headboard. "Woman, if you don't ride my cock right now I promise, I will be riding you in minutes."

I grab my phone and take a picture, then smirk. "Say you're sorry."

"I'm sorry," he says and there's a cracking noise, "I didn't leave," something snaps, "it on," the entire bed shifts, "longer." The bed drops and he's on top of me.

I can't help but laugh and Steve is too. He thrusts into me and ends up holding the bump. Between his thrusting and us laughing our asses off, the bump is all over the place. I can feel my walls tighten around Steve and the way he's panting and grunting lets me know he's close. I grab his face, pulling him to me. I need to kiss him and drown out the scream I know is coming. My orgasm bursts through and Steve swallows my scream.

Steve falls beside me and the other end of the bed hits the floor. Steve starts laughing. "Wait till I figure out what I'm doing to get you back."

"That was pretty good, huh?"

"Yes, but this is better."

"I can't believe you broke the bed."

"I can't believe you tied me up. What did you expect me to do? Lay there and take it?"

"Well, kind of, that's what you expect me to do."

"Hmm, I'm gonna have to think about that," Steve says as he heads to the shower.

"Hey, Beast, we need a new bed."

"So order it and get what you want," he yells from the bathroom.

✣ ✣ ✣

Steve has left and everyone should be walking through the door anytime. "I brought provisions." Kyle holds up two boxes of coffee, decaf and caffeinated. Angelica walks in after him with Maverick and Angela on her heels.

"We're here, feed me," Angelica says and I can't hide the smile on my face.

Ringo walks in behind them. "It's a party! Where's the food?"

"Before we get started, I need help taking something to the curb from my bedroom," I say, straight faced as to not give anything away.

"Hold up! Angela, outside now." Angelica takes her shoes off and is waddling up the stairs with

Maverick right behind her.

"I think I'll go outside with the girls," Adam says and shuts the door on his way out.

"Come on, boys, Maverick is going to need help."

"On it." Kyle grins.

"Following you," Ringo adds.

I head up the stairs and into the bedroom. Angelica has her hand over her mouth, hiding a huge smile. "Somebody was tied up. I'm not sure who was tied up, but someone was tied up."

"Come on, look at the headboard, it's obvious it was him," Kyle states.

"Crys, what happened to the quiet one that watched everything going on?" Ringo asks.

"I got knocked up?"

Maverick grabs me by the shoulders and is looking me over. "Have you lost your fucking mind? You could have gotten hurt and lost the baby. You idiots are supposed to be careful."

"Sure, you don't show that much concern when you're plowing me from the back," Angelica quips.

"Shush, you, she's high risk and was having pain two weeks ago."

"That's the problem, I was in pain. Fucker used a band aid and stuck a vibrating thing to me. I'm pretty sure it went on for hours with my hands in the air. Pay back's a bitch."

"Ah, been there, done that. It's more fun with insertables," Kyle says.

"I'll keep that in mind."

I let everyone know their tasks, then go make lunch while I'm looking at bed sizes and trying to figure what size we have. I grab my phone and call Steve.

"Yeah, Bella, are you okay?"

"Other than my back hurting a little, I'm fine."

"Why are you calling?"

"What size of bed do we have?"

"A California king."

"Perfect. Love you."

I hang up and order the Cortina sleigh bed by Michael Amini, I also order a new box spring and mattress as well as four big, heavy-duty chains from Home Depot. I don't want to change too much for the girls and Steve, but I think the house should have more of Steve and I in it. By the time lunch is done, Maverick, Ringo, and Kyle have the nursery painted and just need to let it dry. They are hoping to start placing the glow in the dark stars and planets, but we'll see.

I get the girls set up on the patio with their lunches since all the adults, including Adam, are in the house. We're all having chicken salad wraps. "Hope everyone enjoys your Maverick approved meal. Since the doc put me on this diet, I've decided to call it the Maverick approved diet."

"You know, when I come here, I look forward to food." Angelica laughs.

"There's nothing wrong with a healthy meal," Maverick and Ringo say at the same time.

"After this, I'm going to have to get a cheeseburger," Kyle says and I laugh.

"Steve would have a hissy fit if he thought I was eating a greasy cheeseburger."

"What? Are you kidding? I've seen that man put away an entire pizza and still look for beer."

"Kyle, I've been cooking for him for almost ten years. I'm pretty sure I know how much he can eat."

After lunch, the guys go back to work on the nursery till I get a text from Marissa letting me know the

Beast is on his way home. I get everyone out of the house and Chinese on the table before Steve walks through the door.

The girls and Adam are sitting at the table eating and I'm sitting in Steve's recliner with my feet up. I've been on them most of the day and I'm starting to feel it.

Steve kisses the girls on the head and says hello to Adam before making his way to me with a smile on his face. He sits down on the floor by my feet and begins massaging them.

"How was your day?"

"Same as normal," I say with a shrug.

"Yeah, so no visitors?"

"I don't really classify Maverick, Angelica, and Angela as visitors anymore."

"They have practically moved in, haven't they? We should just give them a key."

"Oh, no, we are not. Angelica had a field day with the bed while Maverick bitched at me."

"What's he bitching about now?"

"He's afraid we're going too rough and you're going to hurt me."

"Today was a little hairy."

"But it was fun."

"I'm not denying that."

"I got him and Adam to move the queen bed from my old room into ours till the new bed gets here."

"You know you're going to have to sleep right on top of me in that bed."

"As much as I wish it so, I need to take it easy tonight."

"Yes, but if you don't sleep on top of me, I'm liable to squish you."

"Beast, I can't do that and keep to myself."

"We'll figure it out."

"You need to go eat dinner."

"What have you eaten?"

"I had a chicken salad wrap at lunch, then I made an enchilada casserole in the crock pot. The girls didn't like the way it smelled, so that's why there's Chinese in there for you."

"So, other than that, you're feeling all right."

"I've been crampy but just figure it's all the activity."

"What kind of cramps?"

"Nothing crazy, just my sides bothering me a little. I'm okay."

Steve takes a deep breath. "Just take it easy for the next couple of days. When they deliver the bed, stay out of the way. And don't go chaining anything up in the basement."

I smile at him. "I'm already ahead of you. Told Maverick he'd have to set the bed up for me before you got home. "

"Alright," he says and stops rubbing my feet. Getting up, he kisses me on the head. "Need anything before I go eat?"

"No, you're home, so I'm gonna take a shower and lay down."

"Okay, I'll get the girls showered and in bed, then I'll meet you."

It takes me a few minutes, but I get out of the recliner and make my way upstairs. My dinner isn't agreeing with me and I think bed could help.

52

STEVE

CHRISTMAS EVE, AND I'M ON PINS AND needles. Crystal has been up to something and I think everyone is in on it. Brent has been working too hard to keep me at his place all week, even to the point that he enlisted Angelica to come run back up vocals. They want me to sing, and I keep telling them that we are not Kiss and I'm not Peter Criss. *Release Me* is not gonna be another *Beth*.

I had the hardest time figuring out what to get Crystal. I had planned on proposing tonight, but I sorta did that already. So, now I've turned my focus to her and the baby. Everything is baby or pampering related. I had to call the band and make sure they didn't buy any of the things on my list. Angelica had to do a few returns, but hey, they should have asked me first.

I had to leave them today to go and pick up the Christmas Eve presents. I found two of the most adorable puppies I've ever laid eyes on. Chocolate Labs, one with green eyes and one with yellow. They are supposed to be good with kids and protective, so it's a win, win. I've got them in the front seat and they are sleeping soundly as I pull up to the house. I pick them up and put them in the box with big red bows around their necks before walking inside.

"Girls? I'm back."

Mary Beth and Sue Ellen are on the couch, watching Jack Frost, but Crystal is nowhere to be seen. "Crys?" I holler, holding the box up above my head so the girls can't see into it.

"What?" she answers, standing at the top of the stairs. I can see the bump easily now, only eight weeks pregnant and already she looks like we're in the second trimester. The doctors say we are doing well, though, so I'm not worrying.

"Come down. I have a family gift." I watch her come down the stairs and I swear she's starting to get a bit of a waddle already. Once she is standing next to me, I put the box down and the girls go nuts as the puppies yip and wag their tails, giving out kisses.

"Puppies?" She raises an eyebrow.

"I couldn't resist them. I wanted to get us something we could enjoy as a family, and then I realized that we don't have a family pet. Never have. I figured it was high time. I think it's high time for a lot of things."

She looks up at me, confused, as I wrap my arms around her, gently pulling her to me. "You should feel free to start nesting."

She looks at the girls, then to me. "I think it's too soon."

"I think that if you involve them, it will help with the transition, and it will make this place more our home. If Kellie were still alive, I would have had this place gutted out weeks ago. There's nothing here that even says *me*, except that big old recliner you like. It's time we make this house our home."

"Then it has to be everybody doing it together, including Peggy Sue."

I nod, we haven't seen much of her since there are no classes and Kellie died. She was at the funeral but didn't stay long and she hasn't really called. "They are going to be here, tonight, she promised," I say as the puppies escape from the box. "Girls, take them outside. Okay?" The girls run off with their new attractions and I am left holding my Bella. "You feeling up to things tonight? I mean we don't have to do the usual."

"I'm all right, the girls are expecting movies and popcorn, so we're gonna give um movies and popcorn."

I kiss her, loving the feel of her soft body against me, and I get to wondering about all of the things she bought this past week. I didn't get the particulars from the bank, but she did a significant bit of shopping with an online adult store. I haven't said anything because I'm curious what she has up her sleeve, and when she has it planned. The thoughts of sexy lingerie and things that twist and vibrate has my cock growing rigid.

She breaks the kiss and caresses my bulge. "I have cooking to do." She smiles, walking to the kitchen.

❖ ❖ ❖

It's four thirty when the doorbell rings and Peggy Sue announces herself and Harrison. They have Brayden, of course, but he's in a sling across Harrison's chest. "You turning into a couple of hipsters? The next thing you know, he'll grow a beard and be wearing non prescription glasses." I move to hug Peggy Sue, but she bypasses me and heads straight for Crystal. "What am I, chopped liver?" I ask.

"Merry Christmas, Daddy, I just have this icebox cake I made that needs the damn icebox." She holds up a holiday cake. God, I hope she got it right, it was her mother's recipe.

She's talking to Crys when I take Brayden from his father. The boy is quieter than usual and that isn't sitting well with me. "How are things?"

"Going well, I've gotta go out to L.A. for two weeks, though, after the first of the year to do some recording."

"Sounds like fun. Are Peggy Sue and the baby going too?"

"Uh," he scratches his head, looking at my daughter, "I don't know, probably not."

"I used to bring the wife and girls to Aspen whenever we recorded, it was always fun."

"Yeah, but you got a private studio, the label we are with has us sharing a booth. It sucks, but they are the ones paying the bills."

"Right, about that, how is the new house?"

"Nice, prices are good, things are really good." He excuses himself suddenly, going over to Peggy Sue.

"It's like they can't wait to get away from me," I say to Crystal as she's stirring the cranberry apple cider. The house smells of cinnamon and cloves, and the tree looks great with all the popcorn and tinsel. The puppies are passed out on their big fluffy bed and the girls are right alongside them, watching Frosty the Snowman, but Harrison and Peggy Sue just seem like they are up to something.

Crystal pats my chest. "I'm sure it's just the stress of the new house, and living with one another, seeing each other all day, every day."

"Uh huh, I don't know, I just feel like something is going on."

"Don't you think they'd tell you if they wanted you to know?"

"So, you think something's up too? It's not just my imagination?"

"I think you're starting to act like a crazy beast."

"This is the first holiday that I'm completely sober, I may be a little on edge."

"Well, this is my first Christmas knocked up and you're starting to stress me out."

"I'm sorry, Bella, what can I do to help? I'm antsy and can't really sit still. Give me something to do."

"Um, aren't you normally in there watching the movies with the kids?"

"Yeah, and about a six pack deep."

"You need to learn to do the same things you did before without drinking." She turns me around and pushes me toward my girls and the television.

✻ ✻ ✻

Dinner consisted of a tableful of minis. Mini cheeseburgers, pigs in blankets, Swedish meatballs, brown sugar mini sausages in the crock pot, lasagna rolls, build your own pizzas, and garlic pull-aparts that were shaped like a Christmas tree were just a few of the treats of the night. We piled it on thick and watched movies until it started to get dark. Now, it's time to do the presents for the night.

"Okay, I know the family present was the puppies, but we have the others here now. Peggy Sue, Harrison, I know you've been doing what you can to make a go of things and I wanted to get you all something to make it a little easier on you. Aside from paying for the wedding, which I hear is coming along, according to Maverick, I have something that should make life a little easier."

I pull a small box from under the tree and hand it to them. They open it up to find the keys to a brand-new Ford Bronco.

"Daddy, you didn't have to."

"I want my grandbaby in a safe vehicle, as well as his mother. This way, you have a car while Harrison is away too."

"Thank you," Harrison says, hugging Peggy Sue.

I nod as I turn to the girls. Mary Ann got an aquarium for her room with little sharks in it. She's fascinated by them and I want to let her imagination and learning grow as she watches sharks of her very own. Sue Ellen got a telescope since she wants to be an astronomer and work for NASA. I figure it's a good start.

I turn to Crystal, giving her an envelope. She opens it and finds a gift certificate for the spa at the hotel where our love bun was conceived.

"I don't know if we're allowed back there. I don't know if we should go back there," she says with a giggle.

"I talked to them before I got the certificate. They welcome us back as long as we promise not to do a thing or two till we are behind closed hotel room doors."

She doesn't say a word, just smirks. I've given out the presents, but it seems they all have something for Dad for once.

Mary Ann and Sue Ellen give me a pair of silver cuff links and new gauged earrings for my ears. Then, Crystal gives me a fetal heart monitor, so I can listen to our love bun whenever I want. It's sweet. Peggy Sue has something for each of us. The girls open theirs first. They have T-shirts that read *Auntie Squad*, too adorable.

Crystal opens a box, revealing a world's best stepmom T-shirt. I am betting on a T-shirt of some kind, but Peggy Sue just hands me a little envelope.

I open it to find a sheet of paper that says *Coupon, Good for one Grandbaby, redeem July 21st, 2018.* I look up and look at her and Harrison. She puts her hands on her belly and I see the bump already started.

"You're pregnant again?" I ask in shock.

"We found out right after mom died, it's been a process." She walks over to me. "Please don't be mad."

I swallow, looking at Crys. She's got that guilty look on her face. She knew; I can tell. I shake my head.

"What am I gonna do with you girls?" I huff.

"Love and protect us forever." Mary Ann smiles. I just nod, and Peggy Sue hugs me.

❊ ❊ ❊

With the oldest gone, it's time to put the girls to bed. I carry Mary Ann up first and tuck her and Hunter, the green-eyed pup, snugly into bed. Then I come back downstairs for the sleeping Sue Ellen. Her puppy, Jonas, follows me as I carry her with Crystal right behind us.

Sue Ellen stirs as she is put in bed. "Crys?" she asks in her tiny voice.

"Yeah, baby?"

"Now?" she asks, sitting up, suddenly alert.

Crystal scratches her head. "You think he's been good enough?"

She nods, taking my pinky in her hand as she gets off the bed.

"Well, you know the way," Crys says, pointing out of the room.

Sue Ellen drags me out and through the house to where our room is. Then, she passes it and stops at one of the spare rooms. She opens the door giddily.

"Here, Daddy. From Mommy Crystal."

The room is dark, but not entirely. It's lit up by glow in the dark stickers of stars and planets. I can see it's furnished as I turn on the lights. The room is just how I had imagined it in my head when talking to Crystal. Purples and deep blues mixed with clouds and the stars all over to surround the dark oaken crib, matching changing table, a rocker big enough for two, and a swing. On the wall, directly above the crib, are the words *Steven Robert Falcone Jr*. I lick my lips, my mouth is dry. I know it's too soon for her to know for sure, but I'll take it. Some women just know, and I think my woman knows.

"How?"

"How do you think?"

"This was why you wanted me out of the house all week?"

She shrugs. "Maybe."

"I see, it's wonderful. Thank you." I kiss Sue Ellen on the head and then Crystal on the lips. I feel Sue Ellen let me go and she yawns.

"Baby, you need to go to bed before Santa gets here."

She nods and runs off, leaving me with Crystal and the nursery. "It's really just wonderful, and the guys and everyone didn't kill each other helping you?"

"They may have tried once or twice, but I left them with Ringo."

"Ah, Mr. Micromanagement."

"Pretty sure I heard him arguing right along with Kyle and Maverick at some point, but I tried to ignore it. Every time I tried to help, Maverick sent me out of the room."

"Well, with the VOX fumes…" She looks at me perturbed.

"Sorry, my love, it's just that they aren't good for you, I'm so happy right now." I can't stop smiling as I pull her to me.

"Sorry you didn't get to help."

"It's okay, we laid the track. Brent's going to build the next album around it, making it a ballad ensemble."

"At least I did something right."

"Yeah, and now it's time to get you off those feet, into something more comfortable, and into bed. Santa comes soon."

"I'm pretty sure I quit believing in Santa a few years ago."

"Oh, I've never stopped believing, I even put out the cookies and milk, and carrots for the reindeer."

"And who's gonna build your ATV reindeer?"

"It's done and under a tarp in the back yard marked firewood."

"And all the presents that are supposed to be in it?"

"Stuffed in a big red sack right on board."

"How are you doing?"

"Me, just peachy. I'm tickled pink and blue."

"You know what I meant."

I tighten my hold on her with a heavy sigh. "I'm alright, I got through today. We all did."

"Now, we have to make it through tomorrow."

"Yes, with everyone else. I think it will be okay, we'll be okay." I take her hands and lead her back to our room for a short winter's nap.

53

CRYSTAL

I'M OFFICIALLY EIGHT WEEKS PREGNANT today, only six more weeks till we are out of the war zone. We still have to be careful because the high risks never go away, but the percentage on miscarriages drops once we hit fourteen weeks. I gave the girls till the first of the year off since there's yet another party planned. I'm pretty sure we've seen more of the band since they aren't touring than we ever did when they were.

I'm working on getting dressed for the day and I can't get my shorts to button. With a growl, I lay back onto the bed and try to button my shorts again. I look up as Steve walks in.

"I don't think that's going to work," he says with a chuckle.

"If I weren't carrying your beast it would."

"You're telling me with all the shopping you've done, you don't have any other pants?"

"Mine still fit."

"Not anymore."

"UGH!" I get myself off the bed and go into the closet for a dress. I walk back out to the bedroom in a yellow maxi dress with gray chevron and I'm working on buttoning a gray bolero between my ever-growing tits.

Steve's sitting on the bed, looking at me. "Um, you sure you wanna wear that?"

"Is there something wrong with it?"

"The love bun is sticking out."

"There's nothing I can do about that because, trust me, I've tried!"

Steve laughs as he stands and wraps his arms around me. "There gonna spot you."

"I plan to hide between Adam, Maverick, and Harrison."

"Okay, do you need me to do anything while you're gone?"

"You are on little girl duty."

"Right, but there's nothing else I need to be doing?"

"Dinner because God only knows when Peggy Sue will let me come home."

"Okay."

"Are you sure you don't want to trade me places?"

"She needs help because she doesn't know what she's doing with this and she asked you."

"Newsflash, I've never been married nor have I ever planned a wedding."

"You're the closest thing to a momma she's got."

"You aren't playing very fair," I whine.

"It's not about fair."

I pull the beast down to me so I can kiss him and he gets the growl in his chest. We haven't connected in a couple days with Christmas and everything else. He says I need a break, that we were getting too rough.

Pulling back, I smile.

"I love you, Beast, and I'll see you in a few hours."

"Don't have too much fun," Steve says and I roll my eyes before walking away. I'm sure I've left him in a predicament.

We're sitting at the Knights of Columbus Hall. We've just made it through the first tasting of appetizers. I like a couple things from each one, so I finally suggest a trio.

"I really like the idea of the Crostini, you have a few to choose from? This way, they can get different flavors to suit any taste? Pick three and go."

"Cool, how about tomato, basil chutney, fig and ricotta, and the Brie, honey, and prosciutto?" Harrison suggests.

"Those really were the best flavors," I agree.

"Okay, so that's easy. What about the main dishes? There's so much to choose from," Peggy Sue says, looking at the four caterers, who all have something different.

From pasta dishes to a raw bar, Peggy Sue and I start to load up our taster plates.

"Ah, you can't have anything on that bar, nothing raw while pregnant." Maverick kills our fun and I have to leave the yummy, yummy sushi behind.

"We don't want to do anything too fishy, or you all are gonna end up sick," he adds. There go my thoughts on monkfish.

"Carving stations?" Peggy Sue suggests. "The third guy had a tasty turkey and you can't go wrong with beef for Daddy."

"See, you don't need me, you know what you want."

"Yeah, but the hardest part is the cakes." She smiles

as we finish up the main dishes.

I'm starting to get full, but I promised I would help, so cakes and cookies fill the next plate.

"I can't decide!" Peggy Sue whines. "You pick the flavor." She looks at me.

There's lemon, Neapolitan, dark chocolate, red velvet, vanilla, and even an angel food cake, as well as tarts, Madeline's dipped in chocolate, and cupcakes in the same flavors as the cakes. I'm on a sugar high as I'm trying to decide which is the tastiest.

"I think the angel food, it's different. Then do the tarts and Madeline's too."

"What about the groom's cake?"

"Go with his favorite, but a cream cheese frosting. It holds up better and is not nearly as sweet as all that fondant," I tell her.

She seems happy, and that's all that matters, though now, I have to keep a mental list because I want some of this stuff for myself eventually. I take the cards of the caterers we are going with for future needs and slip them into my bag. Just because it's going to be a while off doesn't mean I shouldn't be prepared for when it's our turn.

We pack up, now that we're stuffed to the gills, and head for the exit. Adam cuts us off.

"Crystal, we are gonna have to go out the back."

"Why? What's going on?"

"Reporters are sniffing around. It seems that news of you guys being engaged and having a baby got out."

"How? We've been so careful."

"Imogen put out a press release confirming," Maverick says, looking at his phone, which had been on vibrate.

"Son of a bitch. Well, I'm not going out there while

they are crawling around."

"We have to leave sometime, and they aren't going to leave without their pics of the bump." Maverick shakes his head.

"Adam, pull up right onto the curb and we'll run for it," Harrison suggests.

I sigh. "I'm not running. I'm also not going to be bullied. If Imogen put it out, then I guess it's out." I unbutton my jacket and take Peggy Sue by the hand. "Guess we're coming out in style."

54

STEVE

THREE HOURS. Three hours with three little girls, and one incorrigible Momma. That's how long it's been since Maverick dropped off Angel and Angelica, seems they need babysitting too. Hour one was fine, the girls played some video games and I made lunch with Angelica's help. Since getting together with Maverick, she has really learned a few things about how to man a kitchen. When we used to fool around, I was lucky if I could get her to make me a sandwich, let alone an actual meal.

Now she cooks, cleans, and does the dishes. Maverick really has figured out that to keep her sober means keeping her busy. We are trying to figure out dinner when the girls start pestering.

"Daddy, can we play salon?"

I look at them curiously.

"We wanna do your and Angelica's hair and stuff."

"Um, well… Wait, what have you got there?"

"Makeup," Sue Ellen answers.

"Is that Crystal's?"

They nod.

"No, nope, not happening. Put it back or things will get serious. That's not to play with."

They frown, turning from me, and I feel guilty instantly.

"Steve, why don't you put it back and I'll see what I've got," Angelica suggests, dumping her bag onto the counter. You can tell it's been a while since she cleaned it out. She's still carrying tampons. I can't help but laugh. "Maverick doesn't have you cleaning out your bags every other day? What? Is he slacking?"

"Funny, no. I just dump one bag to the next, is all. Girls, I have some nail polishes and makeup if you all wanna use um."

They light up and drag Angelica and me to the couches where they start with painting my nails black.

✾ ✾ ✾

"Steven Robert Falcone!" I jerk upright to the sound of my name being called and get off the couch where the girls and I were taking a nap. Angelica said she'd make dinner, so I was relaxing with the kids. The hollering is coming from Crystal and I'm not exactly sure why.

"What's the matter?" I ask, coming into the hallway.

"I want you to walk out onto the front porch,. Hell, just open the front door," she whispers, holding what appears to be a bit of anger as she's shaking and her fists are balled up tight.

I roll my eyes and open the door, only to have cameras flicker and flashes go off in my eyes as Adam attempts to get the reporters off the property. Shit, I guess calling Imogen to get in front of the bump wasn't my best idea. I close the door and look down at her.

"Um, sorry. I should have called," I say with a short chuckle in my throat.

She looks at me as if to say, *ya think?*

"Are you okay?" I ask, trying to hug her, but she stomps on my foot and I push back.

"Does it look like I'm okay?" She's pissed. I back off and put up my hands.

"I'm sorry, I called the label because I was warned by Christy that if we got more bad press, it was gonna come out of us in fines."

"And you couldn't have told me before I walked out of this house?"

"How was I to know that they were gonna find ya?"

"We took the Escalade."

"Fuck," I whisper, "I didn't realize. Bella, I'm so sorry."

"You should be, I'm going to bed." She walks by me and I follow her upstairs.

"You eat enough today?"

"I ate plenty," she answers shortly.

"Before you can go to bed, I need to check your sugar."

She purses her lips and sticks out her hand, the middle finger most prominent. "If you must."

I go into the bathroom and grab the glucose meter. I add a strip and code it. When I come back to her, she's bouncy.

"Just a little prick," I say with a smirk.

"Yeah, I've heard that before."

"Not from me, you haven't." I stick her finger and wait for the machine to read her drop of blood. 268 flashes on the screen. Seriously? "Well, you won't be going out to do that again," I say, showing her the machine. "This is not cool. What all did you eat? Raw Sugar?"

"Don't you holler at me! You told me to go. You knew there would be food that I shouldn't have."

"Ugh, you didn't have to eat all of it!"

"How was I supposed to tell her my thoughts if I didn't try it?"

"You're gonna need to stay up and do some yoga or something because you need to work off these calories."

"And you can kiss my ass. I'm taking a shower and I'm going to bed."

"Crys, seriously, you need to wait to lay down till your sugar levels are lower. It's not safe."

She sighs, putting her hands on top of her head. "I'm fine, other than being a little pissed and on a little sugar high. I'm okay, which is more than I can say for you."

I look at her absurdly. "Huh?"

She brings her hand up, her index finger circling in front of my face. "Your face, your hair, and your nails… Did you swap teams?"

"Uh, no, the girls wanted to play. I completely forgot." I laugh. "Don't you like a little eyeliner on your man? I used to wear it back when I was with Renegade War Dogs."

"Yeah, and you were also usually messed up."

"So, it doesn't work while I'm sober?" I ask, pulling her into my arms again.

"Still not happy with you."

"But I'm more than pleased with you." I run my hands down to her ass, lifting her slightly.

"Oh no, you hollered at me," she pouts.

"I hollered at the situation."

"Same thing."

I groan, rubbing her ass. "I'm sorry."

"I can't believe you called Imogen and didn't call me."

"I wasn't thinking. I called Christy, then the girls wanted lunch and to play the Xbox, and then the hair and makeup. I don't know how you keep up with them."

"Well, I didn't just keep up with them, I kept up with you and Kellie as well."

"Again, how? I've had them five hours and I'm exhausted."

"Been doin' it almost ten years, you learn a thing or two after a while."

"I guess so, I'd need like a bottle of no-doze and three pots of coffee with a whole cake."

"I'm pregnant. If I can do it all pregnant, you can do it and be just fine."

"I suppose, but I think that we need some help around here."

She straightens up and rolls her shoulders. "Okay…"

"I'm thinking of calling in one of those Merry Maid services, where they send out a crew every few days who tend to everything you don't want to or simply can't."

She sighs heavily, like in relief.

"What's that for?" I ask.

"I just wasn't sure what you meant."

"What did you think I meant?"

"It wouldn't be the first time."

"You think I was saying a private nanny or some other situation like you started out?" I furrow my brow.

"Bella, I told you, it's just us. No one else. The open relationship I had is over. Any help we get, and there will be help coming in, will be through an agency of some kind. People with bosses other than us."

"I just thought, you know… I can't give you the attention you always need."

"So, I'm going to have to learn that it's not all about me. That's a good lesson to learn."

"That isn't what you're used to though."

"True, but I got used to that over time, and I'll get used to this too."

"And when the times comes that I can't be what you need me to be?"

I look at her, confused. "While I don't see that happening, except for when you have this baby, I guess I'll deal with it like any man in love would. I'll be supportive of you, and buy lotion in bulk."

She covers her face with one hand, trying hard not to smile. She's failing. "How am I supposed to answer that?"

"By kissing me and telling me that you love me, that you want me, and that you will always need me."

She scrunches up her nose. "I love you, but I don't like you very much right now. As for wanting you, I wanted you before you knew I did, and as for needing you… I don't usually need anybody, but today I needed you and you weren't there."

"Bella, I've apologized. I didn't think they were gonna come running the way they have. Though I'm beginning to understand why Brent and Maverick locked down their wives. I just can't do that to you. You deserve to do as you want, go where you want. If anyone in this relationship needs to be locked down, it's me."

"It was different this time. You know how they normally come after you?"

I nod.

"They were worse. You can stick a hand out and scare them. I can't. I've been okay with the pictures, I was okay with the video, but I'm not so okay with them getting so close they can touch me."

My hands fist at her sides. "They touched you?"

"One, but Maverick got him pretty quick."

"They should have never gotten near you with those three guys with you. You and Peggy Sue should barely be in any pictures."

"Peggy Sue shouldn't be, I'm pretty sure it's just me."

I growl in anger. "Adam needs to do a better job, or he's gonna find himself without one. We need more guards."

"The questions were worse."

"What did they say? Ugh, it doesn't matter. I'm gonna have to do an interview. It's the only way to get them to back off."

"They asked if it was my fault that you and Kellie split, they're blaming the baby."

"Sons of bitches. If they only knew…"

"I'm more worried about what it's gonna do to the girls. I can't take them out anymore. I can't do the normal things we used to do."

"I'm gonna get you two more bodyguards, and I'm not gonna let you out of my sight. I'm sorry you've got to go through this, I wish I was a regular guy."

"You couldn't be a regular guy if you tried."

"I could, I could give it all up, sell this place, move us out to like Connecticut or New Hampshire, grow out my beard, start a school teaching kids to play instruments or something."

She just looks at me, biting her lip.

"I mean, think about it, just us and the kids, I don't need all of this, this lifestyle, it's never been me. It was always Kellie."

She shakes her head. "You have obligations and you are not running from them now.

"Obligations? What obligations, aside from writing checks for some people? That I can do from anywhere."

"You have a whole band of obligations."

I huff. "I love them, don't get me wrong, but if things get too hairy for us, we need to think about stepping out. I won't have us lose this baby because of this lifestyle."

"We aren't going to lose the baby, I'll just stay in more."

"That's not fair to you. You are used to going out, being able to leave the house. I can't have you just go into a lockdown, that's not good for you either."

"But I have plenty I need to do here."

"I don't like it."

"We have six weeks, then our numbers change."

"I know... I know." I swallow. "I just wish there was another way to make them go away." My phone starts to vibrate and I look at it. "It's Christy, should I?"

"Probably." She pats my chest and heads for the bathroom.

I answer, "Yeah, Christy... I thought you were supposed to make this go smoothly?"

"How was I to know she was out and about? You didn't tell me she didn't have a full security detail, or that your daughter, Peggy Sue, is also pregnant. They are having a field day with that."

"Fuck, it was no one's business. She's engaged, they

need to back off."

"Well, I got a call from Rolling Stone and Vanity Fair. They want interviews with the two of you, and Peggy Sue."

"My daughter stays out of it."

"They wanna do a mother-daughter thing."

"She's not Peggy Sue's mother, Kellie was."

"Well, stepmother then. I don't know, I just know they want both girls."

"I don't know."

"If you don't give them what they want, they will keep feeding the rumor mill and invading your home and anywhere you go. That means the rest of the band too."

"Shit."

"Do you want to be responsible for them being flagged for their shit too?"

"I'll talk to Crystal, but I can't promise anything."

"You do that, I'll make the calls."

"Christy, I said I'd tr-" the bastard hung up. I head into the bathroom and Crys is climbing into the shower. Her long blonde hair tied up, her breasts full and getting heavy, her bump becoming more obvious... Looking at her, I almost forget my reason for coming in.

She eyes me, then smirks as she closes the shower curtain. "Well?"

"Christy wants us to do interviews."

"And if we say no?"

"They make life hell for the band and us. It's Rolling Stone and Vanity Fair."

"That doesn't make it any better."

"No, but because they are the top of the food chain, everyone else will stop chomping at the bit." I sit on the edge of the sink.

"What else did he say?"

"They want Peggy Sue with you."

"No."

"I said that too, but he's adamant."

"And I'm pregnant. I'm meaner."

"Will you do the interview without her?"

"Yeah."

I sigh. "This is so fucked up, I swear if I didn't know better, I'd think Christy did this on purpose."

"It's always a possibility."

"Except I called him, remember, so I did this to us. It's all my fault, as usual, I'm just a big stupid bear, bumbling around in my cave."

She pulls the curtain open, looking at me. Apparently, I'm having a day because I'm starting to cry. She crooks her finger at me.

"I'm not really in the mood," I say as I wipe my face.

"Who said anything about that?"

I walk over to her. "What?"

"I think someone is getting my mood swings. Have you been taking my hormones?"

I shake my head. "I'm sorry, I'm just gonna go."

"Oh no, you are not. Now strip 'em and help me with my back and hair." She pulls me toward her and almost completely into the shower. I step back, strip off my clothes, and climb in with her.

55

CRYSTAL

THE GIRLS STAYED THE NIGHT WITH Angela because we have two different interviews today, neither of which being something I really want to do. Steve's downstairs, making breakfast, and I haven't pulled myself out of bed yet, mainly because I'm wishing this day was over. Rolling Stone is supposed to be here around noon, so we're having a late breakfast.

I get myself out of bed and throw on one of Steve's shirts. Not like I need to get dressed yet. I walk downstairs and my beast is facing the stove, so his back is to me. I pad up behind him and wrap my arms around him.

He takes my hands in his. "Good morning, Bella."

"Morning, Beast."

"You hungry?"

"Not particularly, but we have a long day."

"I made your favorite muffin and a breakfast casserole that I think you're going to appreciate."

"I don't think I've ever told you my favorite muffin."

"Well, you always go for banana nut anytime we go out."

"Have you really been watching me that closely all these years?"

"Always. I know you take more milk in your coffee than actual coffee, and when you think no one is looking, you're always just a little sad."

"I don't know how I never noticed it." I pause. "Used to be sad, I'm not anymore."

"I know, I've noticed that too, but you still worry." He turns to face me and I'm biting my lip. His mouth connects with mine and I wrap my arms around his shoulders. He lifts and sits me on the counter before pulling back, we're closer to the same height now.

Steve's hands are sneaking up my shirt when I grab them. "Oh, I don't think so."

He smiles at me. "I was thinking about New Year's. Maybe we should let the girls stay at Angelica and Maverick's and it just be us. What do you think?"

"Everyone's going to Brent and Marissa's. It's all the girls have talked about. They want to see Brent without his shirt. I'm telling you, they are just as bad as Peggy Sue."

"Too young. They are way too young."

"Oh, they have Angela in on it too."

"Let them take the girls to Brent and Marissa's for the holiday. Lord knows we've taken Angela enough."

"Um, you can blame Mary Ann and Sue Ellen for that."

"Come on, what do you say? You, me, a new pair of sheets on the bed, and maybe some Chinese?"

"Honestly, I've been trying to figure out how to tell you. I don't want to do any more parties and get togethers, except the wedding, till the annual July party."

"Peggy Sue turns seventeen in February."

"And she's also pregnant. We can do something here, just family, and she will deal with it. She doesn't need some crazy party because it's not like she's drinking or anything."

"You make an excellent point, I just figured I'd bring it up."

"Her wedding is the first week of March. If she wants a party, she can have it then. I'm ready for things to get back to normal. I know nothing will ever feel the same, but right now, I just feel like I'm bouncing from one place to the next."

"No, I agree. I'm kind of getting sick of the impromptu get togethers where everyone comes empty handed. We never do that shit."

"We didn't do that and I still wound up cooking most of everything else. I'm always worn out and I'm afraid it's going to hurt me in the long run. What if we have one of these get togethers and it keeps me from being able to keep up with the girls?"

"I agree with you. No more parties. Starting with New Year's."

"Okay," I say and go to pull him for a kiss when my belly growls.

"Let's get you fed."

"I need to get dressed, just not sure what to wear."

"Put on something comfy because they'll have props."

✢ ✢ ✢

I've never in my life been naked for so many damn people at once. I was able to wear my white cotton panties in a few, but not as many as I'd like. Rolling Stone did our pictures in the parlor. We were on the couch, and in front of the fireplace, as well as some more awkward positions by the Christmas tree that I'd like to never think about again, especially with so many people watching.

I'm in the bathroom, getting dressed, when there's a knock at the door. "Just a minute."

"It's me," Steve says, so I crack the door and when I see that it's only him, I let him in. "Well, if that wasn't completely awkward…"

"Ya think?" I ask, full of sass.

"They're ready when we are."

"I hate Christy for being a prick and making us do this. Good thing he isn't here."

"He's a smart man."

I finish pulling my hair up on my head. "Lead the way." Steve takes my hand and leads us back to the parlor.

"First, let me say congratulations to you both and then, welcome to the big league. How does it feel to be the first member of Fallen Angels to have his own interview with Rolling Stone?" Tye, the reporter from Rolling Stone, asks.

"So far, it feels good, but we'll see. Ask me after the interview and maybe I'll be able to tell you more," Steve answers with a chuckle, but I can tell he's being a smart ass.

"Fair enough. We are here to talk engagements, baby bumps, and new material. Sound good to you?"

Steve nods his head, pulls me to him, and says, "I think we can handle that."

"So, our readers are curious; do you listen to your own music when you two get down and dirty?"

Steve laughs and I'm left to answer. "Truth be told, we enjoy sex and it happens so often that there are no sounds except our own." I crack a smile as Steve face palms.

"Is sex weird now?" Tye asks.

Steve laughs. "We did break a bed, so she's chained the new one to the wall."

Tye raises a brow and looks at me. "Care to elaborate?"

I sigh. "Let's admit it, the man's a beast. I figured if we could break the bed once, I'd need something to help keep the next one safe... Just in case I was feeling frisky. Plus, it's the best form of payback I've found."

"Well, you two obviously like sex. Was this planned or was it an oops after all these years?"

Steve takes me by the hand. "The love bun was very much planned."

"Crystal, did you have an idea of what being pregnant would feel like? How has that changed?"

"Well, honestly, I expected it to be a cake walk. I've watched a few of my close friends go through it and no problems. Pregnancy for me has been something I needed to adjust to."

"Steve, this is your fourth pregnancy, how has it compared to the other three?"

I shift in my seat as Steve answers, "I can't compare them. This has been an entirely different experience, unique and perfect in its own rights."

"You're only eight weeks along, but we have major bumpage, which is what caused the hoopla, so are we safe to say this is gonna be a big baby like it's daddy?"

Steve laughs. "I hope it's not all gas."

I smack his leg. "Again, he's a beast, what can I say?"

"Have you had any strange cravings yet?"

"None that I can think of."

"Has the baby coming inspired any new material?"

Steve squirms in his seat. "Actually, just before we found out we were pregnant, I wrote a song. It's going to be on our next album and Brent's working on some new material to go with it."

"As for your sudden engagement, was this before or after your stint at the hotel and spa?"

Steve clears his throat. "Shit, I thought we were going to get away from this."

I smile and tap Steve's leg. "It was after. Actually, it was the same night he wrote his song."

"Many have speculated about the panties you put on in the lobby. Would you like to tell us the actual story behind the pictures taken in the restaurant?"

Steve looks at me. "Bella, do you want to explain."

I smile as I feel my face and ears burning. "Those damn panties. They were fun, but that was just the tip of the iceberg. I don't want to give away all the secrets, but I rather enjoyed myself."

"Well, as one of the infamous Fallen Angels, you have a pretty well-known face, which is hard to miss in the famously dubbed Angel Has Risen sex tape that the two of you have become known for. Was it an honest act, or were you playing for the cameras?"

"The panties to which she was referring left me in a particular situation and when your woman asks you what you're waiting for, you don't wait anymore. So, yeah, the world got a good look at my cock. Hope you liked what you saw," Steve says.

"Nice answer, thank you for taking your time out today. We hope to hear more from you in the future. That's the end of that. It's been an experience. We will get this taken care of and send you a copy when our issue comes out."

Steve stands and walks the guy out while I just sit and cool off.

I'm laid back with my arm slung over my face when Steve sighs. "Wow. According to Christy, Vanity Fair's going to want to do our shoot in the bedroom. Do we want to do it in our bed or one of the ones down the hall?"

I clear my throat, then stand up. "If Christy wants the shoot in the bedroom, we'll give him a shoot in the bedroom." I look at him with a cocked brow and smirk.

He grabs me by the ass. "I love it when you get cocky." Steve sits me back down before getting down on his hands and knees and starts inching his way up my dress.

I push him backward. "Not happening till we are done. I refuse to look freshly fucked for the cameras."

"But, I just wanted a little taste."

"Tasting always leads to us fucking and I won't be smelling like sex when they get here." He looks like a lost puppy. "We have one more day before we stay locked in bed together with no interruptions. Well, that is, unless we pack the girls some more clothes and have Maverick stop by and get them tonight."

Steve's brain is working in overdrive before he stands up. "I'll be back in ten minutes, you call Maverick."

"You always forget something, you call Maverick and I'll pack them."

"What? They've got everything they need except party dresses and hair clips."

"Oh, beast, you are so wrong."

❖ ❖ ❖

"Excuse me, could one of you move the prescription bottle? It's in our shot," the photographer for Vanity Fair asks.

I look up at Steve and he sees the worried look on my face. He leans across the bed, grabs the bottle, and sticks it in his pocket. He kisses me on the cheek and gets on with the shoot. There are pictures taken on the bed with us together and me alone from all angles. Then a few in front of the picture window in the bedroom.

After the photos, I walk into the bathroom and get my dress back on. I take a few minutes to breathe because I have this strong feeling in my gut that we will be asked about the medicine.

I head back out to see where we're going for the interview. We're told that we look comfy on the bed, so we should just stay here.

"First, thank you for letting us come out to see you, it's a pleasure meeting you," Gina from Vanity Fair says. "You've been part of Steve Falcone's very public ménage a' trios since before he first began with Fallen Angels, in 2014. However, Steve has never actually told us how you met? Care to share?"

"I know this is going to sound cliché, but hey, it really does happen in life. I was actually brought on as the nanny and teacher for his girls."

"So, you were with him during the pizza and beer phase of his career. He does have a history with booze and heroin, but has been clean for nearly three years now. Was it his addictions that kept you two from having children sooner?"

"No, it was me. I just wasn't ready for kids. You know, young and stupid as they say." I smile at her.

"Steve's divorce was kept very quiet, and so has the fact that the two of you are engaged, any reason for that?"

I give a shrug of my shoulders. "I can't say anything for the divorce because I wasn't a part of it. As for the engagement, I just wanted to be able to enjoy it before all the crazy started."

"So, who's the prescription for?"

I look over at Steve, who's beside me, and he nods at me. I bite my lip the look up at Gina. "It's mine."

"Is everything okay?"

"Just peachy."

"How have Steve's daughters, Peggy Sue, age 16, Mary Ann, age 10, and Sue Ellen, age 9, dealt with the new baby news?"

"They've been fine with it. Peggy Sue is happy for us, Mary Ann calls it a peanut, and Sue Ellen, like me, is calling it a beast."

"Beast, that's cute. Are you doing anything specific to prepare the little ones for their new half sibling?"

"Not referring to him as a half is the first thing we're doing," Steve says and I place my hand on his and look at him. Fucker doesn't open his mouth for anything else and when he does, he lets it slip we're having a boy. God damn it.

"A boy, really? Wishful thinking or mother's intuition?"

"Uh, well, um, shutting up now," Steve says.

"Wishful thinking? We have three girls and I think it's time we have a little boy running around like his daddy."

"What's been the best part about your pregnancy since it started? The worst part?"

"Best part is hands down, my sex drive. I thought I

liked sex before, but I love it now. The worst part is having the morning sickness at any time of the day. I think it should be called anytime sickness or something else."

"Can't disagree with you there. You have found yourself defending your relationship since the news came out. A lot of Kellie lovers are blaming you for everything from the divorce to her actual death, which was labeled an accident, but many speculate that it was indeed a suicide, based on a text sent before her death. What would you like to say to those still pushing against you?"

Steve shifts beside me as I look at Gina. I don't feel the tears till Steve's wiping them away. "People are going to say what they want. I loved Kellie as much as I do Steve. Kellie loved her girls and wouldn't ever do anything that would hurt them. For the people against me? So be it, that's a part of life and life is something we all have to deal with."

"That's a good way to put it. I hope we have given you some opportunity to set the record straight. Do come back to us when you've really popped, we'd love to see you again." Gina turns off her recorder. "I apologize for the prescription, but my producer was in here when the camera man saw it, so I couldn't let it go."

"I understand, it's part of the game."

"Thank you for doing the interview."

"It was my pleasure."

"Our magazine hits the stands the first week of January. Do look for it. It's nice to meet you."

Steve thanks her and escorts her out of the room. I lay down on my side and try to curl up, but can't anymore. My belly won't let me. I'm bawling when the bed dips behind me.

Steve pulls me into his arms. "It's okay, everybody's gone."

"I knew Kellie would be brought up, but I didn't think that would happen."

"I know."

"People think it's my fault. They think I'm the reason she's dead."

"We both know that's bullshit."

"Do we?"

"Look, either it was a patch of rain and faulty brakes, or it wasn't. Either way, it's not our fault."

"If I would have just left once you started having problems, she might still be here."

"Bella, you cannot do this."

"How do I not? It's everywhere, I can't open the explorer on the computer and not see something about it."

"If you'd have left, I'd have chased you. It wouldn't have mattered where you went. I wouldn't have stopped till you were mine. If they're going to blame somebody, it needs to be me, so I can tell them to shove it up their ass."

"There will be more speculating now. They saw the medicine and someone said I was having a boy."

He looks at me. "Did I say something?"

"When she mentioned half siblings."

"That just irked me. I'm so sorry."

"It's life. I can handle a thousand interviews for Rolling Stone, but I never want to do another for Vanity Fair."

"I'll make sure Christy knows."

"He's going to hate some of my answers."

"He wanted an interview, he got it."

"So, he did."

56

STEVE

LAST NIGHT WAS A BUST. After all that work up from the pictures and the interviews, Crystal was just too tired. Maverick picked up some more clothes for the girls and then she went to bed, leaving me to contend with a dire set of blue balls.

This morning, I get up and she's still down. I hope she's all right. I have plans for us tonight if I can arrange them. I call the Blue Oyster Bar and Grill and tell them I need a caterer for the night. I'm having all of Crystal's favorite foods prepared and brought to me. Then, after dinner, I thought we could take a moonlight skinny-dip followed by watching the fireworks while cuddled under a blanket by the fire pit.

First things first, I need to make breakfast. I head down and let the puppies out before making a huge fruit salad. We need to eat light so dinner will not leave her overdone and tired. We haven't made love in almost two weeks and I don't want to start the New Year with a dry spell.

I plate the salad and pour the juice, then bring the

tray upstairs. She's not in bed anymore, but I can hear her in the bathroom. I set the tray down and sit beside it, waiting for her to come out.

She's in another one of my T-shirts. Since getting pregnant, she's been stealing a lot of them.

"Good morning, Bella."

"Breakfast in bed?" She watches me curiously.

"Sure, why not? I figure I don't do this often enough for you."

"Did you do something wrong?"

"No, I just want to end the year on high notes and start the year off well."

"Are you sure everything is okay?"

I stab a strawberry and hold it out to her. "Food, eat."

"That doesn't answer my question." She looks at me like I'm hiding something, and I suppose I am, but that's gonna have to wait until later.

"Everything is just fine, Bella, I just thought this would be a nice change of pace. We don't have the girls, so we can do as we please today. What would you like to do?"

"It's weird."

I stand up, wrapping my arms around her. "Different can be good."

She purses her lips. "I still think you're hiding something."

"Surprises, not secrets," I say putting the fork up to her mouth. She takes the bite and closes her eyes happily. I drizzled honey all over it to make it nice and sweet.

"Sugar?"

"A bit of honey and lemon to bring out the sweetness of the fruits. There's granola and fresh yogurt in there too."

"Are you trying to get me hyper?"

"Not purposefully, but you've been craving sweets. I saw how you were looking at those muffins yesterday. I figured I'd look up a healthy sweetie for you and the fruit is better for you and the love bun." I feed her another mouthful before leading her to sit on the bed.

"Have you called and checked on the girls?"

"They are horseback riding with Adam. Apparently, he knows his way around a horse."

"Why is he at Angelica's?"

"Because I am here with you and I don't want the girls without a bodyguard."

"But nobody can get into Angelica's, it's surrounded like Ft. Knox."

"Sure, but they still have to move from one place to another and I just feel better about it if they aren't completely alone."

"Okay."

"Okay?" I smile, handing her a bowl and the fork before picking up my own. A man's gotta eat too. "So, I'm thinking that after we eat, we can do whatever you want today. The house is spotless, so we don't have anything like that to worry about. The day is ours to do with as we see fit."

"Am I to assume you have something planned?"

"For later."

"You wanted to be alone, but you have nothing planned?"

"I made plans for later, the day is yours. Anything you want to do, stay in, go out, mani-pedi, I can have them come out. I know Angelica has a great girl who makes house calls, or we can go to a salon if that's what you want."

She just looks at me.

"You don't have anything in mind? Nothing you wanna show me?" I raise an eyebrow, looking at her. Thinking back to the large adult store purchase from before Christmas that I haven't seen any part of.

"Why would you ask that?"

"Oh, just an alert I got on my bank card from Extreme Restraints dot com before Christmas. I was thinking naughty sleepwear, but haven't seen it yet, so I'm guessing you bought something and have chickened out."

"Or I bought something and somebody hasn't touched me," she snips.

"I tried yesterday, but after all that went on, you were too tired, so I left you alone. I don't know if you know this, but I kinda like it when you get aggressive."

"I wasn't tired yesterday, I just wasn't expecting some of the questions."

"It was draining, which is why we need today to relax and reconnect." I pause. "That is, if you want to."

She looks at me. "I could use a bath." She smiles and stands, taking off my T-shirt. She's standing there in just pink cotton panties and I can't resist. I pick her up and carry her into the bathroom, my lips finding hers. She yields to me, opening her mouth with a little moan. I put her on the counter while I get the tub ready for us, but I have to stop, distracted when she begins to play with herself. She leans back on the sink, rubbing her clit through her panties.

"Fuck me, that's hot to watch," I whimper as I see the moisture collect at the center of her.

Crystal begins moaning, locking her eyes on me as she slides two fingers beneath her waistband, curling them until they are inside her. She bites her lip. "Look at me," she shudders.

I lock eyes with her and she crooks the finger of her other hand at me. I go to her and she pulls me into a kiss.

"Keep your eyes on me," she gasps into me. I keep my eyes open as we kiss and feel her hand grasp me from the outside of my pants. The feeling is insane as she stops long enough to get me undressed. The water is ready and we get into the tub, where she sits on my lap with her back to my chest. Taking my cock into her hands, she leads me to her entrance and is soon riding me slowly.

"Fuck, that feels great," I groan, my hands finding her tits and pulling her against me, making her take me deeper. Opening her up so I can flick her clit with my thumb, I kiss on her shoulders and back as she shatters around me, grasping the edge of the tub, water sloshing all over.

I keep at her, working for my orgasm, when she lifts up and slides down on me again, only my cock slides out, bumping her ass. "I'm sorry," I say as she gasps.

"No, it's okay…" She looks back at me and grinds down on my cock. "Really."

"Are you sure?" I ask, a little excited and nervous. I don't want to hurt her.

"Just go easy, and slow." She leans forward, giving me access to her unused opening. I grab her by the hip and using my other hand, I guide my cock, pushing in little by little. Her hands are grasping the edges of the tub, but she seems okay. I'm inside her and she begins to rock on me. Fuck, it feels good, the tightness around me is unique, like nothing else. I feel pressure against my shaft and realize she's begun to finger herself as I fuck her. I'm glad no one is home because the noises coming from our bathroom might scar them for life.

❖ ❖ ❖

We spend the better part of the afternoon outside, laying by the pool and just working on our tans. Even in December, the UV index is good enough to maintain. She's in her halter bikini, the love bump on display when I hear a twig snap. I turn, seeing a paparazzi trying to get a picture. I'm up in seconds and after the fucker. I give chase and he drops his camera. "Good! Serves you right for trespassing!" I snarl, smashing the camera on the pavement.

I walk back to Crystal and she's sitting up, trying to put my shirt on. "Hey, stop, I got rid of him."

"Maybe we should just go in the house."

"No such luck, you wanted to be outside today by the pool."

"I-I'm good now. Had enough sun." She gets up and heads for the house.

"Bella, everything okay?" I grasp her hand, stopping her at the doors.

"Fine, just had enough of the camera shutters is all."

I wrap my arms around her. "I know, Connecticut calls."

She chuckles. "Not happening, we just need to lay low."

"I wish it was that easy."

"We can dream." She hugs me.

"Well, why don't you go put on some clothes and I'll see what's going on with dinner?"

"I can cook."

"Nope, it's taken care of, just go put on what I laid out?"

"Laid out? So, you're dressing me now? Getting awfully demanding, aren't we?"

"You love it too," I smirk, smacking her ass and setting her in the direction of the stairs.

While she's gone, I check on the order, and it's en route. I grab my clothes from the other room where I stashed them while she was napping and quickly get dressed.

I'm in gray, flat front slacks and a wine-colored dress shirt. I smooth my hair down and it falls to my shoulders. That done, I roll up my sleeves and put on my shoes. I want to look good for my woman.

The food arrives and I get everything plated. The first course is a fig and arugula salad, drizzled with balsamic vinegar and honey. I set the seared filet mignon wrapped in bacon in the oven and the strawberry shortcake made with her favorite angel food in the fridge, for now. I light some candles on the table and wait for her to arrive.

I hear the shuffle of her feet on the floor and look toward the doorway. She's got on little ballerina flats and the pale blue, spaghetti strapped, tea length dress I ordered from Nordstrom. It's got this flowy tank top layer that her cleavage is popping out of, and then it falls easily over the bump while giving her room to move. Her hair is down, falling just to her tits, and she's done her makeup in nudes and blush pinks. She looks elegant, yet comfortable, as she looks around the room.

"For me?"

"For us. Call it the first of our monthly date nights."

She raises an eye. "Date nights?"

"I've been thinking and we have a great network of

friends willing to help us as we help them, so at least once a month, regardless of how hectic things get, we are going to have a night that's just for us. Just like we will have nights that are all about the girls and family time."

"That's gonna be hard with a newborn" She rubs the love bun as I invite her to sit.

"We will make it work, it's important that we do. For us. I won't have us lose touch with each other."

She swallows, looking worried. I just lift her face to mine and kiss her. "I love you."

"I love you," she answers.

57

CRYSTAL

MY FAVORITE FOODS, SOFT MUSIC, AND new clothes. If this man were any more perfect, I'd die. During dinner, we talk about how awkward those photo shoots were and laugh about the looks on the interviewer's faces when I had been so frank about us and our sex life.

He's touched me a few times and my body is tingling, our romp in the tub was a new experience, and the perfect primer for tonight and the toy I bought. Well, one of them. I squirm as he rubs the inside of my knee before getting up with our dessert plates. The angel food cake was perfect.

"So, I thought we could go for a late-night swim, and then watch the fireworks from the fire pit."

"I was thinking you and I could make some fireworks," I say, standing up and leaning on the table. "I have a few things I wanted to show you."

"Do you now?" He's looking at me like the meat I am right now. That's good, he's hot and bothered, maybe enough to let me play how I want. He comes up to me as I inch up my dress, revealing a serious lack of panties.

"Hmm, someone's looking to be awfully naughty."

"Take me to our bed and I'll show you just how naughty." I kiss him and he lifts me, taking me out of the room.

❖ ❖ ❖

I pull out the box from Extreme Restraints dot com and put it on the bed nervously. Steve tilts his head in that curious manner while I open it and tilt it toward him. Inside are a few toys I was curious about, so I bought them.

"A violet wand? New cock rings, a strap on, and vibrating plug?" Steve purses his lips with a wry smile. "For me?"

"Um, well, yes. But the strap on is built for you." I bite my thumb nervously as he looks over the mechanism.

"This is for double penetration?"

I nod. "I was curious, and after this afternoon in the tub... Well, now I really want to try it out."

"You don't think it's too much, I mean with the baby?"

"I feel good now, after earlier. I think if we go easy like before, it will be fucking hot." I crawl across the bed, kissing him. "I'd also like you to try the plug..." He sucks in air, pulling up my dress. "I mean, would you let me?"

He pulls back, the thing was made to stimulate the prostate, and the vibrations I thought would be fun. "As long as you can handle the shaking." He smiles and I feel him put it in my hand.

I nod, looking for the lubricant as he looks over the double penetrator, unhooking the harness and sliding the built-in cock ring over himself and fixing it into place.

"It's snug, but it'll hold." He taps the false cock above his own. He's bigger and thicker, but the dildo will take my ass well while he fucks my pussy.

I stroke him, taking him into my mouth, the plug in one hand while stroking him with the other. I begin to suck his sac, taking his balls into my mouth, one then the other. He's up on his knees, pumping down into my mouth as I lay on my back. My hands now free, I begin to play with his ass, and getting him slick with the lubricant, I start to slide the plug into him and he gasps.

I pop off his cock, "You alright?"

"Yeah." He grabs my tits and begins to squeeze as I push deeper, getting it to the hilt, then I turn the end making it vibrate.

He falls forward some and his cock gets harder, thicker. Christ, I can barely get him in my mouth again. He lifts himself and urges me to my knees, my back to him. His fingers are between my folds and I feel him wiping my slickness to my ass. I hand him a little lube packet, he slicks the dildo, and up on his knees, he's behind me.

"You ready, Bella?" his voice waivers as he shakes some. "Fuck…" He's breathing heavily, he must like the vibe. I made a good choice at least.

"Easy and deep, okay?"

He opens my legs wider. Pushing my head down and getting me on my hands and knees, he guides the cocks into me. I'm filled up and he rocks me slowly, each thrust making my eyes roll to the back of my head. This is one of my better ideas.

We make messy, slow, and deliberate love for the rest of the night. He has me coming as the ball drops and I can't think of a better way to start the new year.

❀ ❀ ❀

I'm the first one up. My Beast worked himself hard last night and I decide that I'm going to make him breakfast. It's been a while since I've cooked the morning meal and I could go for something with ham and cheese. I fry up some of the leftover ham from Christmas and chunk it up, scrambling it into my eggs with jalapeño peppers, spinach, and feta cheese. This is gonna be a killer omelet.

I am just plating the thing when Steve comes up behind me, his cock pressing into my back. "I am not eating a cold omelet, Beast."

"I beg to differ." He turns me around, pulling me to him as he lifts my leg.

I moan as he fingers me, getting me ready. I come undone right there in the kitchen, and he pounces me, pinning me to the stove. His kisses devour my panting gibberish and my head swims in multi-orgasmic oceans as he lifts me, going deeper, coming hard and fast. It doesn't last long, but it leaves my legs unable to hold me up and I nearly drop. He picks me and my food up and sits me in the chair, kissing me.

"Eat, I'm gonna check the mail, we forgot yesterday."

I look at the clock and realize it's after ten. Wow, did we sleep in. I dive into my food while Steve goes off for the mail. That's when I remember Rolling Stone said they'd send the copy.

Steve comes in, tearing into some brown paper. "Is

323

that the Rolling Stone cover?"

He nods as his eyes go wide.

"Is it bad?" I can't help but think it's horrible.

He turns the magazine so I can see it. It shows me standing, naked and facing the camera with Steve blocking my lower half with his head and shoulders as he touches the beast bump. That would have been fine, except they titled the article *Steven's Angel*, semi-imposing wings on me that are half wrapped around us.

"Christ," he whispers.

"Are you okay?" I ask quietly.

"Yeah, it's just- I don't know, a messed up picture."

He brings the magazine over and we go through it together. In every picture, I have wings. "I don't see how they can do that without us agreeing first."

"Creative licensing and we didn't ask."

"Hide it and go get dressed, the girls will be here soon."

Steve nods at me. "I'll be up in a minute."

I get to the bedroom and sit down on the bed. I should be getting dressed, but those pictures have set off a new round of tears. Stupid hormones are getting to be too much to handle. I find myself crying over the craziest things. I was watching TV the other day and cried over the animals that need adopting. I came very close to asking Steve if I could adopt a few.

The bed dips beside me and Steve pulls me to him. "Shh, it's okay. It's not all that bad. It could have been much worse."

"I'm no angel and they're leading everyone to believe I saved you."

"Like I said, it could be worse."

I push him away to stand and start pacing. "I didn't save you. You saved you."

"You made it possible for me to realize that I could save myself. So, in a way, what they're saying is true."

"No, it isn't. If I was the angel, they're claiming I am, then I'd have saved you when I saw all the shit I had to see. When I was the one sitting up at night with sick girls or Peggy Sue with morning sickness. Don't you get it? If I were an angel and saved you, I would have made sure you knew then, but I didn't. That makes me a horrible person." I'm standing in front of him and I can feel my legs getting weak from all the emotions flowing out of me.

Steve catches me just as my legs give. "Angels don't do things for us. They help light the way and you've been my light every day for ten years. Even when I tried to deny it, you were there."

"I'm sorry, I don't see it. All I see is the ten years of hell you went through because I didn't stop it."

"Sometimes we have to run through hell in order to find our happiness. You made it bearable."

"I don't think it works that way, but we can agree to disagree. This is going to get worse before it gets better. I'm going to be the bad guy in everyone's eyes," I say, sniffling.

"What's it matter what others think? All that should matter is what we think. Remember the fuss we got when we came out the first time? We showed them that it worked. We opened doors for people who were afraid to come forward about how they lived, how they love. There's nothing wrong with us and anybody who thinks there is can screw themselves."

"It's going to give bad publicity to the band."

"We'll roll with it."

"We, maybe, but everyone else, I'm not so sure."

"If they want me out, I'll leave. I'll find something

else to do with my time. You're all that matters to me right now. You and the girls."

"You can't leave your band because of me or this. I'm just afraid they will look at us, or well, me, different."

"If they don't want us, then yeah, I can leave. Because we're a package. Where I go, you and the girls go."

Just as I go to speak, Maverick yells up the steps. "Anybody home?"

I look at Steve, then at the door before clearing my throat as Steve grabs me with my knees straddling him and throws a blanket around the back of us.

"Up here," Steve yells, then looks at me. "Don't wiggle."

Wiggle? Don't wiggle? Who in the hell is he kidding? I can already feel him growing at my entrance. I look at him, then down when we connect. Steve groans just as Maverick walks into the room, which also happens to be the same time he's fully erect and pulsing at my core.

"Hey, Maverick, how you doing?" Steve asks as he thrusts upward. I bite my thumb to keep from making noise.

"Fuck, man, seriously?" Maverick asks incredulously. "You could have told me, I wouldn't have come on up."

Steve pulls me forward, which only has him pushing into me deeper. There ain't no damn way he's going to fuck me in front of Maverick. "It's all good, man. What's up? How are the girls?"

"Downstairs," Maverick says, but he sounds a bit more muffled.

"You need to get rid of him, or you are a dead man,

Steven Falcone," I whisper.

Steve chuckles and thrusts into me hard. "Alright, we'll be down in ten minutes or so."

"Great, I'm taking the girls out back," Maverick says and the door closes.

"You've got to be kidding me. You didn't just do that!"

"Oh, I did," he says and continues to fuck me.

I grab his face and kiss him as I match him thrust for thrust. It doesn't take long for my walls to tighten around him. I bite down on his shoulder to keep from being too loud, which only spurs him on. He flips us and I'm on my back with him standing and pumping into me. I grab onto one of the pillows and bite into it as he fucks me harder, deeper, and most definitely animalistically. He's frenzied and rough, but I can't stop him because I'm enjoying it. It doesn't take him long to find his release and he's growling like the beast he is.

He pulls out of me, then leans over, kissing me before heading to the closet. I stand and head for the bathroom to clean myself up. It's as I'm wiping myself that I see it... Blood spots.

"Steve," I shout and it comes out in a crumbled mess. I'm freaking out as he strolls into the bathroom.

"What's the matter?" he asks and I just look up at him with tears in my eyes. He spots the cloth. "Ah, fuck, Bella. Did I hurt you?"

I drop to the floor as he runs from the room, screaming for Maverick. It doesn't take long before he's picking me up and putting me on the bed. I'm squeezing the cloth in my hand for dear life.

Maverick pushes through the door. "What's wrong?"

"Fuck, man, I hurt her."

"What do you mean you *hurt* her?"

"She's bleeding."

Maverick walks over to where I'm laying. "Crystal, I need to look at you, but I'm going to be very careful. Okay?" I swallow and just nod at him. "Steve, I need better lighting, a towel, and a wet and dry cloth." Steve gets Maverick everything he needs, he also turns the light on over us and then starts pacing. "I also need you to come over here and hold her hand. I need you to keep *her* calm."

Steve leans down to me, kissing my head. "I'm so sorry, Bella. I'm so, so sorry." I'm trying to pay attention to him, but I can't.

I feel Maverick lifting my ass and easing me back down on the towel. I tense as I feel him touching me and squeeze Steve's hand.

"Hey, easy," Steve says to Maverick "It's okay Bella."

I feel a wet cloth touch me and then the dry one. Maverick finally looks up. "She's torn a bit, but it doesn't look too crazy. She got you a monitor to hear the baby, right?" Steve nods his head yes before choking the word out. "Grab it."

Steve goes to the dresser to get the monitor and hands it to Maverick. Maverick lifts my shirt up to the curve of my breast before rolling it over my belly. I let out a deep breath as I hear the heartbeat.

"He's still going strong. The next twenty-four to forty-eight hours are going to be crucial. I won't leave if it's okay. I can check her every couple of hours. She needs to stay off her feet. It might even be a good idea for the girls to stay somewhere else just to be on the safe side."

Steve nods his head. "I'll check the girls and call

Marissa."

"I'm gonna get her cleaned up. Crystal, do you have any pads?" Maverick asks, finally talking to me. Steve walks out of the room, leaving Maverick and me.

I nod. "In the bathroom, under the sink."

"And panties?"

"Top drawer on the left."

Maverick gets me cleaned up and dressed, then takes care of the towels and cloths in the bathroom. I'm laying here crying when he squats down beside me.

"Crystal, I'm going to do everything I can to keep anything else from happening. Just have faith and we'll get through this," Maverick says, taking my hand in his and bowing his head. I think he's praying, but I'm not exactly sure. I've sent up the occasional prayer here and there, but nothing like he's doing now.

58

STEVE

"I NEED YOU TO HELP ME," I blurt into the phone as Marissa answers.

"Steve? What's wrong?"

"It-it's Crys, I- I fucking hurt her, I need to get the kids outta this house. Maverick is gonna stay with us to keep an eye on her. Fuck, please?"

"Easy, big guy, we're on our way, okay? Hang in there."

I hang up the phone and collapse into a chair. I can't go back up there. I'll just be in the way. I can't be trusted with her. Damn it. I can't believe I let myself get so rough. I know how delicate she really is, but I've been outta control. I never should have done the things I've done over the past couple days.

It's all risky behavior, all dangerous to the baby if too rough and I've just been pounding away like we're still trying to get pregnant. We still have six weeks of high risk, of possible miscarriage, and I'm just treating her like nothing is going on.

Hunter and Jonas are at my feet, they want to go

outside, so I open the door and find Peggy Sue on the other side.

"Daddy, where is she? Is she okay?" she asks, holding her own little bump.

"I- She's with Maverick, upstairs." I point behind me and she pushes by, heading up as Harrison comes up from parking the Bronco.

"Are you all right?" he asks, putting his hand on my shoulder.

"I- don't know. If she- If I-"

"Steve?" Angelica calls and I turn, the flood gate breaking. "Woah, what's happening? Where's Maverick and Crys?" she asks and I just shake my head.

"She's upstairs," Harrison answers. "There's been a complication."

I nod as she looks at me, concerned. "Steve, you gotta come upstairs with me. She needs you."

"I'm just gonna be in the way. I'm just a stupid bear that can't keep his paws to himself and fucked things up again," I say, heading outside. I need the air.

"Hey!" Angelica yells after me. "You are not just a big stupid bear. Get Kellie outta your head, for fuck's sake. You do something to that woman of yours, you didn't mean to do? Fine, it happens, you get a little rough. You can't beat yourself up for it. She's busy blaming herself right now. You gonna let her do that? Gonna leave her with the fact that she could be losing your baby and you're nowhere to be found?" She pushes me backward. "Stop being a bitch and go up there like the man I know you are. Hold her, cry with her, stroke her hair. She needs that right now. Losing a child is the most terrifying feeling and you're leaving her alone! You selfish prick, this isn't about you!" She slams her fists against me.

"Angelica, what's going on? What are you so worked up about?"

"I know what she's going through, I've been where she is! Okay? She can't-you can't leave her alone, she needs you."

I look at her. When we were together, there were always condoms, so I know she's not talking about me. That leaves Kyle or Brent, because I know she never actually closed the deal with Ringo. "Angelica, who?"

"Brent, all right, two years ago. It's why I switched back over to girls. They can't break your heart. The only person I had was Kyle and Lord knows I couldn't tell his brother. He'd have never forgiven himself." She sniffs, then gasps.

I turn around and see Maverick standing in the doorway. Shit...

"Maverick?" Angelica whispers.

"What?" he answers with a question of his own, fuming. I can't leave these two alone, I don't know what he might do. I stand between them.

"I- I'm sorry I didn't tell you," she pleads. "Please don't be angry."

His face is blood red as he balls up his fist, not answering her.

"Please?" she pleads again as Brent and Marissa's Navigator pulls up.

Marissa is out first, headed straight for me and Maverick's whole posture changes as he beelines for the opposite side of the truck and I have to cut him off. Blake sees me and he's by Brent's side in an instant.

"You can't do that," I say, pushing Maverick back toward the house.

Maverick struggles against me, but I am bigger and put my weight into handling him. "What are you gonna do? He doesn't even know why you're coming at him." I say through gritted teeth.

He growls at me, turning away, then he grabs Angelica and heads inside, yelling for Angela.

Marissa looks at me, confused. "Did I miss something, or was he about to eat my husband?"

I nod my head. "And I can't tell you why. It's not my place."

"Uh huh, well, how is Crys then?"

I just look at Brent, who is still standing at the car with Blake, the twins still strapped into the car. He looks confused, but at the same time, doesn't seem curious enough to ask. Which is good for them.

❊ ❊ ❊

Maverick and Angelica have taken vigil over Crys while Marissa helps me pack up the girls for yet another few days. Brent is with the twins in the living room, keeping an eye on the girls and playing with the puppies.

"So, are you gonna tell me now that it's just us, why Maverick is looking at my caveman with murder in his eyes?"

"I really can't, except to say that it's a tense situation that has only just come to light."

"Right, and it's gotten him in a tizzy. I imagine it has something to do with the current situations going on here?"

"I can't say."

"Confirmation, okay, and if he's pissed, it has to do with my husband and his wife, am I right?"

I just nod. Lying to her isn't working, so I am just not talking.

"Just tell me it was from before we all got together."

"Yes."

"Then it doesn't matter, and I don't care." She picks up the suitcases and heads out of the room.

I turn to follow her when there's a commotion downstairs. I make a break for the steps and practically fly down them to find Maverick's got Brent by the throat, pinning him to the wall. I can't hear them, but I can imagine what Maverick's saying. I have to grab Marissa and pull her back as I watch the light drain from Brent's eyes. Maverick nods and drops Brent, who keeps going right on to the floor.

Marissa breaks free from me and I let her go. She stops in front of Maverick and he says something I can't make out, which has her passing him by and going to Brent. I watch as Maverick steps out the back door and disappears into the yard. I take this moment to go and check on Brent, who's still on the floor with his head in his hands.

"Brent?" I ask gently.

"I didn't know," he answers, shock plain in his voice.

"Hey, none of us did, except Kyle, and you know he wasn't gonna say anything."

"But he should have." He wipes his face as I give him my hand and pull him to his feet.

"Nothing to be done."

"Why would she bring it up now? Why dig out an old wound?" Marissa asks. "What does she gain?"

"It wasn't about her, or about you, it was about me being an ass. She was trying to make a point and it got away from her. I don't think she ever intended for you to know."

"I think it's time you guys go; the girls are all

packed and out front already," I say. "I've gotta go upstairs and stop being such a pussy."

They nod and I kiss my girls before heading upstairs.

I knock on the door and Peggy Sue answers, "Yeah, Daddy?"

"Could I have a few with Crys?"

"Um, sure."

Peggy Sue grabs Harrison and Angelica pats my arm as she walks past.

Crystal is lying in bed, not much different than when I left her, only now she's under the blankets and staring out the window.

"Bella?" I ask softly, afraid to get too close to her, afraid I'll hurt her again.

"Yeah?' she answers distractedly.

"I'm here," I say, sitting on the bench at the foot of the bed.

"Come over here," she calls to me and I hesitate. "Don't make me ask you again."

I swallow, getting up and standing in front of her.

"You're still too far away."

I sigh, sitting on the very edge of the bed beside her. I know what she wants, but I'm afraid I'm gonna do something stupid and hurt her.

"Come here." She scoots over a tad and I slip under the covers, and into the bed with her. "You couldn't have stopped this any more than I could have."

"Yes, I could have, I could have said we had gone far enough after last night, or even before you had breakfast this morning, but no, I had to let my cock do the thinking and now look where we are."

"I could have stopped you just as well as you could have stopped, I didn't."

"I'm just- I lost control, I'm not used to being restrained. I mean it's been nine almost ten years since I had to be."

"It's okay, I keep checking for a heartbeat, but I'm having more and more trouble doing it on my own." My heart begins to race. Is she having trouble because he's dying or is she having trouble because she's tired?

"Are you in pain? Has there been any more bleeding?" My voice shakes.

"I'm just spotting, but Maverick says that may happen for a little while."

"What about pain?"

She shakes her head. "I'm okay.'

I take the heart monitor and get it going. There's his heart, strong like a hummingbird's wings. My whole body relaxes as that sound fills the room. "Thank God," I whisper, kissing her on the forehead. "Thank God."

"What are you freaking out about? I told you he was okay."

"I am just glad to hear it." I kiss her head again. "Glad to hear it."

"What's going on downstairs?"

I chuckle sarcastically.

"Spill it. Are they tearing up my house?"

"No, but it's intense."

"Brent still alive?"

"Yup."

She sighs. "He's gonna fall off the wagon."

"Marissa's not gonna let that happen, you know that."

"This one's gonna be harder to stop."

"I don't have time to deal with his shit again."

"Maybe not, but they came running for us. So, if he needs you, you'll go to him."

"I'm staying with you. I have nothing to offer them for him anymore, Kellie's dead."

She touches my face. "Kellie helped him get clean, but she wasn't the one who helped him stay that way."

I sigh. "I know, but if he falls off the wagon again, there may be no pulling him back."

"Possibly not, but at the same time, you're gonna be upset for not being there for your friend."

I pull her to me with a nod. She's right and I hate it. I hate it because it will pull me from her. I curl around her, stroking her hair. Right now, I just want to be near her, and I pray that the next few days see no other harm.

59

CRYSTAL

IT'S BEEN SEVENTY-TWO HOURS AND Maverick has refused to leave the house because I'm still spotting. He had Angelica bring him clothes. I've slept with a man on either side me, watching over me, and I'm starting to wonder if either has slept. They bring my food up here because they don't want me moving around a whole lot. Maverick prays multiple times a day. Steve moved a TV in the room so I could actually have something to do besides play on the computer, which caused issues with both Steve and Maverick. Every time it got close to my belly, they were moving it backward.

Steve's making lunch, then he's supposed to be helping me into the shower. Maverick said no baths, so Steve said he'd jerk the thing out if he needed to. My Beast is broken and I don't know how to get him back. I'm hoping with us seeing the doctor today, that will help.

Just as I think I've found a way out of the bed, Steve walks in with a tray. "What are you doing?" Steve asks and Maverick's head pops up.

"Um, I need to pee." I look between the guys.

Steve sets the tray on the dresser. "Come on. Maverick, lunch."

"Beast, I can go by myself."

"Yeah, but you can't get off the bed by yourself."

"I can, you just refuse to let me."

"Crystal, stop arguing with the man and let him help you," Maverick orders from the dresser.

Steve helps me into the bathroom, then leaves me to it. I look out the window and contemplate shimmying down the drainpipe. If I wasn't afraid of hurting myself, that's exactly what I'd do. I'm about to the point of stabbing myself in the eye or maybe stabbing one of them. I flush to keep up pretenses and wash my hands.

Just as I finish washing my hands, Steve pops his head back in. "You okay?"

"Want me to do a jig and show you?" I snap.

Steve shakes his head. "Come on, have some lunch."

❀ ❀ ❀

Getting to the doctor was a pain in the ass. Maverick had to take our Escalade and go one way, while Adam smuggled us out in the back of his Chevy Malibu. We were squished.

Steve makes sure to help me sit down before walking up to sign me in. I'm out of the house and even just a little freedom feels good. I'm sitting here kicking my feet when I look over and see the Vanity Fair with Steve and me on the cover. I pick it up and start looking through.

"You've got to be fucking kidding me. Bastards."

I'm cussing when Steve sits down beside me.

Steve groans, "Shit."

"You knew about this?"

"I picked it up when it went live the other day."

"One, when did you leave? Two, why was I kept out of the fucking loop?"

"One, I had to leave at least once a day. Two, we didn't want to upset you further."

I twitch just listening to him. I cross my arms over my chest and turn away from the dick. The fucker is only here out of obligation, then he can sit here while I ignore him. I can't handle the sitting any longer. I stand and start pacing the room.

"Bella, please, sit down," Steve whispers.

I grab Steve's hand and drag him to the bathroom. I don't care who's watching, I can't take anymore. Steve shuts and locks the door behind us. I pin him to the door with my finger in his face.

"You are driving me up the fucking wall. I'm fine! We're going to see the doc, he's going to mess with my girly bits like Maverick has for the last seventy-two hours, then he's going to tell me I'm fine. Do I have pain? Fuck yes, I do. My back and ass are killing me. You want to know what I've been thinking about doing for the last forty-eight hours? Forget it! I'll just tell you. I've been thinking if I could just wrap my mouth around your cock and show you I'm okay, you'd chill the fuck out. But *no*, Maverick is on the other side of me. UGH! I can get up and move," I whisper-shout at him.

"Promises, promises."

I cock a brow at him for half a second before dropping to my knees and unbuttoning his pants. I free his cock and suck him into my mouth. His hand is in my hair as I work my mouth over him. He thinks he's being a dick, but I know what he needs. It's part of why he's being the way he is. I swallow so I can work all of him into my mouth. It's not easy, but I can do it. I grab his sack and roll it in my hands as he pumps me on his cock. His head falls against the door and I know I've got him right where I want him. With my other hand, I grab his free one and stick it on my tit. It only takes four more long, hard sucks and I'm swallowing his seed.

I stand, dusting myself off and trying to push him out of my way. Steve grabs me, lifting me to the sink, and his lips are on mine. I wrap my arms around his neck. He feels good against me. I wrap my legs around his waist. This is what we do. We argue, then we fuck, only this time, I'm not allowed and I know that, and at the same time, I'm okay with it. He lifts my shirt and moves my bra out of the way. He rolls my nipple under his thumb, then pinches it before giving it a flick. He moves from kissing to locking his mouth over my nipple and that's all it takes. His breath mixed with the cold air and I'm coming.

He fixes my top and helps me to my feet before righting his pants. He kisses me, then laces his fingers with mine and walks me out of the bathroom. We're only sitting down for a minute when we get called back.

Doctor Ang takes care of the internal check. Then he does our first 4D ultrasound. Looks like our boy is going to be a thumb sucker. I take Steve's hand as we listen to the whooshing sound of our little beast and watch him on the screen. He kisses me on the forehead. I told him I was okay, now maybe he'll believe me.

Doctor Ang leaves me to get dressed and before I can step down, Steve's helping me. I grab my panties and start putting them on when Steve sighs.

"I know I'm a jackass."

"At least that's something we can agree on."

He laughs and nods his head. I bend over to put my pants on and I hide the sting I still have in my side from our romp that led me to be stuck in bed. I slip my flats on and stand for a minute, just looking at my belly.

"What are you doing?" Steve asks me.

I look up at him with pursed lips. "It won't be long before I can't see my feet anymore."

Steve smiles. "It comes with the territory. Just wait, pretty soon you won't be able to put your shoes on."

"That's not even funny."

He walks over to me and kisses me on the head. "Don't worry, you'll have help." I roll my eyes as my inner thoughts run wild with the bastard helping me sit in bed for seventy-two hours.

Ten minutes later, we're sitting in Doctor Ang's office, waiting for him. He walks in and takes his seat across from us. "I've got bad news and good news. Which do you want first?"

"Is the baby okay? Is Crystal okay?"

"The baby is fine. Crystal is torn."

"How bad?"

"She'll heal, but she will tear again during delivery. Sex is off the table for the time being."

"All sex?" Steve asks.

"I can't do anything?" I ask, then smack Steve. "This is your fault."

"Oral is fine, but you have to watch that as well. Later, it can cause her to pop early."

"Alright, so I can still make her come?"

"Yes, of course, you just have to give her time to come off one before sending her into another."

"Was that the bad news?" I ask and God, I hope so.

"Yes, Crystal, it was. Would you like to know how

big your baby is?" I nod. "Your baby is two inches long and weighs about an ounce. So, it's about the same as an apricot."

"Uh, can I sign up for a C-section now? I'd like to keep my shit intact after he comes."

Doctor Ang laughs. "That's not routine, but it is something we can come back to once we figure out how big the baby will be." He hands both of us a pamphlet. "This has all the information you will need to remember for the tear. Just make sure not to sit too long, nor stand. When you sit down, make sure your feet are level with your heart. Otherwise, your sugar levels have been good. Looks like you had one bad day."

"Thank you so much," I say, standing.

"Thank you."

We finish with the appointment and get home. Maverick is sleeping in my chair. "Oh, hell no!" I shout and Maverick jumps.

Maverick stands, looking at us. "How'd it go?"

"I'm fine, you dipshit, and you are going home. I want my house back and it can't happen with you here."

Maverick looks past me to Steve. "What'd the doc really say?"

I walk over to him, grabbing his shirt and pulling him down so he's in my face. "Listen up and listen good. My body, my rules. I got fucked good and tore a little, but I will heal. As for you, the next time you look past me and talk to Steve like I'm not here, you will go home to your wife nutless."

"Yes, Ma'am, I'll go grab my shit, but you call me if you need anything."

"Good riddance," I say, then turn to Steve. "You ready to talk now?"

"What do you want me to say?"

"Anything! Call me a bitch if it will make you feel better."

Steve is rubbing his temples. "I don't want to fight with you. I don't have anything to fight with you over."

"Whatever! You let me know when you're ready to talk. I'll be in the classroom," I say and head that way.

I'm in the classroom, singing and working to *Crazy Bitch* by Buckcherry, setting out tomorrow's work because I'm ready to get back to the thing I do best. I'm swaying when Steve's arms wrap around me. I stop singing instantly and he picks up where I left off.

The song ends and Steve nuzzles into the crook of my neck. "You've got a pretty voice."

"And you must be going deaf."

Steve chuckles. "You want to talk, then talk."

I push away from him so I can see him. "It doesn't work that way, Steve. I'm not just gonna talk while you listen.

"Then how do you expect me..." He stops and sighs in frustration. "Damn it, this is how you communicate. Somebody speaks and the other listens, then the other speaks and that someone listens. I can't address what's wrong if I don't know."

"Us! We're wrong! We connect and then something like this happens all over again. There are times when I'm sure you know me better than anyone, but this past seventy-two hours? I tried to tell you I was okay and you ignored me and treated me like a child! In ten years, you should have learned, if something's wrong, I'm not lying about it. I'd just tell you."

"You told me that I hurt you. I panicked. So, I just did exactly what the doctor told me to do. You wouldn't stop *bleeding*. I was scared. It's why I didn't leave your side for three days. Every moment that I *was* away from you, I kept expecting to get the call from Maverick."

I walk up to him and look up. "I tried to tell you, but you apparently don't trust me."

"What do you want from me? The bleeding wouldn't stop. I was reacting to that."

"At first I was bleeding, then I told you it was spotting, but I wasn't worried."

"Look, I overreacted, but I'd rather have been safe than sorry. I love you too much to put you through that."

"If we have a miscarriage, then it just means we weren't ready, but I really don't see that happening."

"If we have a miscarriage, then it's my fault and I'm terrified you'll never forgive me."

"What I'm never going to forgive you for is not trusting me. I know my body better than anyone and I'm telling you that I'm okay."

"I don't know what to say to that. I…" He trails off, taking his hands off me defeatedly. "I'll just go." He walks away and I stand here, watching him go. Then, I hear a car pull away. Maverick and Adam have already gone and now Steve. Apparently, I can be alone. I finish up what I'm doing and head for my chair.

60

STEVE

SHE WON'T FORGIVE ME FOR NOT TRUSTING her. There's nothing I can do with that. What am I supposed to do with that? I left her in the classroom, and all I can think of is the taste of sweet bourbon oblivion.

We're already pregnant, I've never had a problem with the booze, so long as I was kept in the right company. My own being the best. Unable to stare at the four walls anymore, I take the keys and I'm out the door, slamming past the reporters camped out trying to get pictures. They attempt to give chase, but I'm too fast and soon lose them on the highway.

I drive out to the strip, and head for the MGM Casino, they were always happy to take my money. I go in and head to the Black Jack table, and here comes the waitress.

"Can I help you?" She smiles, looking me up and down, licking her lips. "Hey, Steve, long time."

Fuck, she's cute, and I realize as she finishes talking that I've had her a couple times. On those nights when I couldn't stand to be in bed with Kellie and came out here to drink and sleep it off.

"Um, yeah. Aggie, right?"

She nods, caressing my shoulder. "You want your usual? Bourbon, neat, right?"

I nod. I play a few hands and even win, doubled my three hundred to six. I'm six drinks in when I wander out of her section. I can't have the temptation, not when I'm drinking and she was getting awful grabby. As I'm headed out, I'm grabbed by the arm and pulled into an alcove.

Long arms wrap around my neck and cherry lip gloss crosses my tongue. I push Aggie back, I remember the lip gloss. "What are you doing?" I ask, wiping my mouth.

"Thought you might wanna party," she says as another girl comes up behind her, a little red head that couldn't be more than twenty-two.

"Um, no, honey, I'm an engaged man."

"Really? You were a married one and it never stopped you," Aggie smirks. "This is Irene, and she can suck that cock like a champ."

"I... Hmm..." Aggie has my cock in her hand, squeezing. My eyes roll, and for a few strokes, I'm there with her.

"You always liked it two at a time," Aggie says and I hear Kellie's voice. I push away, fixing my pants. What the fuck?

"Yeah, sorry, but that's just not me anymore."

The girls pout, letting me pass and I stumble out the door. I make it to my car and lock myself inside. I'm drunk, not sloppy, but enough that I know I'm not driving anywhere far.

I pull out my phone and shoot Kyle a text. "Party at

MGM, you should come."

I climb out of the car and walk over to the liquor store where I buy a fifth of Southern Comfort and a bottle of cranberry juice. I haven't eaten anything and need the sugar to level me.

My phone goes off and it's Kyle, texting me to stay put, he's on the way. I collapse to the curb and start to work on my bottle. I can feel the sweet release of the liquor. I need to be numb, and not think about Kellie, or about Crystal, about the fact that I'm fucking up. I just need this, I need the cold darkness that it brings me.

I don't know how long I've been on the curb, but I hear boots approach and a hand is extended to me. I look up to find Ringo.

"You've got someone at home worried about you."

I scoff, "She's probably reveling in the chance to do whatever she wants. Where's Kyle? I want to party."

"Kyle's with Crystal. You left her home alone. Reporters were in the back yard."

I shake my head. "I thought I'd gotten them to follow me. Man, I can't do this. I thought I could, that it was what I wanted, but it's all fucked up. I'm gonna fuck this all up. She's already said she won't forgive me for not trusting her. So what I do? Prove she can't rely on me. Kell, she knew, she knew I was a hapless bastard. She did the right fucking thing, she got out." I try to get up and slip back down onto my ass. I'm fucked and I know it. Nothing I can really do about it. The damage is done.

"You grow the fuck up and prove her wrong. I was with Kyle when he got the call asking if you were with him. She was crying when we got there. She's worried about you."

I glare at Ringo. "Who the fuck are you to tell me to

grow up? You, the perpetual sober child? So afraid of what the world is gonna think or say that you never move. Me? I take care of business, I make sure my kids are cared for, food's on the table, and my woman, until recently, was satisfied. Fuck, for the better part of ten years, I've taken care of two women plus groupies and cocktail waitresses. I just wanna be able to let it loose once in a while. I've fucking earned it. If I wanna drink, I'm gonna fucking drink. I could be balls deep in two MGM floor girls, but I said no because of Crys. If that's not adulting, then something is wrong, because six months ago, we wouldn't be having this conversation because I'd be too busy getting my tip wet," I growl. "I've changed my world for that woman and she can't see that everything I did was to protect her. Even now, I'm not there because where I am in my head isn't good for her."

Ringo shakes his head at me. "I'm sober because of Brent, but I've stayed that way because I've watched what it's done to everyone else in this band. Crystal is pregnant, she's still learning how to deal with all the emotions. You've just had a big scare and she's dealing with it the only way she knows how. That little one has so much bottled up and it's only natural for her to pop. You wanted this baby, but now you've walked out on her. The only thing she's worried about is you not driving drunk for the girls' sake. If you don't pull out of this funk, you're going to go home to a cold bed."

"She doesn't want me there. I can't fix what she's got wrong with her because she won't tell me. Her giving up on me for protecting her is fucked, man. I love her, but I think that she's just hormonal enough to throw it all away because I overreacted. If my bed is cold, it's because she won't get into it with me." I get up, stumbling to my car. I pull up my Uber app. "I'll go home, but it won't be with you."

* * *

That sun is too fucking bright. I wake up, still dressed and alone in my bed. Fuck, I don't even remember getting home. I look at the floor and there is the rest of the bottle I bought, quite empty. I straighten out and scratch my balls. Crystal, I wonder if she is even here or if Ringo took her.

I head out of the bedroom and check the girl's rooms, empty, at least they never came home. I need coffee before I try and sort through this. As soon as I hit the bottom step, I'm smacked up the back of the head. I turn with a roar and am faced by Kyle, who's pushing me down and onto my ass.

"You irresponsible, selfish prick," he snarls. "You've got it all, have had it all, and you're throwing it away! You call me, knowing the fucked time I'm having, to party? You are lucky I was already fucked, or I might have actually given you the party you were looking for. Instead, I called Ringo because she called me, looking for you. She's been up all night in that nursery of yours, trying to make sense of what she did to drive you to this. She blames herself for every fucked-up thing you do." He is screaming through his teeth, he looks like I feel and has the nerve to yell at me?

I go to get up and he puts his foot on my neck. "You need to pull it together, man. You and Crys, man, you are good, that girl deserves good, she deserves you to make good on your promises to her. You've promised to love her, take care of her and that baby. Are you gonna be a fucking deadbeat drunk? Or are you gonna be a father? Because you can't be both. I won't let you. I won't let you put hands on them. I'd fucking kill you. You understand me? You think you're big and bad, and you may well be, but if you hurt her, hurt your kids, there won't be shit left of you to identify."

I grab his foot, twisting his ankle, and he steps off, hopping backward as I pull myself off the floor. I want to hit him, need to hit something for the pain in my head, but I know that it won't do me a lick of good. I dust myself off and head back up the stairs and toward the nursery.

I open the door to find Crystal with her feet pulled up into the double rocker. By the soft kitten level of her breathing, I can tell she's asleep.

I can feel the anguish fill me and I hit my knees beside her. Pulling her knees toward me, I put my head in her lap. She flinches awake and looks down at me.

"You're home?"

I nod, grasping her sides. "Bella, I'm so sorry. I'm- I don't know what to do."

She's quiet, and I glance up, her hands are protecting her belly while she stares at me. "You need a shower, you stink, the girls are coming home and you're making me sick. The liquor is coming off you in waves."

I sniff, wiping a hand down my face and pulling back to look at her. "I'm sorry." I look into her eyes, searching for the love that she has for me only to see her disappointment and sadness.

I get up and head for our room. Stripping off the clothes from the night before, I toss them in the hamper and look in the bathroom mirror. Fuck, I've got cherry red lipstick on my lip and my cheeks. There's no way she missed it, but she didn't say anything either. I wrap a towel around my waist and head back to the nursery where she's rocking in the chair.

"Crys, I didn't do anything but gamble and drink. The lipstick on me, I turned them down, that's when I called Kyle."

"Okay," she answers quickly, not even looking at me.

"I need you to believe me, Bella. Any fucking thing I've ever done, I was honest about, you know that. You've known me long enough to have realized it. I never kept it hidden, and I told you, it's just us. I mean that. I may not have been able to keep off the liquor, but I stayed away from the strange."

"Believe it or not, I do actually believe you because if you had slept with somebody, it would have been the first thing you said. It's how it's worked for ten years."

I swallow and nod my head. "I love you. You may not believe that right now, but there's nothing that I wouldn't try and do for you. Last night wasn't about you, not really, it was about me. About doing something I could control because I feel like there is little right now where I get to have a say. I drank because it made me feel like the man that could take anything on, but in the end, all I really wanted was for you to forgive me for being so protective. For being so stupid and not being the man you deserve. Last night, I failed you, failed him, and us, and I don't know where we go from there."

She continues to rock in the chair, holding her belly, barely looking at me. She glances my way for a moment, then look away. "You know, in ten years, I've watched you be the best man you can be, I've watched you fall, I've watched you deal with more than any one man should have to, I've watched you be the best daddy to three girls that I've ever seen in my life. I watched you get clean when you laid in bed for hours unable to move, but when you came to me and said you wanted to do this, that you were positive of it, I'm not sure you were ready. I just hope by the time he's here... You are."

I'm in tears as I look at her. I want to pull her to me, feel her arms around me, have her stroke my hair and tell me she loves me, I want so many things, but I'm not the man who deserves them. I don't say anything to her. What can I say that I haven't already? My words haven't been enough to bring her to me, and going to her when I'm not wanted, to be rejected again, will kill me. I turn from her, dropping my head like the scolded child I am and head to clean myself up.

61

CRYSTAL

I KNOW I SHOULDN'T HAVE LET HIM WALK away and I probably should follow him, but right now, I can't console him. I made dinner for everyone before the girls got home. Now, the girls and Steve are in the living room, looking for a movie while I make them popcorn. I figure they will spend some time with Daddy tonight since I plan to start their schedule back tomorrow.

I set the popcorn on the table and Sue Ellen grabs my hand. "Mommy Crys, will you watch with us?"

I smile down at her. "I was thinking a daddy night."

I look up at Steve and he's got his face in his palm when Mary Ann grabs me. "You have to watch it with us. You've wanted to see it too."

"Please," Sue Ellen begs.

"Okay, get up there by Daddy and I'll get me a drink." I turn and head for the kitchen only to almost face plant because I wasn't watching where I was going. If Steve hadn't wrapped an arm around me and pulled me to him, I could have hurt myself.

"Be more careful," Steve says.

I look at him for a long second. I'm starting to miss the us before a baby. "Thank you," I say, pulling myself from his lap.

I get into the kitchen and lean against the counter before making myself a glass of tea. I calm my features and get myself settled on the couch beside Sue Ellen. Steve doesn't say anything, just hits play on the movie. It's *Trolls* and the girls sing and dance a bit through it.

I've glanced at Steve here and there, but when the song *True Colors* plays and it takes everything in me to keep it together. I wipe a tear away, then excuse myself. Walking quickly down the hall and into the bathroom, I turn the water on. I don't want to take the chance on the girls hearing me as I lose it.

Steve and I have problems that we didn't have before the baby and I just don't know how to get back to there. I'm not sure how long I'm in the bathroom, but when I come out and make my way down the hall and to the couch, they're all gone. The movie is on pause at the moment I left, which only brings on a new set of tears.

I walk around the couch to grab the remote and turn the movie off. I set the remote down on the table as I turn to leave and see Steve leaned against the counter, watching me.

"You alright?" he asks.

"I wish, but not really," I say, wiping tears away.

He kind of shrugs his shoulders. "What do you want me to do about it?"

I know I look like some stupid weeping kid. "I want you to hold me. I want you to kiss me. I want us to be the us we were before because at least then, we got along," I blurt out.

He sets his drink down, coming over to me and wrapping his arms around me. "That I can do."

"We suck at this relationship thing," I say through my crying.

Steve strokes my hair. "No, we suck at communicating about this relationship. We've been in a relationship for ten years. I've never been easy to live with. I'm not gonna get easy to live with. When I'm hurt, I lash out, I'm sorry?"

"Our relationship has changed though, and since it has, we've had lots of problems. I'm not good at this pregnant and hormonal thing, I'm sorry."

Steve chuckles. "Nobody is good at pregnant and hormonal. You've got twice the number of hormones running through you and I can't help but be protective like I am. I worry that's not going to change. I worry because I care."

"I don't want you to quit being overprotective or worrying. I just want you to trust me when I say I'm okay, to let me breathe and not lock me down."

He shakes his head. "All I can do is say I'll try."

"Can we agree Maverick doesn't get to inspect or touch me in certain places anymore?"

"Yes."

"Good, because if it was just you in bed with me, I would have been okay. He made everything worse."

"From now on, it's just us."

"Promises, promises."

Steve chuckles again. "That's not fair."

"There's nothing fair in love and war."

"I don't want to be at war with you."

"And I hate being at war with you. So, how do we get past this?"

Steve bends down, kissing me. "We go to bed and I

make you scream."

I lift a brow at him. "Again, promises, promises."

He picks me up and carries me to our bed.

* * *

Steve and I made up, but not in the way we'd both like to. We still have a bit before we are allowed to have sex again. I feel okay, but I know where the scare is. I'm just starting to doze off like the snoring beast cuddled next to me when his phone rings.

"Hey, wake up, your phone's ringing," I say, elbowing him.

He groans, rolling over for his phone. "What?" I hear a pause. "Shut the fuck up. What are you talking about?" He sits up, which has me rolling to my back. I look over and his hand is in his hair. "No, I didn't," he growls. "What do you want me to do about it?" Another pause. "No, she won't do another interview." A longer pause. "I'll pay the fucking fine, but no." I sit up in bed and turn toward him. He sticks his hand out at me, but then grabs my leg, rubbing my thigh. "You do what you gotta do. I'm going back to fucking bed."

Steve hangs up his phone and throws it across the room. I crawl into his lap. "Beast?"

"That was Christy…"

"I kind of sorta figured with the way you were talking."

"They got shots of us coming out of the clinic and apparently our pharmacy records were leaked. It's going to be all over the papers in the morning. Christy thinks we should do another interview. Garner sympathy."

"Maybe we should. If it's out there, we're going to have to talk about it, but it won't be to Vanity Fair."

Steve's got his fingers on his temple and I straddle him so that I can get his full attention. He looks at me.

"We didn't want it out there, but we don't always get what we want. Technically, the problem isn't with you, so it's not like you have a lot to talk about. If we can pick the magazine, it might not be so bad."

"I don't want to put you through another interview."

"You're being overprotective again."

"Who are you thinking?" he questions defeatedly.

"People. It's massive and it's not strictly music. It gets to everyone. That or Ellen. Think about it, if it's something like that, records will fly off the shelf."

"I guess we call their editor. Are you sure?"

"Yeah, I've learned a thing or two over the course of these past ten years. If we go to them, we can usually run down the list of questions and tell them yes or no."

"Right. You're a smart cookie."

"I try."

"I think I broke my phone."

"I think I want to take your mind off it." He raises a brow at me. "I want to *try* something." He gives me this worried look. "Don't give me that look." I bend just enough so my belly is touching his and kiss the smiling fool.

He's very hesitant as I grab his hands that are clenching the bed and put one on my hip and the other on my tit. He shifts under me, which means I'm doing my job.

"Crys, what are you doing? I'm going to hurt you!"

"You ain't gonna do anything to me, but get your tip wet. I want your shorts off and I want you laying down."

"You kind of have to get off me," he says.

I move off his lap, then strip the shirt I'm wearing. He takes off his shorts, throwing them onto the floor before getting into the center of the bed and laying on his back. He's watching me closely.

I climb so I'm straddling him, but I don't move to sit on him. "We're going to take this slow and I'm leading while you follow. We good?"

"Yeah, we're good."

"Do I need to chain you to the bed?"

He laughs. "Would you like me to break the bed?"

"Wouldn't happen this time. I made sure of it." His hands rub up my legs. "If you can't handle it, we stop." He nods at me and I grit my teeth. "Beast, this isn't your first time and I've ridden you more than once."

"Yeah, but this time, I'm afraid you might just break me."

"Then I'll have to fuck you till I put you back together. Right?" He smirks at me, but I can still feel the nervous energy coming from him. "Alright, you're being a pussy. I told you I'm fine and I'll keep being fine, but, Beast, I need you hard so I can use you the way I want to."

His eyes dart around the room. He's thinking that's a step in the right direction. I'm pulled down and he's kissing me. "Sit on my face so I can eat my way to your heart."

"As good as that sounds, this needs to be about you too. You don't get off with me on your face."

"No, but it gets me hard."

I scoot up the bed and the rest of the night is spent with me fucking his face or riding his cock. Both felt amazing, but only one has My Beast biting and suckling me.

I wake up and pull myself from the bed. Last night

was just what we both needed and I'm ready to go again, but I need to give myself time. After relieving myself, I head to the sink to wash my hands. Looking at myself in the mirror, I start to stress.

"God Damn! I'm a fucking Dalmatian. Fuck!" I shout in order to wake the sleeping beast.

It takes about a half a minute and Steve comes in, big cock swinging. "What are you hollering about?"

"I'm a fucking Dalmatian," I say, turning so he can see me.

He's looking at me. "Good look."

I look at him like he's lost his mind and state plainly. "Interview and pictures."

"People lets you keep your clothes."

"Um, they will still want the bump."

The beast wraps his arms around me. "I'm sorry, I got carried away. I'll do better this time."

"No, this time right now, mister. Girls need feeding and I have classes to teach."

Steve kisses me and gets into the shower. I just get dressed and head down the stairs to start breakfast. After breakfast, it's time to get this house back on a schedule.

62

STEVE

MY PHONE SURVIVED. I wish it hadn't, but it did. I get out of the shower and hearing it ring, I answer without looking at it.

"Steve?" It's Christy again, now what does this fucktard want?

"Queen of Africa, actually." I raise my voice an octave.

"No time to play with you, boy. You talk to the wifey about an interview?"

"We'll do People, now leave me the fuck alone."

"Can't, you also have an award show to go to. So, get your asses in gear, People's Choice is the tenth and you will all be present, or I will be forced to consider you in breach of contract."

"I told you we weren't doing appearances. Not until after the baby, you didn't have this issue with Brent."

"The hell I didn't, but you had made your quota for the year already. If you don't make at least four appearances, I can fine you, and consider your contract null and void, dropping you from the label."

I get quiet.

"Now you're understanding me. I'll email the particulars and we will see you on Wednesday in LA." He hangs up, that fucker is holding us hostage. I sigh roughly and get dressed before going downstairs.

I can smell food. Crys is cooking. I usually do the morning meal, but I guess she couldn't wait. She's just plating, and I'm watching, I've gotta tell her the news.

Pregnant and hungry, a good combination for a one track mind. She pays zero attention to me as I stand here. The girls come down and Mary Ann sits at the table, but Sue Ellen goes to Crys, hugging her.

I watch. These kids love her, always have. I smile while they debate her taking her own plate to the table.

"I've got the plates, problem solved," I say, grabbing three plates, putting them on my forearm, then grabbing the last one in my other hand and heading for the dining table. I set the food down as my girls follow.

Not sure how to broach the topic, I just ask the table outright. "So, who wants to go to L.A. this week?"

Mary Ann lifts her head, "Is everybody going? Brent and Angelica too?"

I nod as Crys scratches her head. "Why?"

"People's Choice Awards." I don't look happy. "Christy set it up, I don't have a choice, he threatened our contract."

"Of course, he did," she laments. "Girls, looks like we're going shopping."

Sue Ellen and Mary Ann giggle and bounce, happy as clams. Crys, on the other hand, looks like she could strangle me.

"I'm sorry," I mouth.

"Later," she mouths back.

"Can we go to Disney?" Sue Ellen looks up hopefully.

I look at Crystal, unsure.

"Yeah, can we?" Mary Ann asks. "We were supposed to go last time, but never did."

The fiasco with the tainted water messing everyone up and tossing Brent out of the wagon had killed our plans for Disneyland last time. The girls have never been and it's about time. I just don't know how she's gonna react to it.

"Let me see what I can do."

"Yay!" Sue Ellen shrieks and Mary Ann smiles.

✻ ✻ ✻

As soon as Crystal goes upstairs to get dressed, my phone dings. She's sent a mass message to find out who else wants to go to Disney. The response is EVERYONE…. So much for no more parties or get togethers.

I go upstairs and find her half naked on the laptop. "What are you doing?"

She looks up. "Booking."

"It could have waited for you to put on pants."

"Possibly, but at the same time, it has to be done, or I'll be waiting until the last minute and lose my mind. Any idea what everyone is gonna want to do?"

"Brent and Kyle will be on kid duty since they will want to go on everything they possibly can. That will pull Ringo into the shenanigans, probably Marissa too, so the question is what do you want to do with free, no kid time?"

"You're gonna go on rides with them."

"This isn't about me, it's for the girls. I'm staying

with you. Do you want to hit the spa too while we are there?"

She's ignoring me as she pulls out her calculator and starts to tally up the cost of this little excursion. She keeps asking what we are doing.

"I don't care how much, we have to go shopping, Adam is downstairs and I already canceled Maverick and Angelica bringing Angela for classes."

"But I have to get us booked in a room."

"I like the last one, the El Captain, tell Brent to take the Arcadia, and let's get going. As for everything else, get the all access passes for sixteen days."

"Sixteen? But I have an appointment."

"Sixteen, we will move your appointment. I want to make Peggy Sue's lousy sweet sixteen up to her. She was gone and never got anything good. She's gonna love this."

Crystal pulls up her calendar, looking at it. So, that's the twenty-sixth, which means I have to get back before the doctor closes that day for another appointment."

"All doable with the jet." I bend down, sliding a hand across her breast. "Now, come on, get dressed before I change my mind and just lock us in here for the afternoon." I kiss her neck and ear.

"You can't lock us in here, I won't have anything to wear. I have to find something to go over the ever-growing bump." She groans as I lift her to her feet, taking away the laptop.

"Clothes. Now. Or you will never see this orange monstrosity again."

"I'll just buy a new one. If you lose it, I'll kill you. It has my lesson plans on it."

"It's safe, now get dressed."

"Fine." She shakes her ass at me as she goes into the closet while I call Peggy Sue.

* * *

Neiman-Marcus, Pea in a pod, Macy's, and Lord and Taylor all had zero as far as gowns that Crys was interested in went, then we go past this Mommy and me joint and she steps in front of me, hitting the brake. I guess she likes the look of the place. All pink and blue awnings and a wedding gown for a bump right in the window with flower girl dresses alongside it.

We go inside and every woman that works here seems to be in some stage of pregnancy. They welcome us with open arms, complimentary beverages, and healthy snacks. The girls take a muffin to split and Crystal makes a beeline for the little girl dresses displayed on the racks. They are in all colors and shapes.

She looks at the girls and pulls out like four dresses instantly. Peggy Sue smiles and joins her.

"We can start a dressing room if you like," a woman with a bump just a bit larger than Crystal's offers, pointing as a tall young man comes to be at Crystal's side. "This is George, he will be happy to be your gofer while I, Belinda, can assist with any fit or color questions you may have."

Crystal hands over the dresses as Belinda walks me over to the dressing rooms where there are big cushy chairs and couches. "You can have a seat here and we would be happy to get you anything you need."

"Um, thanks. I'm good, just wanna see what she picks."

Harrison sits, getting comfortable. "This is gonna be a while."

"Of course." Belinda walks away and I watch from the doorway as Crystal loads up George's arms and Peggy Sue seems to have her own assistant now as well.

The girls come and grab me to show me a multi-colored bit of ruffled insanity. While the little girl's dress version is cute, the mommy dress is just too loud, and that's saying something coming from a Rockstar.

"Think Mommy Crys will like it?" Sue Ellen asks.

"I think it is a little much, but you can show her at least." I grab the dress and the matching ones for the girls and head for the dressing room. Crys is there, just now heading into the room. She must have two dozen different dresses between her and the girls. George sets up the rooms for my angels while Peggy Sue is already coming out in a short little cream dress with a high belt, showing off the eight week bump that looks more like a twelve week one. Christ, my baby girl is getting hit with the big babies. She twirls around and while I think it's a little *short,* Harrison likes it.

She beams with a squeal. Lord, I am hoping for just as fast an approval with Crystal. No such luck. The first dress, she can't get over her ass, and the next three, she complains don't show off the bump enough. Complaining as she is, I'm surprised when she gets quiet, looking at Sue Ellen and Mary Ann. The little ones are in these identical dresses, except one is pale pink and the other is pale blue. They are full-on princess inspired gowns, with layers of ruffles and little silver details all over.

"I like these, I really like these." She smiles and the girls sigh, letting out the little breaths they were holding.

"Finally," Mary Ann says, relieved, as Sue Ellen punches her in the arm.

"Be nice."

"Shut up, I'm just glad we don't have to put on any more dresses, jerk face."

"I'm not a jerk face, jerk face."

"Girls, seriously, where do you hear this garbage?"

"Kyle and Ringo," Mary Ann blurts out as I get between the girls.

Oh, brother, the things these two hear when they go to Brent's. "You hear the mouths on these two, Crys? I need to talk to those idiots about what they say. I mean-" I'm rendered speechless as she comes out of the dressing room wearing a cobalt blue gown that slips off her shoulders with lace trim at the bust. The bump is on full display as the dress clings to her hips and falls down her legs. She turns around and the dress is backless with a lacy cut-out from the mid-thigh to the train on the floor. With her hair down, she looks exquisite.

"And here I thought you could never shut up."

I stand with a low growl, walking over and wrapping my arms around her. "When something this beautiful is in front of me, there are no words to express how I feel. Only actions." I press my hardening cock against her back, kissing her bare shoulder.

She clears her throat. "Be good. There are children here, after all."

"You make me want to make a mess of you."

She looks down. "I'm pretty sure you already have."

"Buy this dress, buy it so you can wear it once and I can rip it off you after with my teeth," I whisper against her skin.

"We're not paying this kind of money for a dress for you to tear it up."

"Then buy two."

63

CRYSTAL

FOR THE LAST THREE DAYS, I'VE SHOPPED, booked, and ordered a ton of shit for our trip to California. I had to see the doctor today before we leave tomorrow. He said that the beast and I are both doing fine. Steve made sure to ask how much I would need to sit down if I'm walking a lot. I was shocked by the doc's answers. He said so long as my feet aren't swelling and my numbers are good, I can walk, but rest here and there.

We've had dinner and I'm trying to finish packing everyone before it's time for bed. Steve's outside, making sure everything's locked up since we'll be gone for eighteen days. Sue Ellen's packed and I'm finishing up Mary Ann when arms wrap around my belly.

"We're secured and the pups are at the kennel," Steve says.

"Good. Can you take the cases downstairs and put them by the door? I've got everything packed and laid out for the morning. Meaning, the girls are done and it's just us left."

"I'll grab the stuff, but leave my suit."

"Uh, you kind of need it."

"I ordered something and it's going to be waiting for us in L.A."

"That's all I get?"

"You'll like it."

"Will my dress match?"

"That's why I had it ordered, and don't forget your *diamonds*."

"Just another thing to add to the ever-growing list."

"Wear them so we won't have to pack them."

I push his chest. "Go away, Beast, and do what I said. The girls need to go to bed and that's on you."

He kisses me before grabbing the stuff and heading downstairs. I turn the light out and go to my room. I get mine and Steve's suitcases on the bed as well as a small one for odds and ends. I've got all the undergarments packed for both of us. I don't want to pack the shower shit till we've both had ours.

I'm in the closet, pulling down a few dresses when Steve yells, "Bella, where are you?"

"I'm in the closet," I shout.

"You're not supposed to be up here." He wraps his arms around me and bites my ass cheek.

"Ouch," I say, smacking him.

"Don't put it on display if you don't want it man handled."

"Go, take a shower so I can finish packing."

He picks me up and pulls me off the stool I'm standing on. "Only if you come with me."

"Beast, I have to finish what I'm doing."

"If you could see it, you'd be staring at my caring face."

"Put me down, you over grown ape. I can have fun

later, but I need to finish here. Is your carry-on bag packed?"

"Yeah, I'm all done."

"No, you aren't. Your suitcase is empty."

"Yes, and I'll fill it while we're in California."

"Don't make me tell you again. Put me down!" I say sternly.

Steve lets me slide out of his hands and I turn to face him. "You need clothes, which I'm trying to make sure you have. At least enough for a few days."

"Throw in my jeans and a few band T-shirts and we'll be good to go. Have you washed them since you wore them all?"

I punch him in the gut. "Everything is washed, except what we have on right now. Have I ever not made sure your shit is clean?"

"Ugh, you're snappy tonight."

"I've got a headache and I'm stressed, so yeah, I am."

"When was the last time you checked your sugar?" he asks, concerned.

"This morning. I've been busy."

He looks at me, shakes his head, and walks away. I climb back up on my stool and grab a few more dresses down before moving to Steve's shirts. Steve grabs my hand and stabs me with the stupid needle thing to check my sugar. It stings.

"It's two-forty, not good. We're really going to have to watch what you eat while we're away."

"Doctor Ang said it'd get worse the bigger I got. It ain't my fault I'm carrying a beast that's always hungry."

He sets the meter down, coming over to me and running his hands up my leg, then under my dress before landing on my belly. "Don't let your mommy kid you. She loves eating for two." He kisses me on the belly.

He starts kissing down my belly and I grab his ponytail, pulling him away. "*No*, I told you. I've got stuff to do."

"Alright, what can I do to help?"

"Take your shower and leave me alone."

Steve drops his head dejectedly and walks out of the room. I finish getting everything packed, including my carry-on bag with my necessities. I sit down on the bed to wait for Steve to get done in the shower. He doesn't usually take this long, meaning he's taking care of his need to get off.

* * *

Steve and the rest of the band have to practice for tonight while the rest of us get ready together. We're waiting for them now at the carpet. We're back behind a curtain till they get here. Let's just say there are bellies and babies everywhere in this crowd.

I'm watching and talking to different people I've met over the years. This ain't my first rodeo, it's mostly keeping the girls calm and babies from crying. I'm reminding myself that questions will be coming and fast. Just smile and don't trip.

I jump as I feel hands on my belly till I hear the growl in my ear and know it's my beast. "Took ya long enough. I'm melting out here."

He turns me around and kisses me. "Don't be mad," Steve says and I pull away. He's got his eyebrow pierced, double stud with cobalt blue balls attached.

I open my mouth, then shut it to finally open it

again, "You got to be fucking kidding me!"

"She shit yet? Oh, hi," Kyle mumbles and he's got his fucking tongue pierced as well as his brow.

I look from Steve to Kyle before smacking the both of them. "You went and got this done when you were supposed to be practicing and left me with *MAVERICK!*" I whisper-shout at Steve.

"They broke for lunch. We ended up next to a parlor."

"Dog house, dog house, and a little more dog house."

Steve grabs me by the ass and pulls me to him. "I'm sorry, I was working, just got distracted for a minute or two."

I raise a brow at him. "Did you do anything else to your body that I should know about?"

"No, just dressed exquisitely," he says, stepping back so I can see him. He's got on low slung black leather pants, cobalt blue shirt, a fitted black leather vest, and it's all paired with his black steel-toe boots.

"Did you buy a bike too?"

"If I did?" he challenges me.

My nostrils flare. "Steven Robert Falcone, you better tell me the truth right fucking now."

"You wouldn't ride on my bike?"

I grab his hands and place them on the belly that keeps growing. "Does it look like I could?"

"No, I haven't bought it yet."

"Are you going through a midlife crisis? If you are, you can tell me."

"The only crisis I'm having is keeping these pants in check with you in that dress. Shall we?"

Sue Ellen walks up to us before I can answer. "Can I have my eyebrow done like Daddy?"

I just look at him for a response. He answers her and I smile. "Not till you're eighteen, then I can't stop you."

I grab her hand. "Ignore him, we'll talk about age appropriate piercings when we get home." I look back over at Steve. "We're last. They have Brent going first, then Kyle and Ringo with Angelica following them. I was able to get them to let Peggy Sue and Harrison go, the girls in the middle, then us."

Steve and I make small talk about how our day went as we wait to walk onto the carpet. He asked me if I ate about sixty times. I take a deep breath as we step up to the carpet. I put on a fake smile as the girls start walking and waving for the cameras.

Steve wraps an arm around me and kisses me on the temple. "We've got this, it's a cake walk."

"Yeah, I'm just not ready for the questions."

"They're going to come fast, ignore half and answer the ones you like."

"Not my first rodeo, Beast."

We get the nod and begin walking. Once we make it to the first section, we stop and pose as the questions start.

"Steve, when did you propose?" a reporter shouts.

"On Thanksgiving."

"Crystal, when are you due?"

"July."

"How long have you been trying to get pregnant."

"It took a few tries, but we finally got there," Steve answers, rubbing my belly.

We move on to the next set of cameras and get ready for more questions.

"How are the girls taking their mother's passing?"

"No comment," Steve says and pulls me along. At

the next stop, the questions come again.

"How do you feel about them wanting to reopen the investigation into Kellie's death? Many people believe it was a suicide." a reporter asks.

Steve's body is tense and he steps toward the reporter. I grab his arm and place that hand on my belly to hold him back. "I don't know what you're talking about. This is neither the time nor the place. Call my manager so he can tell you to kiss my ass."

Steve takes me and we stop at the next round, these questions are getting worse and worse.

"Would you like to tell us why you changed your name, Miss Howard, from Hayley Berlet Ayres?"

I swallow and take a step back. That's supposed to be a sealed record. "No, no comment," I say, stumbling over the words a bit.

The next bit is much the same. "Why did you change your name? When did you change your name? Who are you hiding from?"

We make it to the last set and I just hope it's easy questions because I need a bathroom and soon.

"When's the wedding? Have you picked out a dress yet?"

"We've not really talked about the wedding, so that also means no dress yet."

"Are you having a boy or girl?"

"Too soon to know anything."

Once we step off the red carpet and I'm away from cameras, the tears start and I'm heading for the nearest bathroom. I make it into the bathroom and to a stall just in time for my lunch to come back up. I'm holding my hair back and when I'm pretty sure I'm finished, I flush and lean back against the stall.

I step out of the stall and almost run into Steve,

leaning against a sink. "You want me to arrange a car to take you to the hotel?"

"I promised the girls a good night."

"What about the lounge?"

"They want to sit with you."

"Tell me what I can do."

"You can tell me I'm crazy and that I wasn't just asked those questions."

He pulls me to him, kissing my forehead. "I wish I could."

"Those records are supposed to be sealed."

"I don't know how they got them. How do you want to get in front of it?"

"There's only way and I don't want to. I don't want to talk about the hell I endured for all those years. What I did before I found *you*."

"Then we leave it alone, but they're going to keep digging. Bella, I don't want to tell you what to do, but you're going to have to do something. Secrets like this don't stay buried."

"Can't we just have the trip we planned? Can't anything go right for us? Did I do something so wrong that should I feel like I'm in hell?" I drop my head. "I think I need to talk to the band before we take our seats."

"Okay. Come on, let's get you cleaned up." I go over to the sink as Steve slips out of the bathroom.

I walk out and look for Steve. He's standing by a door just down the hall and nods at me. I sigh and make my way to him.

Steve meets me halfway and wraps his arms around me. "Peggy Sue's in there. The girls are with Adam."

"I expected nothing less. Let's just get this over

with."

He takes my hand and leads me to the room. He shuts the door once we are inside and I see the faces that I've come to love as family. They are watching me with disappointment, anger, and disgust.

I swallow hard. "Let me explain before you all judge because I may have a little more in common with you than you think."

Angelica puts her hands in the air and crosses her legs the best she can. Kyle won't look at me. Peggy Sue is leaning into Harrison. Marissa, Brent, and Ringo are just watching me quietly.

I run a hand over my face when I hear Maverick. "You got this, you've already told the man you're going to marry and that's the hardest thing you could ever have to do."

I place a hand on my belly and tell them everything, from the beginning to where I met Steve and Kellie. My parents, the name change, everything, and I watch as their pissed off, disappointed, and hurt faces change.

Angelica gets up and wraps her arms around me. "Welcome to the club."

Ringo grabs me next and pulls me in before whispering, "If you ever need to talk, I'm always here."

Brent pushes off the wall and comes to me. He's never been the hugging type, but he takes my hand. "You know you could have told me?"

"Maybe so, but Steve only just found out. It's not something I ever planned to tell anyone."

He kisses me on the cheek, then goes back to the wall. Marissa nods at me, then gives Brent her hand. Peggy Sue grabs me and she's bawling. "Don't leave us."

"Who said anything about leaving?"

"When people start running from things, they tend to keep doing that," she says and my eyes meet Kyle's. He breaks eye contact. He's the one that's the most upset with me.

"I'm not going anywhere, baby girl. I promise you." Peggy Sue hangs onto me.

"Are we done here?" Kyle asks.

Steve rounds on him. "Is that all you've got to say? The woman pours her heart out and you ask if we're done here?"

I grab his arm. "Beast, it's okay. He has every right to be angry. I lied to him and everyone in here for years."

"Just go, Kyle," Steve says and Kyle shrugs his shoulders and leaves.

I get Peggy Sue calmed down and help her clean herself up. I take a seat beside Angelica because I'm not feeling well. Between the stress, questions, then my past coming back to haunt me, I can't take anymore.

Angelica pats me on the shoulder and Steve says, "We've got this room for the rest of the night. I think you and the girls should stay here with me instead of going out to the audience."

"I agree with Steve," Maverick says and Ringo follows suit with them.

"Steve, we have to perform. Otherwise, Christy's going to…" Angelica trails off.

"I'll be on stage on time. You guys just get out there before they notice," Steve says.

Everyone leaves Steve, Harrison, Peggy Sue, Brayden, and I in the room. "I'm sorry I never said anything," I say to Peggy Sue and Steve again.

Steve wraps his arms around me. "Don't worry

about it. Like I said, it doesn't change a thing."

"Somebody's got to go get Sue Ellen and Mary Ann," Peggy Sue says.

Harrison speaks up, "I'll go." Then he's out the door.

Steve pulls me onto his lap and cuddles me to him. Apparently, we are the ones that weren't ready to be at an award show yet. I hate that they are bringing my shit into this and it just keeps getting worse. I can only hope and pray he doesn't give up on me.

64

STEVE

WE'RE PERFORMING *NIGHTMARE* TONIGHT.
Fitting, seeing as it feels like we stepped into one, taking everyone else with us. One more thing for Christy to come after me for. Another fine, probably. Every time the label has to correct a mess, they are charging me now. It isn't cheap either. Ten grand here, fifteen more there. If we don't start getting this under control, my fines are gonna exceed my royalties and then we'll be in some trouble. I have plenty of money, but a lot is tied up in stock, or the girl's college tuitions. We live off the royalty checks.

We get out on the stage and people are hooting and screaming for us. I'm stripped down to just the leathers and my hair is pulled back and my tats are on display. Angelica is down to this purple half gown, the seven-month bump hard to miss.

"Hey everybody!" she shouts into the mic as she bounces from foot to foot, the music pumping her up. I see the concern on Maverick, but he can't do anything right now. The crowd is hooting and hollering. "So,

379

we'll be doing Nightmare tonight." More screeches and whistles as she laughs. "I'm excited for it live and I gotta say, even more, knowing our boy can hear it too." She rubs her belly and looks at Maverick with a nod.

He smirks and nods as Marissa reaches over and take his hand.

I start the drum beat and Angelica pulls up a stool and sits with a mic. She's just the backup for this one, *Nightmare* is Brent's baby, the song he wrote for Marissa when they were still working things out.

The crowd is eating it up. They love Brent, and when Kyle gets near him, they swoon. Kyle, he's got a lot of nerve treating Crys the way he did. She was always there when he was feeling lonely or misused, she's told me as much. Kellie used to bring it up to get a rise out of me, make me jealous of him. It worked a few times, making me go after him and warn him about messing with my girls without permission. I mean, he and I had shared Kellie once or twice, but Crys was always just mine.

We finish the song and are about to leave the stage when one of the producers stops us.

"Our next act flaked, can you fill in?" he asks Brent and Angelica. They look at Kyle and me. Kyle shrugs and I nod.

"Alright! Thank you," he says, walking off quickly.

"So what are we doing?" I ask Brent and he and Angelica just smile.

"Oh, no, it's not ready."

"It's ready enough, Steve, it's your turn to blow these assholes away." Angelica kisses my cheek. "You got this."

"Brent?" I beg.

"All yours, brother." He turns to the crowd and

introduces me and my song, *Release Me.*

Brent pushes me out of the drummer's seat and hands me the mic as Angelica pulls me to center stage. I'm gonna kill these two. I grit my teeth as Brent starts the low beat and Kyle comes in with the bass. Angelica, for the first time since I met her, picks up Brent's guitar and has a seat. The girl can play, she just never does. I'm nervous, but once the intro ends and the music swells, I'm on point. By the time I'm done, I'm in tears and so is half the crowd.

We get a standing ovation, Brent and Angelica take my hands and we bow as Kyle pulls out and is the first one off stage. He's gone before Ringo and I can make it to the curtains. Fuck, please don't let him do anything stupid. I excuse myself and head to the green room where my family is. Adam is standing outside the room, making sure no one gets in.

"Get the limo, we're done."

He nods, looking at his watch before walking away.

I go into the room and see that Crys and Peggy Sue are both at the sink, trying to fix their makeup. Seems I got them to crying too. Harrison and the girls are playing a game of Uno and not paying much attention to the next act on the TV screen. It's some Jay -Z, Timberlake wanna be.

"The car is coming around, I figure we should get moving," I say finally.

Crystal comes out of the bathroom and looks at me, puzzled. "Aren't you staying for the after party?"

"This bear has done all the singing and balancing on balls that he's gonna. Besides, I'm not drinking, so why go to the after party, especially without you?"

She approaches me, "I don't care if you want to go, I'm sure the others will be there."

"I don't care about them, not right now. Tonight is the first night of our big vacation. You do realize we haven't actually done something like this before? I want to start it off right. With my family. I want to go get Chinese buffet, walk the Hollywood Walk of Fame, and then go back to the hotel, tuck in the girls, and make sweet love to my woman till the late hours. Doesn't that sound better than some after party?"

Peggy Sue snickers, making the girls look up. "Little ears, Daddy."

I hug Crystal, rubbing her ass. "Let's go."

She throws up her hands and sighs. "Okay, let's go."

❀ ❀ ❀

We manage to get into the limo without being spotted, everyone is inside trying to get shots of the celebrities sticking around. We take the limo into Chinatown and wind up at this four-and-a-half-star buffet called Yang Chow. It's elegant inside and the music is soothing. We are seated and our drink orders are taken. I look around and the customers are a mix of Asian and American, casual and some dressed to the nines like us.

The server complements the girls and brings them each a set of paper fans, saying Chinese princesses always had fans. The little ones are tickled pink and the woman gives the final fan to Crys. This one is made of metal and fabric, it's black silk with silver and gold flowers.

"For the expectant mother."

"Thank you," Crys says uncomfortably.

I put my arm around her and kiss her cheek. The

woman nods, then smiles. "Going to be a big boy. Go eat, feed the little ones," she urges us.

Sue Ellen And Mary Ann split up. Mary Ann is stuck to Peggy Sue like glue, and Sue Ellen is following Crys and me around the tables.

"Daddy?" Sue Ellen asks.

"Yeah, baby?"

"What happens if we get spit up at Disney?" She looks to her sister, who I catch giving her a nod.

"Well, what do you mean by split up? You'll be with one of us at all times."

"Well, us kids like to go on rides and it's crowded. What if Uncle Brent or Ringo loses us cause of a groupie or something?"

"Then you'll have to find a security guard."

"I- we need cell phones," she blurts out.

"Oh, I see, so they sent you, the cute one, over to barter, huh?" I shake my head. "Absolutely not! You hear me, Mary Ann, no! You girls are too young. I'll not have you running around like those other spoiled brats with phones."

"Angela has one."

"Not helping your case," I snap back at Mary Ann.

Crystal is laughing so hard she's holding her belly.

"Why do you think this is funny?" I ask.

"Because I agree with them." She smirks.

"Ugh! No, not you too. Don't encourage them." I cry out, piling up my plate and heading for our table.

Crystal sits beside me. "I'm not encouraging, I'm just saying what if they get split up?"

"I kill whoever they were with." I get a disappointed look from the entire table. "Christ, I'll think about it. Can I eat now?"

* * *

After an hour's drive, I'm standing in the electronics section of a Walmart Superstore, listening to my Mary Ann go on about apps like Instagram and Facebook, asking if the phone comes with external memory and what the pixels on the camera are. I'm lucky if I can tell you where the on and off switch is.

"See? Already, Facebook, Instagram, Pinterest. She hasn't even picked the phone yet."

"Beast, she has all that on her Kindle and her laptop," Crystal informs me.

"What? Come on, no! Too young." I grit my teeth, crossing my arms.

"You're kinda out of luck."

"Ugh, listen here!" I shout, getting the girls' attention. "These phones are not toys, they are communication devices, used for keeping in touch with us, the adults in your life. You will relinquish them at any point that you are asked for them. You will not be downloading videos, music, or any other insanity without express permission. Is that understood?"

Mary Ann giggles.

"I mean it."

"Yes, Daddy," Mary Ann says, handing me an iPhone while Sue Ellen gives me a Galaxy 8. I look at the price tags.

"You two are gonna start doing chores to pay for these. Almost two grand just for phones. For fuck's sake," I finish under my breath while Crystal just covers her mouth with one hand and the bump with another, chuckling.

"I feel like I got roped into this when I wasn't looking." Looks from the peanut gallery confirm my suspicions. I just shake my head and run my card, and no, I didn't take the two-year protection plans. I'm not an idiot. I know these kids, they will want upgrades in eight months. Finally done, we head back to the limo and are off to the hotel. I'm beat, and we have an early check out to be at Disneyland's Grand Hotel and Spa for eleven a.m.

65

CRYSTAL

THIS MORNING HAS BEEN CRAZY. WITH three rambunctious little girls and a crying baby, our trip from the hotel to check-in at Disney took forever. Steve was forever telling the girls to chill. Of course, it didn't help. I woke up not feeling the greatest this morning. I'm standing at the counter, trying to check us all into the two separate suites. Angelica, Maverick, and Angela are with Steve and me. Of course, I made sure Adam had his own room in the suite with us. Brent, Marissa, the twins, Ringo, Blake, and Rider have their own. They are all figuring out who's shit is where. The girls are ready to run and I just want a nap.

I am rubbing my head and signing papers when Steve puts his hand on my shoulder. "You ready for a nap yet, Bella?"

I look over at him after I hand the lady at the counter the papers. "I wish, still have to feed everyone, figure out sleeping arrangements, and all that craziness. I need to talk with Marissa as well." I look around, not seeing the girls. "Are you missing anything?"

"Um." He looks around. "Shit, I'll be back." And he's gone.

I head over and take a seat on a bench. Brayden is still fussy, so I pull him out of the stroller and start feeding him with the bottle Peggy Sue gave me just in case. It's no time until Harrison is taking Brayden out of my arms.

"I'm sorry, but Steve will kill me if sees you holding him," Harrison says.

"Does I look like I'm afraid of Steve?"

"You might not be," he complains.

"Boy, I can stop him if he tries anything, now give me back that baby. I'm the one that got to listen to him scream the whole ride."

He looks around. "Nope," he says and takes off running.

I'm bent over with my face in my hands when Steve walks back over to me. "I find three, you lose one."

"He was taken out of my hands," I say not so nicely.

"Well, you shouldn't have been lifting him anyway."

"I kind of had to so he could eat."

"Okay, I located the girls. Where the hell is Marissa and Brent?"

I look up and see Marissa walking out of the gift shop shoving a bag into her purse. "Spotted her, be right back." I walk over to Marissa. "Got something you want to share?" I question her.

"Not yet. Can you keep your mouth shut?"

"I'm pretty sure last night proves I can."

Marissa shakes her head. "I haven't said anything, but I've been getting migraines lately. The last time they were this bad, I found out I was pregnant with the twins. Brent's going to kill me."

I smile at her. "You know what causes that, right? I mean I can sit you all down and explain it like I did with Peggy Sue."

"Ha ha. Apparently, I'm impervious to the depo shot."

"Want to try having to get shots in the ass for fourteen days just to get pregnant? Not much fun. Anywho, I've got your keys here and I'll have all the tickets soon. When you get you to the suite, I've had food delivered for when you want to stay in as well as a few things for the kids and you all."

"You really didn't have to do all that. Brent said to let us know how much and he'll write you a check."

"I couldn't help myself. I was shopping for the girls and saw things everyone needed. I'll check prices again and let you know. It's in my bag."

"Okay, let me get everyone settled and I guess we'll meet for dinner since I have no idea how long it's going to take to settle everyone."

"Unless Steve plans to take the girls out, I'm eating in the room for lunch. Call me when you see your stuff and know what you're doing."

"Okay."

Marissa and I split up. I walk over to Steve, who now has Angelica, Maverick, Adam, and the rest of the gang that's with us. "Are we ready?"

"No one left behind, so yeah."

"Perfect," I say and we head for the suite. We get into the suite and Angelica tips the bellboy before I ever get the chance.

"So, we have four rooms. Steve and I have a king, Angelica, you all have the other king. Peggy Sue can pick which queen she wants, then Adam can have the other. The girls are sharing the sleeper sofa. Everyone has stuff in the living room, just look for your name." Everyone walks into the living room and they are opening bags with their names on them to see what's inside. Inside the bags is a photo album/autograph book, markers and pens, a couple penny holders for the fountains, and power packs to charge phones and such. There's also refillable water bottles with names on them, sunglasses, a rain poncho, first aid kit, Chapstick, sunblock, hand sanitizer, a pillow that says *No Place Like Home* with their names, and at least three Disney themed outfits for each one.

The adults have pretty much the same thing except the outfits and pennies. I did make sure Angelica and Peggy Sue had bump shirts since they are so cute. I look over at Steve. "You going to look at yours?"

He picks it up and wanders into the bedroom with it, so I follow along. He dumps it on the bed. His is almost like the girls'. He has a water bottle for the both of us, but they say *Beast* and *Bella*. His shirts are probably my favorite. They say, *I'm her Beast, I've got biceps to spare*, and *Beast Mode*. I watch as he goes through everything.

I'm leaning against the door as he chuckles. He turns to face me. "Bella, you do too much. Thank you."

I shrug my shoulders. "Had to make sure everyone has a good time."

"If they don't, I'm liable to kick their asses now."

"Kyle never showed, so what do you want to do with his bag?"

"Burn it or let Brent take it. He'll figure it out."

"Are you freaking out?"

"That's a lot of money."

"Not as much as you'd think."

"Enough, considering I know you didn't let the other room go empty handed."

"Would you feel better if I told you I spent less than five hundred on everything."

"I'd say you're lying to make me feel better and I love you for it."

I pull out my phone and walk over to him with the prices of how much I spent on everything. The bags with everything in them tallied up to four fifty-five. I hand him my phone. "Here, take a look." It's also got prices of room and tickets.

He takes my phone and pushes it back into my hand. "You don't have to prove anything to me, Bella. I believe you."

"Sometimes, I do because in cases like this, you look at me like I'm Kellie and I'm not."

Steve sighs and reaches for me. "One thing I'm certain about is that you are not Kellie." He kisses me.

"We need to feed the girls. Marissa doesn't want to meet up till dinner. So I'm gonna unpack the girls and us."

"You should make them help you. They need to start earning their phones."

"It's the first day of vacation, they aren't doing chores because you're being a beast."

He shakes his head. "Where's our stuff?"

"I've got it. The kitchen is stocked and the number for room service is on the counter. Figure out what you want and let me know."

"I can unpack us, you unpack the girls, then we can figure out what we getting for lunch."

"No way, mister. I've seen you pack and unpack one time. I never want to see it again." I smile.

"What? Shorts, socks, and underwear go in a

drawer. T-shirts and jeans hang. How hard is it to put shit away?"

"Grouch, I have it folded in certain ways, so it doesn't get wrinkled and I won't have to iron everything. What is wrong with you?"

"Sorry, I might be tired. I didn't sleep so well last night."

"Then go to bed and I'll unpack later."

He kisses me on the forehead. "I'll go deal with the lunch, I guess."

"Take a nap and I'll deal with it later."

"I'm not one of the girls. Shit needs to be done, I don't have time to take a nap. You don't want my help, fine. I'll go see if somebody out there does," he says, walking to the door.

"Steve," I say and he stops, but doesn't look at me. "You're snapping at me. You also asked me downstairs about a nap. I'm not feeling any better than you, so maybe we both need to take a step back and think about the other for a second. I don't let you pack or unpack because everything ends up wrinkled and I'd have to iron it, meaning double work. I've only got dresses, so they all have to be hung. We've got our stuff from yesterday that needs to be hung. And to beat it all, I'm pretty sure the boy I'm carrying is trying to make me sick from certain smells now. So, can we please not fight over stupid shit today?"

Steve nods his head and walks out of the room, which only makes me cry. UGH! Stupid men know just how to make us crazy pregnant women cry. I start unpacking and I'm just about finished with Steve's clothes when Angelica comes waddling in.

"Crystal, thank you so much for all the stuff. You didn't have to, but the diaper bag is adorable. I so want one," Angelica says.

I wipe at my face after hanging Steve's jeans and turn toward her. "You're more than welcome. You've got one, I was just waiting to hear about a baby shower."

Angelica looks at me. "What has that oaf done now?"

"Nothing. It's just stupid hormones."

"No, he's being snappy." She comes back and I just raise a brow at her. "Maverick was snappy at this point in my pregnancy. Weird things started bothering me. Certain soaps he couldn't use anymore and you know how Maverick is. You can't break the routine."

"They are good at making girls cry, I suppose. But really, I'm okay. I cry over stupid things on TV or songs on the radio."

"It gets worse before it gets better, but it gets better. Right now, I feel invincible. Maverick hasn't touched me in a month, but I feel invincible."

"If I didn't know any better, I'd say that's what is wrong with Steve, but he got it last night."

"Yeah, just don't rub that in, okay? Listen, if you need anything or need talk about anything, I'm right next door and I'm always a phone call away."

"Thanks, but really, I'm okay. I've been doing this for ten years."

"Okay, do you need any help?"

"No, I got it."

Angelica waddles back out of the room. I finish unpacking the girls and myself. I'm working on the toiletries when a smell makes me gag. I take a deep breath and start moving stuff again. That's it, my head's over the toilet and I'm ridding myself of breakfast.

"What's the matter? Thought we were past this. Are you okay?"

I flush the toilet and move away from Steve. "You are making me sick."

"Thanks, thanks a lot. What'd I do now?"

"Something you're wearing. It's the smell, I can't handle it."

"Bella, I don't wear anything. No cologne, no aftershave. Soap and deodorant, that's it. You buy my soap."

I hold my breath and walk over to the sink. I grab the deodorant first and move away before letting the smell hit me. It doesn't bother me. "It's the soap."

"Okay, I guess I'm using yours this week." He starts taking off his clothes.

"What are you doing?"

"Obviously, I need to take a shower." He shuts the bathroom door.

"Sheesh, I just asked a question."

"Strip, little woman."

I look at him like he has two heads. "No, you stink, and the little beast doesn't like it."

He turns the shower on before grabbing the soap out of the dish. "Smell this. Does it bother you?"

I sniff. "No."

"Strip," he says as he gets in and lathers up. I strip my clothes and climb in with him.

66

STEVE

"I'M SORRY I WAS AN ASS EARLIER," I say as Crystal and I pull back the covers on the bed. She's not feeling right, so I canceled us going downstairs for dinner with the clan. Instead, I asked Maverick and Angelica if they would take the girls down to dinner and then to the Disney Light Parade. They need to run off their pent-up energy, so hopefully, they will sleep a little tonight. Crys and I split an Italian combo and chef's salad, so now she just wants to lay here cuddled up and I'm happy to oblige.

"We're all allowed our off days," she says, laying against my chest.

"I know that, it's just that I was feeling kinda useless there, still am. I'm sorta sick of feeling like just the wallet."

She pulls back, looking at me, confused.

"It's not you, it's just a general sense of feeling. It's like Peggy Sue comes up to me, or Mary Ann, and they're like *Daddy, money* and I just pull out the wallet and hand it over. No appreciations, no thank you,

Daddy, we love you and know how hard you work. I know being a parent is a thankless job, it just gets to me sometimes. I mean, doesn't it bother you at all?"

"Kids, they are part Kellie's."

"This is true, I just don't know how to wrangle them, I mean, look at Peggy Sue, *that* never should have happened. We were all at fault for her getting knocked up, then I let her have the relationship? Some parent I am."

"If there's a will, there's a way, I couldn't have stopped that any more than you."

"Is that it then? A grandfather at thirty-two, and again before I'm thirty-three? Will the little ones get pregnant at fifteen too? It's not like I can lock them up." I'm getting worked up, I can feel it. I just can't help myself.

"Can I tell you for sure that they won't? No, I can't. Can I tell you I'm gonna do my damnedest to make sure it doesn't happen? You better believe it." She watches me as I get up and pace.

"They can't stay little girls forever, I just thought I'd have more time with them. This lifestyle keeps me away for so long when we work. It's why this vacation is so important. To spend time with them before it's too late."

I look at Crys and she's laughing at me!

"This isn't funny!" I whine.

"It kinda is, Sue Ellen is nine, Mary Ann is ten. It's funny because your freaking out is marrying them off already."

"God help me, I hope they get married first!"

"We didn't."

"We're different, we've waited ten years to start this life together."

"You gotta think, you lead by example. We're

gonna be lucky if they don't end up with boyfriends and husbands."

"If it makes them happy, fine. I can't be a hypocrite and I would never tell them our lifestyle was wrong. It wasn't. If we hadn't had it, I wouldn't have you now." I smile, sitting beside her.

"You'd have had me, it just would have been in a different way."

"No, I don't believe you would have come to me, not without Kellie's consent. If she hadn't actually brought you to our bed that night, you'd have never let me cheat."

"Like I said, our relationship would have been different. I would have still been the teacher."

"And I'd have ached for you for a lifetime."

"Things happen for a reason. Like I tell the girls, some people come into your life for forever while others are just a lesson."

I pull her to me. "Kellie was a long lesson." I kiss her gently and just as I'm about to deepen the kiss, the door flies open and Mary Ann and Sue Ellen come bouncing in and onto the bed.

"Daddy, you should have seen the light show!" Mary Ann exclaims.

"They had a life-sized Elliot!" Sue Ellen bounces.

"Hey now!" I put my arms out to keep them from falling on Crystal. "Easy, watch out, you're gonna hit your Mom." It came out of me so fast I didn't even think. The girls stop and look at Crystal and me.

"Is that okay?" Sue Ellen asks.

"Can we call you that?" Mary Ann questions.

"I, um…" I look at Crys, who has a hand covering her face, looking rather shocked.

Mary Ann wraps her arms around Crystal. "I know

you're not my Momma, but you've always been a Mom to us."

Sue Ellen nods, also moving in to hug her. I'm not sure what to do.

"Girls, let me talk to your dad?" she finally asks and they pull away with confused little faces. I pat them both on the heads.

"I'll be out to tuck you in shortly okay?"

They nod, looking back at Crystal, who isn't looking at them.

I close the door behind them. "I'm sorry, I don't know where it came from."

"She's quiet, holding a pillow in front of her, she's even rocking a little. "I'm not taking the place of their mother. It's not right, and I wouldn't want somebody to take my place. Sue Ellen has already been having a hard-enough time with it. She's been trying to call me mom since it happened. I just- I don't think it's fair that I take on that name when I'm not."

"This may seem cruel, but biology isn't what makes you their mom. Love, understanding, being there for them when they need you most, that makes you their mom. They are old enough to make the distinction, Mary Ann just said it. These kids love you, they respect you, and I think they want to call you by a name that shows how much they do. My calling you that, well, you are about to be a mother to their sibling, and in all honesty, if they aren't calling you some version of mom, what is he gonna think?"

She breaks eye contact with me. She doesn't like what I have to say, but I can't help how I feel. "These same feelings permeate through me about myself and these girls. I know I'm not here like I should be all the time. I worry that they resent it, resent me, but I've always known you were here, that they love you, and that makes doing this job and leaving a softer thing. They are and have always been, in part, yours."

"Then we come up with something. Not mom, not mommy, and sure as hell not momma. Because it's not fair."

I nod my head. "What do you suggest? I mean these girls have it in their heads what they want to call you and it's not Crystal anymore.'

"I don't know."

"Then why don't we just let them call you Ma? It's close enough, but still not quite there."

She sighs heavily, then nods. "Okay."

I wrap my arms around her. "It's gonna be good. I can feel it. Now, all we need is for you to adopt them and it will all be perfect."

I'm punched in the shoulder hard. "Have you lost your fucking mind?"

"No, actually, the lawyers think we should do it once we get married. This way, no one can say or do anything about the family dynamic. It also protects you and the girls if anything should happen to me."

"And what do you think is going to happen?"

"It's preemptive, I don't think anything will happen, but life happens."

"I don't like it. The papers are already gonna have a field day with this anyway."

"Just think about it."

"Yeah, I'll think about it," she answers unhappily, putting the pillow between us. She's upset, but I can't help that, I can't help the way I feel.

"I'm gonna go put the girls to bed, I'll be back... Unless you want to come too?"

"I'll see you all in the morning, I'm going to sleep."

She pushes down onto the bed and rolls away.

67

CRYSTAL

WE JUST FINISHED BREAKFAST AT *Storytellers Café.* The kids had a blast and well, so did Brent and Harrison. They're only twenty-four and eighteen, so I guess that makes them kids as well. Now, we're all standing outside, trying to figure out who's doing what. The girls, along with Brent, Ringo, and Harrison want to go on the rides. Peggy Sue, Angelica, and I can't, so right now, we are in two groups.

"Angelica's too far along for me to be walking off without her, so I'm sticking with the girls," Maverick pipes up.

"Crys, don't be mad, but I don't want to leave the little ones alone on their first day," Steve says to me.

"Why would I be mad? Go play with the boys." Steve walks over and kisses me before joining the boys. Brent's bouncing on his feet. "Since Steve's going with the boys, does that mean we get Adam and Rider?"

"Yeah, go have fun with the girls," Ringo says and Marissa kisses Brent, then comes to stand by me with the twins in their stroller.

Brent, Ringo, Steve, Harrison, and Blake take off with the three girls. I look around and just laugh. "Who do you think is gonna be worn out first?"

Marissa laughs. "Probably your Beast. Those three are going to run him ragged."

"Angela doesn't sleep," Angelica adds in a creepy tone.

"Steve better learn to keep up, he's got another one on the way."

"So, where are we off too? Doesn't this place have pools so we can relax?" Marissa asks.

"I don't really care. Someone, just point the way."

Angelica opens up the map. "They have a Build-a-Bear."

"Shouldn't the kids be with us for that?" I ask.

"I have to get something for Angela. I don't buy her clothes unless she's present."

"You have one, maybe two. I have to make four!"

"Well, what about you?" Marissa asks as we begin walking.

"I don't want one. I have a life-sized beast every day."

Peggy Sue groans. "I don't wanna hear about that, Ma." I stop midstep and pick up quickly again. Peggy Sue hands off Brayden's stroller to Maverick and laces her arm with mine. "It's good to finally have something to call you besides Crystal. Thank you," she whispers.

I pat her arm. "Don't thank me. It's all your father."

"Well, get used to it because soon it will be grandma."

"Not even funny," I say and Peggy Sue laughs as we walk to Build a Bear.

I made Sue Ellen a Poppy singing, *Get Back Up Again*. It smells like a sugar cookie because Sue Ellen loves them. She's dressed like she was in the movie. I made Mary Ann a Branch with five in one of his sayings. It smells like a cupcake because if we'd let her, Mary Ann would live on them. He too, is dressed like he was in the movie. I made my little Beast his very first Mickey with a personalized message that says *Mommy loves you*. It's dressed in a polka dot sleeper. Finally, I made my big Beast a Spock bear from Star Trek, dressed in his blue uniform and it even comes with a phaser. I added the theme song from Star Trek.

Two hundred dollars later and I'm walking out. Then I get a whiff of something sweet and I want to taste it. "Anyone else smell that?"

Marissa picks up her head. "That's a bakery!"

"Maverick, can we go?" Angelica pleads.

"Quit asking the one with the dick. He can't stop all of us," I say and keep following my nose.

I stop in front of a bakery just around the corner. Sprinkles is the name and the game is to see what I can eat. We all walk in and stand in line. Marissa is first with Peggy Sue behind her, then me and oh my goodness, it all looks so good. I finally decide on a triple scoop sundae with butter pecan, Cap'n crunch, and salty caramel ice cream. I pair it with a fudge brownie and banana cupcake. They put it all in a boat together and drizzle it with chocolate syrup, nuts, and sprinkles.

Angelica walks over with her milkshake and waffle cone ice cream, then looks from hers to mine and then to Maverick. "You're brave and craving." Now she's eating her ice cream and drinking her shake.

"Crystal, you can't eat that." Maverick says just as I go to put a bite in my mouth.

"And who's going to stop me?" I ask.

"Maverick, leave her the hell alone," Marissa says.

"Steve will have a fit with your levels. Come on, let's get you something else."

I hand Peggy Sue my drink. "Hold that." Then I grab Maverick and pull him along behind me and out the door. Once out the door and out of the way, I turn on Maverick.

"Do you remember what I told you I'd do if you messed with me again?" I ask and he just nods. "Would you like to keep them?" Once again, he nods. "Good, so to keep your nuts, you shut up about what I eat. Now, I'm going to sit down and enjoy my snack and you can suck it," I say and make my way back over to the girls.

* * *

We walked around and into more shops for a couple hours before Maverick and Angelica walk back to the hotel. It wasn't long before Marissa and Rider were walking off with Peggy Sue not too far behind, so I told Adam I'd be okay and to go with her.

I've stopped at *Carnation Café* and I'm sitting outside, eating fried pickles, chicken fried chicken, which is just buttermilk fried chicken breast with mashed potatoes, country gravy, and vegetables, and I'm drinking lemonade. I feel like I've been hungry all day.

I'm sitting here, minding my own business, eating, when someone yells, "Ma," and next thing I know, I have arms around me on both sides. I turn to each side to get a look at the smiling faces of Mary Ann and Sue Ellen.

"We went on *so* many rides!" Mary Ann squeals.

"Can I have a pickle?" Sue Ellen asks.

"Of course, where's your daddy?" I ask and Sue

Ellen grabs a pickle.

"Sue Ellen, you just had lunch," Steve says, then kisses me on the cheek before sitting beside me and pulling Mary Ann onto his lap. "Will you sit still?"

Mary Ann is on Steve's lap, bouncing around as Sue Ellen grabs another pickle and sits on my knee. "Did you all have fun?" I ask, then take a drink of my lemonade before taking a bite of my chicken.

"What on earth are you eating?" Steve asks.

"Fried chicken, fried pickles, vegetables, and mashed potatoes. Oh, and I'm drinking lemonade."

"You know that's a lot of complex sugars. Did you bring your meter?"

"Was I supposed to?"

Steve sighs and drops his head. "You sugar is going to be all out of whack tonight, isn't it?"

"I don't know, I've just been extra hungry today."

"No, you're *craving,* and apparently, you want greasy, salty foods. What is *Sprinkles*?"

"Isn't that the place with the cupcakes?" Sue Ellen asks.

I bite my lip and put my head on Sue Ellen's shoulder. "Wow, I can't leave you alone for five hours, can I?" Steve asks.

I look up at him with a pout. "I was hungry."

He smiles at me. "Well, we're going to be having a late dinner."

"Why?"

"Because it's three o'clock and you're eating that."

"I ate about this much at Sprinkles too, and we had just eaten breakfast then."

"What do they have besides cupcakes?"

"Ice cream, brownies, cookies, and sundaes."

"Let me guess, you had a little of everything."

"I didn't eat a cookie."

Steve smiles. "They figured we could meet around seven or seven thirty for dinner at *Carthay Circle*. The food is supposed to be good according to the pamphlet."

"That's fine with me. What are you all doing till then?"

"I was thinking I was going to take the girls back to the hotel, let them change, and sit down by the pool. Where's Adam?"

"Peggy Sue wanted to take Brayden back for a nap, so I made him go with her."

"So you've been all by yourself for how long?"

"About an hour. I've been fine. One person noticed me, but just asked if she could get a picture. I've been fine."

"I know, I just worry. We had to duck and run a couple of times."

"Yeah, Daddy had us under each arm. He needs a new deodorant," Sue Ellen says.

"Yeah, but you kind of call attention to yourself and I try not to. I mean I did threaten Maverick's manhood at one point, but that was it."

"Well, it's hard to hide when it's all of us together at once."

"Brent okay?"

"He was when I left him."

"Who'd you leave him with?"

"Blake and Ringo because Harrison headed back to the hotel. Are him and Marissa alright?"

I look at Steve, confused. "I think so. Why do you ask?"

"It's just funny that she didn't come with us. Brent said she was really excited."

"She had the twins and she's breastfeeding."

"I guess."

I go to take a bite and Sue Ellen has pretty much gone through it all. "Are you sure you fed her?"

"Yes, she ate all of her food and half of mine. I think she's eating for two. She's sympathy eating."

"No, Beast, she's getting ready to *grow*."

"Well, whatever she's going to do, she needs to do it, or you're both going to eat me out of house and home."

"Do I need to remind you that this was your idea."

"What? I'm just saying you guys are eating a lot," Steve says.

"Sue Ellen, can you go put this in the trash over there for me so you can get in the pool?"

Sue Ellen stands, throwing away the trash. I stand and wait for her as Steve reaches for my hand and I put it on my belly instead. He reaches across my belly and takes my hand. I roll my eyes, but pay him no mind. He just called me fat. Dick! Sue Ellen takes my hand and we walk back to the hotel.

68

STEVE

"WHAT DO YOU MEAN YOU DIDN'T PACK ONE?" I start going through the drawers, looking for my swim trunks when Crystal informs me that she didn't bring her bathing suit. "We came to a place full of sandy beaches and crystal-clear oceans and you didn't bring a suit?" I can't wrap my head around her logic.

"Um, no?"

"Why not?"

She furrows her brow at me and purses her lips. "I didn't want to wear it."

"What's wrong with it?"

"It's a two piece."

"And?" I pause as she rubs her growing belly. "Is this about the bump? Why are you ashamed of him?"

"I'm not ashamed of him, you called me fat."

"I did no such thing!" I turn to face her completely. "When did I say something like that? I would never."

"When I was eating."

I look at her, confused, "My rib about you and Sue Ellen eating me out of house and home? I didn't mean it."

"You still said it."

"Bella, I love the way you look. I've fantasized about you like this and getting bigger ever since I got it in my head that I wanted to have babies with you. I've told you before, I find you undeniably sexy like this." I walk over to her and take her hands. "I wanna show off my Bella and her belly. I put that there and I am unquestionably proud of it, and you."

"Well, you can't, I don't have one, sorry."

"Never say can't, there are a dozen shops downstairs, we're just gonna have to go down and get you one, right now. I have plans for us one night this week and you'll be needing one."

"No, I won't."

I sigh, lifting her from the bed and making her follow me out of the bedroom. "Maverick, can you handle bringing the girls down to the pool? We need to do an impromptu bit of shopping."

"Yeah, of course."

Crystal glares at him and me both, then huffs. "I don't need a bathing suit."

"And the next two weeks that we are gonna be here says yes you do. C'mon." I grab her hand and drag her through the suite and out the door.

"I don't plan on getting in, so I'm fine," she continues to argue as we head down the walkways and back into the main part of the hotel.

We find a shop with hundreds of bits of beach wear and accessories. "Jackpot." I smile. "Just pick out like three suits that you like and I'll shut my trap."

"I don't want any," she pouts, crossing her arms.

"Crys, the girls are gonna wanna play with us, and even if you break their little hearts by not going in the pools with them, you are seriously gonna tell me that you're gonna lounge by the pool in the dresses you brought? I mean you didn't pack a single pair of shorts or any tanks, what is that about?"

"My shorts don't fit."

"And who's stopping you from buying new ones?"

"Um, I have dresses."

"While I love the ease of access, there are some instances where pants of some kind and a bathing suit are more appropriate."

"Dresses work too." She stands in the middle of the store just tapping her foot in annoyance.

"Please, humor me and pick out a couple suits. Tomorrow, we're shopping over at the Anaheim Garden walk, Angelica already made the plans. You can get some shorts and stuff there."

She scoffs at me. Looking around, she grabs the two closest suits she can reach and throws them at me.

I sigh and nod, taking them over to the register and paying for them. The girl behind the counter bags them and smiles sweetly, handing them over.

I try to put my arm around Crystal, but she shrinks away from me.

"You seriously are mad because I want you to get the most out of our vacation?"

"I'm not mad that you want me to enjoy myself, I'm upset because you don't listen to me."

"I listened, I heard you say that you think you are too fat to wear a bathing suit, that you're too fat to wear the clothes you prefer. I call bullshit. I don't know why you won't buy new stuff, maybe it's the hormones, but I know if I don't push you, then you're just gonna spend the next two weeks hot and miserable."

"But I'm not hot and miserable. I like the dresses,

they are comfortable. My shorts didn't fit anymore, I just didn't buy any more pairs."

"Until you got pregnant, you never wore dresses unless you and Kellie were together. It's always been those tiny cutoff shorts I love and T-s or tanks. I'm just not getting the wardrobe change."

"I guess it's because I'm not the size I was. I remember when you came in and told us Marissa was pregnant, and how far along she was. I'm only ten weeks and I'm huge. Instead of buying clothes over and over, I can wear the dresses."

I stop us in the middle of the hotel, "Don't you get it? Part of being pregnant is doing the maternity clothes shopping, and I have been looking forward to doing that with you. Kellie never let me, or I was too busy working. I have selfish things I wanna do. I wanna get pics of you like this, I want to see you model little nighties with your bump popping out from between the silks and laces."

"Why?"

"Why? Because this is a little miracle. He's ours and the wonderment of the changes in you are something to be treasured and nurtured. I mean, how awesome are you? You- you're carrying life inside you, a life I helped to put there. That is a remarkable thing, it should be documented, cherished, and celebrated. Perhaps I'm so adamant because this may be your only chance at a child, and while, right now, it doesn't seem all that important, it will and you will miss these moments if we don't take a moment to recognize them."

"I'm sorry I guess I expected a cake walk and I'm not getting that."

I can't help but laugh softly as I hug her. "Bella, everyone has it different, we knew this was gonna be a long road going in. But it does get easier, the first trimester is the hardest. Soon, the sickness goes away, along with the aversion to certain smells and tastes. Then the fun happens, increased sex drive, unusual cravings, bursts of energy. You're not alone either, you have me every step of the way, and Peggy Sue, she's right behind you, so you'll have her to lean on too."

"But mine isn't like others, I have to watch everything I do, everything I eat, I'm so tired of it."

"Once we're out of the high-risk zone, that will ease up too. There haven't been any issues, a couple high days here and there does not a diabetic make. Your blood pressure is stable, and your gaining is on the markers. Everything is going as perfectly as it can be, barring my manhandling of you."

She doesn't say anything, just puts her head against my chest. I lift her face gently by the chin, making her look up at me. "I love you, Bella." I bend down and kiss her. "Let us get you upstairs, out of this dress, and into one of these suits. I want to parade you around like the trophy wife you're eventually going to let me make of you." I grab her ass and press my hard cock against her.

She smirks and just nods, taking my hands and leading me back to the suite.

❈ ❈ ❈

Seeing Crystal in the red tankini set she grabbed sent me over the edge and it right to the floor. I couldn't hold out anymore and we were alone in the suite. She was pleasantly surprised when I jumped her, pinning her to the glass picture window and having my way with her from behind. I'm pretty sure a couple on the beach caught themselves a decent show as I made her come with her tits pressed firmly against the glass.

We get down to the pool and it's about five, the girls are swimming and Angelica is floating on a raft with some sort of drink in her hand. Marissa is lounging and Brent and Ringo are in the water with the girls. It's the first time I've seen Ringo get wet in I don't know how long. I wonder what Brent had to say to get him in the water? I see Brayden with the twins, but I don't see his parents. Harrison and Peggy Sue are missing.

"Hey, you guys, where are the other two?"

"Uh, well, they needed a bit of time together, so I guess you just missed them on your way down." Marissa smiles, putting on her Oakley sunglasses.

"Seriously? You just let them run off to fuck?" I blurt out, getting a few raised brows from some other lingering patrons.

"What? I'm supposed to say no? If it were me, I'd want someone to do me the solid," she retorts. "Besides, they live together, they have one baby and one on the way, they obviously have that little act figured out and it's not like she's going to get pregnant again."

"Ugh!" I throw my hands up in the air.

"Oh, go *ugh* at someone who gives a damn," Marissa snaps with a little laugh. "You need to get over it. Your little girl? Not so little anymore."

I wanna strangle her, but I know Brent would never forgive me, so I storm back over to Crystal, who has seated herself in a lounger and has already ordered us both a drink.

She's chuckling while I seethe. "Beast, why the hell do you think I gave them a queen room and not a king?"

"What's that supposed to mean?"

"The two ing rooms are side by side, the queens are after the king, beside Angelica and Maverick. I didn't wanna hear your daughter randomly one night." She puts her hand on my knee. "I mean, did you really think they were going to go all sixteen days without doing anything?"

I shake my head. "I just don't want to think of my little girl like that, does that make sense? I know she does it, but to see it, or have it paraded in front of me is something else."

"I get it, but there's not a lot we can do about it."

"I know, I know." I turn my attention to the girls, my little angels, the untouched, innocent ones, and say a little prayer that they stay this way a bit longer than their sister did. "Why don't you come in the pool with me, swim, it's good exercise, good for stretching."

"What do I need to stretch for?"

I waggle my brows at her and she rolls her eyes. "At least I tried."

"There's a lot of people in the pool."

"Okay, I get it. Maybe another day." I kiss her temple and dive into the pool.

69

CRYSTAL

WE'RE AT THE ANAHEIM GARDEN WALK and let's just say I'm pretty much shopped out from yesterday with the girls. Once we got into **LUSH, WHICH** has fresh handmade cosmetics, Steve tells me to pick anything I want. Mary Ann and Sue Ellen are behind me and dropping stuff into the basket for them. Sue Ellen picks up one and asks if she can have it. I laugh and show Steve. It's a bath bomb with an inappropriate name, so I'm sure this is going to go over *amazing*.

"Beast, Sue Ellen wants to know if she can have this," I say with a laugh, handing it to him.

"It smells good. What's it called?"

"Sex bomb," I smirk.

"No, no, too young, no. Anything but that."

I have to hold my belly because I'm laughing so hard as we continue shopping. New shower gels, a few of the smells bothered me while I fell in love with others. I hold one up for Steve to smell.

"Do you like this one?" It's called *It's Raining Men*

and smells like honey.

"It's sweet."

"It should be," I say with a smile.

He snatches it from me and rolls his eyes, looking at it. "This place has more sex on the brain than I do."

I laugh and put a couple bottles in my basket. The girls are having a field day, adding stuff in. They've run ahead, but we can still see them as I pull Steve to me for a kiss.

"You know this store is getting better and better," I say, pointing at a shampoo meant to brighten gray or blonde hair. It's called *Daddy-O*.

"Wow, and I thought this was going to be a safe place to shop."

"For you and me, yes. The girls have added all kinds of shit."

"That basket looks like it's getting kind of heavy. Do you want me to take it?"

"I'll be fine as long as the girls quit adding to it." I grab a bottle of the Daddy-O and one of Fairly Traded Honey, adding them both to the basket, then I pick up a conditioner to make my hair silky. I'm checking out the henna hair dyes when Steve brings over a bar for me to smell.

"It smells good. Is that what you're switching to?"

"I think so, if you like it."

"I like it, but you will need a couple till we get home. Beast?"

"What?"

"What do you think about me dying my hair?" I ask casually.

"I think that you're a blonde and nobody has more fun."

I raise a brow at him. "You aren't a blonde and

have plenty of fun."

He looks up at the sky. "But I like your natural colors and I prefer the carpet to match the drapes."

"I could dye that too."

"I'm not sitting in the bathroom to scrub your carpet some ridiculous color. Besides, henna rubs off. I'd rather not have my dick turn purple," Steve says.

"Daddy, why would your dick turn purple if you're scrubbing Ma's carpet?" Sue Ellen asks.

I set the basket at my feet because I'm laughing so hard the belly's shaking and hurting. Doesn't help that I have tears falling down my face.

"Sue Ellen, I can't begin to explain that too, so, um, go get some shampoo and another basket for your Ma."

Sue Ellen takes off and Steve picks the basket from the floor "Good job, Dad."

"How'd I know they were going to circle back like sharks?"

"Sue Ellen is never really far from one or the other of us and Mary Ann has been getting clingy. Last time we had a girl do this, I had to set Peggy Sue down for the talk."

"What? Which talk? The one where they bleed for seven days and don't die or the one about where babies come from?"

"It's one and the same."

"Is it really that time? Aren't they too young?"

"Peggy Sue was almost eleven when she started."

"Alright, I guess we have the talk. Put Sue Ellen down too."

"No! Sue Ellen is still a baby."

Steve chuckles. "We might as well get it over with. Why have to go through it again in less than a year. Two birds, one hairy stone."

"You suck."

"Yeah, but you like it." He bends down, kissing me, sucking my bottom lip for a second.

"Girls, remember?"

"I'm gonna take this up to the counter so the girl can start ringing it up. I guess Sue Ellen is on her way back with empty baskets."

"Did you get everything you need?"

"No, but I'm gonna go grab it after I drop this stuff off."

"Okay, see you in a few."

I grab a few new things for my face like cleansers and a moisturizer, then I grab one of each lip tint, lip scrub, and lip balm. I pick up a new scrub and cream for my hands as well as cream for my feet. I also get a new perfume that smells like a sweet rose.

Makeup! Of course, I have to pick up new mascaras, eye liners, eye shadows, and lipsticks. At least one of every color is now in my basket and Steve is beside me.

"So, Bella, I'm curious. How old were you when you got your ears pierced?"

"When I left home. Why?"

"Well, I was thinking about when Sue Ellen asked about her eyebrow."

"Uh huh?"

"While that's wildly inappropriate for a girl her age, I thought maybe we could let her and Mary Ann get their ears pierced today."

"Okay?"

"So do you think it's a good idea? Good compromise?"

"I don't see why not. Have at it. I'm done, where are the girls?"

He looks around. "Up by the registers. Appears they each got themselves a basket."

"They are their mother's daughters."

We finish up in *Lush*, Steve takes the bags, and we head to *Madison and Co.* so the girls can get their ears pierced. Somehow, they've managed to talk me into getting another ring in my ear and I opt for a bar across the top.

Now, we are heading for *Sockerbit*, a candy store. Steve said he was running to the bathroom, but he'd be back. Told me to pick out enough so that we'd have take home. I grab a tote bag and tell the girls we can get what we want. You name it and we fill the bag with it. Sour, marshmallow, sweet, hard, chocolate, and wrapped candies. I'm working on checking out when Steve comes back.

"Everything okay?" I ask.

"Yeah, breakfast apparently didn't agree with me, then I got a little lost."

"Okay, do you want to go on to the car?"

"No, no, I'm alright now. A little lunch should settle me. I kind of want to hit another shop beforehand."

"Okay, where are we headed?"

"There's this shop here called *Red* that I think you're going to love."

"Lead the way," I say, grabbing the bag from the counter and following behind him. We get to the store and it's dresses. "I thought you didn't like my dresses!"

Steve sighs. "I didn't say I didn't like them. I said I fully appreciate the easy access."

"Then you told me I had to get other clothes."

"I figure I should let you wear what you want."

"Come here," I say, pulling him down to me and

checking for a fever. "Are you sure you're okay? We had a bit of an argument yesterday about this exact thing and you don't usually change your mind like this."

"I'm sure I'm fine."

"Whatever. How many can I have?"

He laughs. "How many can you have? I don't know. Five?"

"Five works for me. Come on, girls," I say and the girls help me search the wrap dresses for the five to get. I ended up with a yellow with branch floral, navy with blue and pink flowers, baby blue with pink flowers, brown with maze like shapes on it, and chevron with multiple colors. The girls are bouncing out of the store to where Steve is sitting on a bench, looking at his phone.

He looks up. "So, did you find five dresses you like?"

"Yup, got them right here." I swing the bag a bit.

"One more shop, then lunch because I'm starving," Steve says and leads us to the *Harley Davidson* store.

I stop outside the door. "I think I'm gonna have a seat while you go look."

Steve asks the girls if they want to go with him and of course, they say yes. He walks over to me. "I'm going in for a new pair of boots." He kisses me and starts walking away.

"I've heard that before," I say loud enough that he can hear me. Steve waves at me and goes on in the store. I'm sitting on the bench, running a hand through my hair while I'm waiting for Steve.

Someone sits next to me, but I ignore them until they speak. That's a voice I know very well.

"I'm a dick," Kyle says from beside me. I smack him for being a dick, but most of all for making me worry about him. "Oww. I'm sorry I freaked out."

419

"I thought you went home."

"No, I just did some visiting with friends."

"You sober?"

"At the moment, mostly. I might've smoked a little pot before I got here."

"How'd you know where we were?"

"Angelica. She always comes here."

"What were you going to do? Wait around for days to see how long it would take us to show up?"

"No, I got her itinerary on my phone. We synced up the other night at the event. I know where you've been every step of the way."

"You have something back the hotel. It won't do anyone else any good. You don't deserve it, but it's still yours."

"You gotta forgive me. Personality defects are not one's fault. Besides," he says, setting a bag on the floor and scooting it to me with his foot, "I come bearing gifts."

"For me?" I ask, pointing to myself.

"Yes."

"Sucking up, are we?"

"Yes," Kyle says again.

"Planning on coming back to the hotel with us?"

"If I'm still welcome."

"You've got two brothers who've got no idea where you are."

"It's probably best if it stays that way."

"Probably, but I'm telling you right now, Kyle Marcus, you do something like that to me again and you will pay, and pay dearly. We clear?"

He nods his head. "We're clear."

I lean over and grab the bag off the floor and open it beside me. He got me shirts with sayings on them. *Yes,*

I'm pregnant, No, it's not twins, Yes, I am sure, Yes, it's a boy, No, you can't touch my belly. My favorites are *First Time Mommy* and *It started with a kiss and ended like this.*

"They're perfect. Thank you."

"You're welcome." Kyle starts to say something else, then stops before sighing. "I just need you to understand that it hurt knowing you know about Brent and me but could never bring yourself to tell me about you."

"I couldn't tell you before I told Steve and if Steve would have never made me take up counseling, he wouldn't have known either."

Kyle nods at me. "I understand that."

"I put it all behind me a long time ago. We're talking like fourteen years ago. That's how long I've been who I am today."

"Then, that's who you are. Who you were doesn't matter. You're the same sweet, caring girl that I met three years ago."

"Are you sure? I want you to be honest with me always. I didn't mean to hurt you. Let's admit it, I'm not completely the same. Not with this thing," I say, pulling the dress tighter around the bump.

Kyle smiles at me. "Me leaving was more about my shit than yours."

I put my hand on his. "You know you can still talk to me, right? Whatever you say stays between us."

Kyle pulls his hand away. "I'm fine."

I turn as the girls start running out and they are all smiles. Sue Ellen is now wearing a pink leather jacket. Mary Ann has a bag.

"I've got boots."

"He bought a bike, didn't he?" I ask and they both giggle. "I'm going to kill him."

"Wait, big man bought a bike? Oh boy."

I'm tapping my foot as Steve walks up with several bags. "I may have bought more than boots." I give him a look that says *no shit.*

"Are you crazy?" Kyle asks. "She can't get on a bike."

"Where the fu-" Steve catches himself and rephrases for the young ears. "Where did you come from?"

"Easy man, I came bearing gifts," Kyle says.

"You know what? It's none of your business," Steve says to Kyle, then looks at me and I know he can see the I told you so face. "I didn't buy the bike. They wanted too much to ship it from here to Las Vegas, but I ordered it. They're building it for us over the next few weeks."

I look at Kyle. "You're out of the dog house." Then I look back to Steve and say,"You're in the dog house."

"But I've got presents."

"I'm starting to get a complex, guys."

"You can open the stuff when you get to the hotel. Kyle, you gonna eat?"

"I want Cheese Cake Factory," I tell them.

"What's that?"

"It's a restaurant that also happens to make the most amazing cheesecake I've ever tasted."

"Alright, lead the way," Steve says.

Cheesecake Factory, here we come. Good food and even better desserts.

70

STEVE

THE CHEESECAKE FACTORY. Whoever came up with the premise for mixing a bar with this decadent dessert and a crazy number of appetizers was a fucking genius. Although, I do believe my daughters will be bouncing off the walls for the next hundred years after having sampled the menu. Crystal too, quite possibly. I think she and Kyle ate like seven different types of cheesecake and there was still more than a dozen to try. I did make her order real food too, but she snaked me by getting the Louisiana chicken pasta, which is Parmesan crusted chicken served over pasta with mushrooms, peppers, and onions in a spicy New Orleans sauce. She shouldn't have the spicy food, but with all the milk, maybe it will offset itself.

The girls got fish and chips and split three flavors of cheesecake. I helped myself to the ribeye and the tiramisu. It was worth the nearly buck fifty with tip.

"So, are you happy, Bella?" I ask as we pile into the car. Adam looks surprised to see Kyle. "Yeah, we picked up a stray."

"I'm plenty happy, why are you asking me?"

"You were cross with me before, was just hoping that had changed."

"I'm still cross with you, you ordered a bike."

"Trike actually, it's an Ultra Glider and it's on three wheels, and I've custom ordered a two-seater side car for the girls and the boy."

"NO! Not, happening."

"It's really cool!" Mary Ann helps. "It's dark blue and chrome and real sturdy."

"No," Crystal says again.

The girls are sitting across from us with Kyle, their little faces turned to pouts.

"You've done it, you've broken their grins," I say with a chuckle.

"Does this look like a face that cares?" She points to her face.

I put my arm around her as we wait for Angelica and Maverick to arrive. Fifteen arduous minutes later and I can hear Maverick's stern tone.

"I don't know why you insist on spending fifteen hundred dollars on shoes you can't even wear right now. That's all I'm saying."

"They were on sale, and I'll be able to wear them in like two months. Besides, do I tell you what to do with your money? No, and I don't hear you complaining when I wear only them to bed."

"Mom!" Angela says as she's opening the door to the truck. "WTMI!"

"Um-"

"Don't even ask," I cut Sue Ellen off before she can finish.

Crystal is laughing her ass off and Kyle is face palming.

"You will not believe the sale I hit! It was- Kyle?" Angelica asks, climbing into the car and across his lap to sit. "Where'd you come from? We were worried."

"Sorry, had to work out some shit," he says as she hugs him and Maverick glares.

We get back to the hotel and Kyle goes up to see Brent and them while I take our girls and Crystal into the park. I could see the fight brewing between Maverick and Angelica and didn't want to be present for it. Adam takes everything upstairs while we go out to the boardwalk and check out the games.

❖ ❖ ❖

With the tension in the room, we decided the rest of the weekend would be spent in our own corners. This kept Kyle away from us and Maverick and Angelica hopefully at peace. I was also hoping that Crystal would forgive me for the bike before Monday since it's her birthday and I have an entire day planned for her. She just doesn't know it yet. I've made reservations and everything.

"Bella, Adam was going to take the girls for a little while today, I thought we could check out the spa, what do you say? They have a massage just for mommy's to be."

"Are you still trying to suck up for getting the bike?"

"No, I was just thinking about how nice it was the last time we went to the spa. You seemed to enjoy it."

"Can I? Aren't I a little big?"

"They say they can accommodate all three trimesters, so I think we will be just fine."

"Okay, so what do I need?"

425

"What do you mean?"

"I'm not going naked."

"Um, why not? I will be and I'll be right there with you."

She pokes my abs and says, "You've got that."

"About the belly again?" I lament. "Bella, you're more than beautiful."

"Trust me, you tell me plenty, but I feel huge."

"But you're not. Not really. We have a ways to go yet."

"I can't help feeling like I am. I'm bigger than I've ever been."

I nod, kissing her. "It's okay, just wear your bathing suit then." I'm a bit frustrated by her mentality, but I am trying to understand it too. I'm just faltering. She wraps her arms around me and I follow her lead, doing the same.

"I know you like to see me, but the staring bothers me."

"They stare because they wish they could look half as sexy carrying Steve Vicious' baby." I lean into her.

"Could you be any more conceited?"

"Probably, just not sure how at the moment. Go put on your suit so I can fight with myself not to rip it off you."

She goes and puts on her suit and we head down to the spa. I set her up with the Elemis Nurturing Massage for Mother-to-Be, it's supposed to be a safe, comfortable experience tailored to relax her. When she finishes that, she's going to have the Mandara Ritual for the hands and feet, which soothes the skin and promotes healthy-looking nails. Her hands and feet get a cleansing, exfoliation, and massage, followed by a traditional manicure, pedicure and polish. She's going to love it, and I do so love to pamper her.

I get a deep tissue massage, an exfoliating facial, and a shave. It's nice.

By the time we've finished, it's time for Adam to meet us for dinner, so we get dressed and I meet Crystal out in the lobby.

"Feeling refreshed?" I ask with a smile.

"I'm waiting on the panties to show up still." She smiles.

"If we didn't have the kids tonight, you would be wearing them."

"Can't help but feel you have ulterior motives."

"Just seeing you pampered and happy, my Bella."

"Okay." Her bullshit meter is on high alert.

I embrace and kiss her. "No motives except to see you happy, and to be happy."

"Okay."

The girls come down with Adam and we head off to the restaurant. Dinner calls.

71

CRYSTAL

IT'S MY BIRTHDAY AND I'M WAKING UP TO complete silence. Maybe, just maybe, everyone forgot. I've never really made much of a deal out of my birthday, but Steve's always done a little something. Kellie would usually make me breakfast, then just act like the day didn't matter. Kyle was probably the only other person besides the girls that made a fuss of my birthday. It was never celebrated growing up, so I figured why start. It only means I'm getting another day older.

I stretch and stand, throwing on a pair of pajama pants before heading for the bathroom and taking care of business. Once I'm finished, I pad out to the living room and head for the kitchen. I need something to drink. Apparently the spa and then Steve being the beast he is, may have dehydrated me just a tad.

I'm leaning against the counter, drinking my juice, when I hear the door of the suite shut. Steve comes walking in, fully dressed, but passes me up. I can't help but stifle a giggle.

A minute goes by, then he calls, "Bella, where are you?"

"Kitchen. What's it to ya?"

Steve comes wandering into the kitchen, wraps his arms around me and kisses me. "Happy birthday, baby."

"And here I was hoping the lot of you forgot."

"Oh no, not at all."

"Am I to assume this is why you've been acting so funny the last few days?"

Steve smiles at me and kisses me again. "Could be. You need to go get dressed."

"What am I wearing? Since I have no idea what you have planned."

"All you have is dresses. Got put on a dress and sneakers."

"Sneakers?"

"You may need them."

"I didn't bring any, just my sandals."

"No problem, just get dressed and I'll take care of the rest."

I pat him on the chest before putting my glass in the sink and heading to the bedroom. I'm just putting my shoes on when Steve comes waltzing in and grabs my purse. "Your pills and everything are in here, right?"

"I don't think my lotion is, but I can grab it."

"Yeah, you might as well."

I go to the bathroom, grab my lotion, then come back to Steve and take my purse to put the lotion in. "Going to tell me where we're going and where everyone is?"

"Everybody is out and that's where we're going, *out*. I have an entire day planned for us."

"The girls?"

"Are with Kyle, Ringo, Brent, and the rest of them."

"That's why Kyle came back."

"I would assume it's because he's sorry. He groveled enough, well not nearly enough, but he groveled."

With that, I just roll my eyes. Seems my beast has been planning something. I take his hand and he leads us to a car. He helps me into the front seat and shuts my door before going to the driver's side. Last time he acted like this, he was trying to get me pregnant.

"I'm already knocked up, you can't do it again," I say with a smile.

Steve laughs, starts the car, and begins driving down the road. I put on my makeup during the trip since he didn't give me time in the suite. It takes about thirty-five minutes before I start seeing the ocean front and another five before he's parking the car in front of *Nick's Laguna Beach.*

"Finally feeding me?" I ask.

"Of course, it just took a little time to get here."

"You've never made this big of a deal before. What gives?"

"Honestly, because Kellie never let me and you're turning thirty, that's a milestone."

"It's just another day."

"It's more than that, really it is." Steve reaches out and takes my hand in his. "I remember how good you made sure my thirtieth was." He has a big smile on his face.

"I'm shocked you remember anything with all the drinking you did."

He smiles. "I remember. Especially that little white thing you wore."

"It was a new one. Disappeared if I remember

correctly."

"Did I demolish it?"

"Haven't you demolished all of them?"

"I'm starving and you've got to be hungry. Let's go see what they've got in here."

Steve pops out and around the car, helping me out. He wraps his arm around me as we walk in. Steve lets them know he has a reservation under Vicious. It takes a minute, but we are escorted to our seats and told the waitress will be right with us. I look over at the view around us since we're sitting outside. The view is fantastic and there's a fresh salty scent in the air. The sound of the waves crashing is soothing and would put me to sleep if I was lying down right now.

"I doubt I'll ever get used to this," I say quietly.

Steve smiles at me. "It's something you should get used to, something you should have been getting used to. I don't know why I let Kellie encourage me to ignore you for so long."

"Kellie was your wife, it was natural for you to spend more time with her."

"Perhaps, but now, my time's going to be spent with you and the girls."

"And a boy."

"And the boy when he gets here."

"It's hard to believe it's already been eleven weeks."

"Yeah, well, it took a lot to get here, but I'm glad we're here. All the times we've been out here, have you ever sat this close to the water?"

"Yeah, I used to take the girls to the beach while you and Kellie were off doing whatever." I smile at him.

He frowns. "Here I was thinking I was taking you to the ocean for the first time."

"I always had two or three girls, I had to keep them entertained. This was the best way."

He nods his head at me. "Yeah, I suppose you're right. Figure out what you want?"

"I'm thinking about the fried chicken and waffle with a fruit bowl and orange juice."

"If that's what you want, then go ahead."

We order and eat in silence, taking in everything around us during breakfast. Sometimes, it's nice just to enjoy the quiet since it doesn't happen much with the girls. I rather enjoy it from time to time. As we get back into the car and Steve starts driving off, I look in my purse for my phone.

"Did you take my phone again?"

He smiles. "No Candy Crush, you'll get it back tomorrow."

"And if the girls call?"

"They won't."

"How do you know?"

"Because they've been instructed not to."

"But what if something happens and they need us."

"Nothing is going to happen. They are going to be fine. They have plenty of people looking out for them."

"Fine!" I say as we pull up to the Montage Hotel in Laguna Beach. "We're not going back tonight?"

"N-no, that's not the plan," he stutters.

"What are you so nervous about?"

Steve rolls his neck. "Let's check in."

"Okay," I say and watch as he checks us in.

We're escorted to a bungalow suite instead of a room. Somebody has pulled out all the stops for today, apparently. Steve opens the door and lets me walk in first and start checking it out while he deals with our stuff and the bellboy. It's done up in a pale yellow. The living room has a fireplace and we have a little kitchen and dining area. There's a set of French doors and I walk through them to find a king size bed in the middle of the room with a bathroom off to the side. The bathroom is beautiful, with double sink, a giant shower, and an even bigger tub. After I'm finished looking around, I set my purse on the table and make my way back to Steve.

I stop as he's wheeling a huge suitcase my way. One I've never seen before. "What are you doing?"

"I have something for you. Come, follow me," he says with a shit eating grin on his face.

"I've been following you for ten years and it hasn't stopped yet," I say, following him back to the bed. He lifts the luggage up before turning to look at me.

Steve wraps his arms around me and kisses me. "Then open your packages."

I smile as I make my way over to the luggage. It's Disney but vintage that looks like it's been tagged all over the world. I unzip and everything inside has been wrapped. Steve sits in the chair by the bed and just smiles as I begin unwrapping. After everything is unwrapped, I have a new pair of black leather boots that come to my thighs and zip up the back, a pair of black and yellow Sketchers, and two new pairs of sandals. He also got me a giclée of the castle ballroom interior from Beauty and the Beast. It's beautiful.

I got new pajamas that are Tinkerbell and say *Fly by Attitude*, eight new tops, a rocker top cut down the front to show everything off with ties on the sides, a Tallulah top that will cover my belly, a Disney shirt with lots of different sayings, and another with Alice on it reading *Calories don't count at Disney*. I'm inclined to agree with this one. He also got one that hits me on the head, it says *My brain is 80% song lyrics.* Then I get into the last three and can't help but smile at them. The sayings are perfect: *Beauty and the bump, The force is strong with this one,* and *Miracle under construction.* I also have three new pairs of shorts as well as three wrap dresses like the ones I just bought, but these are solid colors, and two rompers.

I think I'm done and hit another round of packages. God only knows how he fit so much in here. It's stuff for our little beast. It's all Finding Dory and Nemo themed. A onesie that looks like Nemo, a sleeper that says *Just keep sleeping,* two robes - one is Mickey while the other is Thumper. He also got a board book set and bath toys for our little guy.

My last few things make me smile the most. The fact he knows so much about me is amazing. He got me the twenty-fifth-anniversary edition of Beauty and the Beast. There's a watch that has Belle in it. There's a Beauty and the Beast bangle set, it's three pieces and amazing. One even says *Beauty is found within.* The last thing I open is a Pandora bracelet with a Disneyland charm, three little girls and a little boy on it as well as an ABC charm.

I look over everything once more. I can't help but cry as I walk over and climb onto my Beast's lap and wrap my arms around him.

"Ten years' worth of birthdays and more. I take it you like?"

"I love it all. You're way too good to me," I say, wiping at my face.

"Nonsense, I could live a thousand years and never be as good to you as you are to me." I have no words, so I just kiss him. He stops me and looks at his watch. "I don't know if you want to change into some shorts and a T-shirt, but you definitely want to put on some sneakers for our next little outing."

"Uh, okay? Do you have a particular outfit you want me to wear?"

"No, you can wear whatever you like, but you have to wear sneakers and be prepared to get a little wet."

I look down at my dress. "Give me a second," I say, getting up and grabbing a pair of shorts and the shirt that says *Miracle under construction.* I strip off my dress and slip into the shorts and shirt. I look at Steve. "Better?"

He nods at me. "Perfect."

"I don't have any socks."

He gets up and goes back into the living room before coming back with a pair of his. I can't help but laugh. "They're going to be a mile too big."

"I don't want you getting blisters. Roll them down, nice and eighties style."

I sit down, putting the socks on as he brings me my new Sketchers. "What are we doing that I need to wear these?"

"You'll see in about twenty minutes," he says and I finish getting my shoes on.

I stand and wrap my arms around him again before kissing him and letting him know I'm ready to go.

72

STEVE

THE SAN MATEO IS A FORTY-TWO-FOOT fishing boat used for whale and dolphin watching out of Dana Wharf. It was my next surprise for Crystal. I'd never been whale watching and I thought it would be a great little adventure for us both.

"What do you think so far?" I ask. We've been out to sea for about forty minutes and already seen sea lions and harbor seals, as well as some common dolphins.

"It's amazing." She smiles, looking at the water, I had hoped she would take to the boat well and she has.

As I wrap my arms around her middle, we hear a loud crashing and turn just in time to see a set of humpback whales, as they flop into the water. "You see that, Bella?" I laugh, pointing.

"I saw something, not sure what it was but something." She shakes her head.

"My bad." I realize I'm blocking her way. I turn her and just as I do, the whales flip their tails, splashing water all over the deck and us.

She wipes the salty water from her face and looks

up at me. "What did I do to you?"

"Nothing, my Bella. I'm sorry, that was terrible." I laugh.

"Yeah, you sound like you're sorry."

"I'm soaked too."

"You sound really sorry with that laugh."

I pull her to me and kiss her as the boat makes its way back toward the harbor. "I say we go back to our room and take in a nap before dinner, what do you say?"

"Okay." She looks at me strangely but agrees.

"I don't want to completely overwork you, today is supposed to be fun for you."

"You're not overworking me," she insists, her arms still wrapped around me.

"Okay, then, if you don't want to lay down, what would you like to do? There are museums, art exhibits, and beaches to explore. You name it and we're there."

"The beach sounds nice, don't we have a private one back at the hotel?"

"Yes, I believe we do."

❊ ❊ ❊

A twenty-minute drive and wardrobe change puts us out on Aliso Beach. The tide is just about out when we get out there, making it the perfect time to explore the tide pools. I'm a little nervous about Crystal climbing over all the rocks, but she has better balance than I do!

It's her size, she's got a better hold on her center of gravity than me, even with the bump. We wade in the cool ocean and she educates me about the marine life. Star fish and barnacle, sand dollars and spider crabs. We have to avoid a rock fish because of their poisonous barbs, but it was cool to watch it swim. Ugly thing that it was. She takes all sorts of pictures for the girls and I'm taking all kinds of pictures of her.

She looks radiant out here in the water in her tankini, the bump on full display as she plays and works, the sun kissing her blonde hair and skin, giving it a flush. It takes all of my will power not to just pounce on her right here in the sand, but I have that set for later tonight. It's about five-thirty and I'm starting to get hungry. Lunch was light fare on the dock after the whale watching, so I know she must be starving.

"Bella? You want to get ready for dinner?" I shout as she's a bit off from me at this point.

She nods, slinging her phone on her wristlet and coming back over to me. "Have you had fun?"

"This has been interesting, it is good to learn new things."

"The girls deal with it every day, anytime we come out, go to the beach, have something to do, I always turn it into a school experiment. But then, of course, they get to play."

"We'll get to play after dinner, dessert is s'mores on the beach over a roaring bonfire."

She looks at me oddly. "Is that why you've been so careful?"

"How do you mean?"

"You're watching where and how you touch me."

I bite my lip. "I've been savoring it."

"Should I be worried?"

"I hope not."

I take her hand and lead her inside. "Don't take off the suit, just toss a dress over it," I tell her and she nods. Putting on the hunter green wrap dress I got her for her birthday and a new pair of sandals, she shakes out her hair and fixes her makeup. She looks stunning.

"We're going to Mosaic, one of the restaurants here in the hotel. I put in reservations for a terrace table. It should be a lovely and *private* view."

"No panties are coming, right?"

I smirk, "I have them if you'd like them."

"No," she answers fast, making me laugh outright. "Just making sure there isn't going to be any surprises."

"We are solid." I put my hand on the small of her back and lead her from the room.

We get down to the *Mosaic Bar and Grill* and are seated outside on the patio, the view of the beach is spectacular. People are starting to set up bonfires and the lighting is just spot on.

A lot of the menu items are fish, but we work around it, getting the duck taquitos and mosaic nachos for the starter.

She orders the flame grilled skirt steak, pasilla au gratin potatoes with chimichurri, roasted summer vegetables and the baby greens salad made with local strawberries, dried cranberries, candied walnuts, vine-ripened tomatoes and blue cheese, drizzled with a balsamic basil vinaigrette. Just listening to her order makes my mouth water, so I go with the same.

"Have you had a good day?" I ask, taking her hand from across the table.

"I've had a wonderful day."

"I'm glad for it." I nod my head approvingly. "I know it's all been a bit much, I just wanted it to be a memorable day for you. One you can look back on and say, yeah, that was a good one."

"For the most part, every day is a good one, everybody has their moments. Some just have them more than others. "

"I'm glad that you are a happy soul. It lifts me up in so many ways." I smile. "You've taught that happiness to my girls, to our girls, and you will make a smiling fool out of Steve Jr, I'm sure, and he will be a better man for you having done it."

"Did you take my emotions for the day?" she asks, raising an eyebrow.

"I don't know, maybe, it could be a sympathy thing. I know I started eating like Kellie when she was pregnant. I had to work twice as hard in the gym and still gained fifteen pounds."

She looks at her belly, then at me, "I don't think we have to worry about you gaining weight this time around."

I just chuckle. "Would you feel better if I did?"

"No!" she cries out. "What kind of question is that? I'm not getting blamed for you losing your figure."

"It is a good one, isn't it?" I straighten up, unbuttoning a button on my shirt to show my chest a bit more.

"Cover up before people start snapping pictures. Are you trying to be in the tabloids again?"

"Bella, it's just you, me, and a few couples up here right now. I think we are good." I lean across the table and take her face in my hands, kissing her. When I break the kiss, I ask, "Are you getting wet yet?"

"And if I am?"

I pull her over to me, her chair scratching the concrete. I smirk as my hand travels up her leg.

She pushes my hand down. "Oh, no, no, no, no," she insists.

"Just the way you say no, tells me you really want me to keep going," I whisper, my hand returning, gliding up between her thighs.

"You are being horrible and we are in a restaurant. Stop."

"We are in a secluded spot, and our food has already come, so they are leaving us alone," I say as my fingers graze her center. She's hot and she squirms as I push the fabric of the swimsuit aside. I kiss her neck as I flick her clit.

She bites my ear and I pull back my head, but not my hand. Instead, I go on with my fork and proceed to take a forkful to her mouth with a sly smile. I stop, circling her clit and insist with the food.

"Why are you being mean? What did I do to you?"

"Not being mean, just getting you going before we get back to the beach."

"Pretty sure I'm already there."

I kiss her again, my tongue probing her deeply as my fingers push into her. "Shall we get the rest of dinner to go?"

She only nods as I feel her start to clench up around my thrusting fingers. I wait for her to come before calling over the waiter for our doggy bags.

❀ ❀ ❀

I don't touch her again, not even a hand while we head back to the room. She heads for the bathroom and while she's doing that, I start the bonfire that I set up earlier in the evening and get the blankets laid out for us along with the fixings for the s'mores.

I look up and she's standing there with her dress untied, her tankini exposed, and looking just plain fuckable. My eyes roam over her and it's undeniable that I want and need this woman. I crook a finger at her and she walks over to me. I wrap my arms around her, my face pressed against her belly and her core, so close I can smell her sweet, musky scent. I hook my fingers into the waistband of her bottoms and down they come. Her hands are in my hair while I part her lips, exposing her swelling clit to the cool night breeze. She murmurs and purrs while I lick and suck on her until she can hardly stand any longer. Helping her to the blanket, I lay her down. I've brought out her body pillow to make this more comfortable for her, so she's got her head on it and her body along its length. She coos in approval while I finger fuck her and kiss her. I love to kiss this woman, there is just something in the way she kisses me that sends me over the deep end. It's like I come without having to come. It's almost Tantric. I lose my shorts and finally pull her on top of me and she takes me into her, riding me slowly and deliberately teasing me. She's making up for what I did in Mosaic, but I'm not complaining in the least.

She takes total control of our lovemaking, telling me how she wants me and in which hard, pounding position. I oblige her like the good boy I am. It is her birthday after all.

73

CRYSTAL

THE REST OF OUR TRIP WENT BY SO QUICK I'm already missing it and we just got home this morning. I've managed to get everything unpacked and either in the laundry to be washed or put away. I'm standing at the fridge, pulling stuff out that has gone bad, the garbage can beside me is full and now I'm stacking shit on the counter. We're going to need everything at this rate.

Steve took the girls with him to pick the pups up from the kennel while Adam stays with me. He doesn't usually stay in the same room because I make him do things that he normally wouldn't be doing. The sound of car doors lets me know that everyone's home, and a few seconds later, the front door opens and I hear two sets of puppy feet on the floor.

Steve whistles, then yells for the girls, "Girls, come get your dogs. Bella, what are you doing?"

I turn, setting something else on the counter before looking at Steve. "I was planning on figuring out dinner, but everything has gone bad."

"Even what was in the freezer?"

"A few things, yes."

"I guess we're going to the grocery store. You write me up a list and I'll go," he says before grabbing the garbage.

"Can I just say everything?"

"Do you really want to send me to a store without a list? Do you think that's wise? I'll come home with pizza and beer."

"But you don't drink."

"Exactly."

"How about we go and leave the girls with Adam?"

"Alright, if you think that's wise. They should be okay. They seem to really like Adam."

I laugh at his comment before putting a hand on his chest. "They think he's pretty."

Steve leans back, looking Adam up and down before looking back at me. "What can I say? I'd never hire anybody that doesn't look at least half as good as me."

I scoff at him. "Sometimes, you're so much like Kellie it isn't funny." He looks at me, shaking his head, then picks the trash up and shakes his ass on the way out. Since I think I've finally got everything cleaned out, I grab another bag and stick the stuff on the counter in as Steve comes strolling back into the house. "Do you want to go before or after our appointment?"

"Probably best to go after in case we get anything that might melt."

"Okay if you can handle this, I'm going to make sure I don't need anything for the girls. Sue Ellen grew while we were away, so I'll have to order her some new clothes."

"Okay. Am I saving any of these jars or anything

like that?"

"Nope, just pitch it all." I hand Steve the bag and head for my laptop that's already in my classroom.

We're about a month behind, so I need to make sure I change the lesson plans a bit. As I'm looking at everything we're behind on, I decide we're going to work a little longer each day to play catch up. So, I send a mass text to Peggy Sue, Maverick, Steve, and the girls.

School picks up Monday, be here by eight.

Steve comes walking in not long after the text was sent. "You don't sleep as it is."

"That's because a certain beast won't let me."

"Don't blame me or him for this."

I rub my belly. "I'm not blaming him. It's all on you."

"I'm just trying to wear you out, so you *will* sleep. You're insatiable."

"Greedy? Me? Oh no, mister, that's all you."

"No, I'm not the multi-orgasmic one that gets to come over and over and over."

"Maybe not, but it's your fault I am."

"And you enjoy every single one of them. The claw marks on my back and bite marks on my shoulders attest to that."

"I never said I didn't enjoy it. You're the one complaining about me sleeping, not me."

"Well, I guess we're just going to have to modify the schedule."

"The girls will be going to school from eight in the morning till four in the evening. Mess with me and it goes to five. They are behind and need to catch up."

"I wasn't talking about their schedule," Steve says, walking over and wrapping his arms around me.

"Then what are you talking about?"

"We'll just have to start going to bed earlier. Well, *bedroom*."

"We can't go to bed any earlier than we already do with the girls still awake."

"Then I guess they're going to bed earlier too."

I laugh. "Have fun with that."

"I'll get it done. I'll ground their asses if they don't listen to me."

I roll my eyes and push him away. "Getting them into their rooms isn't the problem."

"I'll tie strings to the door knobs." He laughs.

"You're being crazy. Did you finish in the kitchen?"

"Yes."

"That's why you're in here or are you being nosy?"

Steve smiles. "Well, I came in because of the text and to check on you because you've been running around like a crazy person since we got home."

"Not really, I just wanted to get everyone unpacked and clothes going, then I went to see what we could have for dinner and everything was bad."

"I thought you'd come home and do a little bit of class work, but I didn't expect to come home and you to hit the pavement."

"If I would have waited till later, it would have still been sitting there this time tomorrow. Plus, we had lots of dirty clothes."

"Yeah, but I could have done the laundry."

"Steve, in ten years, when have you ever done the laundry?"

"Okay, maybe not in the last decade, but I've done laundry."

"I'm sure you have something else you need to be doing other than laundry."

"Without sounding like a petulant child, frankly,

I'm bored out of my skull."

"Then why didn't you just say that? You've been making me feel like you don't want me to do anything."

"I just wanna help."

"That's fine, I just figured you had something else you needed to be doing."

He holds his hands out, palms up, and with a shrug, says, "Other than you, I don't do much."

"So, we just need to find something you can do. I'd ask if you want to help with the girls' schooling, but you usually spend time with Maverick and Angelica." I bite my lip and look at him. "We just need to figure out what you can do around here to keep you occupied."

"I'd say I could put baby furniture together, but you had the guys do that," Steve pouts.

I wrap my arms around him. "I wanted to surprise you and you aren't the easiest person to surprise. I can go take it all apart so you can put it back together if that will make you feel better?"

"That's not even funny. I just I don't know, I like doing that kind of shit. I can't carry the baby for you, so it makes me feel like I'm involved."

I take his hand and place it on my belly. "This beast is part of you and me. I'm pretty sure he has more of you than me."

I get this fluttering feeling in my belly as Steve's hand pulls back. "Did you feel that?" he asks, smiling.

"Feel what?"

"I swear the baby just kicked."

"I don't think so, I've been getting these like butterflies in my stomach, but I don't think he's *kicking*."

Steve smiles. "Those butterflies, that's movement. Like a fish swimming in a bowl."

With my brow cocked, I say, "You're nuts. I would

447

know if he's kicking."

"Apparently not because somebody just hit me in the hand."

"I'm not far enough along for that."

"Well, no, it starts at about thirteen weeks and with as big as he is…"

"I think you're crazy."

"We'll find out when we see the doctor this afternoon, but I'm telling you, *that* was a kick."

"Okay, crazy, go see if Adam is keeping the girls or if we're all going. We need to leave in about ten minutes."

Steve wraps his arms around me and kisses me on the cheek. "Okay," he says, then leaves the room.

I sit down in my chair and place my hands on my belly. It does nothing, it's just a belly.

❋ ❋ ❋

After the doctor, who, of course, confirmed that the beast is kicking, Steve and I went shopping, which pretty much wiped me out, so he picked up a pizza on the way home. I ate a salad, then came up for a shower. The only problem is I'm falling asleep standing up. I've been trying to get the shampoo out of my hair for the last fifteen minutes. I finally get the shampoo out of my hair and forgo the conditioner to get out. I barely get dried off before throwing one of Steve's shirts on and climbing into bed.

I'm not laying down for more than five minutes when Steve is wrapping his arm around me. "You up?" he asks, nuzzling into my neck.

I groan. "What else would I be?"

"I'll take that as a no."

"What is it?"

"No, go to bed."

"What do you want?" I whine.

"*Nothing*, just go back to sleep."

I roll over to look up into his face. "Wanna try again?"

He looks down at me, smiling. "I'm horny. What do you want from me? But you're tired."

I rub hand over my face, then through my hair. "You're always horny. You mentioned wearing me down, I think you were trying to wear yourself down."

"That could be very true."

"Let's make a deal, I'll do anything you want in the morning if you let me sleep now."

I can almost see the wheels turning as he ponders this and finally, his gaze settles back on me with a smile. "I think I can live with that." He kisses me. "*Goodnight*," he says very suggestively.

I roll over and he snuggles in behind me after I get comfortable. We fall asleep cuddled together.

74

STEVE

THE SIXTEEN-WEEK CHECKUP. We are out of the red zone for miscarriage now. There are still risks, but they're not nearly as high as they were. Our little guy is just that, a little guy. Crystal was right all along. We are in the exam room and I'm looking at a little pecker on the ultrasound and I am pleased as punch. Crys is crying just a smidge as she holds my hands.

I kiss her head and whisper, "Thank you," as the doc leaves us.

"For what?"

"For giving me what I've always wanted."

"You control that, not me."

"Yeah, well, that may well be, but it took you to carry him, apparently."

"I don't know about that, I think I just got lucky?"

I smirk with a short laugh. "Whatever it is, I'm gonna hold you responsible in part and cherish you all the more for it. Sixteen weeks in and twenty-four more to go. What do you want to do tonight to celebrate the official declaration of gender? We gotta tell everyone, but not tonight, tonight is for us. Adam is already prepared to stay with the girls for a few extra hours if we want."

"We need to spend it with the girls, Sue Ellen will never forgive you."

"Okay, then what do you suggest?" I'm quiet for a half second, then put up my hand. "What about a gender reveal photo shoot?"

"Like pictures?"

"Yeah, I was talking with Adam about you maybe doing some maternity photos anyhow, and since he's becoming something of a fixture here and has his own studio, I thought it would be something cool to do."

"You were talking to Adam?"

"Well, yeah, he's actually a very talented photographer when he's not working with us. He showed me some of the boudoir stuff he's done for couples and maternity shots for women. It's stunning work. I always wanted shots of Kellie, but she was always so busy that she never wanted to."

"You know you could have talked to me first," she says, giving me that look that means I'm about to get what I want.

"We were just talking about it the other day, I hadn't had the chance to discuss it with you. Consider this me talking to you."

"No, this is you telling me what we're doing now."

"Not *telling, suggesting*. I never tell or demand anything."

"So, when did you have this planned for?"

"Will you do it?"

"I wouldn't have asked what day we were doing it if I wouldn't do it."

I bite my lip, wrapping my arms around her. "We

have the fittings on Saturday for the wedding, perhaps Sunday afternoon?"

"Okay, if that's what you want."

"And the gender reveal pics?"

"If we're doing one, we might as well do both."

"Okay, I'll go and talk to Adam, now. Get him prepped. We will need to talk about what you would like to do, how you'd like to do it."

"It's just pictures, right."

"Gimmie your phone." I put out my hand and she gives up her phone as she finishes getting dressed. "This is Adam's website, look at his work, get an idea of what he does and then check out Pinterest for inspiration for our shoot perhaps?"

She looks at the phone. "Am I to assume you already know what you want to do?"

"I'd suggest you look at the bedroom and milk bath scenes as well as the couples. I'd like some of just us and some with us and the girls."

"If you already know what you want, just tell me."

"I want you to be comfortable, to be as into these pics as I am, so look into it, find stuff you like, poses, clothing inspirations, and what not. This is as much for you as it is for me. It's about making you feel sexy, loved, and desirable on a whole new level. It-"

"Dr. Ang is waiting," a nurse interrupts and I sigh as Crystal nods and heads for the door.

The doctor informs us that things look good, that little Steve is growing fast, and that the mild cramping Crystal has been experiencing is normal, just her body stretching and making room for our boy, nothing to be worried about. That's a relief. We've been told to keep on our diet and exercise regimen and to come back in three weeks. At that time, they will check her proteins and hormone levels as well as test the baby for defects if we wish to have those tests run. Crystal and I will have to talk about that. I'm in favor of it, but it's ultimately up to her.

We head out to the car and find Adam and the girls are just getting back from getting ice cream. "You two look like happy clams," I say, taking a bite of Sue Ellen's cone.

"Hey!" she complains. "That's mine!"

"Yup, and it tastes super good too." I chuckle.

She gives me a pout and I kiss her on the nose. "What did the doctor say today?" she asks, looking at Crystal, who's being spoon fed a butterscotch sundae by Mary Ann.

"I don't know? What do you think?"

"I think you're playing with me!" Sue Ellen squeals.

"I wouldn't do such a thing."

"Tell me!"

Mary Ann holds back on the next spoonful of sweetness. "Tell us."

"Sorry, I can't," Crystal tells them.

"What? Why?"

"Your daddy is planning a big ol' photo shoot and apparently, we're telling everyone then, so if you're blaming anyone, blame him."

All eyes turn to me and they are red. I'm in deep caca. "Listen here, ladies, it's no use, I'm not confirming or denying anything." I laugh as they mock attack me in the parking lot.

❊ ❊ ❊

"Daddy, hurry up, I don't wanna be late!' Peggy Sue screams from the back of the Escalade. She and

Harrison have met us at the house and are riding over to the boutique that is handling the gowns and suits for her wedding in two weeks. I'm dragging ass this morning, feeling like my chest is gonna explode. I think I'm having an anxiety attack.

I look at Crystal as I sit on the floor, clutching my heaving chest. "I don't think I can do this."

"It's a little late to think that now, isn't it?"

"I know, I just- I don't-" My breathing is getting labored and it's getting harder to talk.

Crystal grabs my hands and puts them on her ripening belly, "If I can do this, you can do this. I'm the one who has to put a dress on. Would you like to trade me?"

I laugh a little, tears falling down my cheeks. I don't know where this is coming from and it scares me. I rub the belly and put my face against her, feeling him moving. "I'm sorry."

"Because you're having a meltdown?"

I nod.

"Yeah, I've been waiting for it."

I can hear Peggy Sue in the background and I'm ready to strangle her. I tense up and I'm sure Crystal can feel it.

"Peggy Sue! Go wait in the car with the girls!" Crystal hollers and I sigh. Today, I had to fall apart today.

She strokes my hair and I start to calm down. I pull up onto my knees and wrap my arms around her, kissing her belly.

"I'm sorry, I don't know what came over me."

"Honestly, I expected to go through this three months ago."

"Why?"

"Your baby's getting married, that's a big deal."

"It is, I just thought I was handling it better than this."

'I've kinda taken up a lot of your attention, you haven't had the time to have your freak out."

I bite my lip, "Yeah, well, thank God for small favors then." I stand up.

"You'd have been over it by now if you had gone ahead and gone through it."

I blow out air. "I think I'm gonna be okay." I take her hand, "Ready?"

"As I'll ever be."

✵ ✵ ✵

"No!" Peggy Sue whines, "It's not swaying like a bell!" She is adamant that the gowns all have a bell base, like a ball gown. Layers of taffeta and silk are everywhere I turn and her colors are lavender, silver, and black. The tailoring of the suits is interesting, very Disney inspired. High waisted pants, fitted shirts, vests, and jackets. I do have to say, though, that I don't look like an overgrown ape in the cut.

"Miss Falcone, we are doing our best, but with your growing bellies, it is hard to get a perfect sway," the seamstress explains.

"Nonsense. If you all can get it right for Hollywood, you can get right for us Rockers."

Before I can say a word, Crystal starts in on Peggy Sue. "You need to chill, it is not their fault, there is nothing you can do, if you didn't want to get married while you were pregnant, you should have been more careful. You're attitude problem is just gonna make her work slower, is that what you want? I would have already told you to get out."

She's a tad snappy, but not wrong, Peggy Sue is being a brat and needs to be brought down from DEFCON one.

"I'm sorry," Peggy Sue says and the seamstress nods.

"The measurements are good. I will leave allowance in the bodice lacing for the bellies, a lot comes in two weeks." She smiles, looking at me and then Crystal.

"Um, okay? Thank you," I say as I'm helped out of the mockup for the jacket and vest.

Crystal, as well as Angelica and Marissa, are escorted to the back to get out of their gowns, while Peggy Sue goes to change into her own. Harrison is escorted from the room and Adam takes him to the car so he doesn't see the gown.

A few moments later and I cannot contain the tears in my eyes. My little girl is coming out in white and lavender, the dress hugs her belly and her hips, then flows out enormously with layer upon layer of lavender and white fabric. She looks like a princess.

My heart stops, I can't believe this is my little angel. My Peggy Sue. She looks so grown, hard to believe that just a few years ago, I was holding her in my arms to protect her from the bogeyman, and now, I'm going to be handing her off to the man she'll hopefully spend the rest of her life with.

"My little girl," I choke.

"Daddy?" she sniffs.

"You look… I am without words."

"Think Harrison will like it?"

"I think he's gonna love it. Don't you, Crys?" I look over at Crystal, who's just come from the back room and she's smiling.

"She's beautiful, but I always knew she would be."

"My little princess." I go to her and hug her, she hesitates, but yields to me after a moment and it feels good to have her little arms around me if only for a moment.

75

CRYSTAL

IT'S JUST AFTER LUNCH AND I'M TRYING TO finish getting ready for our photo shoot today. I bought all three girls matching dresses and even though Peggy Sue had an issue at first with it, she sucked it up. I'm getting more nervous as the day goes. I know after our family, gender reveal shoot, Steve wants to do a boudoir one. It's going to be weird having Adam seeing me half naked. Kellie wouldn't do this for Steve, and since this is his last one, I figured one time and it's over.

With the way I'm growing, I won't be able to move by the time the little beast is ready to come. Steve's already started being more careful with me and it kind of sucks because I miss the way we were able to connect. I jump as arms go around my belly because I didn't hear anyone come in.

"I'm sorry, Bella. Did I scare you?" Steve apologizes.

"No, I just jump because it's fun," I sass.

"I'm sorry, I was just coming in to see how you were doing."

"Honestly, freaking out a tad."

He looks at me in the mirror, slightly confused. "Why?"

I give him a look. "You really had to choose someone we have to see every day to see me half naked?"

"Well, I figured that he's already someone who knows what you sound like when you come, and we might as well go with someone we can trust. Would you rather it be a perfect stranger?"

"The man already blushes anytime I enter the room. How do you think he's going to act after this?"

"Far more professionally, actually."

"I don't see that happening." I turn to Steve and look up into his face. "Remember when we broke the bed?"

"Yeah?"

"It took him a month to be able to talk to me without blushing afterward."

Steve smiles and shakes his head. "But this is a job."

"And being our body guard isn't?"

"Perhaps he's a bit of a prude."

"I thought he was gay, but I'm starting to think I was wrong. Gay men don't blush because of women."

"I don't know either way. I just know he's a talented photographer, which is why he's here today."

"He's already here?"

"Yes, he's downstairs with the girls, making sure they don't get dirty."

"Peggy Sue in her dress?"

"Yes, it's a little snug."

"It's not my fault that she's growing like me. I've already got to order new clothes."

"You're both having little beasts."

"Apparently so."

I go back to finishing my makeup with Steve behind me. His hands are on my belly where they've taken up residence because the only time our little beast kicks is when his hands are there. When he kicks, I know what it is now because we can see his little foot. After I finish my makeup, I look at Steve in the mirror.

"You've got to move to the side so I can do my hair unless you want to get burnt."

Steve moves to sit on the counter. "Do you need anything, Bella, before I go check on the girls?"

"Nope, just need to finish my hair. I'll need help with my shoes, but I'll bring them downstairs with me."

"Okay." Steve kisses me on the cheek, then he's out the door.

* * *

An hour later, and we're working on the gender reveal pictures. The girls have about driven me insane asking. All three girls are around a box that says *Sister or Brother? Open and you shall see.* Steve and I are some ways behind the box with our hands on my belly as they open it. You will see us in the picture, but in the background.

Adam gets a ton of pictures before he lets the girls open the box. Their little faces are so bright with smiles. He then takes a few of them coming to us and wrapping me in their arms. We take a few family shots with everyone, including Harrison and Brayden. There was also a few done with Steve kneeling in front of me and kissing my bare belly as the girls peek out from either side of me. I do one other with just Mary Ann and Sue Ellen. I'm sitting on the ground with them and they're kissing my belly from the sides. Then I move out of the way so Adam can get a few of Steve with his girls. I don't think Steve has any real pictures with his daughters, so this is a real treat for him. He looks really happy.

Once the girls are finished, it's just Steve, Adam, and I because Peggy Sue takes the girls to spend the night with her. Steve liked that idea. We've not really been alone, so it'll be nice to have a quiet house for a night. Even if it's just to lay around and cuddle while watching TV.

Next, it's just Steve and me together. Steve leaning me backward and going for a kiss, teasing me. Us hugging from the side with Steve's back to the camera and a hand on my belly, one of my arms wrapped around his and the other on my belly. Then we do a couple for the gender reveal. One is us kissing with blue smoke bombs all around us and the other is us holding hands with a pair of little blue booties hanging from our fingers.

Now we're heading for the last part of this shoot, it's all about the food I've been craving. I'm sitting in front of the open fridge with everything you can imagine around me. If I'm not supposed to have it, it's here. Cheeseburgers, fries, fried food, ice cream, cake, even pickles. I make Adam cringe when I dip my pickle in my ice cream, but it tastes so good. Steve gets onto the floor with me and is feeding me. He has a lot of fun with the pictures. So, even though I didn't really want to do them, I am okay because he makes it fun for me.

Steve's downstairs cleaning up as I'm in our bathroom, changing, and Adam's setting up lights out in the bedroom. This is the part that has me nervous. I've changed into a pair of white cotton panties and cotton white top that only covers my boobs. I sit down on the side of the tub as my little beast starts moving around. Steve walks in the room as my belly moves all over the place. I'm pretty sure he's doing somersaults in there.

Steve smiles. "I think you have some indigestion."

"Oh no, that all baby. He's beating the hell out of my insides."

"You're nervous and he can feel it."

"I already told you that. I can't change it."

"Just focus on me. When I'm in the pictures with you, focus on my hands on you."

'This is a thousand times worse than the sex tape."

"How is it you were okay with the pictures for Rolling Stone, but you're not okay with these?"

"Adam wasn't taking those."

"What if I make a deal with you. Let Adam take the shots of us together. Then I'll have him show me how to use the camera for the rest of the shoot."

"He still has to look at the pictures."

"Yes, but then it's after the fact."

"I suppose, doesn't mean I'm going to be any calmer."

Steve's hands go to my belly as he kisses me. "You can do this. It's going to be fun."

I nod and Steve helps me stand. He walks out while I check myself over in the mirror, then follow him out. We start with me lying across the bed, arms above my head and knees gently raised. Adam has me move a few different ways before finally letting me change.

The next outfit is black silk panties with a top to match that makes my boobs and belly pop. Again, I'm lying on the bed, but this time, Steve is over top of me, going for a kiss. I can't help the breath I take the closer he comes to me. These pictures are a lot more sexual and

I know he can tell I'm getting flustered because I can feel my face burning.

After Adam gets enough of us fooling around on the bed and me thinking about all the things Steve could do to me, he moves us, so Steve and I are sitting cross-legged on the bed. Steve has one arm around my back and the other holding my belly. I've got one hand on his back while my other is fisted in his hair and we're kissing. Of course, with us, it isn't just a simple kiss, it's all out sloppy and lots of tongue. Mmm, the things he can do with that tongue.

Steve talks Adam into letting him take a couple of me alone, but it's not till Adam walks out the Steve tells me he wants me naked in front of the picture window, wrapped in the sheer curtain. I do and he takes quite a few of me standing different ways. I hate to admit it, but it is sorta liberating.

Lastly, we have the milk bath. Our bathroom is done up in flowers and candles. Steve helps me change into a purple lacy bra and grown with matching panties. I slip into the tub, then Steve lets Adam know it's okay to come in. Adam tells me to relax and enjoy the feeling of the bath. There are flowers in the tub with the milk. It's soothing and if I weren't all worked up, it'd probably put me to sleep. The pictures in the tub are actually simpler than any of the others. I'm laying with my hands holding my belly, one on top and one on the bottom, with the gown falling off of me, then there's some with my feet on the side of the tub.

There's another with no gown, my panties covered, and my boobs popping, and then one the same way but with the gown. There's a few without the gown and me with a hand over my belly and one in my hair, looking at the camera. The last one is a full body shot, looking down at me in the tub and my gown falling away.

Steve gets all hot and bothered and doesn't give Adam any time to get out as he orders him to leave and is in the tub and kissing me. I fist my hands in his hair as he growls into my mouth.

76

STEVE

ADAM HAD TO GO. The warm water, scented candles, and her body on display was too much for me to take. Water sloshes everywhere as I get her out of the panties and bra, the pads of my fingers running over her smooth skin. She feels so good in my arms, I'm pulling off my soaked clothes as she writhes under me. My aching cock hits the warmth of the water and like a shark, zeroes in on her open legs. I grab her thighs and am working my way into her with long shallow strokes.

She grabs my ass, pulling me in deeper, but I don't want to hurt her. "Steve, if you don't fuck me proper, I swear to God!" she pants, digging her nails into me. I pull up onto my knees and she follows me, turning around and backing up onto my cock, her knees next to mine, she takes me in, and I sigh, sinking in deep.

"Fuck," I grit out, grabbing her under the belly as I thrust harder and she moans, her orgasm mounting. She grasps the sides of the tub as she comes and I hold her till she comes down before lifting her from the tub and carrying her to our bed. I'm not done with her, not by a long shot.

❈ ❈ ❈

I love to watch her sleep. There's just something about it that soothes me, makes me feel calm. She looks so peaceful, serene, and happy. Our boy is active, but he always is when she dreams. I run my fingers down her body, tracing the roadmap her veins have made since the pregnancy. She's self-conscious of them and the stretch marks, but I love every line, every new curve she's gained, they are all proof of the awesome thing she is doing. She's bringing a new life into this world, a child that we are gonna love and if his nursery tells me anything already, we are gonna spoil to all hell. Even the girls want to constantly buy things for him. It's funny, I never thought I'd have any more kids, but now I think a couple more would be great.

I know Crys and I struggled for this little field goaler, and I'm not going to push for more, but if we should find ourselves pregnant again in a year or two, I'd be a happy man. My fingers make their way down to her inner thighs and she opens her legs slightly with a little moan of approval.

"Are you awake, my Bella?" I ask as I kiss down her side. Her hands go into my hair and push my head further south. I guess that's a yes. She's on her side and I push her leg up and back, parting her sensitive flesh to gain access with my mouth. She whimpers, thrusting her pelvis at me. I pull her on top of me, so she's riding my face. Much better, she grasps the headboard as I work her over with my tongue and hands until I'm in need of a good shower.

After cleaning up, I come out and she's asleep once

more. I go let the pups outside and sit on the patio, watching the night sky, wondering what the next few weeks will bring. Peggy Sue is getting married and that is going to be a fiasco. Right now, I sorta miss Kellie. She always had a plan, had something for my idle hands and racing mind to do. I feel bad that she's not going to see her little girl get married.

77

CRYSTAL

"STEVE, I REALLY DON'T WANT TO DO THIS. Can't we say I'm not up to it and you have to stay here to take care of me?"

"Bella, it's Peggy Sue's bridal shower. You're the closest thing she has to a Momma, you can't stand her up."

"Fine, I'll go, but do I have to sleep there. It's not our bed?"

"I said I'd stay the night. So, what are you going to do, come home to an empty house?"

"I could do that, at least I'd get to sleep in my own bed."

Steve smiles and shakes his head. "It's only one night. You can handle it."

"I can handle Angelica's because we're there almost as much as we are home, but Brent's is different. It's so big and I don't know, I just don't like it!"

Steve walks over to me and wraps me in his arms before squeezing my ass. "All the girls are going to be there. You're going to have fun there. He's got a movie theater, gym, I mean he's got all kinds of stuff to play with."

"Seriously? What do you want me to do with a gym? Run the baby out?"

"No, but there are like stretches that Angelica can teach you."

"Not helping! Angelica has like five weeks to go and we're the same damn size! UGH!" I groan.

Steve kisses me. "It's one night, you can handle one night."

"Yeah, you already said that, but I don't see you packing your shit to go," I say with a raised brow.

"Well, I figure I just gotta bring my toiletries."

"The wedding isn't till the afternoon. You need something to wear in the morning. Jesus, why do I have a strange feeling I'll be taking care of four kids when this one gets here?"

"Fine, I'll pack my overnight bag, but you need to go pack yours."

"I have told you today that you suck?"

"No, but you like it anyway."

"I'm getting too fat for all this walking. We're moving downstairs if I get any bigger."

"No, I'll just have to carry you back and forth."

"I'm eventually going to get too big for you to carry around. You know the fact that I'm eighteen weeks and as big as Marissa and Angelica at the end of theirs really sucks!"

Steve laughs at me. "Have you seen me? Bella, I bench press three fifty."

I shake my head, pulling away and heading for the stairs. I can hear him laughing behind me and it's driving me nuts. Doesn't he understand I'm miserable? I'm only eighteen weeks, but look like I'm about to pop.

Marissa had the twins and didn't get much bigger than I am now. Of course, she had Brent as a partner and it's not like he's all that big. But Angelica and Maverick? She's not much bigger than me and Maverick is just under Steve but still not a big baby there. Why must I be the one to carry the beast?

I get mine and Steve's overnight bags packed before finally yelling down the stairs since I can't get my shoes on. I go back to the closet to grab a pair only to find myself sitting on the closet floor. UGH!

Steve walks into the closet, then looks at me curiously. "Bella, why are you sitting on the floor?"

"Because I thought it'd be fun for you to find me this way. Obviously, I was squatting and just kept going," I groan.

"Honey." Steve bends down and stands me on my feet. "What were you trying to get?"

"My shoes, what else?"

"Which ones?"

"The only pair I have that fit when I'm on my feet."

Steve grabs my shoes. "Your gonna have to get you some new shoes, Bella."

"I don't plan to leave the house again till the little beast comes. So, I'm going barefoot."

"So, I managed it, huh?"

"Managed what?"

"Get you barefoot and pregnant in my kitchen."

"Where've you been the last eighteen weeks? I'm always barefoot when I'm home and I've been pregnant for eighteen weeks now."

"Maybe we should skip the shower."

"Oh no, you wanted to do this. So, you're going to spend time with the boys and I have to watch Peggy Sue get some items that will make me rather uncomfortable watching."

"Alright," he says sadly.

❖ ❖ ❖

I've been at the party about two hours and I've noticed a theme with pretty much everything. It's Disney but makes no sense for Peggy Sue. The food is all set up on a table that says *Happily Ever After* and the wall behind it say *Once Upon a Time*. We're sitting here eating now. Marissa came up with some pretty good ideas. We have salad wrapped in bacon, meatballs with Parmesan cheese, pretzel with garlic and herbs, asparagus and bacon wrapped in a crescent roll, skewers with bacon, mozzarella and yellow tomatoes, donut kabobs, pesto crostini and a ham and cheese pinwheel topped with a raspberry sauce.

After we finish eating, Peggy Sue starts handing out bags to everyone with their names on it. She lets me know to open mine first as her, Marissa, and Angelica watch me expectantly. So, I do and pull out a set of yellow satin pajamas with my name on them and a matching kimono. At the bottom of the bag is a smaller box. I pull it out and open it. It's got two beautiful bracelets in it. They are infinity love bracelets. One says *Bride* with a shoe hanging from it and the other says *Maid of Honor* with a bow hanging from it.

I look up at Peggy Sue, confused. "I think I got the wrong box."

Peggy Sue smiles from ear to ear. "That's something I've been meaning to tell you. I'm not getting married tomorrow, you are."

"No, I'm not," I say as Marissa and Angelica walk over and sit on either side of me.

471

"Actually, she's been working on this for months and you are," Marissa says.

"It's all set and it's all paid for."

I look between the two before holding up a finger. "I'll be right back."

I walk to the bedroom where my overnight bag is and grab my phone. I told him not while I was pregnant. The stupid man never listens. I click his name and listen to it ring while waiting for him to answer.

"Hello," Steve says and I can barely hear him for all the loud music.

"Find somewhere quieter."

"Okay, hang on." The roar of the music gets lower as he moves away from it. "What's the matter, Bella?"

"Steven Robert Falcone! How could you? I already said I wouldn't get married while I was pregnant!"

"Bella, what are you talking about?"

"Your daughter just informed me she's not getting married tomorrow, but we are!"

"No, she's pulling your chain." I hear movement and the music gets louder again. "Who the fuck is getting married tomorrow?" Steve shouts out.

Everyone yells, "Surprise!"

I'm standing here, tapping my foot and waiting for him to respond to me.

"But we don't have anything. Everything's been worked out for you guys."

"Steve!" I shout into the phone.

"Yeah, Bella, apparently we've been duped."

"I'm going to kill them all."

"Well, I guess, you'll be doing it as Missus Falcone," he says with a laugh.

"This isn't funny."

"It's a little funny," he says.

"It's the only way we were going to get you down the aisle," Kyle says from Steve's end.

"Tell Kyle to shut the fuck up. Steve, I'm not walking down the aisle when I'm this big."

"Bella, we're here and it's all set, we might as well do this. I don't want to break anybody's heart."

I'm so upset, I can feel the tears running down my face when Peggy Sue comes up behind me. "Ma?"

I wipe at my face before turning to her. "What is it, Peggy Sue?" I ask, still trying to calm myself down.

Peggy Sue is crying. "I'm sorry. I just knew this was the only way to do it."

"I wish you would have asked first."

"If I'd have asked, you would have said no. That's the point. You and Daddy shouldn't have to wait just because mom died. Life doesn't stop."

"That's not why we were waiting."

"Being pregnant is not an excuse to not do this. Please, just trust me."

"I do, but I also want to strangle you."

"You could just pick one of them as my maid of honor and break my heart that way."

"Do you really think I'd ever do that?" She shrugs her shoulders. "Peggy Sue, you've put me in more awkward positions than any one person should ever have to be in. More than once, I got suckered into calming the beast because you knew he'd kill you. I was the one that braved it out and told him you were pregnant and wanted to be with Harrison. Pretty sure I've more than shown you that I love you and when I had planned to do this, even if something happened and it was with a different man, I was always going to ask you."

"Hey, hey! No talks of other men. Are we doing

this or what, Bella?"

"Hush for a second, I'm talking to Peggy Sue."

Peggy Sue pulls me into a hug and the bumps touch. "Give me my bracelet."

"It's with my bag where the girls are. Go get it and let me talk to your dad," I say and Peggy Sue nods her head, sniffling before wiping her face and leaving the room. "She's your daughter," I finally say to Steve.

"Oh, are we finally talking to me again?"

"Don't even go there."

"You didn't answer my last question. Am I getting gussied up or are we disappointing over five hundred people tomorrow?"

"It's too soon and I'm too fat. Why do you think we should do this now?" I ask, sitting on the bed.

"Because my daughter went through all this trouble so we could. She thinks we need to do it now and I happen to agree."

"You were fine with waiting before."

"You were fine with waiting. I'd have married you the day my divorce was final, but I thought you deserved a fairy tale and from the looks of things here... Bella, you've got it."

"UGH! Why must you make me cry when I can't hate you for it?"

"That's not my intention. Just know that I love you and I miss you and if they hadn't stolen my keys, I'd be coming to get you."

"Call an Uber."

"You know they're not going to let me leave. Let them pamper you or whatever they're going to do to you. Just no glitter."

"Glitter?"

"Yeah, I don't trust Marissa and her stripper

friends."

"Is that your way of telling me you have a skinny bitch dancing all over you?"

"Yes, three of them," he says, clearing his throat. "They haven't made their way to me yet."

"Yeah, go have fun with that." I hang up the phone and lay back on the bed.

❖ ❖ ❖

The night went much like you'd have expected, strippers, food, presents, inappropriate toys, and other fun games. The closer we get to time, the more nervous I get. I've never even seen myself getting married. I know I told Steve yes, but honestly, I figured that was enough for him. It's not like I thought he would push to go through with it. He had just gotten divorced and lost his first love. I was second fiddle and just figured it'd stay that way. Yes, he wanted me pregnant. Was that because I told him I couldn't have babies or because he wanted one?

Angelica's girls have finished my makeup and hair, so now, I'm sitting on the bed, waiting till it's time to get my dress on. My little beast is going nuts because I can't seem to calm my nerves. I can't handle sitting anymore, so I stand and start pacing the room. I'm on my about my tenth pass, when the door opens and Kyle sticks his head in.

"Check," Kyle says.

"What are you doing in here?"

"What'd I say? Check, I'm checking on you?"

"More like annoying me."

"The man of the hour sent me in to make sure you're okay."

"Do I look okay?"

"No, actually. You look like you'd be running out the doors if they weren't guarding them."

I fall into the bed with a pout and try to keep from crying. "This isn't supposed to happen for me. I just figured as second fiddle, I'd never have to worry about this."

"Well, honey, step up to the plate because you just became first place."

"We're fine like we are. What happens if we do this then end up like him and Kellie?"

"Something tells me that he and Kel were like him and Kel before him and Kel got married. You also forget that Steve was a sixteen-year-old kid at the time."

"We're already changing so much with a baby. What happens if he decides we aren't enough?"

Kyle looks at me and laughs. "Then I guess I'll have to bury him in the desert and keep you for myself." He chuckles. "Come on, Crys, that man loves you like nothing else."

I smile as he sits beside me. "You are going to make a girl very happy one day. I just hope she deserves you because that will be a tall order to fill." I put a hand on my belly as the little beast starts kicking again. "I know Steve loves me and I love him, but that isn't always enough."

Kyle stands up, looking at me. "Have you looked at me? I did not put on this outfit for you to not walk down that aisle to get married."

I look Kyle up and down. He's wearing a white shirt under a royal blue suit with a yellow vest and bow tie. "You do look kind of snazzy."

"That's right. Now, we're gonna blot your face and get you into that behemoth of a dress over there, then we're gonna get you married."

I nod and stand beside him. "Okay."

"Alright."

78

STEVE

TALK ABOUT A WHIRLWIND. From the instant, I found out I was getting married, I've been in something of a haze. People have been talking to me, but I'm not sure what they have been saying. I'm smiling and nodding, which seems to be doing the trick, so far. Ringo had his hands full with Kyle, who had his hands full of the strippers, and Maverick looked like his head was gonna explode. I'm not sure where Brent went. I think it's been weird for him to be in Angelica's house, but that's not my problem, that's his. Me, I'm high, hooked on a feeling of elation. I'm getting married to the girl who said yes.

In less than two hours, I'll be standing at the altar, outside under an arbor of roses and lilies, pledging my everlasting love to her. I'm terrified.

Having managed to break away from the rest of the guys, I find myself pounding on a bedroom door. It opens and Kyle is standing on the other side.

"Dude, what are you doing here?" He holds the door closed against me.

"I need to talk to her, please," I beg.

"You can't see her. It's bad luck, man."

"I don't give a shit about luck, I want to see my girl."

"Can't, man." He's struggling against us both and loses the battle, then I've got my hands on her face and my tongue in her mouth as I push my way into the room.

"I'm gonna just…" Kyle says, his voice fading in the fog in my head as the door slams shut.

"I needed to see you, make sure you were here," I pant, coming up for air as my hands slide under her robe and down her sides, grabbing her by the ass firmly.

"I'm here."

I nod, smiling like a fool. I pull at the curls of her hair, take in the golden shadow on her eyes, the deep red of her lips, which I'm sure is smeared across mine. "I had my doubts, but seeing you now, I couldn't be surer of anything in this world."

She pulls away from me. "If you're having doubts, we shouldn't do this."

"Bella, a little doubt, after my track record, is normal, I woke up and I was lost, in a haze, but the moment I found you, touched you, it all fell away and the world became crystal clear, for you. Crystal, I love you, I adore you, you are my world, and I hope that I can someday mean as much to you as you do to me."

The tears fall and I don't know what to do except pull her to me. I lift her face with a finger under her chin and kiss her again, deeply, wanting to distract her from her sorrows, from her doubts and her trepidations. "Bella, Bella, Bella, you're my love, my inspiration, the air I breathe," I whisper, kissing her again and again.

"I can't help but be afraid that if we do this,

everything changes."

"The only thing that changes is your name. We're still gonna be us, still gonna be the same family we were, except you will be seen as my wife with all the respect that it entails."

"In my heart, I know that, but in my head, I've seen all the hell you've gone through in the past ten years."

"Yeah, hell that I endured from misplaced loyalty, but that's not what this is. You and me, we've spent a decade building this relationship, it's high time it was given wings to fly."

She sits on the bed and I sit beside her, taking her hand in mine. "What happens if you change your mind a year down the road?"

"Bella, I've been in love with you for seven and a half years, knowingly in love. That's when Kellie first called me on my shit about it. Peggy Sue's tenth birthday party when you baked the cake. That was the day I admitted it to myself. If I've been in love this long, not knowing you felt the same way, do you really think I'm gonna go anywhere now that I know you love me too?"

"We can't get married now, though."

"Like hell we can't," I whisper-shout. "Nothing is stopping us."

"You ruined my makeup."

"Oh, bother! ANGELICA!"

✤ ✤ ✤

I was thrown out of the room and now I'm standing at the altar, Maverick at my side, Brent and Marissa are at the stage, and a familiar intro begins. The opening sequence to *Beauty and the Beast*. There must be five or six hundred people here. Executives from the label, including Christy, all walks of media, snapping pictures, taking video. Bloggers, social media guru's, other musical artists that like to make a splash. I even spotted Brent's parent's in attendance. It's a who's who of Hollywood and music industry faire. My eyes sail over the sea of faces and connect with Angelica, who's first down the aisle, followed by my girls and Angela, sprinkling white rose petals down the red carpet, then all sound seems to stop and my head is full of cotton as Kyle appears with my Bella. My Crystal. Her long, full, yellow gown is a replica of Belle's from the animated *Beauty and the Beast* and is cut generously enough that the belly is concealed as she comes toward me. She smiles, holding her bouquet of red roses and yellow lilies with splashes of baby's breath. My heart feels like it's beating in time with her steps, and only as her hand connects with mine, do I become aware of the cameras around us once again. But I don't care. I'm with my Bella.

The ceremony is a blur, we take our vows and we kiss for the crowd, then again for ourselves at the end of the walkway. Right now, I have her tucked away in an alcove, trying to find my way under all this dress.

"I can't stand it anymore. I swear I'm going to tear it off of you," I growl, my head buried in her shoulder.

"Your daughter would kill you." She smiles, running her hands through my hair, tormenting me further.

"I just want to ravage you till the sun rises, is that so bad?"

"No, but they're waiting."

"Fuck, right, the cakes…" I sigh, "And all the food. Can't they do all of that without us? I mean c'mon, what about us says traditional anyhow?"

"Three little girls."

I groan, knowing she's right.

We escape from our hiding spot and emerge to the crowd and are instantly hit with camera shutters, then Adam appears and the cameras all go away as he, Blake, and Rider make a perimeter around us. I notice that the food is all French, from the crostini to the lobster bisque in shot glasses with Bella and Beast written on them. Everything is themed this way, and it has Crys tickled pink. The cake is impressive, it has the beauty and the beast silhouettes and on top, the rose under glass made of sugar, so it can be eaten too. The groom's cake is a beast head and a Belle head, only it looks more like Crys, and it too says Bella and the Beast.

"Peggy Sue really busted her hump," I whisper as Crystal squeezes my hand in approval.

Somewhere in the distance, someone clinks their glass and I look up. It's Kyle, he's standing and he's got a glass of champagne. We had to serve it, too many people to not have alcohol present.

"I'd like to make a toast to the happy couple!" Kyle starts. I'm not sure I want to let him continue, but Crystal keeps me from stopping him. "To those who know me, you all know that marriage, weddings, all this... It doesn't mean all that much to me." He waves his hands above his head. "Hell, I'm the first one to slam my fists together and tell you love lies. Now, I'm not changing my position, but I am here to say that for these two, love is clearly horizontal, and primal, and something they are riding out and sucking the marrow out of. If only we were all so lucky. Keep it up, you two, you give hope to the crazies. Cheers!"

"Cheers!" go up from the crowd, and I'm not sure

what to say or think. I look at Crystal and then to my girls, who are starting to wind down.

"Think we should probably think about cutting the cakes?"

"Probably."

We cut the cakes and while I was a good husband, and fed my wife sweetly, I'm wearing angel food and devil's food accordingly. I go to the bathroom to clean it up when I'm joined by Angelica.

"What are you doing in here?" I ask, surprised to see her.

"I wanted to say I'm proud of you. You got a good woman there and don't you forget it."

"I won't."

"Good, now, we're keeping your kids for the next week and sending you and the wifey back to your fun little hideaway at Laguna Beach. The jet is fueled up and a car will be waiting for you when you land. I already called and talked to your doctor, it's perfectly safe to fly, on our jet at least."

"What about our clothes and stuff?"

"You're all packed. Adam, Peggy Sue, and Harrison took care of all that last night. Now, kiss me and go, before I pee myself."

I smile, kissing her cheek and heading out to find my wife.

"Get up slowly and don't make a big deal out of it," I whisper to Crystal when I find her sitting at our table.

She looks at me like I'm nuts. "What?"

"The band threw in and got us a week's stay at that little hotel in Laguna Beach, we leave now. C'mon, let's go get your purse."

"We have to say goodbye."

"No, if we do, then the paparazzi is gonna figure it

out. I want us to be hidden away, don't you?"

"But the girls?"

"Won't even notice, they're half asleep."

"We'll call them tomorrow?"

"Sure, video chat if you need to."

"Okay."

We get up and head to the bedroom where her purse was and find, to our surprise, a fresh, clean change of clothes. Jeans and a polo for me and stretchy shorts with a Tallulah tank for Crystal. Plus, sneakers for us both. Bless Angelica.

✾ ✾ ✾

"So, here we are back at Laguna Beach," I say, laying back on the bed. It's about ten p.m. when we finally arrive in our bungalow. "What, oh what, are we gonna do for a week?"

"Sleep." Crystal smirks, trying her damnedest to conceal her laugh and failing miserably.

"Sleep? Yeah, maybe after the tenth orgasm of our newly wedded night." I sit up on my elbows and watch her.

"Well, if you had your ideas of what we were going to do, then why ask me?"

"I know to what end we are going to come, I was looking for suggestions on how you would like to get there." I crook a finger at her.

"You know I'm not prone to coming when you tell me to," she says, inching away from me. That will not do.

"Hmm, oh, but you will get accustomed to it if I can help it." I hop up, chasing after her as she makes her way out of the bedroom and into the living room. I catch up to her about the dining room and get her cornered at the table.

"C'mon, Bella, you know you wanna play," I say as I close in on her, rounding the table.

"I'm supposed to have a head start, I've got a beast in me."

"Yeah, me too, and he wants to play." I tear around the table and grab her, pressing my cock into her back.

"Well, you caught me," she says, defeated.

I spin her around and look into her eyes. "Hello, Mrs. Falcone," I whisper as I kiss her gently. She kisses me back with more urgency, more passion, and I lift her, cradling her into my arms and carrying her toward the bedroom. The do not disturb sign I put outside will be there all week long.

~THE END~

ABOUT THE AUTHORS

J. Haney was born and raised in Kentucky, currently residing in Greenup County, Kentucky with her family, where she is the proud momma to Jessalyn Kristine and co-owner of Proud Momma Designs, which she runs with her amazing Momma. J. Haney's work tends to lean toward sweet and sexy, with suspenseful undertones, giving her readers something to hold onto.

S.I. Hayes was born and bred in New England, currently living in Ohio. Running around Connecticut, she used all of her family and friends as inspiration for her many novels. When not writing Paranormal Drama or Erotic Romance she can be found drawing one of many fabulous book covers or teasers. To see them check out her web site. www.sihayes.com

The pair met while working for a former publisher and became fast friends, their split dynamics and views on life, family, and love, in general, led to the idea of *A County Fair Romance*. They now bring you *A Sex Drugs and Rock Romance*. They do hope to bring you more of their shenanigans in the months to come, so keep your eyes open and a fresh pair of panties close by... You know, just in case.

J. Haney Links:
Website Facebook Street Team Twitter Pinterest Goodreads Instagram TSU Google + YouTube Spotify

S.I. Hayes Links:
A Writer's Mind, More or Less
The 131 Preview Review
Facebook Website Twitter

Made in the USA
Lexington, KY
24 September 2017